# SHADOW ENDER

## HAYLIE HANSON

# SHADOWENDER

THE LUMINAUT TRILOGY

BOOK THREE

## HAYLIE HANSON

Cover Designer: Emilie Haney
Interior Art: Kristen Hildebrand
Editors: Katie Phillips & Amy Williams
Interior Formatter: Michelle M. Bruhn

*To my parents, who can never say*

*I didn't dedicate a book to them.*


*And to Ty, Aaron, and Evie.*

*You're simply the best.*

# CHAPTER 1
# CALLIE

SO, I'M IN JAIL, I guess.

I'm pretty sure this room is a high-tech jail cell. Single cot. Weird plastic space toilet. Super-obvious cameras or bio-scan devices—whatever the blinking red lights are—mounted in the upper corners of the room, monitoring my every move.

I rise from the cot on rubbery legs: the lights move. I sit down, dizzy from a rush of blood to my head: the lights move. I grab my forehead and groan as the world's worst headache overtakes my skull: the lights track the rocking motion of my body. Rows of bulbs glare overhead, so bright they're almost blinding. It's not helping the headache. Like, at all.

Basically, this place has jail written all over it. Better than a torture chamber, right?

On second thought, maybe I shouldn't speak that into the multiverse. ...

Speaking of the multiverse, how did I wind up on this side of it?

Everything prior to this moment is fuzzy. The last thing I remember clearly was Diving through a multiversal gateway from Tremurheim to escape the Queen Beyond the Stars—the

Prime Shadowmancer who killed my friends, Nate Ormandi and Heike Rykjiersen, before she almost killed me too. I crash-landed in the desert heat of Ensolorada, lost under a boiling-hot sun with no relief in sight. But just before I succumbed to sunburn and exhaustion, I was rescued. After that...

Hazy flashes, muffled bleeps, medical equipment, and the sound of voices. A floating sensation. Hands holding me steady. A bright light—

*Light.* I stand too rapidly, black clouding my vision, and grip the cot rail until my limbs cease shaking. My backpack with my Light Cores is nowhere in sight. And more importantly, I have no idea what happened to my mechs, Nemo and Diver. My last memories are Nemo desperately trying to shake me into consciousness on a dune and Diver's brokenness and fear as his inner Light dimmed.

*Luminaut, we are fading...*

"I cracked his Prism and left him in the desert." My heart plummets to my toes as the reality of my massive screw-up comes into focus. "I abandoned him."

"Hey, Callie's awake!" A familiar voice reaches my ears.

"El?"

The boy sits on top of a bunk across the room, dangling his legs over the side. A broad smile stretches across his face, still splotchy-pink under his silver-blond curls; a remnant of the horrific sunburns he suffered on the dunes. But otherwise, he's all right.

"El! I'm so glad you're okay!" I don't move more than five steps before I'm bounced back against the toilet wall. A transparent yellow shield appears out of thin air, spreading from floor to ceiling with a low *zrrrmm* before fading away. I pick myself up from beside the toilet and blink hard, clearing stars from my eyes.

"Are you okay?" El hops off the bunk. "I forgot to tell you there's some kind of invisible wall blocking you off."

"The idiot dramora spawn only figured it out after he ran into it four times."

Ah, Toran Rykjiersen is here too, in all his scowling, cantankerous Seer glory. I hadn't noticed him on the bottom bunk with El's feet hanging off the edge. Shadows cast a dark parlor over his similarly splotchy face. "I'd hoped you were dead, but alas."

Nice to know where we stand. "Glad you're feeling better, Toran."

"I don't feel better, I feel awful. Especially since I'm trapped in jail with the sorceress who killed my sister."

Really? We're back to the sorceress thing? I grind my teeth, forcing myself to overlook the jab. Toran just lost his sister and home world in the space of a blink, of course he's raw and edgy.

"I didn't kill Heike. I did everything I could to save her. The Queen Beyond the Stars took her and—" I gulp before I utter the next name on our list of deceased friends, one more painful than it should be for a guy who once hunted me across the multiverse. "And Nate."

El's gaze falls to the floor, his slender shoulders rolling forward toward his heart. He loved Nate like a brother. I want to comfort him, but yeah, force field wall. Take a mental hug, okay El?

"My sister never would've been out there on the Hem, fighting Darkness, if it weren't for you." Immense grief and barely-contained rage swallow Toran's blue-gray eyes. "You promised her freedom and adventure, but all she found was pain and death. Everything that happened to her is your fault."

Toran isn't letting go of the blame-Callie narrative anytime soon, is he? I breathe deep, in and out. *Cut him some slack, he's been through a lot. We all have.* Heike was my friend, but Toran lost the only person he's ever loved.

*And I lost Nate* ... whatever he was or wasn't to me.

"I know you're rock bottom in terms of grief right now, and we'll make a plan to avenge our friends. But we can't do any of that until we get out of this jail." Think like Nate — make a plan, plus three backup plans. I've seen enough movies about jails to know sooner or later somebody's going to come for us. We need to be long gone before they do. "First things first. Diver, Nemo, and my Light Cores are missing. Our rescuers healed our injuries, but why put us in jail?"

"I heard some people talking when they brought me in," El replies. "One of them said you might have stolen something."

"Why would anybody think I stole something?" I pace back and forth beside the force field. "That's totally ridiculous. *They* stole something from *me*. Now, how do we get out of here?"

"The only door is on your side of the invisible wall, and there's no windows or vents." El blows a frustrated raspberry. "Escaping isn't going to be easy."

"You think places like this are *easy* to escape from?" Toran glowers.

"I'll try to Light blast the door down," I suggest. "Once we're out, we'll get our bearings. El, you're good at scouting. It can't be hard to find a gigantic mech, a tiny mech, and three glow sticks, right?"

El nods. "No problem. Then we'll figure out where the monster lady went and tear her to pieces for killing Nate and Heike."

"Exactly." El's next steps align perfectly with mine. "Toran, use your Water Manipulation to ice out the mechanism controlling the force field."

"No."

"Okay. Fine." I guess Toran *wants* to stay in jail. "I'll Light blast that, too."

El snorts. "You mean Toran's not helping? Wow, *so* surprising."

Way to go, El, impressive comeback! No wonder he and Nate got along so well. It hurts a little more every time I'm reminded he's gone.

"Shield your eyes," I announce. "This is going to get really bright."

I reach inside for my Light. The power glows under my heart, a flickering flame igniting as it races through my arms into my palms. The door is basically a rectangle-shaped indentation in the far wall with no handle or threshold. Moving my hands in a circle, I form a Light orb, take aim, and —

*Ping-swish.*

The door opens. My Light instantaneously zips backward through my body as I stare at the people coming into my cell.

Three guard-looking dudes armed with laser blasters and wearing some kind of glowing yellow energy-shield armor stand on either side of the human equivalent of a fox: a lanky man, about fifty, with a long face, shifty amber eyes that border on yellow, and reddish-brown hair I'd say was wavy if it weren't so frizzy. When he narrows a glare on my face, a frown creases his deeply tanned brow.

"Come with us," Fox Face commands.

"Who are you? What's going on?" I glance between the four men cautiously. Laser blasters aren't my favorite thing, and Fox Face is giving off untrustworthy vibes — and not just because he resembles an animal with a reputation for deceit.

"Come with us willingly or we'll use force." Starting with the threats already, Fox Face? Not a good look, just FYI. The three guard-guys step forward, brandishing their weapons, and something tells me those lasers aren't set to stun.

"Don't hurt Callie, you dümfo!" El rushes to protect me, but the force field *zrrrrmmms* and bounces him back. He crash-lands in Toran's bunk.

"Get off me, dramora spawn!" Toran shoves El to the floor.

"Chill out, both of you." Seriously, these guys are carrying actual weapons over here, and they look like the shoot-first-ask-questions-later type.

The way I see it, I've got two options. I can use my Light to blast these guys into the dunes, but that will get me arrested again in a heartbeat. Or, I could go with them, then escape when I've got a better grasp on the current situation. It may be a simple misunderstanding. If I'm lucky, Fox Face might know what happened to my Light Cores and mechs, too.

I don't trust Fox Face or these guards, but the second option seems better than the first.

"Fine." I shrug. "I'll talk. But first, power down the blaster things."

"Absolutely not." Fox Face shakes his head.

He's not letting up. Figures. Time to play the innocent-but-savvy card. I clasp my hands and give him a pleading look. "Please, sir, I'm just an unarmed teenager! Don't shoot me! I'm sure the recording devices hidden in this room would agree that rough treatment of children is the epitome of cruelty."

Fox Face presses his lips and nods stiffly at the guards, who power down the blasters and stow them in hip holsters. Sweet, that actually worked! I hop off the cot, and the guards surround me on all sides.

"You'll come back, right?" El calls, his eyes wide with uncertainty.

"I won't leave you behind, I promise." The second the words cross my lips, the cell door *ping-swishes* behind my shoulders.

Fox Face leads me into a small, airy room that's less cell-like, even though it's still weirdly white and windowless. A chair sits in the corner, made of orange, plushy fabric and covered in red-and-purple pillows, and beside it a small, round table graced with a delicate tea kettle and cup, both vivid blue and intricately painted with flowers.

We're going to have tea? Nice!

"Let's get started, shall we?" Fox Face saunters ahead and sits in the chair, pouring himself a steaming cup of spiced tea.

"May I have some tea?" I ask. "I'm a little thirsty."

"Not a chance." Ugh, should have known this was too good to be true. The three guards flank me, and Fox Face puffs himself up like he's some kind of head honcho. "I'm Manu Carosti, a Cordonanza City Guardian."

Cordonanza. Must be the town we're in. City Guardian sounds like police or politics. Judging by the fancy tea set, the sleek vest-shirt, five billion gold rings (okay, overstatement), and the silky, pressed pants this guy is wearing, I'm gonna guess politics.

"I'm Callie James, regular human teenager," I introduce myself. The guards breathe heavily down my neck. "Is all the firepower really necessary?"

"I'll be the judge of that, not you." Manu sips his tea with quiet confidence. "Tell me how you stole Mariasol Zaira's World Diver and three Light Cores."

Manu thinks I stole Diver and my Light Cores? Wow, has

there ever been a mix-up.

"I didn't steal anything. The World Diver is mine, and I found the Light Cores on my own."

"I don't believe you." Fox Face Manu nods to the guards, and they power on their blasters. This escalated quickly, didn't it? "I searched *years* for one single Light Core to provide stable power to our city. You were found in the desert carrying three, piloting a mech that disappeared over sixty years ago with a rogue Luminaut turned criminal. Thank the stars we were able to recover everything before you wreaked even more havoc."

"Everything?" My palms release a deluge of sweat, and my heartbeat thunders in my ears. "Even my World Diver?"

"The mechs, the Light Cores, everything."

He has Diver and my Light Cores! That son of a buzzkill! If Fox Face has my mechs and Light Cores, what else does he want with me? Blackmail?

"Where's Diver?" I meet his gaze, hoping I look calmer than I feel. "And what did you do with my Light Cores?"

"*Your* Light Cores? I think not." Manu leers over the rim of his teacup. "I have no idea how you came to steal one Light Core, let alone three, but power sources like that are of more benefit to Cordonanza than they ever will be to you. Regarding the World Diver, broken, ancient tech is of no use to anyone. It will be properly disposed of shortly."

*Properly disposed of?!* Somehow, through a landslide of panic, I form words. "Diver is not garbage to throw away, he's my mech and he needs me."

"It's not a discussion we're having." Manu waves his hand as though batting away my feeble protest. Rude. "If you stole three Light Cores, it stands to reason you can steal more. Be amenable to my terms, and I'll make sure you're given a lenient sentence. I might even be able to get you exonerated completely, should you be willing to divulge certain information."

Holy extortion, Batman. This is worse than I thought. I've got to get out of here with El and Toran, and find Diver before he's turned into scrap.

The three guards form a semi-circle, their blasters shoved between my shoulder blades. Beyond them the door is wide open, leaving the most obvious escape route exposed. *So* crafty of you, Fox Face. Your machinations are just a chef's kiss. Now, how to get past the edgy guards?

Come on, Callie, think of a plan… distract and run. Simple enough, right?

"Okay, fine. You win. I'll talk," I say, feigning browbeaten defeat.

"I knew you could be persuaded." Manu flicks his wrist, and the guards lower their weapons. Good, good, everyone's being chill. But I have to time this exactly right.

"I'm ready to confess that I—oh my gosh, what is *that*?!" I scream, pointing at a nondescript spot on the farthest wall.

When Manu and the guards turn to look, I drop to my knees, pretending to cower on the floor. Calling my Light into my hands, I build two orbs, one per palm.

"Did you really think that was going to work?" The derision in Manu's voice is too marked to miss.

"No, but this will." I leap to my feet, throwing one Light orb in one direction, the other opposite. They spin in circles, bouncing like glittering pinballs with lightning speed. My captors instantly scatter, shrieking and terrified.

"So long, suckers, I'm bailing." I dart out the door, and with a *ping-swish,* it closes behind me.

My footsteps echo through the pristine, white-walled corridor as I sprint for my old cell. At last, I spy the open door and race into it, sending a gigantic orb of Light flying at the yellow force field. The barrier crackles and sparks, shutting down with an electricity-zapping *zzzrrrmmm*. Lights flicker overhead, and the blinking red scanners pulse in and out.

"Come on, guys, we gotta go," I announce breathlessly.

"What happened?" El leaps off his bunk, but Toran (predictably) doesn't move.

"That guy, Manu Carosti, has my Light Cores and he's disposing of Diver." Who knows what happened to Nemo, but if Fox Face was willing to toss Diver like a used napkin, Nemo's fate is equally dire. "We'll come up with a plan to find the Light Cores as soon as I rescue my mechs."

"What did you do to that man and his guards?" Toran peels himself away from his bunk and glares at me with narrowed eyes.

"I locked them in another cell, but they'll figure out how to escape, so make haste, or whatever old-school Tremurheim phrase you prefer." I saunter away, El trailing close behind. Toran catches up a moment later. He must've decided escaping jail with me is better than staying locked up.

"How do we get out of here?" El asks.

"A detail she didn't consider," Toran grouches.

"Oh, you're welcome, Crabbypants, for getting you out jail, it was nothing." I continue my march forward, past the cell where Manu and the guards' muffled cries can be heard through the closed door.

"We aren't out of jail, we're in the corridor." Details, but sure. Toran's gaze darts toward the source of the screams. "Are you sure they're unharmed?"

"Totally, I just scared them a little." Or maybe a lot. Should I have kept my Luminaut powers hidden? A sinking feeling tells me this might come back to haunt me sooner than later. "Let's find an exit. Pronto."

"Who are you?"

Two women appear at the end of the long hallway as if out of nowhere: one older, one young, both dressed like royalty. Emerald crystals stitched into the fabric of the elder's flowing gown glitter even in the harsh light of the jail. Intricate braids of black hair streaked heavily with gray twist on top of her head, secured by a gem-studded ornament that resembles a crown, and her beautiful, dark brown skin creases around her eyes and mouth, adding to her regal affect. At her side is a tall girl about my age. Gauzy, shimmering pink fabric floats around her willowy frame like a cloud covered in flower petals. She's as beautiful as her older companion, with light brown skin, brunette curls, hazel eyes, and a face like a pixie from an ethereal garden.

"You have *no* idea how glad I am to see you two," I say with a relieved grin. "I'm trying to find an exit, and—"

The older woman's brown eyes blaze bright green, and vine-covered branches shoot from her wrists, grasping my arms before slamming me against the wall. All the breath is knocked from my lungs, and I'm pinned so tight I can't move a muscle. The ground shakes beneath our feet while vines and branches wrap tight around El's legs, rooting him in place.

So, she's a Seer. An Earth Manipulator, probably. Wonderful. This is just my luck, isn't it?

"She's a Seer!" No, really Toran? You think? His eyes glow blue, and he calls the scant moisture in the air into his hands, forming twin daggers.

"Eeep!" The girl's eyes burn diamond-white at the sight of glistening ice knives. Before Toran makes a move, lightning sparks shoot from her fingertips, taking Toran down. He convulses on the ground, speechless.

"Please, stop!" I cry. "Let us go!"

"No." The older Seer's vines tighten around my neck while simultaneously encasing El in roots, and Toran's teeth chatter as electricity rockets through him.

Outmanned, outmaneuvered, and trapped in less than thirty seconds—so much for a quick escape.

"I'm Serai Eradah, High Guardian of Cordonanza," the Earth Manipulator announces. "Tell me everything you know about the three Light Cores that were brought into the Hall of Guardians, and what happened to Mariasol Zaira."

# CHAPTER 2
# NATE

"WE HAVE TO ESCAPE. We'll die if we don't escape."

Heike curls herself in a ball around her Light lantern, as though Callie's fading orb inside is the only thing tethering her to life. I float nearby, staring at the surrounding Darkness with abject horror.

*Wow Nate, isn't it ironic that you're suddenly horrified by this crap show of your own making?* Yes, yes, I know. Listen, I've had some realizations come to light since I was last down here, okay?

Come to Light, get it? Because of my suppressed Light powers.

Okay, it's not the best time for my puns. Both of us are fading, and fast. Heike's face grows more corpse-like by the second, and any glimmer of Light reignited in me has been weakening since I was snatched away and chained by Queen.

"I'm working on a plan." If I weren't bound up, we'd be long gone, but the Shadows around my ankles and wrists are tight as a vise.

"We're going to die." Heike sniffs, her lips quivering at the corners.

Should I promise her we're going to make it out? She doesn't seem like she'd buy into coddling. El wouldn't either. He'd snort and call me a stupid dümfo before punching my arm or something.

I miss that kid. My chest aches to be away from him, not knowing if he and Callie made the Dive. Priority numero uno is finding them before Queen carries out the evil scheme she promised to enact: capturing Callie and El and torturing them in the Shadow Plain while I play Good Guy Luminaut in exchange for their lives, making sure Darkness triumphs.

Now her royal awfulness is somewhere multiplying her army of sentient Darkness Shadowmancers, recharging her power battery until she's strong enough to turn every world in the multiverse to ash, a cataclysmic event I've got to help Callie stop.

"Focus up," I tell Heike. "I can't take us anywhere until I get free, and I have no idea how to do that. Help me think of a way out, okay?"

"Is there a key somewhere?" Heike stops crying now that I've given her a task to accomplish.

"A key? Hmm …" A key seems too easy. "I don't think Queen made a key."

"But she knows you'll find a way to escape." Heike dares to meet my gaze. I don't know if I've got the Shadowmancer's eyes or Nate's eyes, but she doesn't look away in fear. "And then she'll kill everyone we love."

"We won't know if she was bluffing or telling the truth until we bust out," I say. "But we're going to do it anyway."

"That'll lead the monsters straight to our friends," Heike counters. Shadows slither around her Light lantern, yet for all their menace, they can't get close to the Light.

Interesting.

"I wish Callie were here," Heike sniffles. "She can kill the

Darkness with her Light powers."

Kill the Darkness with Light powers. There it is, the key I need to break free. Darkness—regular Darkness, not Queen herself or the hideous Shadowmancers she's created—can't survive when confronted with Light. Callie blasts it away, scatters it, sends tentacles crumbling to ash and vapor. If all that's holding me in place is Darkness, well, have I got news for you.

"I have an idea." An idea that might be horrible for everyone involved, but it's better than nothing. "I'm going to use my Light powers to free myself."

Heike stares, her eyebrows pinched together. "*You* have Light powers? Callie told me a lot about you, but not that."

"It's a new development. Callie didn't know until right after Queen attacked the Beacons, and—" Hold on just a minute. Something inside my chest leaps, a weird skip-hop around my heart. "Callie talked about me? What did she say? Was she, like, Nate's an irredeemable sleaze-bag, or was she like, he's not so bad anymore, or …"

Heike shrugs. "Mostly she said you're a heartless monster who lied and betrayed her." Ouch. But I should have expected that, considering all the villainous scheming I did in California. Heike pauses, then adds, "And also, you're a good kisser."

"Really?" It's got to be the worst possible moment for this conversation.

Heike wipes tear tracks off her cheek and nods. "Something about ten out of ten."

"Ten out of ten?!" Way to go, Ormandi! The skip-hop sensation leaps all the way into my throat this time.

"Aren't we trying to escape?" Heike gives me a pointed look.

"Yes, escaping, right." Sticking it to Queen on the way out. "So here's the plan. I'm going to get out of these bindings using

Light powers. Then we're going beyond the Veil."

"What if the monsters follow us?" Heike asks.

"They'll follow, trust me." Not getting attacked was never an option. "It's a matter of keeping the upper hand."

"How?" Heike recoils from the Darkness closing in, turning her body so her lantern shines bright. The reprieve is only temporary.

"We're going to the one place in the multiverse Queen least expects." The place of my deepest pain and my greatest loss, where I was humiliated, defeated, and shamed. Where I made the worst mistakes of my human life—and my Shadowmancer existence. "We're going to Verona Beach."

"California? That's Callie's home."

"Mine, too." Despite all the horrible things that happened, it was—and is—the only home I've ever had.

"Really?" Guess that's another detail Callie was too busy eviscerating me to mention. "But why are we going there? Shouldn't we warn Callie, El, and Toran about the monster army?"

"We should, and we will." If we play our cards right, this is going to work. It *has* to work. "We've got to throw Queen off our trail first. Get her lost in the woods, you know?" Heike nods sagely at the forest analogy. "Then we'll find a way to join Callie, El, and Toran in Ensolorada without a Light Core or a World Diver."

"Aren't those things… essential?" Heike gives me a weird stare out of the corner of her eye, the kind that says I'm about to get us killed.

Minutes away from death, and middle schoolers can't quit the sass. It's admirable.

"If there's a rule, there's a way to break it," I argue. "My mom

Dove to California with just a World Diver, she didn't have a Light Core. We just have to find out how she pulled it off."

And I know exactly who to ask—if he'll speak to me. Dad's another person I didn't part with on good terms. The list of people who would slam the door in my face is much longer than those I can rely on for help because, as you recall, I was a raging slime ball not too long ago. But I'm not going to admit that to Heike when she's counting on me to save her life.

"So, we're going to go to California to evade the Queen Beyond the Stars and her monsters. Then we'll figure out how to find Callie, El, and Toran and warn them about the danger, even though we don't have a Light Core or a World Diver," Heike surmises. "And we're going to escape from here using your Light powers you didn't know you had until recently."

"That's correct."

My scheme doesn't seem any more plausible or safe than Heike's summary made it sound, but I don't foresee any way Queen could predict my next move. Terrible plan it is.

"Watch out, I'm gonna do the Light thing." And hopefully I won't pass out like I did the last time.

Heike shields her eyes with her palm while I reach deep inside, searching for the Light just under my undead heart. I haven't used my powers since I saved El on Ictari but I feel it, little more than a stubborn ember in the midst of dying coals. Yet Light can't answer my call when surrounded by so much Darkness.

"Where are your powers?" Heike lowers her hand. "Did you use them?"

"Not yet." Where's Callie when I need her to help me figure this out? Did she teach herself to be a Luminaut with absolutely no guidance? She's even more impressive than I thought.

Heike purses her lips. "Are you *sure* you can do this?"

"Do you want me to answer, or do you want me to try again?" What is it with preteens asking questions? Yeesh.

Heike shields her eyes. "Try again."

Okay, Light, let's go. It's the bottom of the ninth and we're losing. I need to pull a major trick play out of my back pocket. I close my eyes, reaching for the power. Come on, Nate, make Light work for you like your life depends on it—Heike's certainly does.

*Come on, come on, come on …*

Light glows, warming me as it trickles through veins and arteries. The power wants to obey, but my Darkness doesn't like it, fighting back tooth and nail. A miniature war rages, the kind that causes agonizing pain—almost as bad as Queen ripping the left half of my face open with her fingernails. I grit my teeth and push through.

*Light must win. Darkness is death.*

Light reaches my hands, glimmering brilliance cutting the oppressive Shadows. But it's not enough to free me.

*It's too much, I can't do it.*

No, I'm not giving up. This is one time I absolutely cannot fail, not when I'm this close to saving Heike. She doesn't deserve to die down here.

*More, more. Just a bit more.* Light moves like a faint breeze billowing a sail. That's it, baby powers, we can do this.

But the closer I get, the more Darkness rages. My vision blurs as pain like electric shockwaves rockets through every muscle, every bone, every place Light touches. Darkness—my Darkness— isn't going down without a fight.

Head up, Nate. If you fail, Heike dies, and not one single person is going to die because I screwed up. Think of El and Callie. Think of how I can't let them get hurt again because of my mistakes.

Think of Mom.

*Nate, my stars …*

Her invisible hand reaches through Light across space and time. The pain of raging tension evaporates, and I'm filled with the warmth of every good thing she meant to me. Darkness draws back as Light rushes through my arms until it bursts in my hands as powerful as anything Callie has thrown my way.

Chains of Darkness fall away. At last, I can move.

"You did it!" Heike grins when she sees I'm free to move around. "I watched the Light through my fingertips, I wanted to make sure you were telling the truth."

Digging myself out of the liar hole one person at a time, I guess. I help her maneuver upright since we don't really stand in the Shadow Plain, just weirdly float.

"Let's get out of here," I say, "before the Shadowmancers figure out I'm free."

I take a quick look around, gauging if any of Queen's legions are on our tail, but the first thing I notice isn't lurking phantoms slithering through the endless sea of Shadow.

There's less Darkness in the Shadow Plain than there was before.

From the moment I was Turned, the amount of Darkness in the Shadow Plain has been static. But when I look back at the spot where Queen imprisoned me, there's a loss of Darkness mass. I destroyed it with Light, as though it never existed at all.

Darkness *can* be eradicated forever, but only from inside the Shadow Plain. And that, right there, is how Callie saves the multiverse. Finding her just became a lot more imperative.

"Where do you think you're going, Nathaniel?"

Crap. It's Queen and a pack of monstrous new Shadowmancers, staring at us like we're about to be the main course at a feast. Heike stiffens behind me as even more Shadowmancers emerge: a dozen, twenty, almost forty.

"Back away slowly," I murmur over my shoulder.

"I can't walk down here."

Solid point. "Just follow my lead." I glide backward, pushing Heike, keeping my eyes on Queen and her Shadowmancers.

"You didn't think I'd let you escape unscathed, did you?" Queen asks, her smile like a spider.

"Actually, I did. Because you assume I'll lead you straight to Callie." The Veil to the human world appears in my peripheral. As long as I make it across first, I'll maintain the edge. "Do you think she's going to be easy to capture? She almost blasted you into the Tageveld the last time you saw her."

"Nate, what are you *doing*?" Heike jabs my side with a finger.

Just trust me.

"Calliope is young and naive," Queen taunts. "You are too. Both of you remain blinded by human weakness."

"You got one thing right." I back up farther as Shadowmancers slink forward, their glowing red eyes zeroed in on my face. "I've always had a very specific human weakness you blocked from my memory."

"They're getting closer." Heike's voice quakes. Another couple inches back, even nearer to the Veil than before. Timing is everything.

"Failing to eradicate your Light was an error," Queen replies, so casually I'd assume we were about to go get coffee. Her minions circle menacingly, Shadowy tentacle mouths reaching for us. "But errors can become beneficial when used to my advantage."

I force the Veil to show me Verona Beach. The muffled sound of the crashing waves and crying gulls reach my ears. Keeping my hands behind my back, I grin at Queen and her Shadowmancers.

"You know, for once we agree. Errors can be beneficial when played the right way."

I hurl the residual Light in my palms at Queen like I'm throwing out a batter heading into first, then grab Heike and push us through the Veil into Verona Beach.

Seagulls become as loud as sirens. Pounding waves thunder through my ears, remnants trickling into the swash zone around my ankles and knees. Sunshine bears down, mixing with the salty spray of ocean breeze. Everything about the briny smell of the Pacific and the sensation of warmth mixed with crisp, wild wind tell me one thing: I'm home.

"Are you okay?" I touch Heike's shoulder. "We're here. We made it."

With a sinking feeling, I realize we emerged at the absolute peak of summer tourist season.

Hundreds of people mill around the beach: kids running through the surf building sandcastles, adults lounging under awnings drinking beer or soda, locals walking their dogs. The scent of Coppertone mixes with grilling hotdogs and burgers, and surfers drag boards down to the water, leaving tracks in the sand.

If Queen's Shadowmancers follow us, every one of them will die.

"Come on." I grasp Heike's elbow, helping her stand. "We've got to get off the beach. It's not safe."

"Is this California?" Now that she's not about to be ashed, color and life return to her cheeks. "This is amazing! What's that thing over there?" She points to the pier. "I smell food, I'm starving. Is this the ocean? I've never seen so much water in one place! Callie told me she surfs, what does that mean?"

She's as bad as El with the stream-of-consciousness questions. No wonder middle school teachers always look fried by the end of the day. "I'll explain everything once we're at Dad's place."

"Your dad lives here?" Heike's wide eyes settle on the stilted lifeguard tower. "Is that his house?"

"No, it's this way." I march up the sand toward the towering Verona Beach cliffs. A narrow pedestrian path snakes up the craggy bluff before cresting into rolling green hills covered in bungalows and 1960s era beach cottages — my old neighborhood. No honeyed feelings accompany the sight. It hangs over me like a judge's gavel before delivering a sentence. Dad's sentence on my past, specifically.

"I bet he'll be happy to see you," Heike says with a grin.

Bet not, Boy Scout's sister. With any luck, Dad will let me explain how I need his help to reach Callie before he sets my head on fire with his Manipulation.

If I don't get lucky … to say I'll be burned extra crispy is an understatement.

# CHAPTER 3
# TORAN

PAIN LIKE I'VE NEVER EXPERIENCED stabs all the way to the bone as I lay convulsing, twitching, and pulsing on the floor. My teeth grind together. I cannot unclench my jaw. The backs of my eyes burn as though they'll pop from my head any second. No words form. All I perceive are sparks.

"Dunes, are you dying?" The young Seer who attacked stands over me. I can't see her face through the blurry haze, but she sounds genuinely concerned. "Mama, I think he's dying."

The older Earth Manipulator, Serai, turns to my attacker. "Remove the electricity, Ayla. I've warned you about using your powers in public."

Ayla flicks her wrists, fingers twirling delicately. Sparks fly into the air before fading away. I breathe in and out, residual pain snaking through my limbs and chest as the numbness wears off.

Yet the pain squeezing my heart remains, if only in a different form. Nothing can change the fact that my sister is dead.

"Are you all right?" Ayla offers a hand to help me stand. "I apologize for electrocuting you. I saw the ice daggers and was startled. I only meant to give you a bit of a zap. It appears I overdid it again."

"Again?" I blink hard until my vision clears. "Lands Beyond, you're a menace."

"Menace? How rude! I've apologized well, haven't I?" She tilts her chin, sucking on her bottom lip.

"Well or not, I don't accept." I wobble to my feet before crashing to the ground, my legs useless with residual shock. Instead, I crawl down the hall on my elbows. There is no world in the multiverse in which I would willingly stay near Callie or these deadly Seers a moment longer than I have to, and wherever this hall leads, it's away from them.

"Where do you think you're going, Water Manipulator?" Serai's vines extend from Elion to catch me, pinning me to the floor. Dramora spawn!

"Let us go." Callie's plea squeaks through the branches. "I can't breathe. Please."

"Which one of you is the Luminaut?" Serai looks between Elion and Callie. "The sand ogre over there is a Seer, which became evident when he tried to stab my daughter with ice knives."

Sand ogre? Who is she calling a sand ogre? I am no ogre, whatever that is.

"Well?" Serai tightens the vines' stranglehold. "Answer me."

How is she controlling vines? Ah, there are seeds embedded in the jewels on her wrist. Clever. Perhaps I can find a water bottle to sling about my neck. That would make it a fair fight.

"How do you know—" Callie gasps and gags "—one of us is a Luminaut?"

"Because a World Diver crash-landed in the dunes the same night three Light Cores mysteriously appeared in Cordonanza." Serai looks between Elion and Callie with narrowed eyes. "Since neither of you are Mariasol Zaira, I assume she sent her protégé on a misguided mission to seek my help."

"It's her." I lift my arm not pinned to the floor and point at Callie. "Callie James. She's the Luminaut."

Serai stares at me for a long moment. I can't read her, but I was never good at ascertaining ambiguous expressions. The older Seer faces Callie. "Is that true?"

"Yes, I'm a Luminaut." From her bindings, Callie's fingers fill with Light.

Serai eases up, her stony expression softening. Vines and crackling branches retract, growing smaller and smaller until they disappear back into the seeds from which they came. Callie slumps to the ground, sucking in deep breaths, and Elion gradually stands, coughing. I rise, unsteady on my feet. The trembling in my legs erases any hope of running away.

Dramora spawn!

"Where is Mariasol?" Serai looks between the three of us. "Why did she send you instead of coming herself?"

"Uh ... she ... um ..." Callie stammers.

If she's going to dawdle, I'll answer. "Mariasol is dead."

"Toran! Use some tact, dude!" Callie stares, her big brown eyes widening.

"What? Am I not supposed to say dead people are dead?"

Serai startles at my reply. Even though the ground beneath us has stilled, she sways sharply. Ayla catches her mother's arm before Serai recovers, tall and strong once more. Her expression shifts from obvious shock to aloof calm.

"I'm well, my stars." Serai pats Ayla's hand. "This is unfortunate news. Is that why you've come? To inform me?"

"No, she passed away years ago," Callie says. "I never met Mariasol."

Serai tilts her chin. "Then who trained you as a Luminaut?"

"Nobody trained Callie, which is why she's a dangerous fool who destroys everything she touches." I make another attempt to spin away, but alas, my legs. I tumble to the floor.

With a quick bump, the stone tile under my chest sends me flying upward. My shoulders slam against the wall, and Serai's face appears before mine, a glint like steel in her dark brown eyes. "That's a fairly serious accusation. Would you care to explain?"

"No, I do not care to explain anything to you."

"I see." Serai raises two stone tiles to pin my legs, trapping me worse than before.

I do not like Earth Manipulators at all.

"Callie isn't dangerous," Elion pipes up. "Toran's mad because the monster woman killed his sister, and Callie couldn't stop her."

Serai glances at Elion. "Monster woman?"

"The Queen Beyond the Stars," Callie says. "She's the reason we lost Toran's sister, Heike, and our friend, Nate."

Serai's face turns ashen. Floor tiles form a chair to catch her movement and steady her, including the ones holding me trapped.

Finally, a chance to escape! I haven't hobbled far before Serai flicks her wrist and the tiles move again, pushing me backward on a wave until I'm up against the wall where I started.

Lands Beyond, I *loathe* Earth Manipulators!

"No one is leaving. I'm taking all three of you under my protection. I need answers about Mariasol Zaira, the Light Cores, and especially the Queen Beyond the Stars." She speaks to Callie. "Did Darkness follow you through the gateway into Ensolorada?"

"Not that I saw," Callie answers. "But I don't think it's far behind."

Serai's face is as hard as raw ore. "Darkness is *never* far behind."

Farther down the hall, muted yelling behind a door intensifies, and the man who took Callie for interrogation—Manu Carosti—emerges with his three guards. All of them are angrier than a dramora that missed out on a hunt. Serai spots him immediately, a muscle near her eye twitching.

"Do not speak to him. Any of you." She looks swiftly at me Callie. "Did he see your powers?"

"I, uh, might have launched some Light orbs into the air before locking them in that cell," Callie admits. "As a distraction."

Serai purses her lips, visibly annoyed. "I wish you hadn't. No more powers. Understood?"

Clearly, Serai thinks there will be consequences if Manu knows the truth about who and what Callie is. The man means nothing to me, but Serai doesn't like him. Callie doesn't like him, either, and Elion will hate anyone Callie hates.

Any enemy of my enemy is a potential friend. Perhaps Manu will prove useful.

"I've got this situation under control, Serai," Manu barks. He and the three guards approach at a quick march. "Your interference is not needed."

"What situation is that, Manu?" Serai grows as cold as one of my favorite ice pikes when Manu stops in front of her. "The fact that you ordered three teenagers with no outstanding warrants removed from a MedFac and taken to a containment center without permission? Is that the situation?"

"Only two are teenagers," Manu argues, his tone marked by derision.

"Fine. Two teens and a child. Although, I'm not sure that makes the optics any better."

"That isn't what I mean, and you know it." Manu points a slim finger at Callie's face. "That one is a Luminaut. Three Light Cores were taken from the girl's pack by the MedFac team who treated her." The guards behind him mumble to themselves before Manu glares, and they become quiet. "Furthermore, a World Diver and another sentient mech were recovered from the dunes with footprints leading to the exact location the girl and her friends were found."

Friends? Elion might like her well enough, but not me. "Callie isn't my friend."

Everyone turns to stare at me with surprised or angry expressions, depending on the face. Serai is the most displeased, second only to Callie and Elion.

"Thank you, Toran, for clarifying." Serai is anything but thankful. In fact, she's livid I spoke out of turn. Serai faces Manu, folding her hands in front of her. "You think this girl is a Luminaut? She's no older than Ayla, and harmless."

"I know she's a Luminaut because she used her powers on me," Manu informs Serai. "Before I'm through with her, she's going to find me a fourth Light Core."

"I'm not going to find anything for you," Callie announces, to Serai's obvious chagrin. "You stole my Light Cores. I need them back before—"

"Light Cores?" Serai interrupts Callie with an over-loud laugh, then smiles through gritted teeth. "You're still a little sun-sick. A transport crash in the middle of the dunes at the height of day is more than enough to disorient a person."

It would be an advantageous time to run away while everyone is distracted. But no matter what I try, the tiles hold my feet captive. Instead, I sway sharply to the side before catching the wall.

"Skuddima take me, you droppings of addle-headed nargush, spawn of Mist and dramora." The worst swearing I know blends together. Everyone, including the emotionless guards, stare at me strangely.

"See what I mean? Completely disoriented." Serai places a hand on my shoulder. Her nails dig into my skin, a warning to remain silent, before she shifts her thin smile to Manu. "These are Ayla's friends from Oasis III, they've come to visit for a few weeks. Thank you for recovering them from their ordeal—although, I don't know how a transport crash in the desert fell under the oversight of the Energy Department. But I'm sure you have a good explanation for maneuvering outside your jurisdiction, one you won't mind discussing at our next Guardian forum."

"Oasis III? Lies. That girl was piloting a World Diver, she has Light powers, and she arrived with three Light Cores." Manu might be smarter than I initially gave him credit for. "She's a Luminaut as surely as you don't let your daughter have friends, even ones from Oasis III."

Behind Serai's back, Ayla winces.

"All this talk of Luminauts is dangerous." Serai steps forward, staring Manu down. "Are you jumping to conclusions over a few coincidences, or is it the Light Cores themselves that captured your conspiracy-driven mind?"

"Your past association with Luminauts is no conspiracy," Manu spits back. "You managed to convince the Hall of Guardians you had nothing to do with Mariasol Zaira's escape, but my father never believed it, and I don't either."

"Speaking of your father, he was removed from his position as Guardian for doing the very thing you're doing now, wasn't he?" Serai grins when Manu's tan face blooms red. "I know you started building a power extractor for the Light Cores without the votes or funds. Light from the Cores can't replace our failing solar coils, and your design requires at least four. That's one more than three, in case arithmetic is too complex for you."

"There's a map to the Rognaga where a fourth Core is hidden," Manu counters. "I intend to make use of it."

Serai rolls her eyes. "A map written in an ancient, indecipherable language nobody can translate. The Rognaga is a myth. Mariasol Zaira couldn't find it, you think you can?"

"Mariasol never found it because you helped her abandon her Luminaut duty, and—"

"You have a map? Can I see it?" My desire to escape is overshadowed by my desire to see said map and to try my hand at decoding this supposedly indecipherable translation. Language encryption and decoding were my favorite hobbies in Tremurheim. Besides, it isn't like I can go anywhere with Serai's Manipulation ensnaring my feet.

"It's been a mystery for thousands of years." Manu takes a glass rectangle from his pocket and taps it. A visual picture of the map floats in the air above the glass, as tangible as anything solid. Even Callie and Elion, whose home worlds are more technologically advanced than Tremurheim, look impressed.

"That's some awesome tech!" Callie exclaims.

"It's a comm," Ayla says. "We'll be sure to replace yours, since it must have been lost during your accident."

A cursory glance at the floating map reveals the problem Manu and countless generations before him have had in translating it—a problem that, for me, is mere reading.

"Ancient, indecipherable language?" I bark a laugh, ignoring Serai's cautionary glare. "It's written in old Tremurheim runes. Of course you can't read it."

"Tremurheim runes." Manu fixes me with a pointed stare. "How do you know that?"

"Quite the wit, this one." Serai fakes a chuckle to hide an ominous glower sent my way. "He's obviously joking. Tremurheim? Such a place doesn't exist."

"Yes, it does." How dare she say my home world is a lie?

"Is Tremurheim some unknown slang for Oasis III?" Manu sneers, disbelief plain on his narrow face. "I haven't kept up with all the new words young people create. Perhaps you're better versed, Serai, since Ayla is, what, seventeen now? Hard to remember how long it's been since the expedited adoption was approved under that veil of secrecy."

"I was born in Oasis III. My mother owned that mine as well as the mines at Oasis I and Oasis II. Now I own them. Tremurheim doesn't exist in Oasis III or otherwise." Serai steps forward, her fingers twitching as they curl around her seeded gemstone bracelets. "It's *especially* not your place to make insinuations regarding my daughter."

Manu has nothing to say in response. He stares at Serai with hate like I have never seen.

"I know you're lying about that girl being a Luminaut," Manu hisses like a skuddima sucking a victim's breath. "I refuse to be intimidated into silence."

"This discussion is over. Stay away from the Light Cores." Serai turns on her heel and Ayla obediently follows behind — no hint of sparks or rushing wind. "All of you, come."

At long last, the stone tiles release my feet and I'm free. Callie and Elion trail after Serai and Ayla without a word of protest. Manu catches my eye while the others march away.

"I'm Toran Rykjiersen," I say quietly once Serai is out of earshot, "and I'm from Tremurheim, *not* Oasis III."

"I see." A smile spreads slowly across Manu's face until it gleams under the artificial lights. A swift nod of acknowledgement is more than enough to communicate my understanding. He will contact me. I must be ready.

"Toran, keep up!" Serai calls. "Our transport is waiting!"

As much as I don't want to follow orders, accomplishing my goal will go twice as fast if I keep my enemies close. Without another word, I leave my spot on the wall and catch up to Callie, Elion, and the Seers.

# CHAPTER 4
## NATE

"COME ON, DAD, OPEN UP."

I bang on the door with my fist. Isn't he home? He never goes anywhere in the summer, except the public library. My station wagon rusting in the carport means he still walks everywhere, too. Weird old science hippie. You can take a man out of the Bay, but you can't take the Bay out of the man.

"Maybe he isn't here," Heike says.

"He better be. We're easy targets for Queen, waiting out in the open like dorks." I knock again, mentally preparing for whatever happens next. Will Dad be happy to see me? Or will he fireball me over the edge of the nearby cliffs?

The latter is most likely.

"No soliciting!" At last, Dad's angry growl reverberates through the door. "How many times do I have to tell people: read the sign!"

"Hey, Dad!" The door swings wide, and I force a smile to counteract his obvious shock, an expression growing darker and angrier by the second. "I'm probably the last person you expected to see standing on your porch, but—"

Instead of greeting me, Dad goes full Fire Manipulator. His

yellow-orange Seer's Eye burns like flame, and with a click of his pocket lighter, he launches a ferocious fireball at my head. Heike and I barely duck in time. She screams, terrified. Fire Manipulation is particularly horrifying the first time you see it.

"Okay, I deserved that," I say.

"What are you doing here?" Dad storms down the steps and backs me onto the lawn with more speed and agility than I anticipated. Dry grass scorches under his blazing feet. "Go back to your Dark realm, Shadowmancer. I have no more Light Cores or World Divers for you to destroy."

I guess I'm not forgiven for setting his kitchen on fire and raiding his basement. I didn't figure I would be, but he's a smidgen angrier than I anticipated.

"I'm not here to cause trouble." I hold my hands high, the Light I used to free myself from the Shadow Plain still glowing in my fingertips. When he sees it, Dad stops in his tracks. Even with the Seer's Eye, he's suspicious.

"How do you have Light in your hands?" Dad snarls. "You're a creature of Darkness."

"And a Luminaut, too. It's a both-and situation. Very complicated. I'm still processing. Can we—"

"How do you have my son's face?" Dad isn't going to let this go without some kind of scientific explanation his mind can rationalize. "Nate died a long time ago. A monster exists in his place."

I don't blame him for thinking I'm playing charades in his kid's human skin-suit. The look in his eyes that night when I stood in the kitchen remains burned in my memory, as fresh as if it happened yesterday. When Dad saw what I chose to become, it was like he watched me die all over again.

Would it matter if I said the part of me that was Queen's

unquestioning servant died that night, too? I doubt it. Dad is still Dad. He doesn't want to hear some long-winded, emotional word-vomit of an explanation.

"I can take human form. And I can also be—well, you saw it. But I'm leaving Darkness behind. For good." Awkward pause. Neither of us makes a move. "Could you put the Fire Manipulation away?"

"Once I'm certain I won't have to use it."

Yeesh, okay. Time to eat the biggest crow I've ever had to swallow.

"I need help." I keep my hands in front of me so Dad sees I'm no threat. "I wouldn't have come home if I didn't know you'd have answers."

"Answers to what?" Dad arches one of his silver eyebrows.

"How Mom got to California with Diver. Specifically, how she Dove without a Light Core." I take a step, just a small one. Dad's fire doesn't flare—positive progress.

"Who is the girl?" Dad nods at Heike. She shrinks under the ferocity of his gaze.

"It's Callie's Seer's sister." I nudge her with my elbow. "Heike Rykjiersen, this is my dad, Richard Ormandi."

"H-h-hello." Heike barely forms the word.

"Callie is alive? And she found her Seer?" At last, the fire around Dad dies, and his eyes fade from yellow-orange to their normal coal-black, coming to rest on the scars marking the left side of my face. "What happened there?"

"Long story."

Another pause settles between us. "Was it Callie?"

"No." I shake my head. "Someone else."

"Ah." He's quiet. Thinking. Dad's always thinking. Heike looks between us, tension etched on her face.

"Look, Dad, I'm sorry. I just—" I purse my lips. "I didn't know where else to go."

Dad's never been physically imposing—he's a distance runner, not a baller, and I've been taller than him since I was fourteen. But that doesn't mean I'm not intimidated by the calculated shrewdness on his face. Mere minutes have passed in his presence and I'm already lost, struggling to navigate a relationship with somebody I never really knew in the first place and understand even less after all I did wrong.

"Get inside." Dad gestures to the open door. "And before you do anything else, take a shower. You both smell like death."

"Thanks, Dad." I lob a grin his way, but he avoids my gaze, scuffing out the scorch marks on the lawn with the toe of his sneaker. Maybe a long shower is a good idea.

*Drip, drip–drop.*

I watch the last droplets fall from the faucet. It's cold, standing here, but I can't bring myself to move. Probably because when I emerge, I'll have to face Dad again, and I don't know if I'm ready.

Something tells me he doesn't want to face me, either.

"Better get this over with."

The shower curtain screeches when I push it aside. I wrap a towel around myself and step into my old bedroom where Dad said I could find fresh clothes.

Whoa, it's actually my room.

None of my stuff has been touched, not even the chewed-up homework pens and notebooks. My Cal Bears cap hangs on a hook next to my favorite Giants cap, my bookshelf is dusted, filled with fantasy paperbacks and Little League trophies, and my bag with my catcher gear lies on the floor. My dresser contains all my old clothes, right down to the threadbare socks. I grab some beach shorts and a Sonic Youth t-shirt to throw on.

Dad's been in here to clean, but not much else. It's like he made a living memorial of the day I "died."

*"He always talks about you, and he has pictures of you everywhere. He misses you a lot."* It's what Callie said when I asked if Dad remembered me. The look in her eyes was gentle, and a little sad — the first time I ever noticed how beautifully they shine in the sunlight.

If he missed me so much, attacking me with fire is a funny way to show it.

The sound of muffled laughter from the living room reminds me that, despite the tightly wound ball of mixed emotions tumbling through my useless chest cavity, I've got an agenda. I run my hands through my damp hair as I enter the living room.

"Hello, Nate!" Heike sits on the couch with a huge mug of tea and a plate of triangle-cut sandwiches. "Richard gave me food."

Dad cranes his neck, catching my eye. He's got tea, too. "I would have made you coffee, but I didn't think you needed things like caffeine in your current state of existence."

As subtly snide as expected. Maybe Callie lied about Dad missing me — or protected me from an unpleasant truth.

"Too bad, I miss coffee." I sit on the floor near the wood stove because Heike's taking up most of the couch with her slouchy, crisscross applesauce posture.

"Richard found me California clothes." Heike gestures proudly to her new outfit — cutoff shorts, a gray hoodie, and black flip-flops.

"I ran an errand while you were both cleaning up," Dad explains at my weird look. "She's near the same size as Callie, it wasn't hard to guess."

Heike is the same *height* as Callie, but Callie's build is that of a long-limbed surfer, slight curves forming her waist and hips — uh, ahem. Anyway, Heike is rangy, like her brother.

"Let's get down to business." Dad sets his teacup on a side table, one with my senior picture on top. He slams the frame facedown before fixing me with a glare. "You want to know how your mother got to California without a Light Core, correct?"

"Yes." Guess we're jumping into the deep end, head first. "So, how'd she do it?"

"She and her previous Seer — an Earth Manipulator — opened a gateway in the ground, and Mari used all her Light, channeled through Diver's Prism, to Dive. They had to be extremely precise given the unknown nature of the experiment. Anything less, and both your mother and Diver would have been lost."

"But it can be done," I say. "Diving without a Light Core."

"It isn't a matter of can and can't, it *should not* be done." Dad knows exactly what I'm thinking. "What your mother did was extremely dangerous. That's why I never put the idea into Callie James's head. You should get it out of your head as well."

"Unfortunately, I don't have another option, and abandoning Callie is a risk I won't take."

My plan to throw Queen off Callie's trail seems to have worked, but only temporarily. Her poisonous words slither through my mind, culminating with a shudder: the things she said she'd do to Callie and El fill me with fear like I've never known.

"You suddenly care what happens to Callie James?" An impenetrable wall of stone erects itself around Dad's face. "I was under the impression you'd do anything to destroy her Light, even ruin the lives of everyone in Verona Beach that cares for her."

Dad picks up a stack of newspapers and tosses them to me. Callie's face, in official school photos and candid shots provided by family and friends, graces the front page of them all. Stark headlines tell a bleak story.

*Local Teen, Calliope "Callie" James, Still Missing Two Weeks After Mysterious VBHS Gym Fire. No Evidence of Human Remains Found in Rubble*

*Coast Guard Has No Official Statement for Paranormal Light Phenomena Witnessed the Night Calliope James Disappeared*

*Somber Prom: VBHS Upperclassmen Honor Calliope James with Candle Lighting Ceremony While Local Surf Community Holds Memorial Paddle-Out*

*Bereaved Parents of Callie James Refuse to Make Plans for Funeral Service: "We believe she's alive, and she's out there."*

Hello, guilt and shame, you're appropriately on time. Everything lurches forward, indescribable pain searing my insides. I was so blinded by lies and anger that I couldn't see— didn't want to see—the horror I brought upon Callie, her family and friends, the whole town.

"I'm sorry."

Heike snatches the papers from my hands, staring at pictures of Callie, the gym, and other random journalistic shots telling the aftermath of Callie's Dive.

"Your newfound regret won't make things right." Dad's eyes glint like onyx. "Now you owe me answers to my questions."

"I figured." Vulnerability shrinks me in Dad's presence. Tough, Nate, you made this mess. It's time to start cleaning up.

"How long have you had Light powers?" Dad folds his arms. "Or was I mistaken earlier?"

"Nate has Light powers," Heike blurts, looking up from the

newspapers. "He's a Luminaut. The Queen Beyond the Stars called him one."

"The Queen Beyond the Stars." Dad blinks hard, like he can't believe the name he just heard. "Is she serious?"

"She is." I force the Shadows in my mind to part, to remember exactly what happened. "I knew I was a Luminaut before I Turned to Darkness, but I didn't want to tell you. I thought it would make you more sad about Mom. Or maybe I was scared to call it what it was. I wanted to find Earth's Light Core before I said anything, but Queen found me first."

"But what does the long-dead Prime Shadowmancer have to do with you?" Dad's next question is more than a little fearful.

"She's not dead. Not in the technical sense, anyway." My confirmation is a nightmare made real for Dad. His face drains of color, turning ashen.

"She lives?" Dad isn't interested in my confession so much as he's horrified by Queen's existence.

"Yes. And she's going to find us and kill us. Slowly." Geez, Heike, why do you sound so nonchalant about it? A small smile appears on her lips, but then again, it could be that she's still noshing her sandwiches. She holds the plate out to Dad after popping the last one into her mouth. "Can I have more to eat, please?"

"Help yourself in the kitchen." Dad rests his chin on his balled fist while Heike hops up to get more snacks. When she's gone, he turns to me. "Are you still working for the Queen? Following her orders?"

"No." It hurts that it's the first thing he assumes, but I also can't blame him. "The reason she gave me these" —I gesture to the tiger stripes on my face—"is because I started acting on my own. And I'm still acting on my own."

Dad stares at the scars, how deep they are, how raw. When Queen was cutting my face apart, trying to torture me into loyal submission, she probably didn't think my scars would be the key to getting people to believe I'm being truthful. It's a miscalculation in my favor.

"So how do you plan to reunite with Callie, now that you're acting on your own?" Dad switches topics. "Will your Luminaut powers be involved?"

"You got it." I steel my resolve against the bomb about to explode in my face. "I'm going to use my car to Dive. And your Seer powers."

"Absolutely not." Boom-boom, mushroom cloud. Called it. Dad shakes his head so fast his neck cracks. "I'm not opening a gateway so you can kill yourself and that girl Diving your old car to—where is Callie?"

"Ensolorada."

"Mechs like the World Diver are made with a rare type of bronze and contain crystals only mined in Ensolorada that channel Light, allowing them to pass through multiversal gateways unharmed." Dad rubs his neck where his joints popped. "Your old car is not made of that particular metal, nor does it contain a Prism crystal."

"I don't care if the car gets trashed. It's got to get us through one gateway, one time. And we'll improvise a Prism." Heike's Light lantern still glows in a far corner. I move to pick it up. "This works. We'll amplify the Light with incandescent bulbs, Christmas lights, anything."

Dad stands and takes the Light lantern, staring at the shimmering orb inside. Uncertainty fills his eyes. "How strong is your Light?" he asks. "Have you practiced with it?"

This is *not* the right time to admit I suck at anything Light related. "I've used it enough times to scare Queen." Which is true. "I'm not as controlled as Callie." Dad's jaw hardens. Backpedal, Nate. You're losing him. "But it's the only way to get to Ensolorada. I'll do whatever it takes."

Dad remains quiet, his expression unreadable. He's got an uncanny way of masking every emotion on his face so I can't tell what he's feeling. It's a strategy I perfected the last few years of my human life, a helpful trick when doing Queen's bidding, but I'm sick of those games.

"I can't risk this kind of gamble." Dad hands me the lantern. "I'm sorry. It's impossible."

"No, it's not." I carefully check my desire to roll my eyes, but this kind of ambivalence is so Richard Ormandi it's killing me. "Highly unlikely isn't impossible, and you know it. You're just afraid to try."

"Don't I have a right to be afraid?" Dad hugs his arms around his middle, personal armor against my chaotic schemes. "First, you set my kitchen on fire as a Shadowmancer after trying to destroy Earth's Light Core. Then you show up on my porch looking just like my son who sailed away forever, claiming you're actually a Luminaut. To make matters worse, you want me to leave the world where I have every single memory of Mariasol, all so you can jump you car off the cliffs, hoping you'll conjure enough Light to Dive your derelict vehicle through a multiversal gateway."

"I'm sorry, what?" Back the train into the station, Dad. "Did you say jump my car off the cliffs?"

"Was that really the only thing you heard?" Dad groans and sinks into his chair. "I thought you were smarter than this, better at strategizing. But you've always had a habit of proving me wrong."

Ouch, Dad. If I'd hoped things would be different, I was dead wrong. Which is a good pun (*dead* wrong, get it?), but I'm not in the mood to laugh at myself right now.

It was a mistake, coming here before finding Callie in Ensolorada. What was I thinking, making such a stupid call? Dad's not wrong to say I should be better at strategies. I *know* I can be better, more calculated with my maneuvers. Am I really *that* emotional when it comes to decisions that involve El and Callie?

Don't answer that.

"Did somebody say we're jumping off the cliffs?" Heike comes back, her plate loaded with a random smorgasbord of snack food: pita crisps, Oreos, some grapes, and a bag of shelled pistachios. Counter surfing for the win.

"We're not jumping off the —"

"Yes, we are," I interrupt before Dad contradicts the plan I'm committed to, whether I like the plan or not. "The gateway to Ensolorada is hanging in midair. Lucky us."

Dad snorts derisively. "The gateway's location makes you anything but lucky, if you ask me."

I didn't, but thanks, Dad.

"How will we Dive through the gateway without a World Diver?" Heike resumes her seat on the couch.

"I already told you, we aren't —"

"We've got a Subaru," I interrupt Dad again.

"What's a Subaru?"

"I can assure you, it is *not* a World Diver," Dad snarks.

Okay, enough. I rise, and Dad meets my gaze. Time to say what I have to say and leave the ball in his court.

"Coming with me was never on the table. If you want to stay here, that choice is yours." I retreat to my room, pulling on my

Giants cap and stepping into flip-flops. "Where are the old Christmas lights?"

"What are Christmas lights?" Heike asks when I emerge.

"Don't worry about it." I glance at Dad once Heike dives back into her tower of Oreos. "Well? Did you keep them?"

"You're serious about doing this?" Dad places his hand on my face-down senior picture.

"Yes, I am. I have vital information Callie needs to destroy the Shadow Plain, and I'm going to give it to her, even if it means pulling dangerous *Back to the Future* stunts with my car."

"Nate, listen to me, I—"

"I didn't come here under any misguided notion we'd have some big, happy family reunion," I go on. "Too much went down between us for that. All I ask is that you open the gateway so Heike and I can Dive. After that, you never have to see me again."

Dad winces slightly, a betrayal of softer emotion, something he never allowed me to see, even when I was human. He picks up the picture frame and sets it right. "The lights are in the shed out back."

"Cool." I spin on my heel and pass through the kitchen—newly remodeled since the fire I started—and down the steps into the back yard.

No matter what Dad thinks, I have to get back to Callie. I just hope my speech was enough to convince him to open the gateway to Ensolorada. If not, my chances of success plummet to absolute zero.

# CHAPTER 5
# CALLIE

"THANKS FOR BUSTING US OUT of jail. That was awesome of you. Anyway, where's my World Diver?"

The words are out of my mouth before the door to the transport—basically, a flying, egg-shaped shuttle—has a chance to close behind me. I should probably be less abrupt about Diver's whereabouts, especially since Serai just bailed us out of a jam, but I can't take it back now.

A mech driver asks Serai her destination, and she takes a glass tablet out of her pocket, one that glows yellow when she taps the screen. It looks just like the tablet Manu used to show us the hologram Rognaga map. Ayla called them "comms."

"You mean the ancient, last-known World Diver you destroyed in the desert?" Serai taps on her tablet, and the mech driver responds with a monotone affirmative before the transport rises into the air and zooms away. "Most likely being disassembled for tech scrap at the Hall of Machines."

"Disassembled for scrap?!" I lurch forward in my seat. "I can't let that happen. Is the Hall of Machines where they took Nemo, too? I've got to go there and—"

"You'll do no such thing." Serai shoots me a humorless glare.

"You revealed yourself as a Luminaut to one of the most corrupt politicians in Cordonanza, one who would manipulate your powers to gain another Light Core for himself. Until I say otherwise, you'll be laying low, working on a solution to the Darkness trailing you."

How does she not understand? I can't do anything about Darkness and Queen until I have my mechs, safe and sound. "I totally get that I kinda sorta started an apocalypse. Accidentally. But my mechs aren't scrap, they're my friends. I need to find them."

"Considering that it's a matter of time before Shadowmancers from another dimension attack my city, I'm the only person who will decide what is needed." Serai isn't much for negotiation, is she? All I'm asking for is two robots—one of which is fifty feet tall, but details.

"Maybe I could find Diver and Nemo for Callie," El suggests. "Then she can stay at your house like you want and make a plan about the monster woman."

"That is a fair compromise." Ayla flashes a grin across the transport. Ayla gets it, why doesn't Serai?

Toran looks up from massaging the red spots the tiles left on his heels and snorts disdainfully. "Even if you found the World Diver you couldn't repair him, and the headache otherwise called Nemo can rot in the dunes for all I care."

"What's a Nemo, and why is it a headache?" Ayla looks between me and Toran.

"I told you not to talk to me." Ah, the angry badger is back! Watch out, Ayla, he bites.

"Let's change the subject." It's aways a good idea not to get on the bad side of the people who could toss us back in jail, even if Toran seems intent on getting vine-strangled. "How does that skeevy dude, Manu, have a map to Ensolorada's Light Core written in Tremurheim runes?"

"Yes, how *does* he have that map?" Toran pauses his foot rub, suddenly interested. Languages and maps are his favorite things, besides disparaging Nemo.

"It's a map to the *supposed* site of the Rognaga," Serai corrects me. "Ancient Lore has long been Manu's obsession, especially buying, selling, and trading banned artifacts."

"So the map is something Manu shouldn't have in the first place," I conclude.

"Precisely. The last known person to see the map was Mariasol until Manu showed up with a copy, shouting about hunting Light Cores at otherwise productive Guardian forums." She pauses, adjusting her bracelets so the seeded gems don't get caught on her skirt. "According to legend, the Rognaga is a labyrinth that hides Ensolorada's Light Core. It is said to be unsolvable. Anyone who tried to navigate it met a horrific death, and the location of the maze was lost to time and memory."

I nudge Toran with my elbow. "Hey, can you say 'Beacons of Tremurheim?'"

"Of course I can say it." Oh look, there's the point, flying over Toran's head. "I'll admit, however, that it sounds like a very similar scenario."

"One we solved before." Getting my hands on Manu's map just became another task to add to my increasingly long to-do list.

"If the Rognaga still exists, only a fool would attempt to enter it." Serai swishes her hand through the air in a way that reminds me of Dr. Ormandi. "Mariasol knew better than to risk our lives chasing fantasies through endless dunes."

"But Manu said everyone wanted her to find the Light Core anyway. Is that why she left Ensolorada?" I ask. "Did she know the Light Cores are the keys to releasing the Queen Beyond the Stars and her powers?"

If Mariasol knew the truth, she never mentioned it in her journals. Dr. Ormandi never mentioned it, either, but he had his own agenda in helping me, and it wasn't guiding teenage Luminauts to make good choices.

"Understanding the destruction she'd unleash if she were to find Ensolorada's Light Core is one of the myriad reasons Mariasol fled." Serai's face tightens briefly before smoothing into detached chill. "I've spent the last sixty years protecting her secrets, and I have no intention of betraying her now."

Serai is older than sixty? Wow, she looks *great* for her age. The medical tech in Ensolorada must be as advanced as everything else.

"People in Cordonanza have an unfortunate tendency to forget what shouldn't be forgotten and remember what they should forget," Serai adds darkly. "You should learn to forget certain things as well."

"'Certain things' being my mechs and Ensolorada's lost Light Core," I surmise.

Serai's succinct nod confirms my suspicion. "I'll take care of Manu and his schemes. In the meantime, you are going to make Darkness mitigation your primary objective. Are we agreed?"

"You've definitely made your point." Acknowledgement without explicit agreement—doesn't mean I'm *not* going to find Nemo and Diver the first chance I get, but the fine print isn't relevant.

"Excellent." Serai settles back next to Ayla. "Here we are. Home at last."

The transport glides smoothly to a stop in front of the most swag penthouse I've ever seen. Gigantic windows let in deepfake sunlight that blocks the light of the moon and stars far overhead. Lush, private gardens surrounded by marble walls encase the perimeter, and crystal sculptures flank the front entrance, reflecting prisms of color across the glossy white steps. Once we're inside, the swank-factor continues. Everything is bright and airy, pleasantly cool despite the heat outside. Creamy furniture with earth-toned pillows, rugs in complementary hues, and tinkling chandeliers occupy my vision, as well as dozens of mechs ready and waiting to take shoes, offer beverages and snacks, and direct people into a plush sitting room with million-dollar city views.

"Keep all water away from this one," Serai instructs a mech as she gestures at Toran. "I won't be stabbed by an ice dagger while my back is turned."

"What if I'm thirsty?" Toran argues.

"I'm quite certain you aren't," Serai argues right back, and Toran scowls at being fully called out. Another mech offers Serai a cup of spiced tea. "Comms have been ordered for all of you, as well as appropriate wardrobes for the heat. Mechs will show you to your rooms, so please, make yourselves at home."

"Uh, thanks," I say. "That's really nice of you."

"I would hardly be Cordonanzan if I were less than hospitable. It is shameful not to welcome guests properly." Serai sounds slightly offended I would doubt her generosity. "Now, please excuse me."

"Where are you going, Mama?" Ayla takes a knitted shrug from a mech, draping it over her bare shoulders.

"To contact the Hall of Guardians regarding Manu and the Light Cores, and conduct preliminary damage control. No doubt Luminaut rumors are already wildly circulating." Serai looks tired just thinking about it. "If anybody needs additional comforts, you'll have to see to them. And until I say otherwise, no one leaves the estate."

Serai whips out her comm, tapping the screen, and a bearded man's face appears in the air. An intense conversation ensues as she strides down the hall, disappearing behind a door. As soon as she's out of sight, a glowing yellow barrier appears over the front entry and the surrounding windows, similar to the force field in the containment center.

Force fields, great. This robot rescue caper just got a lot harder.

"Is anybody hungry?" Ayla approaches with an eager smile. "Our mechs can bring you anything you like, or I can make you something myself. I'm getting to be a very good baker, I'd be happy to—"

"I'm not hungry." Toran ices Ayla with his infamous death-stare before marching down the hall with a mech on his heels, directing him into a nearby bedroom.

Ayla chews on her lips, then squeezes them together a few times. "Dunes. He hates me," she murmurs.

"Welcome to the club. Don't worry, Toran hates everyone." I don't know if my reassurance makes Ayla feel better, but she stops squeezing her lips.

"I didn't mean to zap him," she promises.

"He came at you with ice knives. Self-defense is valid." When I smile, she smiles back this time. "How do you make electricity with your hands? Something to do with your Manipulation?"

"Yes, I'm an Air Manipulator." Ayla swirls her hands. A soft breeze stirs the air, and tiny sparks dance on her fingertips. "Air is full of electricity. I can call it into my hands and discharge it wherever I wish. But I tend to go overboard without meaning to. The last time I zapped somebody was at my old school. A boy and I had an altercation …" A small shudder ripples across her shoulders, and the wavering breeze blowing through the room hastens, clinking the chandelier. "Mama allowed me to learn at home afterwards, and I've been much happier."

Happier? Homeschooling Ayla because she had problems with a bully is one thing, but actively discouraging human contact is another. From what I've seen, this is a case of the latter.

Speaking of things Serai discouraged … whether I can trust Ayla to help me is uncertain, but I've got to take a chance anyway. She seemed to be on my side in the transport — was it all for show?

"Listen, Ayla." I sit next to her. "I know your mom said to forget Diver and my other mech, Nemo, but I need to find them. It's my fault Diver is broken, and I have to fix him. I can't prevent Darkness from taking over the multiverse without him. He has memories of his Luminauts before the Lightbridge was destroyed." I search her, trying to gauge whether she understands. "Does the Lightbridge sound familiar?"

"Of course." Ayla nods. "All Ensoloradans know about the Lightbridge and the Light Collective era. Before the Severing."

Severing. As in, the multiverse was hacked to pieces by Queen's Darkness, and Light was broken forever. Such a simple word to describe what must have been cataclysmic beyond measure.

"What happened to the Lightbridge is a cautionary tale of Luminauts abusing their power," Ayla goes on. "I know Mama comes across as strict, but if anybody saw you using Light, it wouldn't end well. There's still an active warrant for Mariasol Zaira. You'd be considered equally as dangerous."

"I won't use my powers in public," I promise. "But no matter how dangerous people might think I am, Queen is worse, and I was serious when I said I can't defeat her without my mechs.

Diver is more than just a multiverse-hopping vehicle. He's—"

"Your friend." Ayla sighs wistfully, as though that word is something she wants more than anything. "Despite what Mama thinks, I agree you should try to find him. But—"

"I understand your mom has rules." Implicating Ayla in Diver and Nemo's recovery mission would be completely unfair. "I just need you to disable the security system and call a transport to take me to the Hall of Machines. That's all."

"What I was going to say is that Mama will have put a transport alert out by now, forbidding them to dock here unless the signal originates from her personal comm. And my comm can't access the force shield." Ayla gestures to the faint yellow glow on the door and windows. She gives me a sad look. "I'm sorry. I can see your Diver and Nemo mean a lot to you."

"Let's steal Serai's comm." El sprawls out on the floor in front of the couch. "Then we'll be able to control the force shield, not her."

"You automatically jump to petty theft?" He spent too much time around Nate. Besides, Serai would hogtie us with vines before we got within ten feet of her comm. "There's got to be another way to bypass the security and get where we need to go …" An old-school way. "If we can't call a transport, can we travel to the Hall of Machines on foot?"

"Theoretically, yes," Ayla replies. "But I don't know what the Hall of Machines looks like. I haven't really been anywhere since I arrived in Ensolo—" Her eyes get big and she sucks in a breath, sparks flying around her fingers. They disappear when she closes her hands into tight fists. "I mean, since I came to Cordonanza from Oasis III."

Weird slip. Meh.

"I saw the Machine Hall thing." El rolls around on the floor, reaching for something under the couch Ayla and I are sitting on—a dust-encrusted piece of what looks like candy. "What's this? Is it food?"

"It's disgusting. Please don't eat it." A mech whizzes up, removes the garbage from El's hand, and whizzes away. I've got to get a housecleaning mech to trail after Nemo and remove his filth from my path—as soon as I free him from wherever he's held captive. "How do you know you saw the Hall of Machines?"

"I looked out the transport windows while you were busy arguing with Serai about the labyrinth thing. There was a humongous building below us with all kinds of signs for robots around it." He takes a savory-smelling meat and vegetable roll from a mech who anticipated hunger based on El's willingness to ingest garbage candy.

"Yes, that's the Hall of Machines, I'm sure!" Ayla claps her hands, smiling.

I catch El's eye. "Do you remember the path?"

"No, but all the streets are laid out in squares," El says. "You can find *anything* in squares."

Just like El to let everyone think he's not paying attention when his focus is right where it needed to be all along. "Can you scout us there on foot from street level? You already scouted a Light Core at the bottom of a dark, twisting mineshaft. A giant building full of robots on a grid shouldn't be hard."

"Sure, I'll scout for you. I can scout anything." El puffs his chest proudly.

"Awesome!" I give El a high five. "All we have to do now is figure out how to get past the force shields."

Ayla rises from the couch. "May I make a suggestion?"

"Go for it," I say.

"Mama may have a poor opinion of Manu Carosti, and for

good reason, but he doesn't *always* tell lies." She twists her fingers together while she thinks. "Cordonanza's solar coils are, in fact, failing. Mama has been securing votes to design new, sustainable solartech. Manu wants to build his power extractor for the Light Cores."

"Yeah, he made that obvious." I'm still not over that leech stealing my Light Cores and saying *I* was the thief. "But I'm not sure what that has to do with shutting down your mom's security system."

"There's a point, I promise." Ayla paces in front of the windows, looking out across the vast city of sparkling marble fountains, luxury gardens, and gleaming transports. "Because the solar coils are failing, Cordonanza has power curfews and planned electricity cuts. There's a small window of one hour, just before sundown, when the power goes out city-wide."

"And that benefits us how?"

"We can sneak past Mama's security measures during the power cut." Ayla leaves the window and faces me with a conspiratorial smile. "We have a generator to keep necessities running, but the console that operates our force shields is not considered essential."

"Awesome! Thanks, Ayla." I sling my arm around her shoulder, giving her a side hug, and she practically beams.

"One problem." El points to the tops of the glistening white skyscrapers beyond the windows. "If there's no electricity or transports, how are we going to get down to the street?"

"I'll use my Manipulation to channel the air currents," Ayla suggests. "We'll float to the ground easily."

"Won't you be in huge trouble with Serai if we get busted?" Getting caught sounds way more sketchy than relying on Ayla's untested Manipulation skills to escape.

Ayla giggles. "I will not be busted. I'm a person, not a vase." Okay then, cool. "Mama will understand when I explain the situation. She would never hurt my friends."

"Seriously?" That sounds like a blissfully naive estimation of Serai, but what do I know?

"Diver is your friend. Mama always says how important it is to help friends, even when it might seem wrong or dangerous," Ayla assures me. "I'm happy to help you, my new friends."

She *wants* to be friends, that much is obvious — openly defying Serai's hardcore rules is her olive branch. I'm not going to refuse help, especially help from a local. Even if Ayla's never been to the Hall of Machines, she knows the customs and culture of Cordonanza and can help El and I avoid trouble.

"The fact that you electrocuted Toran makes us automatic besties," I say with a smile. "I appreciate any help my friends give. Thank you."

"You're very welcome, Callie." Ayla throws her arms around me and hugs a little too tight before pulling away.

"I'm still really hungry." El and his bottomless stomach interject themselves into the conversation. "Can I have more to eat?"

"Of course!" Ayla remains all-too-eager to assist. "We have plenty in the kitchen. Let's see what the mechs can cook for us."

"Cool. I'll be there in a minute." El catches my eye, unspoken communication passing between us. He has something to say and doesn't want Ayla to hear.

"Yeah, we'll catch up," I add.

"As you like. The kitchen is through the far door, opposite the dining solarium." Ayla practically floats away, her flowery skirt billowing behind her as if blown by an invisible breeze.

Once she's out of sight, El turns to me with a look that's clear and piercing, almost Nate-like. "Do you really trust her to help us save Nemo and Diver?"

"She's our one-way ticket out of here." I shrug. "What other choice do we have?"

"She could rat us out to Serai," El says. "Just like Toran could rat us out to—well, anybody."

"Toran is a non-issue. He'd rather rot in the sun than help me find Nemo and Diver." He's never hidden the fact he hates my mechs.

"I don't know about that." El shifts his gaze down the hall where Toran stomped off. "He was really interested in the map to the Rognaga and where the Light Core is hidden. If he finds out we're escaping, he'll try to come too."

"Toran doesn't trust anyone except himself," I remind El, "and never does anything unless he benefits in some way."

"Do you think Ayla's the same as Toran?" El pulls his knees into his chest, searching me with his gaze.

"No, I think she's sincere. She wants to help."

"If you trust her, I trust her," El replies. "Nate trusted you too, before the monster lady took him away."

"You think Nate was a good judge of character?" I might have laughed at the suggestion before, but after Nate fought Queen on Tremurheim so we had a chance to escape—and the aching apology he gave Diver through his Light before he died—I wonder if maybe El's right.

"He made a lot of mistakes, but he admitted them." El's big brown eyes are suddenly glassy. "He wanted to make things right with you. And he'd want you to find Diver and Nemo and beat the monster lady, even if it means trusting Ayla. He believed you're the only person who can win."

"I hope he was right." Nate was wrong about a lot of things, but he told the truth about Queen when it mattered. Am I another one of his many misjudgments? Or something he was right about all along?

I only hope Ayla's as trustworthy as I think she is. Because as much as Nate was wrong, I've been equally wrong about things too — with disastrous consequences.

# CHAPTER 6
# TORAN

"INCOMING TRANSMISSION from Manu Carosti."

At last! I scramble to grab my comm from the table beside my bed, next to the picked-over plate of food a mech brought in with some disgustingly sweet juice. Serai was serious when she said I wouldn't be allowed any water—not even to drink.

"Hello, this is Toran Rykjiersen." I hold the glass rectangle up to my mouth. "Hello. Hello?" But the comm doesn't show me Manu's face or let me hear his voice. Dramora spawn!

This is already a disaster, all because I accidentally fell asleep instead of learning how to use my comm. Long curtains fell and covered the windows once the sun came up, making my room comfortably cool and dark as Misty night. I couldn't help but doze off, spinning my internal clock of sleeping and waking completely backward.

The only tolerable thing about residing in a nocturnal desert the rest of my days was knowing Heike would be with me, safe from Tremurheim's dangers. Now, my future stretches before me as bleak and barren as the sand dunes.

I have one future worth living for: I will avenge my sister. All else is loss.

"Incoming transmission from Manu Carosti," my comm says again.

"Yes, I know." How do I get the comm to show me the transmission? A blinking dot pulses beside the featureless comm-person-thing, hovering above the glass. Do I press the air beside the blinking dot? That sounds stupid, pressing air, but I don't see an alternative. I try it, and finally, Manu's floating frown appears.

"Took you long enough to answer," he grouches. "Don't tell me you were still asleep. Early risers accomplish more than lazy, sleeping sand ogres."

"I was awake, I just—" What's a good excuse that doesn't make me seem like a lazy sand ogre? "My, er, comm was being difficult."

Manu nods like he believes me. "Comms are touchy, especially if the avatar interface is acting up. Let's get down to business." Yes, let's. I like that Manu doesn't waste time. "You said my map of the Rognaga site is written in Tremurheim runes."

"Yes, although the runes I saw on the map are ancient, from before the Clan Wars. It's a style that fell out of favor during Assimilation—"

"I don't need a history lesson." Manu cuts me off and rolls his eyes impatiently. "Can you translate it or not?"

"Yes, I can."

"Good."

Manu disappears, and the map I glimpsed in jail floats in the air above me, as wide as my whole room and glowing with runes like twinkling stars. A twisting, turning labyrinth unfolds in the shape of a diamond with a massive hole at the center, as if a boulder fell from the height of the tallest tree in Tremurheim and cut a bottomless pit into the forest floor. In the top corner of the map are sets of coordinates and directions, and shimmering lights mark three corners of the winding path inside the maze, each one drawing closer to the center pit. It is intricate, carefully carved, both terrifying and beautiful.

How long did it take to make this labyrinth of stone? And *who* could have made it, all to keep a Light Core hidden? It's too complex for human miners and masons to have created this work of art. Just looking at the Rognaga is dizzying. I can't imagine trying to solve it. No wonder Serai said any who tried met a terrible death.

"All right, Toran from Tremurheim, get translating." Manu's voice cuts through the solitary floating map, reminding me I cannot simply stare at the Rognaga in awe. He's expecting me to work.

"My labor isn't free," I say.

"Payment, yes. Of course." The map disappears, and I'm faced with Manu's scowling head once more. "What's your price? A couple thousand credits? Ten thousand? An internship at the Hall of Guardians?"

As if I want money or power. All I'm interested in is one thing.

"The Luminaut, Callie James, is the reason my sister died." I swallow hard, choking on the lump of grief stuck in my throat. "I want to make sure her Light never harms anyone I care about again."

"So she *is* a Luminaut!" Manu can't conceal his glee. "I knew Serai was lying." He rubs his hands together, his smile stretching across his narrow face. "As you wish. I'll get rid of her Light powers."

"Can you really do that?" I don't see how Manu could take away Callie's powers as a normal human. Something like that seems to be the magic of other Luminauts, Seers, or worse, Shadowmancers.

"Ensolorada's Record Halls house all the Lore regarding Luminauts, World Divers, and the ancient Light Collective," Manu's tone takes on an impatient edge. "When I promise I can make it so the girl never harms another person with Light, believe me, I know what I'm talking about."

If there's one thing more powerful than Light, Shadow, or Elemental Manipulation, it's knowledge. I'm ignorant of the Lore, so it stands to reason Manu knows something I don't.

"Then we have a deal," I say. "What, exactly, do you expect from me?" I sit on a plush chair beside the window. The curtains are drawn, which means the Ensoloradan sun hasn't set, but once it does, I risk being overheard. "Do you want me to translate a path for you to find the Light Core yourself?"

"Here's where things get tricky," Manu replies. "Only a Luminaut can survive the Rognaga and reach the Light Core at the center. As much as I want to find it myself, I wouldn't make it out alive. Luckily, my father realized this before he got himself killed."

"That's why he sent Mariasol Zaira in search of the Rognaga with Serai." It makes sense now. "And instead of finding the Light Core, she ran away with the World Diver."

"You catch on fast." A sneer reveals Manu's gleaming teeth. "Mariasol and Serai were meant to complete the Rognaga sixty years ago, the first time the solar coils failed. My father outfitted them with everything they'd need, trained them to survive harsh conditions, all on the agreement they would bring the Light Core back to Cordonanza and end the crisis. But Mariasol betrayed us."

"His first mistake was trusting a Luminaut." Bitterness

making my tongue raw.

"Trust is a dangerous game." Manu's yellow eyes grow hard above his leer. "Serai allows less-fortunate Cordonanzans to suffer the current power crisis while she sits in her crystal estate, holding out for votes. But I don't believe all of your kind are similarly cruel. I trust you'll translate the map, find the Light Core in the Rognaga, and bring it to me."

He needs me, a Seer, to find the Light Core? "But you just said only a Luminaut can retrieve the Light Core from the —"

"Yes, that's part of our deal." Manu cuts me off. He has a bad habit of interrupting. "I can't hold up my end of the bargain until you and the Luminaut finish the maze."

"No." The word is out of my mouth quicker than a nargush swooping on its prey. "I refuse to do this with Callie."

"The problem is" — Manu's malevolent glower sends a shiver of dread down my spine — "you're a ward under Serai's protection, as is Callie James. Conspiring to defraud your benefactor carries a strong penalty. It would be a shame if word of this conversation got out to the right people ... or wrong people, depending on how you look at it. Am I making myself clear?"

I don't like being at Manu's slippery mercy, but there's no other choice. It's a small consolation that my partnership with him is temporary.

"You're perfectly clear," I murmur.

"I'm sending you a copy of the map. The Luminaut can't know it came from me. Say you accessed it from the Record Hall on your comm." Manu glances down, his hand moving rapidly back and forth, and my comm glows yellow, a tiny version of the Rognaga map appearing on the glass. "Once she finds the Light Core, contact me. I'll take care of the rest."

"One last concern. I, erm, don't exactly get along with Callie." Two brawling dramora trying to tear each other's throats out get along better. "And she has no interest in hunting Light Cores until she locates her lost mechs."

"That's your problem. Don't make it mine." Manu's eyes flash darkly. "Find her mechs and gain her trust. I need the fourth Core in my hands before the next forum vote, or my last chance to build this extractor slips through my fingers." Manu leans forward until only his face can be seen above my comm, glaring with menace. "Get me what I want, or I'll find somebody else to translate my map."

"That's not necessary." I gulp, my mouth suddenly dry. "I'll feign friendship with Callie."

"Good." Manu nods as though he was expecting my answer. "Off you go, Translator Toran."

The transmission ends and my comm goes dark, save for the glowing mini-map of the Rognaga in the far corner of the glass.

Forest spare me, how am I going to pretend to be friends with Callie? We argue constantly—she never thinks through a single thing, rushing headlong into trouble. On top of her impetuous personality, she's stubborn to a fault about her mechs, both of which I hate. There is nothing redeemable about those idiotic nuisances she loves so dearly.

But the key to winning her trust and finding Ensolorada's Light Core *is* her mechs. Without them, there's no going forward.

Lands Beyond, this will be painful. I need a drink of water to clear my head, not this awful juice that makes my teeth sticky. I pocket my comm and open the door, intent to find the kitchen before Serai or a mech catches me.

No lights provide a path to see down the surprisingly dark hallway, and no mechs roam the premises. That's odd, given how bright and full of activity the house was when we first arrived. Now it's so dark I can't see anything except—

Except a small orb of Light glowing in the entry hall, accompanied by hushed voices.

I hang back, observing. Callie stands huddled in a semi-circle with Ayla and Elion. Callie and the boy have changed into practical Ensoloradan clothing and sturdy shoes. Ayla wears yet another ridiculous dress, but instead of pink flowers, it's pale blue, puffy, and hits at her knees, revealing walking sandals instead of fanciful slippers. Everything about their conversation feels conspiratorial.

Yes, they're definitely making escape plans. It's a good thing I found them when I did or I might have missed my chance to enact Manu's plot.

"Where are you going?"

Callie startles at my voice, Light flaring fiercely in her palms. Electricity gathers in Ayla's hands when she whirls around to face me, and Elion groans.

"I told you he'd find us and ruin everything," the boy laments far too loudly.

"Shh, quiet." Callie jabs him with her elbow before turning her scowl onto me. "Go back to bed, Toran, this doesn't concern you."

"Are you escaping?" I approach cautiously. Sparks crackle in Ayla's diamond-white Seer's Eye, and I have no desire to be electrocuted again.

"Like I said, this doesn't—"

"If you're going to find Nemo and Diver, I want to help." I'm interrupting the way Manu interrupted me, but I can't let them turn me away.

"Excuse me?" Callie narrows her eyes suspiciously.

"Yeah, excuse me?" Elion assesses me with more shrewdness than I'd given him credit for.

"I want to help you find the lost mechs."

Callie doesn't reply. Instead, she laughs, a spray of spittle flying from her lips before she covers her mouth with a Light-filled hand. Why is she laughing? Nothing I said was funny.

"I'm sorry." Callie wipes her eyes and presses her lips to stifle another laugh. "I just — I thought I heard you say you want to help find Nemo and Diver, but clearly I need my ears checked."

"Checked for what?" Ayla inspects Callie's ears with concern. "They look fine to me."

She doubts my sincerity. Dramora spawn, I shouldn't have tried to kick that menace Nemo so many times! I must act swiftly — and act well, which is infinitely harder. "I've had time to think."

"Uh-huh." Callie nods for me to go on.

"And I thought if you miss Nemo and Diver the way I miss —" I can't bring myself to say Heike's name. It sticks in my throat, and I swallow hard to prevent a lump from forming. "In any case, one of us should be reunited with our loved ones."

"That's very kind, Toran." Ayla smiles, a genuine expression. The sparks leave her eyes, but not the sparkle. At least she isn't laughing at me like Callie, or incredulous like Elion. "We welcome your help."

"Do we?" Callie arches an eyebrow. I think she would rather accept help from a screeching skuddima.

"Of course!" Ayla nods emphatically. "Why wouldn't we accept help from friends?" If I can get Ayla on my side, perhaps Callie will follow.

"I agree." My lips quirk when I look at Ayla, an attempt at a grin. Smiling feels too unnatural, but a grin will suffice. She smiles brightly enough for both of us.

"Except Toran and I aren't friends," Callie says, "and we never have been." As much as I'd like to argue, she's correct.

"Plus, he hates Nemo," Elion adds. Again, correct.

I'm not going to succeed if I don't shift their focus. How would Heike have handled this? She was far better at navigating social situations.

"I don't have to like the mechs to have a change of heart about helping you find them." Lying is repulsive, but that, at least, is true. I'm just conveniently omitting *why* I've had a change of heart. "Please, we must go before the sun sets."

"Crap, you're right." Callie sighs. "Fine, you can join the mech heist. But don't even *think* about pulling any sketchy shenanigans, got it?"

"Toran will not do shenanigans, whatever that is," Ayla says, reaching for the door. "Come, Mama will wake soon."

The moment Ayla touches the handle, a yellow force shield activates across the threshold, and a piercing alarm tears the air. No less than seven guard mechs, all of them wielding active blasters, whiz into the entryway, eyes as red as flames.

"Attention: security compromised." The mechs form a line, aiming their blasters. "Attention: security compromised. Seal all exits."

Callie whirls on Ayla, panic in her eyes. "You said the security systems weren't connected to the backup generator."

"They aren't. Usually." A gale blows around Ayla until her fear swallows the air. "Mama must have added them to the control panel."

"Where's the control panel?" Callie looks around frantically. "I need to blow it sky-high."

"We don't have time." Is there any water in this wide, airy

room? Ah, a fountain beside a wall of windows. Just what I need. I stretch my hand, reaching for the water in the basin, and my element responds. Water flies through the air, and with a flick of my wrist, it covers the mechs and freezes.

"Attention: secur—" The mechs cannot finish their warning. Instead of firing on us, they topple to the floor, covered in ice.

"I don't like to admit when you're cool, Toran, but that was *really* cool," Callie says.

Ayla tilts her head. "Cool because he made ice?"

"No, it's—never mind. Let's figure out the force shield and get out of here."

"You won't be going anywhere."

Serai appears in the hall, her green Seer's Eye backlit by even more security mechs. Vines fly forward to ensnare our wrists and ankles.

"Mama, no!" Ayla's electricity zap the vines.

Serai frowns, annoyed. "That's enough, Ayla. Now, stand back." All the while, the new group of mechs circle in.

"I will not. I promised to help my friends." Ayla's voice wavers, but she stands strong.

"Hey, that looks like a control panel." Callie spots a square on the ceiling covered in blinking dots. Serai panics, her vines shifting directions to catch the Light in Callie's hands.

"Don't even think about it, Luminaut."

Callie ignores Serai and launches her Light. The panel crackles and shudders, then makes a defeated hiss. The force shield fades before the rest of the mechs fall to the floor, blasters useless.

"Hurry!" Ayla aims a gust at the door and blows it open.

"Stop! All of you!" Serai flexes her fingers, creating more vines, and the stone tiles beneath our feet rise up, moving us away from imminent escape.

"Cover your eyes!" Callie creates a Light orb so bright it's blinding and blasts the tiles. Marble flies everywhere, stopped only by the thick curtains covering the windows.

"Go, now!" I push Elion out the unlocked door. Callie and Ayla follow before Serai commands more vines or tiles to snare us. Ayla creates a suction vacuum to pull the door closed, and I call forth water from a fountain over the garden wall. The hinges freeze solid just as Serai's vines creep under the door.

"Mama will get it open soon." Ayla faces the blazing sunset transforming the desert sky to a wondrous bonfire of orange mingled with pink, red, yellow, and glittering gold. Just beyond the last rays of the sun, stars shimmer in the purple sky above.

Perhaps Ensolorada is prettier than I assumed, if only for brief moments.

"At least Callie blew the backup control panel," Elion points out.

"But once the power cut ends, it won't matter." Callie stares at the docking port just beyond us, the Cordonanza cityscape devoid of transports. "Ayla, how long do we have?"

"A few minutes at best. But don't worry. I'm here to help."

"How could you possibly help? We're thousands of feet high with no way down." When I look at my fellow Seer, she's already closed her eyes, a placid look on her face.

"Don't think. Just do." Ayla repeats the words like a whispered prayer, as if to assure herself they'll work, despite her doubts. "Air moves, air bends. I am the air, the air is me."

A rush of wind rises over the edge of the platform, sending loose potted plants and leaves from the garden flying far and wide. I barely remain standing as the wind picks up speed, and an uprooted fern almost slams into my head.

"What in Lands Beyond are you doing?!"

Air moves in a spherical shape, and suddenly my feet leave the ground, followed by Callie and Elion, all of us suspended in the swirling orb Ayla has created. She levitates in the midst of stray leaves and flower petals, debris catching in her curls until she looks just like a Tremurheim tree sprite—one whose magic brings mayhem and death.

"Ayla, stop!" I cry out, but she can't hear me. She hovers, hands outstretched, a look of intense concentration on her face. Soon we will die in the midst of flying plants and snapping leaves. Death by a pot to the head is not a dignified end.

"Ayla, you have to do something!" I can agree with Callie sometimes. Now is one of those times.

"I am doing something," Ayla says. "I'm helping my friends."

Another whoosh sends all of us rocketing over the edge of the platform, plummeting toward the streets of Cordonanza.

# CHAPTER 7
# CALLIE

FALLING, FALLING, FALLING through the air to our collective deaths.

Trees, flowers, and gleaming transports docked at bays and ports at street level come into startling view as the glistening pavement grows closer by the millisecond. My reflection in the tops of the vehicles becomes larger and larger, sickeningly detailed. It would be awesome if those transports would rise into the air and open up for us before we hit the ground, but the power is still out. Nothing—no one—is saving us.

I mean, Ayla could totally save us, but she seems to have forgotten she's an Air Manipulator at the worst possible time.

"Ayla!" I shriek. "Help!"

"I'm trying!" Ayla shrieks back.

"Can you try faster?"

"Callie!" El plummets just a few feet away, and Toran screams every Tremurheim obscenity he knows.

After everything I survived, I never thought I'd meet my end as a flattened puddle of goo on the pavement, but here I am, facing down that very demise. Slamming into the ground is really gonna suck as a last conscious sensation.

Not all hope is lost. I estimate there's about two-and-a-half seconds left before *splat*. Plenty of time for Ayla to get it together, right?

"Come on, Ayla, Manipulate some air!"

Ayla's wide eyes flicker between white and hazel, mouth open in a silent scream of terror. I reach out and grab her hand.

Two seconds.

"You can do this." I *need* her to do this because I really don't want to go *splat*. I highly doubt El and Toran want to go *splat* either.

One-and-a-half-seconds.

"I c-can't!" Ayla stammers around tears.

"You can." She has to believe it, or we're doomed.

One second.

Ayla squeezes my hand and lets out a shriek — of pain, fear, or exertion, I don't know. Suddenly, her eyes shine like a thousand diamonds caught in the moonlight. As if launched from a spring tethered to the pavement, air bounces up to meet us, rocketing us upward until we're steady and still, then gently lowers us to the street below. I come to a stop on pale blue paving stones arranged in a geometric pattern, cool and smooth beneath my cheek.

As soon as I get my feet under me, I reach up and fling my arm around Ayla's shoulders. She's a bit taller than me, close to six feet. "You did it, bestie!"

"I'm terribly sorry for frightening you." Ayla looks ashen. The cloud-like blue tulle on her skirt trembles along with her legs, and her eyes fade back to hazel. She glances up at her mom's looming penthouse with a look of dread. "Mama will be furious."

"Furious" is an earth-shattering understatement on Serai's emotion Richter scale.

"We'll worry about your mom later," I say. "Let's focus on finding the Hall of Machines, okay?"

"Never. Do. That. Again." Toran stops and catches his breath between each word. Not even Ayla's sunny smile counteracts his furious scowl.

"I will maintain control next time, I promise," Ayla replies. "I've only ever done that with myself, not three other people. It changes the air flow immensely."

"You like throwing yourself off tall buildings?" Weird hobby, but whatever floats your boat.

"I don't *like* it, but it is good practice. One day, my future Luminaut and I may find ourselves in trouble, and I should know how to save us, don't you think?"

I don't have the heart to tell Ayla I'm the only Luminaut in the multiverse, not when she sounds so hopeful.

"At least we're not dead." El takes in our surroundings. The moon is almost fully in the sky, which means deepfake sunlight isn't far behind. "Come on, let's go find the machine hall place."

El isn't wrong about things being easy to find on a square grid—or, his uncanny knack for scouting is more advanced than I realized. His talent exceeds even my Luminaut instinct about navigation. Brightly animated, holographic street signs spring to life and transports leave their docks, zooming overhead while the artificial sun rises to simulate morning, but nothing distracts him. El takes turn after turn, block after block, sometimes going straight, sometimes altering course, but never once backtracking. He moves so fast the rest of us have a hard time keeping up.

"There it is. That's the building I saw in the transport." El comes to a halt at the end of a tree-lined block. "The Hall of Machines."

"Hall" seems like an inadequate word to describe the biggest building I've ever seen in my life. The heights of white marble spires reach past the artificially curated sunlight, touching brilliant galaxies of stars and a purple-blue moon. Beyond the gigantic bronze doors, people and mechs meander through lush gardens bursting with colorful flowers, shrubs, and blossoming trees. Holographic signs for robotics courses, personal mech repair specials, and exhibits on Ensolorada's tech history hover every few yards. It's like a college, tech store, and museum combined.

And part of it is on fire.

*Thud-kick* goes my pulse at the sight of billowing smoke, and the acrid scent of corroded metal and singed wires stings my nostrils. Please, *please* let it not be the part of the Hall Nemo and Diver are trapped in.

"Lands Beyond, it smells awful," Toran announces.

"I hope everyone's all right. Let's see what's going on." Ayla crosses the main thoroughfare and approaches a group of people wearing matching blue-and-gold uniforms. Several sleek mechs are grouped along with them, hovering and beeping back and forth anxiously. "Pardon me, but can you tell us what caused the fire in the Hall of Machines?"

"Did you forget comms?" One of the uniformed people looks surprised we haven't heard the apparent news. "The entire small mech lab is on lockdown."

"I'm sorry to say I *did* forget my comm," Ayla replies with a look of dismay. "How did the fire start?"

"I work in that wing, daylight shift," a uniformed woman says. "Some unidentified personal mech—no class code, unknown model—went completely feral during the power cut. It got brought in from the dunes a while ago, and when no owner could be located, we marked it for decommission. The thing lost its sun-sick mind when our programmers tried to catch it."

Oh, no. If that doesn't scream "Hi, my name is Nemo," I don't know what does.

"How did a mech start a fire that big?" My heart thumps against my ribs, and my palms sweat at the thought of Nemo trapped in a blaze.

"It just … attacked everything." The woman shakes her head, half amazed, half disturbed. "It tore apart any mech it didn't recognize, and when human programmers came near, it went for their hands or throats. Tech scraps were everywhere, wires and chemicals … all that flammable material combusted when the power came back on." She shows us her left hand, raw with bloody scratches. "I was lucky it went easy on me."

Shredding somebody's hand when they come too close? Trademark Nemo. I swallow hard, worry knotting tight in my throat.

"Was this mech very tiny?" I ask. "Small enough to sit on your shoulder? Claws for hands? Kind of boxy-looking?"

"That's exactly what it looked like," the woman replies. "How did you—"

I don't stick around to answer. Instead, I dash away, panic rising along with the smoke gushing from the right side of the gigantic building.

"Stop! You can't go in there!" The Hall of Machines techs calls after me, but I don't care. I'll run headlong into the flames to make sure Nemo survived his own vengeance.

Sparks, char, and soot blow everywhere, and water-laden drones buzz through the choking black plumes, dropping their payloads one after the other. High-tech, fire-resistant mechs surround the entrance, warning everyone to keep back until the fire is out.

"Callie, wait for us!" Ayla jogs to my side.

"I'm going in," I announce firmly.

El frowns. "You're not making a plan first?" He's used to Nate having four primary plans, plus two backups.

"No time for a plan," I say. "Nemo is trapped in there, and possibly Diver, too. The only thing I care about is finding my mechs."

"It seems foolish to go in unprepared," Ayla agrees with El.

"It is. But Callie is often foolhardy when it comes to Nemo and the other lumbering hunk of scrap." Toran nods at the water drones dropping tank after tank into the blaze. "I can direct the water a lot more efficiently than those machines. The fire will be out in no time."

"We still have to get past the fire mechs by the doors," Ayla points out.

Toran flexes his fingers and glances around, his Seer's Eye glowing blue when he notices a nearby fountain. "There's water over there. I'll ice them so they can't halt us. Then you three can find Nemo while I put the fires out."

"You hate Nemo. Now you're making plans to save him?" El narrows his eyes, instantly suspicious. "What's wrong with you?"

Yeah, why *is* Toran suddenly being helpful? He's never been this cooperative the entire time I've known him, even when Heike was around. I can't help wondering what it means that he's suddenly developed a conscience.

Toran's nostrils flare impatiently. "Are you going to stand around questioning me, or will you let me remove the obstacles around the entrance?"

"Fine, ice the mechs," I agree to his suggestion.

With a swish of his hands, Toran draws water out of the

fountain basin and sends it gushing around the mechs at the entrance, freezing in an instant and sticking them tight to the stairs. We race past them into the Hall of Machines, a strong gust of wind slamming the doors behind us. Ayla grins, pleased with herself.

"I can be helpful as well, you see?"

"Helpful?" Toran sneers. "You just closed off our best escape route from a building currently on fire. How is that helpful?"

"You're a Water Manipulator, I thought fires weren't a problem for you." Is Ayla sarcastic or just pointing out the obvious? Regardless, Toran and perceived sarcasm don't mix.

"My problem is the fact you could have killed us once already, and may yet again."

"Take the stick out of your butt, Boy Scout," El snaps. "Worry less about Ayla and more about finding Nemo and Diver."

Wow, it's like I'm hearing Nate Ormandi snark from beyond the grave.

Ayla's eyebrows shoot up her forehead, and she faces Toran, deeply concerned. "Is that true, Toran? I've never heard of placing sticks in one's orifices, but perhaps it's a custom in Tremurheim. No wonder you're so taciturn and unpleasant. You should call a MedPro."

"There is no stick up my—up there." Toran's cheeks blaze pink. "And I'm not unpleasant."

"You are *very* unpleasant," Ayla replies, her voice as light and floaty as her skirt.

"Quit pondering the size, breadth, and sharpness of the stick lodged in Toran's backside and focus." Remember how my littlest mech is trapped in a raging inferno? "We've got to figure out where the fire's coming from because that's where we'll find Nemo."

Easier said than done. The Hall is a huge space with vaulted ceilings, cylindrical columns covered in screens full of information and advertisements, and floating holograms blaring over-bright, over-loud announcements … but no fire. Weird. It's like it disappeared, only a faint whiff of char remaining.

"There it is." El points at a closed door to the right, tiny tendrils of smoke creeping from the gap between the floorboards.

"I'll take care of the door." Ayla's rush of wind blows open the barrier. Instantly, plumes of black smoke rush into the entry. Further down the corridor, flames flicker from inside an open laboratory.

There it is. The place I'll find Nemo. Unthinking, I race for the open door.

"Callie, wait! You won't be able to breathe!"

Sorry, Ayla, not slowing down. Not when Nemo is trapped in a fire all alone.

Smoke chokes me the second I cross the threshold into the burning lab. My eyes sting, welling with tears. Okay, maybe I should have slowed down and waited for Ayla and Toran, but it's too late for caution. I shield my eyes with my arm and push forward into the blaze.

"Nemo!" I call for my little guy over the roar of fire. Flames lick around my legs, and I hop and skitter out of their path. "Nemo, where are you?"

I peer through the smoke, unable to see anything except fire climbing higher and higher before water drones blast through the burned-out roof. But where one fire dies, another appears a moment later. All I sense are flames and my rising panic—no Nemo.

"Nemo!" The blaze growls and snaps louder than the whirring drones. How will he ever hear me?

"I'm here!" Ayla's gale at my back almost knocks me down, but finally the smoke clears. And there, in the midst of chaos and carnage, is Nemo.

He speeds past in and enraged blur, moving between shattered mechs and pulverizing their heads with his claw hands, rubbing salt in the wound of his kills. Once he's sure his adversary is destroyed, he hauls kindling to toss on top of the multitude of bonfires blazing across the vast expanse of what used to be a tech lab. As soon as a drone drops a load of water on Nemo's pyre, he scream-whirs at it, shaking his claws in rage before wheeling off to desecrate more useless mech corpses.

I've never seen Nemo like this—so full of anger and violence. There's nothing left for him to lose, and he's digressed to his basest instinct: to destroy as much as he can, however he can, before the inevitable end.

"Nemo!" I run headlong into the charred remains of the lab. El follows close on my heels.

"Nemo, it's us!" El cries, waving his arms to catch Nemo's attention.

A few more steps put me right in Nemo's path. "Nemo, it's me. It's Callie."

Nemo stops in his tracks at the sound of my voice, dropping his armful of kindling. A different kind of whir-shriek fills the smoky air—not one of rage, but of pure joy.

"Oh, Nemo." I run to him as he speeds toward me, clamping himself tight around my ankle  before he climbs into my waiting arms. I tremble in relief and happiness, and don't care that his claw hands digging into my shoulder and neck hurt a little. Nothing hurts as much as the thought of losing him forever. "It's okay, Nemo. I'm here. I've got you. I won't let anyone take you from me again."

"Hey, Nemo!" El gives Nemo a pat, and my mech jumps from me to his second-favorite human, embracing him too. "I'm so glad you're okay!"

"A tiny mech did all this?" Ayla sends more smoke flying skyward, keeping it away from our group.

"I'm not surprised. He's a dramora-forsaken menace." Toran hangs back, always wary of Nemo taking a swipe at his face. Good call.

"Nemo is his own force of nature." I pat the mech now cozily resting in the crook of my neck, the picture of pure contentment in his favorite snuggle spot. "Tiny but mighty."

"Amazing!" Ayla watches Nemo but wisely doesn't try to touch him. Toran being here makes Nemo growly, and I don't think he's in the mood to deal with new people. Instead, she smiles at him a safe distance away. "He's an adorable companion mech. The way he sits on your shoulder reminds me of the little olinís people kept as pets back in Aure—" She catches herself again, weirdly startling as if she almost said something she didn't mean to admit. "Back in Oasis III."

That's the second time she's made that face when talking about Oasis III. It's starting to get weird.

"These drones are the most terrible fire extinguishers I've ever seen. No aim at all." Toran directs the payload of water onto the various fires with his Manipulation, effectively dousing the flames until all that's left is wet char and smoke.

"We don't have many fires in Cordonanza." Ayla shoos the rest of the smoke out of the lab. "Perhaps you could lend your skills to the fire brigades, if you need permanent employment."

"First you try to kill me, now you're suggesting employment opportunities?" Toran stares at Ayla, blinking hard. He really doesn't know what to do around a person like her, does he?

"One mech found, one to go." I hold Nemo at arm's length. "Do you know where they took Diver, Nemo?"

Nemo nods enthusiastically.

"Can you take me to him?"

More enthusiastic nodding.

"I knew I could count on you." Nemo has a memory like a steel trap—just ask Toran's ankles. I set him on the damp floor. "Everybody, follow the mech."

Nemo takes off like a shot down the corridor. El races along with him while the rest of us trail behind, taking twists and turns deeper into the Hall of Machines. At last, we come to a halt in front of a set of bronze doors. And, of course, they're locked tight. Whatever the Hall of Machines hides behind these doors, they don't want anybody getting inside.

"I don't see a lock or handles." El runs his hands over the worn patterns etched into the bronze. "No hidden mechanisms either."

Nemo bangs on the door, whir-squealing. He looks at me and points, like I have to get through to what's on the other side immediately.

"Let me try something." Ayla's eyes glow white, and she places her palms on the door. It groans until the hinges pop, and swings wide into a cavernous opening. "There! I built up the air pressure from behind."

"At last, the Air Manipulator proves helpful," Toran mutters.

"I have been very helpful all evening, thank you," Ayla says. "So have you, except I didn't make a snide remark about your help. It must be the stick up your butt."

Toran's back to staring and blinking. The eye twitch is worse.

"Nice work, Ayla." I toss a few Light orbs into the darkness. "Okay, let's get Diver back online. Ready?"

"Ready," El agrees.

I step into the darkness, anticipating the sight of Diver looming beyond the shadows, but what I see instead is—

Statues?

# CHAPTER 8
# NATE

"FIFTY-FIVE, FIFTY-SIX, fifty-seven …" I work my way down the strand of Christmas lights, touching each bulb with my glowing index finger. Boulders of knotted muscle encircle my tensed shoulders, anticipating a Darkness attack that will catch me unaware — and unprepared.

"Fifty-eight, fifty-nine, sixty — "

*Cling cling clank.*

"What the — ah!" I startle, spinning around on the hood of my car. What made that noise? Is it Shadowmancers? Has Queen arrived with a legion of monsters to tear the place to pieces before Heike and I can Dive?

It's sunny and pleasant on the street. No trace of Darkness. I whip around, examining the corner of the backyard visible from my spot on the car. No Shadows. No Queen. Nothing but the cement patio where Mom used to soak in the sun on her lounger and the orange tree I'd harvest when she was sick. (All that vitamin C and D cured her cancer, right? Nope.)

A squirrel hops across the tin carport roof. Its bounding steps make the same clanging sound that unnerved me before it leaps into one of the DeLuca's trees hanging over the fence.

"Just a squirrel. Calm down." I resume the slow, careful pace of my Lighting (capital L kind of Light), willing the knots in my shoulders to untwist themselves.

To say I'm wound tight is an understatement. Focusing on souping up my Subaru with Light requires mental stamina—and all I'm worried about is Queen launching an attack when I'm in the middle of prepping my escape to Ensolorada.

It would be a typical Queen move to hang back at the Veil with her ravenous monsters, waiting and watching, strategizing a way to make sure I fail. It's what she taught me to do with Callie—and she made sure I was a pro.

A creak over my shoulder, and I leap to my feet. "Who's there?!" Christmas lights clatter to the ground, and I aim with both glowing hands, ready for the impending attack. It's not like I can Light blast anything without passing out, but it looks semi-intimidating.

"Is there a problem?" Dad opens the side door and gives me a weird look. He holds a box in his arms.

Creaky hinge. Dad really needs to put some oil on those things. I lower my hands and sink onto the hood, picking up the lights I dropped.

"You scared the crap out of me." It's strange to be terrified without a pulse, but the phantom hammering in my chest almost feels real.

"Apologies," Dad says. "I found more lights for you in the hall closet."

"Thanks. I just hope it's enough."

Dad finishes descending the steps with a painful grunt and sets the box next to my thigh. He picks up a Lighted strand. "What is the purpose of your experiment?"

"To amplify Callie's Light in Heike's lantern." I continue

working my way down the original strand. I have a vague recollection of helping Mom string these exact Christmas lights along the gutter when I was a kid, but that would be a happy memory and Darkness didn't let me keep any of those.

"Your own Light isn't strong enough?" Dad watches the flickering sparks dance in the bulbs. My Light looks different than Callie's. Hers is gold and glittery, mine is pearly, almost silver. "Is it corrupted by Darkness?"

"I don't know. I just know I'm not as strong as Callie." I finish up and set the lights aside, moving on to the box Dad brought out.

*Nathaniel ... I'm coming for you ...*

I still at the sound of my name on the breeze. Only Queen calls me Nathaniel.

An icy shudder runs along my skin, and I look back and forth. There's no sign of the Veil, nothing resembling Darkness. No trace of Queen's razor-sharp smile or her burning eyes.

"Do you see something?" A frown creases Dad's brow.

"No, it's—I could swear I heard Queen say my name. Taunting me. There's nothing there." One last tremor up my arms before the chill is gone. Must be more wound up than I thought. I reach into the box Dad brought only to find tangled wires and bulbs in a coiled ball. Talk about a Clark Griswold mess. "Geez, Dad, when was the last time you used these?"

"It's been a few years." A few years? No joke.

"Can you help untangle them? It goes faster with two people."

Dad wordlessly unravels one end of the Christmas lights while I tackle the other. "Despite all the hours I spent teaching you sailing knots, you remember remarkably little," he says.

"And you remember remarkably little about the difference

between a slip knot and a fire hazard."

Dad actually laughs. "Your quick wit remains, I see." He works quietly for a moment, tension thick between us. "I'm surprised how much you're still *you*, despite all your time in the Shadows."

I want to tell him the Shadow Plain didn't make me an entirely new person, but we both know that's a lie. I'm not the Nate Ormandi who went sailing that day and never came home — the Nate obsessed with finding answers, rendered static by grief. Neither am I Queen's Shadowmancer servant, determined to destroy Light for all I misguidedly believed it took from me. I'm both Darkness and Light, not living but not dead.

"It wasn't long for me." My tongue feels thick, and I can't find words to express anything else. Dad looks up, confused. "All my 'time in the Shadows.' Time is static in the Shadow Plain. Minutes feel like years. Decades go by in a blink." I unravel a few lights still caught up in each other. "Everything is permanently paused, just like me."

"Paused, but not gone. And you never were." Dad finishes unknotting the last bulbs and shifts his gaze, looking between the Light in my hands and the scars on my face. "You're going to have to make a choice, you know."

"What choice?"

"Whether you're going to fully embrace your future as a Luminaut by returning to Light, or if part of you will forever be tethered to Darkness, paused and unable to move forward."

Yep, there it is, the poorly-timed dad-speech I should've guessed was coming. And yet, he's not wrong. The unsustainable duality of my existence has been obvious since the moment I remembered my Light powers. Some truths, even two opposing ones, can exist in tandem — but not Luminauts and

Shadowmancers. Not life and death. What's been balanced on a razor's edge will eventually tip. I've got to reconcile this conflict before somebody else makes the choice for me.

The somebody else in question being Queen.

"Speaking of making choices …" Let's get back to the choice I left in Dad's hands. "Are you going to open the gateway to Ensolorada for me and Heike?"

"I never gave you confirmation, did I?" I can't read Dad's expression, but when could I? Then he softens and reaches for me, grasps my forearm, squeezes tight.

Is this affection? Acceptance? Or something else?

"I'll go finish packing," Dad says, hobbling up the steps.

"Packing?" I catch his eye. "Why are you packing?"

"I'm not Diving to Ensolorada with only the clothes on my back." When I startle at his reply, Dad grins over his shoulder. "Did you really think I'd let you do this on your own?"

"Yeah, I did." He made it clear I'm an idiot for attempting this Dive, calling me irrational and foolhardy, or some other Richard Ormandi-ish language. "Why'd you change your mind?"

"Because you don't have a Light Core, and you don't have a World Diver. Therefore, you definitely need a Seer." He pauses mid-step, a strange quirk playing about his mouth. "By the way, the girl—Heike—seems to be under the impression you're doing all this because you harbor romantic feelings for Callie."

The Christmas lights almost fly out of my hands. "Watch it, Dad, these are fragile!"

Dad smirks. "Are they? I see."

What does he see? Nothing, that's what.

Or maybe… something that's getting harder and harder to deny.

Since the moment I met her, Callie has taken up an obscene

amount of my mental real estate. Her smile warms me like the August sun, and if my heart could beat, it would skip every time she says my name. Queen sensed the real reason I wanted to come topside to Verona Beach so often, and it wasn't just scheming to steal Light Cores from Luminauts. Her shadowy awfulness has no qualms about exploiting me emotionally—especially when it comes to Callie.

I might not have been able to protect Mom from cancer, but I'll use every trick in my playbook to protect Callie from Queen.

"Listen, I sank that ship a long time ago." My newfound truth about Light and Darkness doesn't change how I lied, manipulated, and threatened Callie as a Shadowmancer. "All I care about now is keeping her safe from my mistakes. I'll do whatever I can to help her defeat Queen. My feelings—romantic or otherwise—don't matter."

"I don't know." A faraway look clouds Dad's eyes. "I'd say feelings matter a great deal in how much we're willing to sacrifice for the people we care about." He blinks, and the look disappears. "Heike has been asleep on the couch since she devoured my entire pack of Oreos. I suggest you wake her while I load the car. I've calculated a solid trajectory and if you're a halfway decent driver, we'll hit the gateway."

"Thanks, Dad." I had no idea Dad was good at physics. I guess I'll find out his skill level the hard way.

"I'd like to leave in fifteen minutes," Dad adds.

Fifteen minutes? Not much time. Maybe that's better. Gives Queen less time to find us and less time for me to get all nervy and back out. I wrap the strands of Christmas lights around Heike's lantern, my Light amplifying Callie's Light inside, just like I hoped. It's sickeningly weak compared to the amount of Light it takes to open a gateway without a Light Core—this decoy

Core, plus everything I've got, and it might not be enough.

Too late for doubt. Fourteen minutes and counting. I affix the fake Light Core to the dash, Light bouncing off the car's mirrors. It'll be … something. Enough? Who knows.

I come in from the carport and spot Heike snoozing under a blanket on the couch right where Dad said she'd be. Her mouth has Oreo crumbs around the edges.

"Hey." I give her shoulder a shake. "Wake up. We're Diving soon."

Heike opens her eyes, oddly dark and red-rimmed. Her whole face drains of color until it's corpselike and gray. Then she blinks, and her eyes look blue-gray again, familiar ruddiness coloring her cheeks. Must be imagining things… or Darkness is playing mind games.

Doesn't bode well for our Dive, does it?

Heike tosses the blanket off her legs before stepping into flip-flops. "Is it almost time to jump your car to our deaths?"

"Nice sarcasm, dork." Speaking of dork middle-schoolers, I should take my Cal Bears cap to El. That kid's probably torched without sun protection, and Mom's home world is an actual desert. Sunscreen might be useful to have on hand, and extra clothes too. I quickly load my backpack, taking one last look around. What else do I need? Anything I can use to prank Boy Scout? Telling him my old Tolkien paperbacks are Earth's history books would be—

"Aaaahhhhh!"

A bloodcurdling scream shatters my thoughts. I rush from my room out the front door, Dad hot on my heels. The shriek came from somewhere close by—a neighbor's house, probably. Despite the glare of the late afternoon sun, the sky grows darker, more forbidding, and the salty ocean breeze blowing across the cliffs smells rotten, like putrid fish left to decay in the sun. Slithering dread slips down my spine, and in the pit of my stomach, nausea.

The world isn't right. There's been some sort of … infestation.

"What is that?" Dad asks behind my shoulder. Does he feel it too?

"I don't—oh, no."

The Veil appears suspended in the air, spewing twitchy, pulsating Shadowmancers. They move up and down the street, sniffing out inner Light in all the humans enjoying the afternoon with their tentacle mouths. Just when I think this next monster will be the last, another follows close behind—a leaky faucet of nightmare creatures ready to turn the whole town to ash.

"Somebody help me! Ralph! Help!"

Dad's neighbor, Barb DeLuca, lies on the ground, pinned by a Shadowmancer. Its elbows that look like knees bend while it's tentacles caress her face. Her dog barks frantically at her side.

"Help!" Barb shrieks again. The Shadowmancer licks her terrified tears and hisses with delight, a sound like shattering glass.

"Barb! Run for it!" Dad goes full Fire Manipulator in one click of his lighter, sending a gigantic fireball flying. The Shadowmancer faces Dad with a defiant snarl, abandoning Barb in favor of a more potent Seer. Her yapping dog takes off down the street. Smart dog.

"Come on, get up!" I rush over, pulling Barb to her feet. She's shaking, hardly able to speak. If Barb DeLuca can't speak, the situation is dire.

"M-Marlene." She looks around, terrified. "Where's my chorkie, Marlene?"

"The dog will be fine." Seriously, Barb, focus up. "Get in the car and drive as fast as you can."

She doesn't move, just stares. Something in me pushes against my tongue, and under her heart, a flicker like a tiny flame appears. *Make her get in the car. Make her drive away and save herself.* A quiet voice, almost subconscious, whispers in my mind, suggesting I force Barb to move against her will—to obey me instead of her fear.

What's happening? Is this voice Darkness or Light? Why can I see a flame in Barb's chest? Why am I even *looking* at Barb's chest? Get it together, Nate.

"Rick?" Barb remembers she's the neighborhood gossip as she stares at Dad battling an increasing number of Shadowmancers crossing the Veil into Verona Beach. Her voice breaks through my creeping thoughts of control. "Good lord, the man's on fire! Make sure he doesn't ignite Marlene!"

"Barb? What happened?" Barb's square-shaped husband, Ralph, rambles out the door. He stops short, his small eyes growing bigger than I thought possible when he sees the Shadowmancers and Dad's fire.

"Get out of here. Now."

Ralph actually listens to me. He pulls his car keys from his pocket, shoves his wife into the passenger seat, and starts the ignition quick as a flash before speeding up the road like a bullet. They only stop once for Barb to grab her dog off the curb before rounding the corner out of sight.

"Dad!" If I don't step up to the plate, Dad's going to slip, and Shadowmancers will take full advantage of a tired Seer. Light flares in my fingers, and at the sight of it, the monsters slither toward me. "Get Heike in the car, I'll keep them on the run."

Dad nods. "Be safe."

I race up the street, baiting the Shadowmancers to chase me.

Mailboxes turn to ashes before my eyes, cars crumble, and rooftops slowly disintegrate as the twitchy Shadowmancers stretch their limbs in every angle but the right one, destroying any object they find.

"Hey!" I yell over the screams and shrieks of terror. "Come get me! Look! Sparkle hands!" Attack my shiny fingers, and leave the general populace alone.

I need Light like Callie has, the kind that lifts her into the air and shines brighter than a galaxy of a billion stars. She could wipe these things out with a flick of her wrist. All I can do is resort to Little League taunts, and it's not enough.

"Nate!" Dad calls from the driver side of my car, speeding up the block. He puts it in park and climbs out, joining me on the street. "It seems your plan to distract them failed."

I peg Dad with a scowl that could rival Boy Scout's. "I don't need unhelpful observations right now, okay?"

"Understood." Dad jerks a quick nod. "My preference is to get the monsters away from civilians before we make the jump, but you're the Luminaut."

*Except I'm not a Luminaut. Not really.* But right now, a Luminaut is what everyone needs. Fake it until you make it, right?

I reach deep inside, pulling as much Light through the depths as possible past the barrier of Darkness until it's screaming through my veins. Soon, the familiar urge to fall to my knees and lose consciousness will take over.

*You have to hold on, Nate. Darkness can't win.*

It's not my inner voice telling me to stay afloat but Mom's, calling through the Light.

*Mom, help me. Please.* I can't fight Shadowmancers alone. I'm not strong enough. And I'm scared.

*You can do this, my stars.*

Can or can't, I *have* to do this or all of Dad's neighbors—maybe all of Verona Beach—will become piles of ash. I raise my hands, but my swaying vision makes me nauseated. I swallow a dry heave.

*Come on, Light. I'm tired of begging. Just work.*

A stream of Light shoots from my hands, hitting a group of Shadowmancers tearing apart a house across the street. The monsters scream, a sound worse than crystal shards scratching a chalkboard, before they disintegrate. Spinning around, I hit even more monsters ashing a door. One last Light blast flies from my hands, annihilating the remaining Shadowmancers chasing an SUV trying to escape the carnage.

Everything buckles under me, and my knees hit the pavement. Sickness twists my stomach, and I gag around something wet sticking in my throat—what is this stuff? I don't have anything in my stomach, I don't eat.

Sea water. Gallons of it, spewing from my lips. I guess I'd have plenty of that in there.

"Nate!" Dad's distant voice calls. "Quick, get up. We have to Dive."

"That was *almost* as good as Callie!" Heike chimes in. Why the snark? Why now?

"Get back in the car and stay there!" Dad again. Heike groans in annoyance when he points to the back seat.

"I … I can't …" Words fail.

"Come on." Dad tries to lift me, but he's not as strong as he used to be. "One last obstacle to overcome."

"One last …" *Obstacle* is too big for my sluggish tongue. My entire body is on fire with pain as Darkness swirls around my Light, trying to choke it. Light is stronger, but the battle—no, the *war* going on inside me—threatens to end my Dive before it begins. I drag myself to my feet and slide into the driver seat, fingers fumbling for the seatbelt.

"You have to drive farther up the block first," Dad says. "We won't get to the proper speed from this distance."

"What's proper speed? Eighty-eight miles an hour?" I know, I know. Couldn't resist.

"No." Dad snorts. "Fifty to fifty-five."

"Okay. All right, yeah." Reality sinks in. My hands shake as I put the car in gear. Heike clings tight to the driver's headrest.

"Don't drive fast, please," she moans.

"Buckle up. Because we're going to go fast." I spin the car around again, facing the cliff, and Heike flops over in her seat with an *oomph*. Maybe now she'll listen to my seatbelt admonishment.

"Drive straight, build up as much speed as you can until you hit fifty to fifty-five, and you should be able to break through the fence and hit the gateway," Dad says. "While you're driving, concentrate on your Light. You'll need quite a lot."

Quite a lot is more than I have, and my Light seems to have vanished inside my fear.

"I wish Callie were here." I stare at the cliff, at the churning white-and-blue ocean below—the ocean that will kill Dad and Heike if I don't succeed. I'm sick and want to throw up again, and I don't think I can do this. "I wish Mom were here."

"Callie and your mother aren't here. You are." Dad looks me in the eye. "The only Luminaut in this car is you. The only person who can make the Dive is you. But you must make the choice."

"If you're going to Dive, you might want to do it now," Heike adds, clicking her seatbelt. "Because they're coming back."

How does she—oh crap, Heike's right. The Veil materializes

outside the rear window, and dozens of Shadowmancers emerge, their sights set on my car.

No time to doubt, get sick, or be scared. I slam my foot on the gas, and we peel away down the street. The fence and the cliff get closer and closer with every second as my car gains speed.

Thirty, forty, fifty miles per hour on the speedometer. Fifty-five—

Shadowmancers slither around the car, reaching for the hatchback with their tentacle mouths. The roof becomes ashes, particles floating away on the sea breeze.

The fence is a few yards away, and beyond, open air.

"Now!" Dad tosses a fireball out the window. A shimmering gateway appears in the space between the cliff and the horizon—sand dunes under a blanket of brilliant stars, and above, a purple moon. A gleaming city of white rises in the distance, beckoning us forward.

"Hurry, Nate!" Dad's struggling to keep the gateway open. The Light in the lantern and Christmas lights isn't enough to maintain it. Dad needs more juice—he needs me. I call for my Light, begging it to fill my body and connect to the gateway.

"We're going to die now," Heike announces with remarkable nonchalance. Darkness and Shadowmancers attach themselves to the back of my car, slithering for the open roof.

"Nate! Focus!" Dad grabs my arm with his hand that isn't on fire.

My car breaks through the fence, splinters flying like snow flurries. Some catch fire, some turn to ash. The front wheels leave the cliff's edge.

*Please, Light, I need you to work.*

The back wheels leave the cliff. My tires spin on air.

*I have to find Callie. I have to see El again. He needs his hat. I've got to give him his hat.*

Their faces fill my mind, and I see them in the white city under the stars. I'm going to find them, no matter what. Darkness won't win. That little dingus will *not* get sunburned on my watch.

Light glows under my heart, flaring to life. I channel it, concentrating it outward, forcing the power to remember El and Callie, to help me seek them in the vast unknown.

*My stars …*

Light overtakes everything: the Shadowmancers, the fire, the car. Air becomes Light itself, and the cliff and ocean fade from sight. Dad's fiery gateway widens, the dunes and stars materializing until Light swallows them, too.

There's a flash like an explosion, bigger and brighter than I imagined Light could be. Everything physical is gone, only Light remains.

I don't know where we are in space or reality. I can't see Dad and Heike. I'm lost in Light, aware of only power, until—

*SLAM*

My car comes to a jarring halt, the force of a brick wall smashing into the hood. I'm thrown against the steering wheel, and something dark and swirling spills around the windows. Did we make it through the gateway? Or did we land in the ocean, succumbing to our last living moments before death?

"Dad … Heike." They don't respond. No one does.

Light fades, and everything goes black.

# CHAPTER 9
# CALLIE

"STATUES?" El climbs up a wide stone pedestal, inspecting the bronze object. "Nemo wanted us to find statues?"

Pairs of bronze people occupy each podium as far as my Light reaches. Sometimes a man and a woman, sometimes two men, sometimes two women, but always only two. There doesn't seem to be an obvious connection between them in their frozen states. No signs of love, conflict, or camaraderie. Just blank expressions on cold bronze.

"Why so many? And who are these people in the first place — El, quit hanging on that guy's arm, this isn't a jungle gym."

"Sorry." El swings from the elbow of a nearby statue. One of my Light orbs follows him down, and he lands with a thud in front of a placard at the base of the podium.

"This might give us a clue." Ayla bends down to read the dust-encrusted placard. "Luminaut: Eoghan O'Brian, Earth. Seer: Alanna Ariadna, Fire Manipulator, Aureloria. World Diver Number 12." She straightens. "They appear to be an ancient Luminaut and Seer dyad, possibly Light Collective era or earlier. Oh! Look at this!" Ayla picks up a long, crystal spear with a scimitar-like blade from the base of the statue. "Mama told me about this! It was made for Mariasol, when she was training to find the Rognaga."

"Whoa, rad!" El picked up more 90s slang from Nate than I thought. He reaches for the spear, but I gently brush his hand away.

"That's sharp, and longer than you are tall."

"Perhaps he'll fall on it and test the effectiveness." If Toran's making a joke, he needs to work on his delivery.

"Eat your own ears, stupid dümfo," El snaps. "Why don't *you* test it on your face?"

I step between the two before they exchange more barbs. "Nobody is going to test sharp objects on each other, okay?"

"I'll keep it safe." Ayla glances around the darkened space. "This must be a depository for all things related to Luminauts and Seers of the past."

"Are all these statues Luminaut and Seer dyads?" I send Light orbs floating through the vault, each one lighting a statue briefly before moving on to the next. An all-too-familiar Luminaut and Seer come into view, the kind-yet-logical Luminaut with long black hair and her Water Manipulating Seer who moved Mist like a magician. The people I saw the Light Collective murder in Diver's memory.

A shudder runs through me as I remember Diver's Earth Manipulating Seer screaming in agony. Her Luminaut's face was so full of rage I felt it as if it were my own.

"Why keep all these Luminauts and Seers a secret like this?" I wonder.

"Because people want to forget they exist," El suggests.

"Forgetting the ugly parts of history and locking them up forever instead of dealing with the discomfort? That sounds familiar," I snark.

Yet looking around at the statues, I know not all of the dyads in the vault were members of the Collective. Some of them gave their lives defending the multiverse, first from the Collective's cruelty and later from Queen's Darkness—a task they ultimately failed.

"Why not acknowledge the good people who cared while condemning evil all at once?" I gaze at the long-dead Luminauts and Seers cast in bronze, dusty and abandoned. "We can learn from the Collective's mistakes so they aren't repeated, but we shouldn't condemn the people who sacrificed everything for Light."

"I agree. But according to Mama, the rest of Ensolorada does not." Ayla sighs. "It's very difficult to change how people feel. And Mariasol Zaira running away didn't help."

"I didn't meet Mariasol personally, but I have a hard time believing she'd abandon the only home she'd ever known without a second thought—not unless she believed staying would make everything worse. What now, Nemo?" My tiny mech emerges from the depths of the enormous vault, making all of his angriest growls. "We're having an extremely deep discussion here, and besides, Diver isn't in this dusty old room."

Nemo is relentless. He wraps his tiny arms around my ankle and pulls as hard as he can.

"That menace doesn't know where the World Diver was taken, he's just being belligerent." Toran aims a kick at Nemo, who retaliates by whizzing around to pinch him before taking refuge between my feet.

"Nemo is not a menace, he's adorable." Ayla smiles. Toran scowls. Hello Grumpy, meet Sunshine.

"Look, Nemo, I know you wanted to help," I tell my mech, "and I appreciate the thought, but there's nothing in here besides statues."

"This place isn't just full of statues," Ayla says. "The air at the back of the room feels enormous, as high as the moon."

"The back of the room?" El, Toran, and I look at Ayla. "Does this place keep going?"

"Yes, much farther. And I sense … a door. One bigger than the Hall of Machines main entrance. Walls don't allow air to seep through, but doors do." Ayla furrows her brow in concentration. "Beyond it is … heat. Air from the desert. But something in between is taking up space."

"What something?" I look at Nemo, who gestures to the darkest part of this hidden museum. "Something like …"

*Diver, are you here?*

The tiniest spark of Light cries out for me, an answer from the depths.

"He's down there." I build twin Light orbs and throw them far, far, far. They come to a stop above a familiar shape, one I know as well as I know my own heart. A mech lying crumpled and defeated, the most forgotten thing of all.

"Diver!"

I run as fast as my legs will carry me, dropping to my knees when I reach him. This scrap heap is nothing like Diver. There's no warmth, no sentience. The faint Light that called me feels imagined. Tears sting my eyes, and a sob breaks free.

"Diver. Oh, buddy, what did I do to you?" I rest my forehead on Diver's dome and cry. Nemo crawls into my lap, trying to comfort me. It's useless. "I'm sorry. I'm so sorry."

"Hey, Diver!" El calls the lifeless mech as he races toward us. "Wake up, Big Guy!"

*Big Guy.* What Nate called Diver. Searing pain erupts fresh, a gaping wound I don't think will ever heal. All these senseless deaths and losses, and what do I have to show for it? An abysmal track record of trying to save people I care about from Darkness — and failing.

"See? Hopeless wreckage." Toran paces the length of Diver's frame, shaking his head. "There is no salvaging him, and it would be a waste of our time trying."

I don't need you spouting off inconvenient truths right now, okay Toran?

"Poor old mech." Ayla places a hand on my shoulder. "It's good you're here for him."

"Is it?" I ask bitterly. "He's like a broken toy that got tossed in the trash, and it's all my fault." Tears pour down my cheeks, and I stretch my arms against Diver's cold head, wishing I could take all of him into my arms. "I messed up so bad, Ayla. I never do anything right."

"Didn't you say we should learn from our past mistakes?" Ayla kneels at my side and touches Diver's lifeless head. "He may look bad, but you'll know what to do."

"What we need to do is leave." Toran jerks his chin at the distant door. "Come. The Diver is a lost cause." He marches away without a second glance over his shoulder. A total lack of compassion is so on brand for Toran, isn't it?

I sniff a little, wiping my cheeks, and turn to Ayla. "Why couldn't you have been my Seer? Toran is the worst. You're a decent human being."

She laughs and sets the crystal spear aside before she hugs me too tight. I don't mind, I could use a good hug right now. "I've already seen my Luminaut in my Sight, and he's a boy. One with dark hair, surrounded by smoke and sunlight. But I'm so glad we are besties instead."

"You saw your Luminaut?" I tilt my chin. "How is that

possible?"

"Very possible, and he's coming soon," Ayla says. "But let's not worry about him yet. We have a World Diver to fix."

"Yeah, you're right." Fix Diver first. After that, Ayla's Luminaut needs to get himself to Ensolorada and help me track down some Light Cores.

"Hey, I found something!" El's voice comes from the farthest point back. There's a click when he touches something he's definitely not supposed to.

"El, what are you —"

A rumbling earthquake shakes the floor followed by the deafening groan of corroded metal being forced to move: scraping, scratching, bending, and bowing. At last, a crack of brilliant moonlight appears, revealing miles of rolling dunes beyond a door tall enough and wide enough for at least four Divers to walk through at once. A desert breeze blows away the heavy daytime heat, and stars and galaxies as bright as dawn shimmer against the deep purple night.

"This is amazing!" El runs outside, throwing his arms wide under the blanket of stars."Why are you hiding everything with fake sun?"

Cool lavender moonlight spills into the vault, making it bright enough to get to work. I set Nemo on my shoulder and climb up Diver's side onto his neck. The hatch door remains unlocked.

"I'm going into the Crow's Nest," I announce. "With any luck, I'll figure out how to get Diver working again."

"I want to help!" El climbs up after me, and Ayla behind him, clutching the crystal spear tight.

"I do as well!"

"Some of my favorite books are in there." Toran follows too.

Party in Diver's head, I guess. I toss open the hatch. "Be

forewarned, it's a tight squeeze. And you're not allowed to make fun of the mess."

"Ayla Alindia! What do you think you're doing?"

Ayla's entire body becomes as still as one of the lifeless statues flanking the vault. "Mama?"

A miniscule sliver of light created by the open door frames the outline of Serai's form. The marble columns holding the vault's ceiling shake with every step she takes, and the stone tiles on the floor create a conveyor belt to rocket her forward. A tidal wave of branches and vines rush from Serai's extended hands, reaching to ensnare us.

"Inside, now!" I hop inside the Crow's Nest with Nemo. El follows, landing hard with an *umph,* then Ayla, and Toran last. Rapidly sprouting vines crisscross over the hatch just as I pull it closed, latching it tight. I toss a few Light orbs so we can see, then stare at Ayla. "Oh, my gosh, dude. I thought my parents were strict, but your mom is next level."

"This is a disaster." Ayla wrings her hands, covered in tiny electric sparks, and does her lip-sucking anxiety thing as she walks circles through piles of old maps, ration boxes, and Toran's mini library.

"Watch out for the books!" Toran shoos Ayla from his precious loves, stacking them neatly in his arms.

I wade through the mess until I reach the Prism, staring at the broken crystal. "If I can figure out how to repair this crack, Diver will — theoretically — be back online, and we can ditch Serai in the dunes."

"Mama is an Earth Manipulator, you think she can't track us through a desert full of sand?" Ayla looks as defeated as I did when I saw Diver's brokenness. "There's nowhere to hide."

As if to emphasize Serai's seriousness in getting to Ayla, metal groans and the Crow's Nest shifts. Nemo flies off my shoulder into a pile of garbage, which, luckily, is his favorite thing. Toran sways, Ayla falls over, and El clings tight to Nate's old album crate. I barely remain standing.

"Forest spare me, I hate Earth Manipulators," Toran grouches.

"She's trying to unlock the hatch." Ayla wraps her arms around her middle.

"I guess that means I've got to work fast." I heave one half of Diver's broken crystal Prism into position. Now, how do I repair this? My robotics class didn't teach me anything about magical, sentient robot programming, just the regular Earth-brand robots that require all their functions to be coded. Think, Callie, think.

Another jolt rocks the Crow's Nest. Serai's hardcore, isn't she?

"I estimate we have three minutes until the World Diver is tied up by vines," Ayla announces.

Fantastic.

"Do your mom's powers work on metal?" El asks.

"I don't know if Mama's Manipulation includes metal," Ayla replies. "But I don't want to find out."

Me either, bestie.

The Crow's Nest shakes, and it won't be long before Serai tears my mech apart. All right, let's recall how to bring a sentient robot to life. I brought Nemo to sentience, and he doesn't have a Prism. He just happened to be in the path of Earth's Light Core when it fell out of my backpack.

If Light made Nemo become self-aware, maybe Diver's Light needs a jump-start. I put my hands on the Prism crystal. It's still a little off-kilter, but it'll have to do.

"Please, Diver," I whisper to my mech as Light spreads from my heart, down my arms and into my hands, filling Diver's

Prism. Closing my eyes against the brilliance, I call for more Light, then even more. As much Light as I have, if that's what it takes.

*Please, buddy. Come back to me.*

"Lands Beyond, are you trying to blind us?" Toran cries.

"Callie, what are you doing? It's too bright!" El sounds pained, and Nemo whir-squeals in protest, but I don't stop. Diver's Light *has* to be here. I can't have felt his spark if he was completely gone.

*Diver, show me where you are.*

I'm diving, falling, sinking into the lost void of ancient time, searching for anything that feels like Diver, like Light. At first, there's nothing but the sensation of my mind plunging further away from the reality of the Crow's Nest, thousands of miles from El and Ayla's panic, Toran's terse muttering, Nemo's shrieks. I'm floating on nothingness, lost in a sea of unknown space.

I become vaguely aware of my physical body being jerked roughly from side to side. Distant cries for me to come back to the present, to show a reaction to what's happening to my friends.

But I can't leave. Not yet. Desperation keeps me sinking, but hope keeps me tethered. And there, as far into the deep as I can plunge my mind and Light without losing connection to my body forever, is a flickering flame.

*Diver?*

Luminaut!

"Diver!" My voice is so far away I might as well be across the multiverse from myself. *I'm so sorry I lost you, buddy.*

We were worried Luminaut would not come. We were frightened and alone.

My heart hurts to feel Diver's immense sadness. *I'm here now, and I'll never leave you. It's time to wake up.*

Diver's Light glows, gaining power and intensity. A swirl of sparkling Light fills the void, overtaking the darkness. Memories congeal and take shape, becoming enmeshed with the Light, and voices and pictures of the past stitch back together in the brilliance of rising Light. I fly upward, giving Diver my courage to step into himself.

When I arrive back in the present and open my eyes, Diver's Prism glows bright. The crack at the top is held together by a thin thread of my Light, and Diver's voice warms my heart.

*We are glad Luminaut found us.*

Finally, I've got my friend back. *I'm never letting you go, Diver. I promise.*

"Callie, we have a problem …"

I turn and spot exactly what Ayla means. Yeah, *major* problem. Serai's vines turn the hatch door. In moments, she'll be through.

*Diver, I need you to stand up and get rid of these vines. Can you do it?*

Diver is more than happy to test his legs. *Yes, Luminaut.*

With a metallic creak, Diver breaks free of the vines and branches encircling him. Slowly he rises, and the casing around the Crow's Nest falls away, revealing the stars, the desert beyond, and Serai. Her green Seer's Eye is practically on fire as she stares at her shredded vines littering the vault floor.

"All of you *will* come down this instant and answer for what you did to my home!" Serai's voice carries into the night, piercing the glass with startling clarity.

Yeah, she's mad we trashed her house. Figures. I look between Toran, Ayla, El, and Nemo, who was riding on El's shoulder. "What do you think we should do? Run away into the desert? Or face off where we stand?"

"I vote face off," El says, rubbing his palms with violent glee. Nemo whirs in agreement.

"Desert," Toran replies succinctly. "That is my vote."

"I don't vote for either," Ayla counters, shaking her head. "You underestimate Mama's advantage in the dunes. I say we—"

In the distance, a bright flash of Light like an exploding star pierces the fabric of the nighttime sky. Something dark flies a short distance through the air and skids to a stop on the dune face, residual Light wrapped around it's wheels—

Wait a minute, is that a station wagon?!

The Light inside the car feels instantaneously familiar. It once called for refuge across the multiverse, connected me to him in our hands clasped tight: a promise to heal the past through a future of tenuous understanding. A Light not my own. A Light that's …

"He's here!" Ayla's anxiety evaporates, and in its place, sheer joy. "He's finally here! My Luminaut!"

"Your *what*?!" Toran's face is the picture of shock. "There's a second Luminaut?"

Before I ask Ayla what she means or comprehend why I feel the Light of a person I know to be dead shining in the middle of a car flying straight from my world, something else catches my eye. Almost as soon as the desert sand settles and the Light in the station wagon fades, sinister shadow follows behind.

"What is that?" Ayla shudders, wrapping her arms around herself as she looks at the sneaking phantoms. "It feels … cold. And evil."

"We know what it is." El's eyes darken, and his face twists into a grimace.

It's Darkness.

# CHAPTER 10
# NATE

"NATE, WAKE UP."

Consciousness breaks through the black when someone touches me, the warmth of their palm spreading across my shoulder. Slowly, awareness returns, pulling me like a riptide toward wherever I've landed. There's pain in my head—and everywhere else. I'm tired. So, so tired … like the weight of a thousand bricks is tied to my eyelids.

"G'way." I smack the hand on my shoulder, ignoring a low buzz in my ears. I don't know where I am or how I got here, but something smooth and billowy rests under my cheek. A pillow? Makes sense. All I want to do is sleep. "Five minutes."

"Who does that boy think he is? Five minutes—nonsense." The speaker *tsks* their tongue and gives me a rough shake. "Come on, Nate, get yourself together."

Dad, alive and crabby. I open my eyes, and the world takes shape through bleary fog.

What I thought was a pillow is an airbag. I'm not in my bed, but the driver's seat of my car. They horizon beyond the dunes stretches into infinity, filled with so many stars my mind can't comprehend them. In the distance, a glimmering white city rises toward the pale purple moon.

It all comes rushing back in an instant—the Shadowmancers chasing us, Dad opening a gateway to Ensolorada in thin air, driving the car off the cliff face, and my Light powers …

A pile of glass, corroded metal, and singed wires on the dash—the remains of Heike's lantern and Dad's Christmas lights. Did the decoy Light Core work? Or did my Light overpower everything and take us through?

"Are you okay?" I ask Dad.

"As well as can be expected, given what we survived." Blood drips from a cut on his forehead before pooling above a silver eyebrow. Otherwise, he seems all right. "I must say, that was impressive. I didn't think you had it in you."

"Me either." I push aside the airbag and stare at the sand dunes, the stars, the city. "This is Ensolorada, right? We made it?"

"'Made it' is a relative term." Dad snorts. "Miraculously, you've managed to avoid killing me twice with your various schemes."

"Third time will be the charm, I promise." I rub my eyes, still blurry with exhaustion, and turn around, searching my back seat for the last member of our escape crew. "Heike? You good?"

"I'm alive, but not good." The girl in question peeks her head up from the floorboards and gives me an I-will-kill-you-in-your-sleep scowl to rival her brother. "You're the worst driver I've ever met."

"You're from Tremurheim, I'm the only driver you've ever met." Am I surprised the middle schooler is snarking me the first opportunity she can? No. "You're welcome for saving your life. Again."

"I didn't say thank you."

"Whatever. We won't be driving again anytime soon, since the whole front of my car just got crunched by a sand dune." I unbuckle myself. "Feel like hiking to that city, Dad?"

"Do we have a choice?" Dad wrinkles his nose, unbuckling himself too. "It's farther than it looks, I'm certain."

"Probably." But if Callie and El are there, we don't have another mode of transport. Hiking it is. "Come on, Snark Girl, we're going for a walk."

"That's not my name."

"Wow, *Heike*, you don't say!" I take the keys out of the ignition and pocket them. Even though the car is totaled, it's instinct.

As soon as we step onto the dune, a wave of blistering heat washes over me. Wow, it's hotter than a sauna out here, isn't it? I can only imagine what a furnace this place is in daylight. When Mom described her home world as "toasty," she was not being understated.

"It's hot." On the nose, Heike.

"A correct observation," Dad dryly concurs.

"I'm so glad you survived near-death twice, all so you could enlighten us with that riveting assessment." I shoulder my backpack and adjust my Giants cap on my forehead. "Since you don't like Snark Girl, let's go with Captain Obvious."

"I don't like that either." Wow, that's a Boy Scout-level expression.

"You know, I used to wonder sometimes how you and your brother were related, but when your face looks like that, I can see—get down! Now!"

A Shadowmancer sneaks up from behind, its tentacle mouth grasping the air near Dad's face. I grab Heike's arm roughly, shove her behind me, and call all the Light I can muster to fill my hands. A click of Dad's lighter, and fire races across the sand. Shrieking, the Shadowmancer disappears behind the Veil, unleashing a torrent of monsters in its wake.

And of course, the moment I need my Light to work, all I've got is sparkle hands. Nice, powers, way to be inconsistent. Well, sparkle hands can still throw punches. Let's see how solid these Shadowmancers are. I leap on top of one sneaking up behind Dad and tackle it to the ground.

"What are you doing?" Dad's fire sends a couple more monsters screaming into the Shadow Plain while I pummel the one I've got pinned.

"Bashing this thing's head in, what's it look like?" A few more hits, and the Shadowmancer disintegrates in the brilliant glow of Light. "Now I just decapitated it with my fists."

"I don't know whether to be proud or deeply disturbed." Dad lets loose a flame on a few more. "They're relentless, aren't they?"

"Yeah, because Queen's got an endless supply." As long as she keeps creating them from Darkness in the Shadow Plain, we'll never not be outnumbered. "Where is Heike?"

"I'm hiding behind the car!" Smart, but why aren't these things going for her? She's the easiest target—no powers, not even trying to fight, just sitting beside a half-buried tire.

"Look out!" Dad throws a fireball at some Shadowmancers about to sneak up on me, and I rush to take down another coming up fast on him.

These things are getting smarter, and I'm so physically exhausted I can't control my powers. I didn't think I got tired anymore, but as I beat up my latest Shadowmancer opponent, every muscle in my arms and shoulders screams at me to stop.

"I'm running out of steam." I slip away from another

disintegrated pile of dreadfully departed Shadowmancer ash.

"Agreed." Dad's sweating, his teeth clenched tight. "But allies are short supply."

"We need backup, ASAP." Specifically, we need Callie. I felt her Light through the gateway, so I know she's here. But not … here. Not present at this moment. My Light called to hers across the multiverse before. Maybe I can do it again. I reach deep into my power, searching for anything that feels like her.

*Callie, where are you?*

Please, far-superior Luminaut, come help us fight. Dad and I don't have long left.

*Hang on, I'm coming. Try not to get ashed in the meantime.* The Light of another Luminaut calls across the desert, and distant rumbling shakes the sand. I scramble to the top of the dune, scanning the horizon. Silhouetted against the starlight and the glowing white city, the dark outline of Diver marches forward.

"Dad, she's on her way!"

"Who's on their way?" Dad asks, wiping ash from his brow.

Before I answer, chaos explodes.

Sand rises into the air when Diver crests the dunes, crashing down around the Shadowmancers. Lightning strikes go *zzz-splat* on the tops of Shadowy heads, and finally, Light bombs rain down from above as Diver comes to a groaning halt. Callie and another girl—a tall one with long curls, light brown skin, and *way* overdressed—appear on Diver's shoulder. Hot on their heels is Boy Scout in all his scowling scowlery. The fancy new girl levitates herself to the ground, her eyes glowing white—clearly, she's another type of Seer. She moves her hands, and a miniature cyclone sweeps a group of Shadowmancers away into the night.

"Nate! What are you doing here?" Diver puts Callie and Toran on the ground. As soon as her feet touch the sand, she Light blasts half a dozen Shadowmancers as easily as breathing.

"Hey! Thanks for showing up!" I smile when she comes to my side. "Epic entrance, by the way."

Callie takes out some more Shadowmancers, then stares at me and the Light in my hands. Wow, her eyes are pretty in the moonlight. "How did you — I mean, I thought you were —"

"You're finally here!" Fancy Girl assaults me with a hug. She squeezes so tight I'm pretty sure a couple ribs snap. "I'm so excited to meet you!"

"Let go!" I wriggle free of Fancy Girl's grasp and throw my hands up when she moves in for more unwanted touching. "Don't hug me."

"Why?" Fancy Girl shoots bolts of menacing lightning at some Shadowmancers behind me. "Aren't you happy to see me?"

"I don't know who you are." And I'd like to forget the hug-attack thing as quickly as possible.

"Is that another Seer?" Dad calls from his position on the other side of the car. "I could use the assistance."

"Two Seers," Boy Scout corrects him. "But there's no water for me to assist, even if I wanted to."

"Toran?" Heike suddenly recalls she's got a pulse and a voice. She peeks over the half-buried hood of the car and smiles bigger than I've seen her smile since Queen took us into the Shadows. "Toran! Brother! You're all right!"

"Heike?" Boy Scout stops in his tracks. His face contorts into pure shock, like somebody shot him in the gut. He stumbles weakly to his knees before picking himself up and bolting for his sister. He gathers her into his outstretched arms, on the verge of smiling.

Yes, really! Boy Scout, smiling!

"Heike, my sister, I thought you were dead!"

"I'm sorry I couldn't get here sooner." Heike squeezes him tight.

"How did you survive? Did the Shadowmancer hurt you?" Toran looks his sister over for distress, then glares at me.

I didn't do anything except save her life, so you can keep your accusatory frowns to yourself, Toran. And while you're at it, go suck eggs.

"I've never been better," Heike says with a grin.

"If we could pause the reunion momentarily," Dad announces with his last thread of patience. "I'm elderly, and I need help *now*."

Loud and clear, Dad.

"Hey, Princess Airhead." Good one, works way better than Fancy Girl. I take the Seer's shoulders and spin her towards Dad holding down the entire battle himself, while Boy Scout stands around chit-chatting with Heike. "Shadowmancers. Imminent doom. Go. Fight. Win."

"Oh, I see!" Princess Airhead grins. Who is this weirdo? Why is she grinning? "Don't worry, I'll be back!"

"Please, don't be back." Once she twirls off like a ballerina-meets-live-wire, I face Callie. She looks like she's—relieved? Confused? I can't read her. "So, uh—how've you been?"

Callie glances down the dune at the remains of my Subaru. "Is that your car?"

"It is. Long story."

Her eyes pop when she realizes who's causing the firestorm, now mixed with Princess Airhead's lightning. "Is that your *dad?!*"

"It is. Also a long story."

"We thought you were dead." Callie pauses Light blasting Shadowmancers long enough to meet my eyes. Her gaze softens, and my heart skips (metaphorically). Does she want to hug me?

Princess Airhead can get lost, but if Callie wants to hug me …
"How did you get here? Like, obviously your car was involved,
but … Verona Beach? Why?"

"I made a small detour before I—watch out! They're coming
up fast!" Shadowmancers swoop in, reminding me we don't have
time for conversation. Callie's on top of the threat, sending orb
after spinning orb flying at the monsters. They turn to ashes and
Darkness vapor before they know what hit them.

"You're gonna have to teach me how to do that," I say.

"Are you still a Shadowmancer, or are you a Luminaut?"
Callie flicks a glance at my sparkle hands. "What's going on with
you?"

"I don't know what I am, but I'm giving the reformed, ex-
heartless-monster thing a try." I point at the creatures of Shadow
she's blasting into oblivion. "Those, however, are Queen's new-
and-improved Shadowmancers."

Callie's expression plummets. "You can't be serious."

"Believe me, I wish I was—"

"NATE!" El leaps from Diver's ankle to the sand and runs for
me at top speed.

"What are you doing, dingus?" Did he seriously climb all the
way down Diver? "Do you have a death wish or something? Get
back up there where it's safe!"

"You're alive!" El does what he always does and completely
ignores every smart thing I've ever said. He has Callie's little
mech, Nemo, on his shoulder, and the robot whir-squeals when
he sees me. Does that mean he's happy, or is he going to attack
my ankle?

"Don't try to hug-assault me like Princess Airhead, or I'll—
ow!" El punches me right in the stomach. Not what I was
expecting. I double over in pain, almost dropping to my knees.

"Why? Just—why?"

"Because you let us think you were dead, you stupid dümfo!" El aims another punch, but I raise my hand, blocking him. "Where were you? Why didn't you come find us?"

"I was trapped in the Shadow Plain. And what do you think I just did, dweeb?"

"El, you're an unprotected pile of ash waiting to happen." Thanks, Callie, for reminding El he's almost toast.

"I'm on dingus protection duty." Those who can't fight can babysit.

"Elion?" Heike peels herself away from her brother at the sight of her friend.

"Heike!" El's eyes get big and sparkly when he sees Heike, and they run for each other. Instead of punching Heike, El gives her a giant hug, and she hugs him back. She's a whole foot taller, but neither seem to care.

"Aw, it's so squishy and sweet, I'm melting." I grab both of their shoulders and shove them behind my body, holding my Light hands to the side to keep the Shadowmancers away. "Stay back, and don't get any more dangerous, dumb ideas, *El specifically*. Got it?"

"Heike, come back here! He's not safe!" Toran attempts to coax his sister away from me, but I'm a lot faster in out-maneuvering him.

"You worry about finding water to help Dad and Princess Airhead with the Shadowmancers." I think Boy Scout and I need to have a talk later about which scenarios are safe and unsafe. "I've got the middle schoolers. Believe it or not, I'm a decent babysitter, and I—El, if you don't quit trying to sneak off to look at Shadowmancers, I'm going to drop-kick you across three-and-a-half sand dunes."

"Harm her, and you'll regret it," Toran threatens.

"Yep, got it." Thumbs up, butthead. Shove one up yours, why dontcha?

Toran marches off to join Dad and Princess Airhead down the dune, and Callie turns to me with a half-smile. "You'll drop-kick your babysitting charges across the dunes? Your skills are truly unmatched, Nate."

"Thanks, I know," I reply.

"You're so humble about it, too."

"Humble is my middle name."

Callie blasts Shadowmancers while Dad and the other Seers take care of the rest down at the base. Toran found a small amount of water—condensation from my car exhaust, I think—that he's using to violently freeze and impale. As quick as they came, the Shadowmancers retreat through the Veil, like they were never there at all.

Why such a rapid departure? It's too easy.

"Hello!" Oh great, Princess Airhead is back with Dad and Boy Scout. At least she didn't try to hug me this time. "We've gotten rid of the monsters down the dune."

"Almost done here." Callie raises both hands, sending Light blasts far and wide across the desert. Any remaining Darkness flies away into the night.

None of this makes sense. Why doesn't Queen keep sending Shadowmancers to weaken Callie? She told me to my horrified face she'd capture and torture Callie and El to blackmail my servitude. Why give up her prize so easily?

I don't like it. Not one bit.

"A small-scale attack compared to what we saw in Verona Beach." Dad comes to my side. "Are you hurt?"

"No, I'm good." I turn to the kids at my back. "How about

you guys?"

"I'm fine!" Heike practically skips to Toran's side and huddles there like a chick under the wing of her frowning, cranky mother hen.

"My hands got scraped up climbing down Diver, but I'm okay," El says.

No injuries all around is a small relief. "Come on, let's go. Queen could show up any second, so—"

"Who are you?" El stares at Dad. They face each other for a moment in a weird size-up standoff.

"I'm Nate's father, Richard. Who are you?"

"I'm El, his best friend in the multiverse."

"Hey there, Dr. Ormandi." Callie approaches Dad. If I had to pin the look on her face, I'd say she was beyond angry. Furious, even. The Light around her takes on a malevolent gleam. "Are you surprised to see me alive?"

"Very much relieved." Still, Dad shrinks away. He's usually so direct, it's awkward to watch him evade eye contact. Is he scared of her powers? Doubtful. Unless he has some other reason to be afraid.

Speaking of fear, we should all be afraid of Shadowmancers showing up, but nobody's interested in immediate dangers.

"Relieved I wasn't killed by the Queen Beyond the Stars when I found each new Light Core?" Callie arches an eyebrow. "Because the Light Cores are the keys to her prison, after all, and each one that's found allows her to gain even more of her full power."

Ah, that's the reason she's mad: Dad withheld key intel before her first Dive. Honestly, that tracks.

"You're angry that I didn't tell you everything about Darkness," Dad defends himself. "I thought we'd have more time. I didn't expect you'd have to Dive before I could explain the whole truth."

The truth is that we could get attacked by Darkness. But who cares? Just me, apparently. "Maybe we should—"

"Didn't tell me everything?" Light flares ferociously around Callie. "You flat-out lied to me. Said the Light Cores were just missing pieces of some mythical bridge that got destroyed eons ago, not purposely hidden so Queen could never be released into the multiverse. You told me Luminauts were benevolent protectors of Light, but I watched Luminauts slaughter innocent people in Diver's memories. So what, exactly, did you tell me that was true?"

"Nate's father lied to you? And you're surprised?" Toran scoffs like Callie is the biggest idiot he knows. "Duplicity is family trait, I suppose."

"What's your family trait, Boy Scout? Blaming everyone else for your problems?" I can take Callie calling Dad and me liars, but Toran better shut his pie hole. "Without us lying Ormandis, your sister would be dead. Or is myopia a Rykjiersen trait, too?"

Toran balls his hands into fists like he's going to start a fight. Just try it, Boy Scout. "Take care not to insult my sister, you nargush-infested—"

"I'm sensing a lot of tension," Princess Airhead speaks up. "Perhaps we should travel back to Cordonanza and have a nice pastry together. I'm always more angry when I'm hungry, but feel so much better when I eat something sweet." Princess Airhead looks between us all, her hazel eyes bright. Everyone seems a little too shocked by her obliviousness to contradict her. "Oh, I forgot! Introductions first. I'm Ayla Alindia, Air Manipulator. Callie, do you already know my Luminaut?"

"What the—" Is she talking about me? No freaking way, man.

"I'm not jack squat to you."

"But you are!" Princess Airhead—Ayla—insists. "You must be disoriented from the Darkness attacks."

"I'm not disoriented, you're delusional."

"Nate Ormandi, a *Luminaut*?" Toran's barking laugh flies from his lips. "You're joking. That monster of Darkness is the furthest thing from a Luminaut that exists."

Remind me to punch this guy in the throat later.

"Nate, Ayla, Toran, please." Callie glares, impatient. "I'm trying to get to the bottom of why I was lied to and tricked into undertaking a life-threatening quest, not hashing out this Luminaut-and-Seer stuff, okay?"

"Can we hash out the Shadowmancer stuff instead?" Any takers? No?

"Shadowmancer stuff—does that include you? I don't even know what you are." Callie narrows her eyes at Dad and nods. "Dr. Ormandi owes me an explanation first."

"I didn't trick you." Dad pinches the bridge of his nose. "I would never knowingly—"

"Luminaut, is your name Nate? Same as Elion and Callie's lost friend?" Princess Airhead *just* put it together that the Nate everyone's been talking about is me? She claps her hands like a cartoon princess about to sing a song to some dancing squirrels. "How wonderful you aren't dead after all! Now we can all be best of friends."

Oh for the love of— "You need a *massive* reality check, Princess Airhead."

"My name isn't Princess Airhead, it's Ayla."

Facepalm.

"Enough! All of you!" Dad tosses his hands high in frustration. "Nate's right, more Shadowmancers could be gathering for a strike, and we're standing in a highly exposed area, arguing over details that can be addressed later."

"Nobody's arguing you lied to me," Callie retorts. Better go get some burn ointment, Dad.

"Fine. I deserved that." Dad's eye tics. "The point being, there are powerless children out here, and—"

"Who are you calling powerless, old man?" El stares defiantly at Dad, and Nemo shakes his fist.

"We're all powerless to stop the coming Darkness." Heike's being creepy now. Great.

"Stop interrupting!" Dad's eyes flash like he's about to burst into flame. "I swear, if one more teenager interrupts me before I've finished speaking, I will—"

It's not teenagers that interrupt Dad, but the whooshing *zurrrmmm* of airships overhead. The sand beneath our feet sifts with violent quickness until we sink into the fine grains knee-deep. Something about the sand is solid, almost sentient, holding us in place.

In the midst of the airship lights, a woman with glowing green eyes appears. Creeping, writhing vines cover her arms, which I'd think was interesting if said vines didn't immediately shoot from her wrists to tie our hands behind our backs.

Next time, people should listen to me when I tell them we've got to scram.

"Please, no, Mama," Ayla murmurs.

Mama? The Seer with the vines is Princess Airhead's mom? Talk about the apple falling *very* far from the tree.

"Many apologies for trapping you like this." The Seer's tone says she's anything but sorry. Armed guards with handcuffs and blasters descend from the airships, moving quickly to encircle us, weapons pointed at our faces.

"However," the Seer stares at us, Machiavellian and calculating, "I have to inform you that you're all under arrest."

# CHAPTER 11
# TORAN

HEIKE IS ALIVE.

It's a miracle I never thought possible, more than I dared to hope. I was prepared to dwell forever in the chasm of her loss after the Shadows swallowed her before my eyes. But she's here, as though we'd never been parted at all.

However, our reunion is not a happy meeting. If Darkness attacks weren't awful enough, now we're tied up by Serai's vines, and guards move swiftly to arrest us. The last thing I'll let anyone do is part me from my sister again.

"Toran, help me! I can't break free!" Panic chokes Heike, and her voice squeaks as she struggles against the vines.

"Hold still. I'll figure out a way to free us, I promise." How I'll keep said promise, I don't know. The only water available to fight off Shadowmancers was a tiny amount from the remains of Nate's car, and that's long gone.

"Mama, you can't do this to my friends!" Ayla pleads, but her cries fall on hardened ears.

"We aren't having this discussion, Ayla." Serai motions for the guards to move in closer, bronze handcuffs at the ready. "The situation with the Luminaut has to be contained before word gets out to the wrong politicians. I tried being reasonable about this, and my estate in Sky District was destroyed. I have no other choice but to—"

"That's Mariasol's son and husband." Callie's proclamation stops Serai in her tracks. The Seer holds up her vine-covered hand, and the guards pause. "Are you seriously going to arrest them?"

"Ah, we're not so bad when we present an expedient end to a predicament," Richard, Nate's father, mutters under his breath.

"Shut up, Dad, you wanna stay tied up?" Nate has a good point, for once.

"You're her family?" Serai stares at Nate and his father, her gaze lingering on the former. "Dunes, you look just like your mother. It's uncanny."

She's distracted, and the guards she brought don't know what to do without a clear set of orders to follow. Excellent. This buys me time.

Reaching with my Manipulation, I search for water below the dune. Bubbling fountains scattered throughout Cordonanza indicate water is coming from somewhere—most likely underground wells and springs. If I can call it to the surface, I'll be able to slice through the vines, and Heike and I can escape. I press my cheek to the sand, feeling for water. The thick, hot earth blocks the flow of anything that could be underneath. I try again, concentrating harder.

"Toran," Heike whispers, "what are you doing?"

"Shh." I sense something, so deep it seems fathomless, but it's there. A gentle trickle giving way to a wide chasm—a whole sea under the sand.

*Come to me, water. Rise to the surface and find me.*

Slowly, like Mist creeping through the forest, the water obeys.

It pushes through the sand, upward against all logical flow. At last, a small puddle forms under my cheek.

Yes, this is working! More puddles spring up, and more still. Serai turns away from the Ormandis when she realizes what I'm doing, and the guards panic as the sand beneath them turns into muddy silt. Callie, Nate, Richard, and Elion shift the best they can in their restraints to get away from the rising water, but there isn't anywhere to hide.

"Stop this instant, Toran Rykjiersen, or you'll regret it," Serai warns. Her vines tighten around my wrists and ankles, cutting off blood flow to my feet and hands, but it doesn't matter. Water can function as my hands. With a flick of my chin, frozen spikes cut through my bindings.

"I will not stop." I call water into my hands, forming twin pikes. The guards immediately descend on me, and I swing hard. Water gathers around Serai's ankles, freezing her in place.

"Toran, get us out of these things!" Callie cries.

"As you can see, I'm busy." Two of the guards snap my pikes with their force shields, and I'm weaponless. Dramora spawn!

"That's a clever trick." Serai sends a cascade of small rocks along the dune to crack her ice bindings. "But you're entirely unprepared for such games."

Sand from the dunes rises up to engulf me, looming over my head until the moon and stars disappear from sight. There isn't enough water to safely cocoon my body or form a wall of protective ice. Terror jumbles my guts. I'm done for.

"Diver, help!" Callie calls.

Before I'm smothered, the giant mech's hand swipes the falling sand, scattering it far and wide. I make another set of ice pikes and take a headlong run at Serai, but she breaks them with shooting branches.

"Didn't I warn you?" Serai buries my puddles with her Manipulation. Fresh vines wrap around my entire frame, rooting me where I stand, and the guards aim their weapons at me, awaiting Serai's order to fire. "You need quite a bit more training before you attempt something like that again."

"Hey, listen up!" Callie's voice slices the tension between me and Serai. Every single guard goes completely still, and they face her in silent unison.

"Put down the blasters," Callie commands. Her voice takes on an unearthly, reverberating quality, as though it permeates flesh and bone all the way to the guards' inner thoughts. I've seen her do this before, when she forced the Volorad to perform that idiotic chicken dance so we could get Heike out of Gravenskov's jail.

"Yes." The guards speak in odd unison and put down the blasters.

"What's going on?" Nate looks between the guards and Callie, staring at the latter with increasing fear. "How are you—"

"Power down your force shields," Callie says. The guards power down the force shields. "Get back on the airships and stay there."

The unarmed guards march back to where they came from, leaving Serai to fend for herself against two (alleged) Luminauts, three Seers, and a giant mech.

"Nobody wants to fight anybody." Callie's voice and eyes return to normal when she looks at Serai. "Please, let's just talk about this."

"Callie, what did you do?" Nate stares at her, blinking hard. "How did you get those guards to do what you said?"

"She used Persuasion on them," Serai answers for Callie, horrified and enraged in equal measure.

"Of course I did. They had live blasters pointed at me and my friends, and were about to fire on Toran," Callie argues.

"You used *Persuasion*?!" Nate shudders. "What is *wrong* with you?"

"Fool of a Luminaut." Serai looks at Callie and shakes her head. "What you just did erased any leniency I might have shown."

"Why?" Callie tilts her chin. "What's wrong with—"

"Finally!" Richard ignites, fire burning through his bindings, and his joints crack and pop as he drags himself to his feet. "Took me a minute to find my lighter. Arthritic hands." A blaze races across the sand, encircling Serai. "If you'll kindly let my son and his friends go, I'd appreciate it."

"A Fire Manipulator?" Serai flicks her wrists, and desert sand suffocates the flames as fast as they appeared. "How fascinating. Unfortunately, I can't grant your request."

"I had a feeling you'd say that." Richard holds a flickering flame in his palm, reflected in his flashing dark eyes. "What a pity."

Earth and fire race for one another, and while Richard and Serai battle, I find one last puddle she didn't obliterate with sand. I call the water into my bound hands and form a saw-tooth knife to free myself, and next, my sister.

"Thank you, brother." Heike rubs her wrists, which are raw and red.

"Wanna get the rest of us, Toran?" Callie wears a hopeful grin.

The only thing I "wanna" do is flee with Heike to safety, but my rectangular comm pressed to my chest in my vest pocket reminds me I made a deal with Manu, and he needs me to find his Light Core—which means I need Callie to solve the Rognaga.

So I cut her bindings and then those of Nate, Ayla, and Elion. Now they're all in my debt, which is exactly where I want them to be.

"Thank you, Toran." Ayla's smile shines in the starlight. An odd clench tightens my insides, one that rises all the way into my throat. I look away quickly and it's gone.

"Come on, Seers, Dad needs an assist." Nate tries his best to get his Light to make an orb like Callie's, but he's woefully incompetent. "This is freaking impossible!"

"You just haven't been taught." Callie launches a Light orb high and wide, aiming at nothing in particular.

"Yes, yes, very nice. At least that part of your power isn't murderous. Next time, aim for the Earth Manipulator trying to hogtie my dad with sentient vines." Nate rushes off before she can reply. "Hang on, Dad, I'm coming!"

"Me too!" Elion charges in, but not before depositing Nemo safely behind.

"What are you doing?" I yell after Nate and Elion's backsides. "We need to leave while she's distracted!"

"Murderous? What are you talking about?" Callie sets Nemo on her shoulder and stomps after Nate.

"This is ridiculous!" I rake my hands through my hair, squeezing tight in frustration. "They're asking to get caught!"

"I agree." Ayla agrees with me? At last, a person with some sense!

"We need to go find the Light Core," Heike adds.

How does my sister know we need a Light Core? I didn't say anything about my secret plan to hunt Ensolorada's Light Core. But regardless, she's right.

"Stand back," Ayla cautions. "I'm—I'm going to try something. It might be dangerous, and Mama may be terribly angry with me."

"Then why do it?" I ask.

"Because my friends need me to do it. My Luminaut needs me to do it." Ayla is resolute, her bottom lip firmly fixed despite the rest of her shaking with nerves. "Our Luminauts are our brothers and sisters by Light. Wouldn't you do anything to save Callie from danger?"

Never in a thousand ages would I call Callie my sister, let alone my friend, nor would I lift a finger to save her from idiotic dangers of her own making. But whatever Ayla has planned will provide us a means to escape, so I say nothing besides, "Heike, come, out of the way."

As soon as I'm safely out of the path of Ayla's crossfire, she rises into the air, and a strong wind blows across the dunes. Richard's fire races every which way across the sand, completely uncontrolled, and Serai ducks and dodges the flames, her vines disappearing. Callie, Nate, and Elion shield their eyes from the spinning air and sand.

"Ayla! Cease this immediately!" Serai shouts over the gales.

"Dad! El! We've got to get out of here!" Nate reaches for his father and Elion, both of them physically weakened in the face of such intense winds.

"Diver! I need you!" Callie calls for her largest mech, clutching Nemo tight against her chest.

"I'm sorry, Mama. Not this time." Ayla doesn't hesitate. Electric sparks coalesce around her until fierce lightning strikes tear the air.

Diver finds Callie and lowers his hand. She yells over the wind and lightning. "Come on, everybody up!"

I fight against gusts, and Callie pulls Heike onto Diver's palm first. I board next. She passes Nemo to my sister, then cups her hands around her mouth. "Nate! El! Ayla! Dr. O! Let's go!"

Nate reaches Diver, hanging on to the mech's finger while he stretches his hand for Richard and Elion. Ayla zaps the sand several more times, creating a deep fissure in the desert to separate us from Serai, before she comes down and joins our increasingly crowded perch.

"We must go." Ayla pants from the exertion her storm took to create. "Mama will recover quickly and attack."

"EL! DAD!"

Vines ensnare the ankles of the two people not yet touching Diver, pulling them away from Nate. His eyes widen, and he springs after his father and the boy, but Ayla snatches his wrist and tugs him backward.

"Luminaut, no!" She's stronger than I thought, considering Nate is so athletic.

"Let me go!" Nate's eyes are darker than dark, almost black. Darkness peeking through the facade? Or helpless anger?

"Diver, get us up," Callie commands, and she joins Ayla in pulling Nate aboard. Diver uses his other hand to cup Nate safely in his grasp, and the four of us ascend the giant mech.

Richard and Elion shout for Nate, vines dragging them across the sand mercilessly until they disappear into the crevice formed by Ayla's lightning. Serai watches from the other side as the rest of us mount the World Diver's shoulder, and the mech lumbers into the desert night.

"Tell him to put me down, Callie. I'm going back for them." Nate struggles against Diver's firm grip.

"No way," Callie argues, roughly pulling Nate through the Crow's Nest hatch door. It locks tight the second Callie slams it shut. "You're going to hurt yourself if you don't calm down."

"*You're* one to talk about hurting people." Nate yanks on the hatch. "You seriously used *Persuasion* on those guards? Didn't anybody ever tell you how the Light Collective used Persuasion? Murder, blackmail, extortion, more murder. Mom said it was banned in Ensolorada ages ago."

"Okay, that's a fair point. I promise I won't use it ever again," Callie says. "Now can you please come away from the door?"

"Nope." Another hard pull. "Open up, Big Guy. I have to get Dad and El before they're choked to death."

If the World Diver hears, he does not comply. The door remains locked.

"Mama wouldn't choke them." Ayla sits primly on the Crow's Nest couch. "She'd just lock them inside the estate while she uses every resource she has to hunt us down."

"Because imprisonment is *so* much better," Nate snaps.

"Ayla said they won't be harmed, we have to trust her." I take a step toward the Diver's Prism, and all eyes turn to me. "Going back means we risk capture as well, and that accomplishes nothing. It's not worth the trouble at the moment."

"Thanks for the advice, Boy Scout, but I'll decide what's worth the trouble for myself." Nate resumes tugging on the hatch door with rapid speed.

"Boy Scout?" Ayla frowns, confused. "His name is Toran. And he is, unfortunately, correct. It would be best to give Mama a wide berth until things calm down."

"Nate." Callie places a gentle hand on Nate's shoulder. "I know you're worried, but there's nothing we can do right now. Let's make a plan together, okay?"

All the fight leaves Nate. He slumps under Callie's touch and stumbles into the Crow's Nest, the picture of defeat. "Fine. Plans. Talk to me."

"Since going back to Cordonanza is not ideal," I begin, "why not hunt down Ensolorada's Light Core?" The opportunity to accomplish my plot with Manu unfolds even as I say the words. "By the time we find the Rognaga and extract the Light Core, Serai's anger will have cooled and we can rescue Richard and Elion."

I have no intention of rescuing Richard and Elion, and it occurs to me that this is the first outright lie I've ever told—and I did it as easily as breathing. I've always said I'd never deceive others the way I was deceived by the Village Council, but that's exactly what I'm doing now.

I glance down at Heike, sitting cross-legged on the floor at my feet. She's here, safe. Why not run away, and leave dangerous people with even more dangerous powers behind forever. Forget Light Cores and all the trouble they've caused—or the multitude of lies I'll have to tell to keep everyone on my side.

But if I don't see the hunt through, Manu will not follow through on his end of our deal. I can't allow Callie's Light to cause Heike even more harm.

"One issue with your Light Core hunting plan, Toran," Callie says. "We don't have a copy of the map to the Rognaga."

"I, uh, I found a copy. I was looking at Lore on my comm and came across it." Another lie. Callie and Ayla are obviously shocked, but Nate shrugs.

"Maps and Rognagas and Light Cores, oh my!" His tone betrays impatience. "Anybody want to explain why I should care about this instead of going after my dad and El right freaking now?"

I take my comm from my pocket and tap the Rognaga icon in the corner of the glass. Instantly, the Crow's Nest glows with the entirety of the map floating above our heads.

"Look. These runes give directions to finding the labyrinth in the desert." I point out the words in the far corner of the map. "And these guide competitors through the maze itself." I gesture to the runes written throughout the map.

"This is an incredibly dangerous undertaking, and we're not prepared." Ayla presses her lips. "We need desert gear and clothing, first aid and medical supplies, food, water rations. And you and Callie are the only ones with comms. Speaking of which …" Ayla rises and takes Callie's comm, then mine, her fingers dancing along the glass. "There. Mama is blocked from transmitting and receiving signals, which will make us harder to trace."

"Could we sneak back into Cordonanza and get the supplies we need?" I ask.

"It's unwise," Ayla replies. "But perhaps small drone transports could deliver them to the World Diver. They often make deliveries at remote outposts in the dunes."

"That all sounds great, except none of it explains why Toran has a copy of a map nobody's supposed to have in the first place." Callie narrows a glare on me, growing more suspicious by the second. "Serai said the Rognaga map Manu had is contraband. How did you happen to 'find' it randomly browsing Lore on your comm?"

I open my mouth, hoping to conjure a quick lie, but Nate saves me the trouble of speaking.

"I don't give a crap who Manu is or how Boy Scout got his mitts on something illegal. What I want to know is how you expect five people who don't get along in the first place to survive *that*?" Nate points at the terrible labyrinth above our heads. "The odds are not in our favor."

"According to Lore, only a Luminaut can win the Rognaga." I formulate a plan swiftly. "Ayla, Heike, and myself will stay in the Crow's Nest and guide you through, using my comm transmitting to Callie's."

"So, I'm going in alone," Callie surmises. "Fantastic."

"Not alone." Ayla grins at her alleged Luminaut. "Nate can go in too."

Callie hesitates, then says, "I don't think that's a good idea. Nate can't use his Light consistently, and he might still be a Shadowmancer."

"Thanks for the vote of confidence," Nate deadpans. "However, Callie's got a point. I'm a half-Luminaut at best, and the other half is a monster."

Callie winces. "I didn't call you a monster."

"It was implied," Nate says with a shrug. "Regardless, we've got trust issues, and throwing us into a death maze together isn't going to solve them."

"But two Luminauts going in, even one at half-strength, increases the odds of beating the maze," Ayla reasons.

"Or it increases our likelihood of getting screwed," Nate counters.

"What is screwed? We don't have screws in us. Although Toran does have a stick up his butt."

Nate snorts.

"Let's talk seriously." Callie paces back and forth, thinking aloud. "Even though I'm the better Luminaut, Nate's a better strategist, especially on the fly."

"Hey, I make pretty sparkle hands." Nate waves said sparkling hands in Callie's face. She pushes them out of the way, but a small smile curves her lips.

"Nate will get better at using Light if you teach him." Ayla looks between the two Luminauts. "The Record Hall kept the footage of Mariasol and Mama training for the Rognaga accessible to the public. I'll pull it up for you both to watch. I believe we can make this happen!"

They're agreeing with my scheme? Have I died and entered the Lands Beyond? I don't know how to react except to stand there, stunned this is actually working.

"I don't want to rain on anyone's parade," Nate announces in a way that means he is going to rain on a parade, whatever that means, "but Darkness followed me through the gateway, which means Queen's on our trail. If Callie and I get lost in the maze, that's gift wrapping her two Luminauts with a bow on top."

"And even if we win, Manu still has my other three Light Cores," Callie adds. "That complicates things."

"The more I hear about this Manu guy, the more I don't like him," Nate observes.

"Oh, he's like, super gross. Big-time slime ball."

Doubt creeps into their words. This is not good.

"Just listen!" I toss my hands high, and draw everyone's attention back to the map. I need to remind Callie of Phase Two of her plan—defeating the Queen Beyond the Stars.

"We can't worry about Manu, and we can't rush back to find Richard and Elion until we have this Light Core. Distractions mean we've already lost." I face Callie, willing her to remember what she herself said she wanted most. "You need to end Darkness so you can keep your loved ones safe. Isn't that why you Dove across the multiverse in the first place? This is how you do it. Not arguing or fighting—taking action."

"He's right," Heike adds.

I wait, barely breathing, for her response. Callie is the Luminaut who commands the World Diver. If she says we are finding the Light Core, the rest will follow.

"All right then, we're going to the Rognaga to find

Ensolorada's Light Core," Callie announces. "As much as it pains me to say it, Toran's right. It's the only way we can eventually defeat Queen."

Finally! I've won! Perhaps I'm better at lying and schemes than I thought.

"I'll order our supplies." Ayla borrows Callie's comm, and taps away on the glass.

"Hooray, a death maze. Just what I always wanted to do on my first trip to Mom's home world." Nate reclines in the Luminaut's chair. "If you need me, I'll be here, having an existential crisis."

Nate can have an existential crisis all he likes. My plan is working.

Heike touches my leg, getting my attention. "We must speak. Alone."

"Of course." I glance at Callie, perusing desert gear with Ayla. "Heike needs air. Tell the mech to unlock the door."

Callie grumbles something about saying please before tapping the Prism. "Diver, open up the hatch, *please*."

A lock clicks, and Heike and I slip into the desert night, sitting side by side on the Diver's shoulder. She looks up at the stars, the pale purple moon reflecting on the dunes. The openness of this world feels scary — Tremurheim is enclosed by forests and Mist, for better or worse. Out here in the vast desert, we are insignificant grains of sand beneath the infinite expanse of sky.

"Are you sure you want Callie to do the Rognaga?" Heike speaks first.

"I understand if you're worried," I say. "Callie is your friend, and —"

"Callie is no longer my friend." Heike shakes her head. "She could have saved me back on Tremurheim, but she didn't. She let the monsters take me." My sister's face hardens like stone. "What kind of friend does that?"

"Oh, Heike." Relief washes over me, and I put my arms around her. "I'm so glad you finally see the truth."

"You were right all along," Heike says with a sad sigh. "I should have listened to you."

"It's in the past." My heart swells, and at last, a smile reaches my lips. "I promise Callie will never harm you again."

"Is that why you're sending her into the maze?" Heike gives me a sharp look. "We both know Nate won't let anything happen to her. He betrays his weaknesses too easily."

"No, I need her to win. For now." I glance over my shoulder, making sure nobody comes close to the door. "I made a secret plan with a politician in Cordonanza, Manu Carosti. He's the one who gave me the map of the Rognaga. After Callie finds the Light Core, he'll arrest her and take her Light powers away."

"Arrest her for what?" Heike furrows her brow. "Can he do that?"

"It's part of the deal we made. He needs four Light Cores for his power extractor, and I need Callie's powers eliminated for everything she did to you."

"Excellent." Heike smirks, a steely gleam in her eyes. I've never seen her wear this kind of expression, all coldness and spite. "I didn't know you had it in you to play such games."

"I would do anything for you, Heike." I put my arm around her slim shoulders. "Just promise me you'll keep this between us. If Ayla finds out ..."

"Why do you care what Ayla thinks?" Heike tilts her chin. "For your plan to work, you can't be soft."

I balk at her words. Heike, telling *me* not to be soft? "I've never been soft. I don't intend to start now."

"Good." My sister yawns and stretches her arms above her head. "I think I'll go back inside and rest."

Heike makes her way across Diver's shoulder into the Crow's Nest, but I remain staring across the desert, content to be alone. I've never needed anyone besides Heike, and soon we'll put an end to this terrible time—one I'd like nothing more than to forget forever. Soon, we'll be free to live our lives in peace.

All I've got to do is make sure Callie James and Nate Ormandi survive a death maze and emerge with a Light Core in hand. It can't be *that* difficult, can it?

# CHAPTER 12
# CALLIE

"TELL THE MECH TO GO three degrees right." Toran sits in Diver's Seer chair like a Navigator King on his Crabbyface Throne, reading runes on the Rognaga map and bossing me and Diver around like he runs the place.

I'm trying to hold it together, but Toran is *seriously* making it difficult to believe we're a real-life Luminaut and Seer dyad. My fingernails dig into the soft leather of my Luminaut chair, a poor attempt to keep my mounting frustration in check.

"I already told him to go three degrees right," I say through gritted teeth.

Toran scowls. "Then why is he not doing it?"

"He *is* doing it."

*Is the Seer accusing us of things that are not true, Luminaut?* Even steadfast Diver's on edge over Toran's new overlordship. If I could read the map myself, Toran would have the privilege of hiking through the dunes in Diver's wake, or riding on Diver's shoulder with Heike while she waits for drone deliveries to arrive with our supplies. As it stands, nobody but Toran can make sense of the ancient language or the archaic sentence structure of the map's directions.

So it's up to Crabby McButthead to guide us. Bummer.

*Can you stop talking to each other in my head? It's weird.*

Oh, and Nate can hear Diver's conversations with me, too. We figured it out when I was griping about Toran to my mech, and Nate joined in to air his many grievances.

*If you didn't want him to talk to you, you shouldn't have given him that Light memory in Tremurheim,* I tell Nate via Diver's Light.

*I didn't do it on purpose.* Even Nate's Light voice sounds annoyed.

*If telepathic Light communication with mechs irritates you, Luminauting is going to be difficult.*

*What I'm irritated with is Princess Airhead telling me the exact same thing for the fifth time in a row. Wanna trade Seers?*

*Absolutely. Ayla is cool, Toran is the worst.*

Nate's internal laugh sounds just like his real one. *Yeah, Toran can be a massive –*

*Luminaut and Not-Our-Luminaut must stop talking so much,* Diver interrupts. *We are trying to concentrate on the Seer's directives.*

Oops. At least Nate didn't teach Diver yet another four-letter word. My mech has learned a lot of those in the last twenty-four hours. *Sorry, Diver.*

*Apologies, Big Guy. And you can call me Nate.*

Diver is quiet for a second, his Light computing this information. *As you wish, Not-Our-Luminaut-Nate.*

Nate groans on the couch behind me, and I laugh into my hand. As per usual, Toran whips his head around to scowl.

"What's so funny?"

"Are we headed in this direction for a while?" I ask instead of answering Toran's blunt query. "Because there are things I need to do before we arrive at the Rognaga site."

"It's a straight path the rest of the way," Toran replies.

"However, the dunes are growing steep. I sincerely hope this old scrapheap is up to the task. Which I doubt."

Nemo whizzes up when Toran insults his mech buddy and whacks him hard on the ankles. Before Toran aims a retaliatory kick, Nemo whizzes off, whir-laughing.

Guess who's thrilled to have Nemo back and who's not?

"Did Nemo score another point?" Nate asks. I make my way to the couch, my tiny mech trailing me with an air of smug satisfaction.

"Of course. Nemo is an expert ankle-swiper." I take a seat on the floor and set Nemo on his favorite shoulder perch. A copy of the Rognaga map Toran sent to my comm floats in the air between Ayla and Nate on opposite ends of the couch. Ayla is as prim and perky as ever. Nate slumps in his seat like he wants to die for real.

"It's good you joined us, Callie. I was just about to go over the Rognaga map with Nate," Ayla says.

"For the sixth time," Nate mutters.

"It's better to be over-prepared than underprepared." I nudge Nate's knee with my elbow. "Come on, you love plans."

"What plan?" Nate asks. "All I've seen is this map from every possible angle until I want to stick a fork in my eye."

"Don't do that, Luminaut, you would severely injure yourself," Ayla cautions. Nate groans. The holo map expands over my head with a flick of Ayla's fingers. "As you can see, the Rognaga has four quadrants. The first three quadrants have a safe house at the terminus." Ayla points to a little blinking dot in the midst of the twisting labyrinth.

"Like I'm going to recall the exact location of those blinking dots when I'm focused on not dying in the middle of a death maze." Nate gets along with Ayla's upbeat cheerfulness about as well as I get along with Toran's blunt rigidity.

"Don't be so broody," I tell him. "Besides, I'll be there, too."

Nate pinches the bridge of his nose, just like Dr. Ormandi. "I'm not broody."

"You are very broody, Luminaut. Anyway, the goal is to reach each safe house before sunrise," Ayla continues. "Otherwise, the desert sun will get so hot your blood will boil you alive."

"Can I be boiled alive now, please?" Nate deadpans.

Ayla's face contorts into a look of dismay. "Oh, dunes, no! It would be a dreadful way to go! You aren't serious, are you?"

Nate sighs deeply, counting down on his fingers. "Lightbulb of awareness clicking on in five, four, three, two …"

"Of course you aren't serious, you're teasing me again." Ayla laughs once she catches on to the joke. "One day I'll learn to tell when you're teasing me."

"Sure, you will."

"Let's go on with the lesson." I want to know as much as I can about the maze, even if Nate's annoyed with the repetitive conversation.

"Every night, we'll link our comms," Ayla continues. "Toran, Heike, and myself will help you find the quickest path through the quadrants to each safe house until you reach the center Pit where the Light Core is hidden. Once inside the Pit, the map is vague about how one acquires the Light Core. Toran said there's some language about Light being alive, but that doesn't seem right."

"That can't be right. Light isn't sentient," I say. "A Luminaut has to control it."

"I agree, but that's all it says." Ayla shrugs her slim shoulders.

"How did ancient Tremurheim runes make their way onto an Ensoloradan map anyway?" Nate stares at the Rognaga holo, intense concentration creasing his brow. "Does anybody know who wrote it? And why encrypt it in the first place?"

"What makes you say it's encrypted?"

"Because after the Severing, Ensoloradans wouldn't be able to read Tremurheim's language and vice versa—the cartographer literally used an unbreakable code," Nate says. "If Boy Scout hadn't serendipitously come along, the labyrinth would've stayed hidden forever. Someone went to a *lot* of trouble to make sure nobody finds this Light Core."

"Food and water rations arrived." Heike drags a package up the steps from Diver's shoulder, and an egg-shaped drone flies away into the night. "The last one will be desert gear."

"Awesome. Something for you guys to eat besides leftover Tremurheim hardtack." Nate takes the heavy packs from Heike and sets them near Diver's Prism. "I'll wait for the rest of the gear outside."

Heike doesn't complain about Nate trading places and flops into the Luminaut chair next to Toran.

"Wanna hang out with Heike, Nemo?" I set my little buddy down, but he shakes his head vehemently, whizzing to hide behind Ayla's ankles.

Wow, that's … interesting. Nemo and Heike were best pals when we were crossing the Hem of Tremurheim. Why the shift?

"Nemo and I will sort the ration packs and watch holodramas, won't we?" Ayla gives the tiny mech a pat on the head, and he clamors for her to pick him up. Maybe he'd just rather chill with Ayla.

"I guess, um, I'll wait for the desert gear with Nate."

Ayla practically beams. "Yes, that's an *excellent* idea."

Don't start shipping me with Nate, okay Ayla? The Rognaga is nothing more than a mutually beneficial partnership. End of story.

But the truth is, Nate's right. We have trust issues, and I don't actually know much about him—I know who he wanted me to think he was, acting on Queen's orders. But Nate himself? Other than the obvious broody sarcasm, which I suspect is yet another front, he's a mystery: one I'd better solve quickly, before we're reliant on each other for survival.

"Mind some company?" I join Nate on Diver's shoulder.

Nate startles, eyeing me like my presence isn't unwelcome despite uncertainty about my motives. He scoots over, giving me a wide space to sit. "I was just stargazing. Nothing nefarious, I promise."

"It's beautiful out here." At nighttime, the heavy heat evaporates, and a pleasant breeze slips across the dunes, blowing my hair away from my neck and shoulders. Stars glitter above our heads like a blanket of diamonds, and the hazy lavender moon shines bright enough to see for miles across the desert.

"I see why people in Ensolorada use 'my stars' as a pet name," I say.

"It's more than a pet name," Nate corrects my assumption. "Ensoloradans say 'my stars' about the people most precious to them. Mom only ever called me and Dad 'my stars.'"

"Is it cool for you to be in your mom's home world? Or mixed feelings?" Maybe my question is too bold, but Nate doesn't seem to mind.

"Bittersweet, I guess. I always wanted to come here, just … under different circumstances." He gazes at the lavender moon, his eyes full of grief as wide as the sky.

"I like your shirt. Sonic Youth is really cool." There, much better topic to lead with. Just a casual getting-to-know-you observation, not let's-rehash-your-greatest-trauma.

"You like them too?" Nate glances at his tee and grins. "They're one of my favorite bands."

"I thought you liked Pixies," I reply. "You played one of their albums when you found us in Tremurheim, remember?"

"That's right. Then you immediately took me prisoner and threatened to Light-blast my head off."

Yeah, I did do that. Kinda yikes, looking back. Does he want me to say I'm sorry?

"I have a lot of favorite bands." Nate circles back before I can apologize. "I got this shirt at a concert in LA. Dad was livid I drove there by myself. He grounded me for a month."

"No wonder he has an eye twitch problem." I grin across Diver's shoulder. "I thought I gave it to him when I brought a welder into his basement."

Nate smiles around a half-laugh, and my heart does the stubborn *kick-thud* thing it's always done when his dimples are in close proximity.

"No way, he perfected the I-hate-teenagers look on me first." Nate cocks his head, his lips curving. "You seriously got a welder down those rickety stairs without breaking your neck?"

"I had a lot of help from Diver. Otherwise, I'd have broken every bone in my body."

The way we naturally fall back into conversation, his sly wit and contagious impishness always making me laugh… it would be easy to forget everything that transpired between us won't require some serious hashing out.

"Nate, I wanted to ask—"

"Callie, there's something I need to tell you."

Awkward pause. I wait for him to decide if he's going to speak first. Nope. "You, uh, have something to tell me?"

"Yes." Nate pulls up his knees and rests his elbows on them.

"I learned something critical about the Shadow Plain when I was escaping with Heike. I think it's the key to ending Queen for good."

"What is it?"

"The Shadow Plain can be destroyed, but only from the inside." He pauses, letting this revelation take shape in my mind. "She chained me with Darkness, and I freed myself with Light. When I did, there was a permanent loss of mass. Less Darkness than before. When you destroy Shadowmancers out here in the human world, it doesn't matter because Queen's power comes from the Shadow Plain. She can always make more. But if the Shadow Plain is destroyed, we cut the head off the snake. Her power becomes finite, and once she's out of juice, boom. You take her out."

"But how does a Luminaut get inside the Shadow Plain without an invite from Queen?" I rest my chin on my balled fists, ruminating. "Maybe there's a gateway Toran or Ayla can find."

"I don't think there are gateways beyond the Veil." Darn, a dead end. "But that doesn't mean one couldn't exist, if we figure out how to make one. Ayla can research the Lore for information about gateway creation while Toran's busy with his map."

Nate thinks quicker than he can speak, his tongue charmingly tripping on his words. It feels like a peek behind the veneer of the Nate he shows others to the Nate he is inside. My eyes are fully open, always wary of Darkness, but right now, I think he's trying to be something different. Something more … true.

"I like that idea," I say. "It's a good plan."

"Aren't you glad you have a reformed heartless monster on your team?" Nate smiles. *Kick-thud* — okay, stop. He's cute, get over it.

"I'll keep you around on a trial basis. And by that I mean the whole death maze thing." I pause, holding my breath, shoulders tensed by my ears. I've been dying to ask this question since I saw his car fly through the air, trailed by Darkness. "So, uh, when you went to Verona Beach, did you see my family?"

"Sorry, I didn't," Nate says. I release a breath through pursed lips, my stomach lurching like I got punched in the gut. "I was trying to throw Queen off my trail and, obviously, mend some fences with Dad. But as far as I know, they're safe."

"As far as you know …" Which means he doesn't know. Not really. I gulp down a pit of anxiety rising into my throat. *If they're not safe, it's all been for nothing.*

"Listen, Callie." Nate's gaze finds me. I used to think his eyes were black, but now I see them with no mask, no pretense. They're dark brown, little flecks of amber peeking through the edges. Way prettier than they have any right to be. How easy would it be to fall into them?

"You might not believe me, and that's okay." His voice is almost rough. "But I want you to know I would *never* do anything to deliberately hurt you or your family again."

*Zrrrrmmmm*

A carrier drone arriving with a package distracts us before I reply — with affirmation or otherwise — to Nate's promise. The package falls onto Diver's shoulder, and the drone flies away as unceremoniously as it came.

"Huh. That was anticlimactic." Nate watches the drone disappear into the vastness of the desert night. "Guess that's our signal to go get prepped for the death maze."

"I'll check our navigation with Toran. We should be there soon."

Inside the Crow's Nest, Ayla has sorted the food and water and packed backpacks for me and Nate. Toran remains front and center, watching the dunes pass. His shoulders hunch like twin icebergs on either side of his neck, the reason immediately apparent. Ayla is engrossed in some kind of Bachelor-esque reality show on my comm. Actors floats above her like a television in thin air. Even Nemo's into the story, utterly transfixed.

"No, Chara, don't let Xandis take you to Star Fest! He'll break your heart once he secures your fortune!"

"Can you stop narrating? I'm trying to concentrate." At least Toran asks Ayla semi-nicely instead of snapping.

"It's just so infuriating to watch a kindhearted girl like Chara throw her love away on that no-good—oh! You're here!" Ayla smiles when she spots me and Nate. "Did you enjoy a lovely chat under the stars?"

"As lovely as your floating soap opera," Nate snarks. "Don't let us interrupt the thrilling conclusion of Chara and Xandis, the skeevy fortune hunter."

"They can wait. Look! I have something for you!" Ayla hops to her feet and retrieves the crystal spear we found in the Luminaut and Seer vault. "Here, take this with you into the maze." She holds the weapon out to Nate. "It belonged to your mother when she was training for the Rognaga."

"This was Mom's?" Nate's Light fills the spear as soon as he touches it, silver-white and pearly. He stares at the weapon, an unreadable look in his eyes. "I, uh—thanks, Ayla."

Remind me again why Nate gets the cool Seer? Seems unfair. Just saying.

I open the package of desert gear, all of it practical, rugged clothing and shoes, very Star Wars-flavored. "How close are we to the maze entrance, Toran?"

"It is just over the top of this dune," he answers.

"Awesome." But awesome is the last thing I feel. My heart thuds, my stomach clenching tight. "Diver, stop at the top of the dune."

*Yes, Luminaut.*

Ayla and Heike hold up a bedroll blanket for me to change while Nate slips behind the couch, and we're kitted out as soon as Diver crests the dune. I join Toran up front, staring out the windows in search of this death maze, only to find …

Nothing. Just miles and miles of flat sand, stretching like a beige lake toward the horizon.

"Are you serious?" I spin and glare at Toran. "You took us the wrong way!"

"Boy Scout betrayed us all?" Nate feigns a gape-mouthed gasp. "I can't believe it! The audacity!"

"The maze should be there." Toran rechecks his map, genuinely confused. "I followed the directions perfectly."

"Perhaps the Rognaga is so ancient it crumbled into dust," Ayla suggests.

"Or Toran's map is a counterfeit intentionally circulated to mislead anyone searching for the maze." I don't know exactly how Toran got this copy of the Rognaga map, but it would make sense that fakes were planted to keep the maze's secrets — well, secret.

"It isn't a counterfeit, it's the real thing." Toran *really* hates being called out.

"How do you know?" I cross my arms, thrumming my fingers. "Care to explain?"

"I—" Toran's lips disappear into a hard line. "Trust me, it's not a fake."

"Well, *that* changes everything." Nate's dripping derision could fill a sarcasm sea. "Don't worry, everyone, Toran promised it's the real map. We don't need to ask questions or deserve explanations. Let's all go back to trusting him, just because." The dark glower in his eyes reflects his Light spear like gleaming steel. "I left Dad and El to an unknown fate in Cordonanza for this wild goose chase. We're sitting ducks out here, waiting for Queen and her Darkness to exploit us."

"Too heavy on the bird analogies," I say.

Nate waves his hand through the air, another Dr. Ormandi move. "The point is, everything I'm trying to prevent, Boy Scout just compromised."

"The maze is hidden," Heike announces.

Everyone stares. Her undone hair covers most of her face, but when she lifts her head, the curtain of red-brown parts. Her gray eyes flash, dark and storm-like. So … not Heike. I shiver at the sight of them.

"It makes sense, doesn't it?" The storm breaks, and a bright smile stretches across her face. I must have imagined the other look. "Go outside and see if I'm right."

Okay, why not? Nate and I shoulder our packs, and Diver sets us on the sand.

"Hidden death maze! Where are you?" Nate calls into the breezy night.

"I don't think the Rognaga can hear you," Ayla says. Nate facepalms.

"Ask the mech." Toran stares angrily across the desert like he can force it to give him what he wants by scowling. "Ask him if the Rognaga is here or if we're lost."

"Fine." I'll try Toran's way, since we're rapidly running out of options. "Diver, is there a death maze hidden in this flat expanse of nothing?"

*Luminaut and Not-Our-Luminaut must get away from here.*

Whoa, that's unexpectedly terse. Nate and I exchange a look. *What do you mean, Big Guy?*

Diver's Light is absolutely terrified. An invisible wall slams down between us so I can't see his memories. *Luminaut needs to leave. This place is not safe.*

Diver did this before, on the Hem of Tremurheim when he didn't want me to find the Light Core in the Beacons. It was there his Luminaut and Seer met their horrific fate at the hands of the Light Collective. Did something similarly awful happen here?

*I'm not going to ask for a memory. I just need to know if a maze is hidden under the sand.*

Diver hesitates, torn up about how to respond. *Light will show the way forward,* he says at last.

Light will show the way? Hmm …

I spin a couple of quick orbs between my palms and scatter them far and wide over the flat sand until my Light is indistinguishable from the stars. At first, it doesn't look like anything is going to happen. Then the orbs stop, still as a photograph in the nighttime sky, before plunging into the sand below.

A ferocious rumble shakes the dune and the sand lake parts, falling into paths and tunnels and screeching, screaming corridors. A set of stairs materializes, leading down, down, down before disappearing into the deep. Stillness like impending death fills every square inch of air. The maze is as wide and deep as a trench in the sea—the entirety of it encompasses what feels like the whole desert. Bends, curves, and edges lead straight to nowhere, and rising from the earth a short distance away, a jagged, horned gate pierces the nighttime sky.

Yeah, that looks like a death maze.

"That's it. I'm out." Nate spins on his heel, marching back to

Diver.

"You can't be out." I rush after him, leaving Ayla and Toran staring at the Rognaga in disbelief. "We won't find Ensolorada's Light Core if we don't try."

Nate points the tip of his spear at the horned gate. "We won't find the Light Core anyway, because that place is going to kill us."

*Not-Our-Luminaut is right.*

I don't need Diver to start agreeing with Nate at the worst possible time. "We don't have a another choice," I argue.

*Luminaut always has a choice.*

"Believe it or not, I care about survival—yours, particularly." Nate's piercing stare burrows deep. "We'd be walking straight into an obvious trap with no easy way out if things go south. Is that really a risk you want to take?"

*Once again, Not-Our-Luminaut is right.*

Knock it off, both of you.

"You promised you'd never hurt me or my family again, and we both know I can't protect them from Queen without this Light Core. Or was that just another lie?" Nate winces at my words. "If you're serious about rebuilding trust, this is how you do it."

Nate glances at the screaming maze over my shoulder, fear etched across his face, before he shrugs. "If this is what you choose, this is what we'll do."

I don't like the way his voice sounds, like his grave opened up and he's staring down into it. But there's no time to question him.

"Diver," I command, "if the Seers or Heike asks you to pick them up or put them down or take them somewhere, follow their directions."

*Yes, Luminaut.* Diver's immense sadness at my choice squeezes my heart, but I know that no matter what, he'll do what I ask.

*I'll be back, Diver. I promise. I'm never abandoning you again.*

There's no mistaking Diver's doubt. *We hope that is true, Luminaut.*

"Don't let Toran kick Nemo into the dunes, okay bestie?" I give Ayla a quick hug while Toran scoffs in the background.

"Be careful." Ayla hugs back too tight. "There were some little books I saw in your pack, do you want to leave those with me for safekeeping?"

Little books? Oh, Mariasol's journals. The one thing Manu didn't think was important enough to steal. "No, I'll keep them with me."

"Very well." Another tight hug before she turns to Nate with arms outstretched. "Good luck, Luminaut!"

"No hugging!" Nate leaps backward.

"Why not?"

"Because you don't know the difference between a hug and a chokehold."

"You're all wasting time." Toran breaks up any hugfest before it can begin. "When you reach the gate, contact my comm and I'll guide you to the first safe house."

So much for encouragement. Thanks a lot, Toran. Ayla floats up to the Crow's Nest on a breeze, and Toran barks for Diver to pick him up, leaving me, Nate, and one creepy-looking staircase leading into the darkness of the Rognaga.

"Ladies first." Nate gestures to the stairs with his spear.

"Age before beauty," I reply.

"We're both seventeen," he counters. "My birthday is June twenty-fourth. You're approximately six months younger."

"I mean, technically, I don't think your age can be—"

"Let's leave my extended study abroad at Shadow Plain

Darkness Academy out of the equation, okay?" Nate peers down the steps, which are more than wide enough for two people. "How about we go at the same time?"

"That's fair." I make two Light orbs in my palms, and together we begin our descent.

Yikes, this place is a dungeon pit of doom. It's never a good sign when the bottom of the steps is lost in so much gloom I can't actually see them. Even my Light and Nate's glowing spear can't penetrate the dark. And what happened to all the shrieks and cries we heard standing on the dune? The maze has gone silent.

This is bad. Just bad, bad, bad.

"Is your birthday really June twenty-fourth?" Small talk keeps me from getting too creeped out by this endless staircase.

"Yes," Nate says.

"Did you know your zodiac sign is Cancer?"

"Seeing as my existence is one long study in dramatic irony, that makes perfect sense." Nate holds his spear like a torch, but the blackness surrounding us is tangible, blocking out the moon, stars, and the rest of the desert as though they had never existed. "What are you?"

"Capricorn, I think."

"Isn't that a goat?" Nate laughs. "So, are we a match?"

"Why do you care?"

"Why else would you bring it up?"

"Listen," I say, pointing a Light-filled finger at his sternum, "I'm *not* flirting with you."

"I'm not flirting with you either. And if I *was* flirting, which I was not, I would be way more awkward than this."

"Awkward? You?" Keep talking. Light topics. Don't think about how the endless staircase fills me with foreboding, or the fact we still haven't hit a landing, or that the horned entry gate has disappeared. "I don't remember you being awkward."

"That's because I was flirting with you as a Shadowmancer. Mr. Dark, Deceptive, and Devious has game." One step farther, then another. "My attempts at flirting are Dad-level tangents about Giants trivia or talking about this dead whale I found one time when I was Light Core hunting on the skiff."

"What makes you think I'd ever want to hear about something so offensive and vile?" My nose wrinkles involuntarily. "But seriously, tell me about the dead whale."

"Oh—I see what you did there." Nate scowls like he smelled rotten eggs mixed with cabbage and is trying to hold back vomit. "Please don't tell me you're a Dodgers fan. Any team but the Dodgers."

"My family bleeds blue and white."

"See, this is why I would never flirt with you." Nate's voice is only sound on the staircase. All else is eerie silence. "Even Satan needs a fanbase, right?"

"That's true. Giants fans exist." Our steps match each other's, and across the stair, I catch his eye. "At least we know any flirting would come to nothing."

"Right, because—"

"AH!"

The staircase falls away. Nate barely catches the edge of the stair with his right hand, and I latch on to his left arm. My legs dangle dangerously close to the blade of his spear, but it's less deadly than the nothingness beneath my feet. My palms let loose a deluge of terrified sweat, and I white-knuckle his wrist like my life depends on it.

"Nate! I'm slipping!"

"Hang on!" But he's slipping too. His grip on the stair gets looser with every passing second. "Don't let go. I'll pull us out."

"Nate. I can't. I'm—"

My fingers slip away. The bloodcurdling scream in my ears barely registers as my own, and I plunge into the endless dark.

# CHAPTER 13
# CALLIE

*"OOF.* THAT SUCKED."

Good news, my fall into the dark isn't all that hazardous. Just as my life flashes before my eyes, my feet connect with dirt and I topple onto my butt. Which hurts, but I'm not dead, so yay! Survival is awesome!

Unfortunately, Nate still dangles above me, hanging on to a stair with one hand, his Light spear in the other. I'm not saying it's impressive he has the upper body strength to hold his weight steady with one arm, but, um, yeah. I wouldn't say it's *not* impressive either.

"Callie!" His voice grows frantic. "Are you all right?"

"I'm fine." I pick myself up and rub my aching tailbone. "It's like, four feet to the bottom."

"Really?" Tangible darkness engulfs everything around me except for a tiny spark of Light coming from the tip of Nate's spear. "What a fake-out."

"Yeah, it looks way worse than it is." Hopefully I'm not inviting some kind of monster attack by saying so. I have an annoying habit of announcing I'm safe, or blah-blah isn't so bad, and then bam! — monsters.

"Cool deal. Watch yourself at the bottom."

"Wait, let me get out of the—"

His fingers slip from the stair and he drops. But I forgot that when I'm holding on to his dangling arm and wrist, a four-foot drop for me is much farther for him. Nate lands roughly, legs buckling under him. His arms fly out to the side and he accidentally snags my waist, sending both of us to the ground. His Light spear clatters at his side.

"Ow." Nate sprawls out. "Just FYI, that was more than four feet."

"I realized that after you said you were letting go." I lay there for a moment, catching my breath from my unexpected second fall, until I realize what's under my cheek isn't stone. It's his chest, and those are definitely pecs under my palms.

"Are you going to get off of me anytime soon?" Nate asks, his gravelly voice rumbling against my ear. "Or are you just happy to see me?"

"You're going with *that* line? You can do better." I lean back, scowling. That smug grin on his face needs to quit being so hot, especially since he caused all this unnecessary awkwardness. "We agreed, no flirting."

"You're the one laying on top of my chest, cupping my pecs," he argues.

Cupping his pecs? Yeah, right! He's living in fantasy land.

"You pulled me down in the first place." Which is true, he can't deny it. "And I was *not* cupping your pecs."

Except I *kinda* was … not that I'd ever admit it aloud. I've been down this road with Nate before, and it more-than-kinda didn't work out.

But that was then, and this is now—and he's a Luminaut. Kinda.

"It isn't my fault you miscalculated the drop." *Kick-thud* dimples — nope, stop. "Don't you have to be good at math to build robots?"

"You have a witty comeback for everything, don't you, Jerk Face?" I scramble to my feet. "Quit being belligerent. We've got a death maze to solve."

"You're right about the maze." Nate stands too, brushing off his pants before he retrieves his spear. "I'm disappointed the best you've got is Jerk Face. I'm at least a Slime Ball or a Dirt Bag."

"I'll work on expanding my arsenal of insults for you."

"Aw, shucks, I'm honored." He peers into the near-total darkness surrounding us. "Any idea where we are? Is this the death maze?"

"I can't tell." I form a series of Light orbs to illuminate a path. "Isn't there supposed to be a horned gate at the entrance?"

"The ominous, horror movie gate holding back screams of terror from our deepest nightmares? That gate?" Nate grins again. "Or are you talking about the gate to my blackened, undead little heart you were so gently caressing just a second ago? A gate otherwise called my pecs?"

Oh, brother.

"Stop making everything about your pecs." Now that half a dozen Light orbs are circling above our heads, I pull my comm from my pocket. "Toran and Ayla haven't tried to contact us."

"He said to start the comm link once we were at the gate. This clearly isn't the gate." Nate holds his spear high, Light bouncing off of his bicep that I'm totally not staring at. "Maybe you should contact them, just in case. We could get lost easily down here."

"Good call." I strap my comm into an armband of my desert gear. "If we had a little more visibility, we could find our way — uh-oh."

Hands—hundreds, if not thousands of hands, all of them slimy, rotting, and oozing sludge—emerge from the walls, from the floor, from every corner and dark crevice. They crawl, slithering forward on putrid fingers, moving en masse toward me and Nate.

"What the—!" Nate shouts a string of obscenities as he swipes at the grasping hands with his spear. They fall under the crystal blade, crumbling to ash and dust, but even more pile up to take their place.

"Okay, time to get out of here." I Light blast a mound of hands forming a claw to reach out and grab me. Even more hands rush around my ankles and start climbing up my legs, gagging me with their noxious scent. Nauseating familiarity overwhelms my sense of smell, but I can't pinpoint where I've smelled it before.

"The stairs are too far to reach." Nate hacks away the corpse-like hands trying to climb his body. With every second that passes, more and more hands gather, threatening to topple us. Their slippery, disgusting fingers latch on to the skin of my arms, my exposed calves, inching closer to my hips. Time's running out before we're engulfed entirely.

One more trick. I aim a Light blast into the dark and fire. I don't know what's hiding down there. I might awaken an even worse monster than this swarm of sentient hands. I just hope whatever's down there is *not* an even bigger, nastier, meaner hand.

My Light hits solid rock, bombing through with a crackling crumble. On the other side, moonlight floods the massive gate made of carved horns.

"Look! The entry gate!" I point through the small opening my Light blast made in the wall.

"Look! A cave-in!" Nate deadpans, gesturing to the stairs

above our heads. What was once a small-ish hole has widened. Sediment falls into our hair as the stairs tear themselves apart.

If we don't escape, we'll be crushed by zombie hands *and* rocks. Fantastic.

"Now's a great time to use that exit I made." I shoot a couple Light bombs into the ever-growing pile of hands, sending them flying. They melt into smelly piles of slime and dust.

"On it." Nate rushes forward, leaping through piles of hands and cutting them down, his spear moving like a scythe. I follow at his back, blasting as many hands as I can while huge chunks of the staircase fall, burying the zombie-like creatures.

But not all of them.

Hands rise through the rubble to pursue me, grabbing my ankles tight, trying to pull me back into the dark.

"Help!" I cry. But Nate's already gone, and if these hands don't kill me, the cave-in will.

Did he seriously just ditch me? Who was I kidding, thinking he'd changed for good? I swear, if I live through these hands, I'll—

"Callie! Hang on!" Nate reaches back through the hole, stretching as far as he can. I grasp his wrist tight, throwing Light orbs at hands rushing at me like an open floodgate. With a swift tug, Nate draws me out of the hole to safety just as the rest of the staircase collapses.

I stand and bend over, hands on my knees, catching my breath. *I'm alive. I made it out. Nate came back.*

He came back …

"Are you okay? Did they scratch you?" Pale moonlight betrays Nate's worry. "The fingernails on those things could be infectious."

"I'm fine." Surprisingly, none the worse for the wear.

"That's a relief." The anxiety on his face recedes. "I'm not exactly down to do this death maze alone. I need you to be okay."

*I need you to be okay* … I never pictured Nate saying that and meaning it. A different kind of warmth spreads through my stomach, unraveling a knot of tension I wasn't aware of until now.

"How about you?" I ask, looking up and down his frame. "Any new scrapes?"

"No." But he doesn't bother to check. A grave look hovers over his eyes. "Did you smell it? When we cut them down and they became ash?"

"I smelled something gross, that's for sure." I gag, remembering the putrid scent left by the hands.

"It was Darkness." Nate meets my gaze. "That smell is Shadowmancer ash."

The decayed, rotting reek of ashes after I Light blasted Queen's new Shadowmancers in the desert is *exactly* where I smelled the horrible stench made by the monster hands.

"Those things weren't a Shadowmancer." More likely the first trap in the death maze, or a fatal warning to keep out.

"No, they weren't," Nate agrees. "But the question is, what is Darkness doing down here in the first place?" He jams the end of his spear shaft into the ground, pounding out a quick beat as though trying to keep up with the pace of his thoughts. "If all the traps in the Rognaga are controlled by Darkness, that's information we need. How could we find out for certain?"

Realization dawns on both Nate and I.

"Diver," we say in unison.

Nate smiles. *Kick-thud* – seriously, again?! "Can you access his memories remotely?"

"I can try." Speaking of people trying to access things —

"Incoming transmission from Crabby McButthead," my comm announces.

I tap on my comm interface, and a hologram of Toran's absolutely enraged face appears, along with Ayla, Heike, and Nemo.

"What in Lands Beyond were you doing?" Toran can really let loose with the fury-gripes, can't he? "We've been trying to contact you for twenty minutes!"

"We had an unexpected detour getting to the main gate," Nate replies. "My spear came in *handy*." I see where he's going with this.

"*Hands* down, that was the worst staircase ever," I say.

"Gotta *hand* it to you, we made a good team." Actually, all hand jokes aside, we really did make a good team back there.

"Why are you talking about hands so much? Did you hold hands? Oh, I hope so!" Ayla's hologram smile flits between the two of us.

"No, Ayla, sorry."

"Well, it *is* early, I suppose," Ayla replies with obvious disappointment.

Only Heike holds back, watching us with a hardened jaw and frosty eyes that remind me more of Toran than his bubbly, charismatic sister. A look that's completely normal on Toran is strange, almost unsettling, on her. A shiver runs down my spine before evaporating into the warm desert night.

"The hands are likely some idiotic pun they've decided is funny." Toran waves his hand (ha!) through the air, which is code for this-is-stupid-and-we're-moving-on. He pulls up the map and zeroes in on the Rognaga's first quadrant. The floating hologram faces disappear, replaced by labyrinthine tunnels, paths, and dead ends.

"You're located at the entry gate." A blinking dot appears on the hologram map, marking my comm. "I've worked out the route to the first safe house."

"I can't put my *finger* on it, but something tells me the Rognaga is going to be a lot more *hands*-on than we anticipated," Nate says. "Don't you agree, Callie?"

I snort a laugh.

Nate motions toward the gate with his glowing spear. "Should I go first? Or do you want to take the lead?"

I form a few Light orbs, holding them just above my palms in case I have to launch them at more disgusting, Darkness creatures. "I'll keep an eye on what's in front of us, you watch our backs."

He nods. "Let me know if you need a *hand* up front."

I sense this running gag is going to last all night.

Before us, the massive Rognaga gate rises toward the moon and stars, piercing the purple, sparkling sky with inky foreboding. No crossbars or grate bar us from entering, simply a wide space between two imposing posts.

Here we go. Death maze time.

I step past the gate, looking around. So far, nothing besides a long stretch of corridor. Nate follows, crossing into the maze too.

"See any monsters? Booby traps? Torture stuff?" He holds his spear high to peek at our gloomy surroundings.

"No." It's remarkably calm and quiet. "Nothing."

"Huh." Nate lowers his spear, the Light inside piercing the shadows around his face. "Talk about overselling it."

Behind us, metal crossbars release, and a wall of steel slides across the open gate. With a thud, bars fall into place, and a heavy, clicking lock shuts tight. We have no choice but to go forward.

"Welcome, competitor, to the great and glorious Rognaga," a disembodied female voice announces, echoing down the abandoned path. "You are in Quadrant One. Eight hours remain to reach the first safe house. Moon and Stars guide you through."

No matter what happens, we're trapped. Either we reach the first safe house or the death maze lives up to its name. "You still think the maze was overselling it?"

Nate gulps audibly. "Not at all."

"All right, let's begin." I bet Toran just *loves* being in charge and telling us what to do from the safety of Diver's head. "Go forward along the path until it reaches a T, then head left. Once you make the turn, alert us for the next set of directions."

"Forward to the T, then left. Got it." I send my Light orbs ahead of me for visibility. Oppressive darkness draws in tight, like a grave closing in overhead.

"Hey, Princess Airhead, I have a job for you," Nate says. "Instead of encouraging sneaky hand-holding, use Toran's comm to research how to open a new gateway into the Shadow Plain."

"Oh, yes! That's a fantastic idea!" Some muffled shuffling. "Toran, I need your comm."

"But, I—oh, fine! Just take it! As long as you keep the menace very far away from me."

Nemo whir-squeals a hearty laugh. Toran's going to beg to switch places with Nate tomorrow night, mark my words.

The maze walls seem to touch the stars, jagged and claw-like, narrowing in until the sky is no longer visible. The orbs I launched to brighten the way stop moving, hanging stationary in the center of our path. Claustrophobic tightness wraps around my chest.

"Something's wrong," I tell Nate.

"What do you mean?" he replies at my back.

"Look at what my Light is doing — or not doing." The stilled orbs resemble faded light bulbs as the gloom gathers on all sides. "The walls are creeping closer and closer."

"But the maze *isn't* shrinking. Look, I'm holding my spear like this." The weapon rests in a horizontal position across his waist. "There's a roughly two-and-a-half feet of space on either end. It's been that way since we left the gate."

"What gate?" I point over Nate's shoulder. "It's gone."

There's nothing behind us but a rock wall that seems to be sneaking closer with every step we take. No trace of the gate. No crossbars and steel door, no carved horns rising skyward. Just solid rock on all sides, boxing us in.

"We can hear everything you're saying. What's going on? Why did you stop?" Toran demands over our comms.

"Something probably bad," Nate answers.

With no warning, the rock wall trailing us gains speed, rumbling and crashing through the path. The maze shakes and rattles, and my Light orbs vanish in a plume of Darkness as the sides close in to crush us.

"Okay, that's *definitely* bad," I say.

"What is bad?" Toran commences freak-out mode right as the wall behind us reaches our ankles. The three panicked voices on the comm fade, and all I hear are rocks crunching over the pounding pulse thundering through in my ears.

Nate and I race for the end of the path before moving walls trap us forever.

# CHAPTER 14
# NATE

I DON'T KNOW WHO in Callie's life decided she should play volleyball for VBHS—if that was a choice she made or somebody made it for her—but she missed her true calling as an elite sprinter. No joke, she can *hustle*. I'm six-three compared to her five-eight with way longer legs, and she's outpacing me by almost half a foot. Must be all that running through the waves, swimming, and balancing she does as a surfer.

Then again, we're fleeing for our lives as a rock wall tries to crush us. Anybody would run at top speed in this scenario.

"The Darkness is back," Callie pants.

"I see that." It's the only thing visible in front of us or above—a blanket of swirling Shadow blocking out the moonlight and stars. Even the far wall ending in a T is hidden.

Just like the Shadows controlling the sentient zombie hands, this Darkness doesn't behave the way Darkness should. Callie has at least five orbs whizzing around her head, and I've got a Light-filled spear, but the Darkness makes no attempt to attack our powers. Darkness is the enemy of Light, it ought to be turning us to ashes. It's definitely working in tandem with the Rognaga to prevent us from going deeper, but it's not outwardly aggressive to Light.

So what is this Darkness, exactly, and what's the endgame? Because destroying Luminauts is obviously not it.

"There's Darkness in the maze? How?" Toran speaks over the comm, remarkably calm. It's not the best moment for analytics, okay Boy Scout?

"Just tell us if we turn left at the T or if the whole trajectory of the Rognaga changed." If one wall moves, all the walls probably move.

"Of course you do, why would the maze change?" Toran makes a dismissive snort as if I'm wasting his time with irrelevant questions.

"Oh, you know." Callie aims a Light blast at the Darkness, scattering just enough for us to see the T-wall is approaching fast. "There's only an entire maze wall trying to crush us."

"No, there's not." Thanks, Toran, but you're not down here to see the impending doom. "There's nothing on the map except Callie's comm, heading the right direction."

"Well, *we* can't see anything at all." Callie's Light orb fades into the Shadows. "We're completely in the dark." Did she make a pun on purpose? Probably not. "How much farther?"

"You're approaching rapidly," Boy Scout says. "Slow down."

"How rapidly is 'rapidly?'" A little more detail would be helpful here.

"You have a few seconds, probably," he replies. Again, vague. Not helpful.

"It's blocking their path," When Heike's voice comes through, it's almost insidious, filled with something … cold.

"Stop talking!" Light surrounds Callie, finally scattering the Darkness.

The T-wall appears right in front of our faces, two feet

between us and solid rock.

"Oh my—ah!"

We skid into a hard left turn, barely missing a face-first collision, and stumble forward as the gate wall rockets into the T, sending rock shards and debris flying. A small crevice makes a good hiding spot, and we press ourselves inside, avoiding anything big enough to take off our heads.

After a tense moment, the dust settles, and the Rognaga grows silent. Callie and I remain in the crevice, her breath sticking in her throat.

"Are you all right?" It's dark in here, except for the Light in my spear. I hold it up to see her face.

"That was too close." Callie leans against the rocks behind her, trembling. Her skin is so pale I can count every freckle on her nose and cheeks.

"Rest for a minute," I tell her.

"There's no time to rest!" Toran's protest comes in loud and clear. Can't you just hear his nostrils flaring? I sure do. "There could be a thousand more traps between you and the safe house, and you already wasted twenty minutes walking down the stairs! This is unacceptable! Get back out there, and—"

"Boy Scout, you're at a ten. Gonna need you to dial that down to a two," I say. "Callie needs a breather, so we're taking one."

"I understand." Ayla might be more perceptive than I give her credit for. "Let us know when you're ready to proceed." She mutes the transmission, and all that remains is silence.

"Are we safe in here?" Callie's voice pierces the quiet. Her wide-eyed gaze darts around the crevice. "There's no Darkness bats hanging above our heads, waiting to swoop down and turn us to ash with a single bite?"

"Let me check." I raise my Light spear, scanning the top of the crack in the rock. "No bats."

"Hooray for small wins." Callie inhales deeply, fearful tension releasing itself from her shoulder muscles. "I don't think I like this death maze."

"I concur." I lean against the wall behind me and force a breath. It feels like an anvil is tied to the base of my neck, pulling everything inside me toward the ground. This was only trap two—technically, the first inside the Rognaga itself. How are we going to make it to the center Pit alive?

"Can I ask you something?" Callie says.

"Should the Giants have won the '89 World Series? Yes."

An adorable wrinkle creases Callie's nose. I mean—her nose is nice, and I've always liked her freckles, and—okay, I'm stopping now.

"Eww, no. This is serious." She searches me like she's mining my depths for an answer. "You can sense Darkness, right?"

"Usually, yes. But I couldn't sense anything back there or under the stairs until it was too late. It came out of nowhere." Which is disturbing, because if I'm losing my ability to sense any Darkness at all, Queen could sneak up on us unawares.

"So it's not just me." Callie sucks on her bottom lip absent-mindedly. "I can always sense Darkness too, but this is weird. It's like it's ... behaving in a whole new way."

"We need more information about this maze—why it was built, who built it, everything we can learn." Diver's Light may be the key. Might as well take a chance on a hunch. "You there, Big Guy?"

*We are here, Luminaut and Not-Our-Luminaut.*

*"Diver, do you remember when the Rognaga was constructed?"* Callie's voice appears in my mind.

*Yes, Luminaut.* Diver's hesitant answer.

*"Can you show us how this maze was built?"*

Diver barricades our minds from accessing part of his. It's a protection mechanism—I know about those all too well. Whatever Diver remembers about the Rognaga, it's a deep wound that's never healed.

*Diver, this is important. Show us what you know.* Callie doesn't get that pressing forward like a battering ram is going to make her mech erect an even denser wall to keep her out, but I get it. I've stood in Diver's place, with everyone trying to get me to acknowledge a hurt so deep that all I wanted to do was close myself off to everything and never feel again.

*"How can you come out here and practice for League playoffs like your mom didn't die four days ago?"* They didn't know that all I could think about, all I breathed and tasted when I wasn't on the baseball diamond, was watching her take her last breath.

I channel the origin of Diver's wound, the barrier he holds between us and his pain. *I know it hurts,* I assure him. *Nobody's going to force you. But if you can, we need to understand some things about the maze. There's Darkness down here, and it could hurt your Luminaut.*

Silence greets me on the other side of Diver's spark, a point-blank refusal. But at last, I get a reply. *The maze is not meant to be won. Only a Luminaut can reach the Pit, and even still, Luminaut and Not-Our-Luminaut should turn back.*

*That's not going to happen, Diver, we —*

I force my thoughts to overwhelm Callie's frustration. *We know it's dangerous, but the Queen Beyond the Stars is more dangerous. The last thing we both want is for Callie to get hurt.*

Callie softens, and a question lingers between us. Do I really mean what I say, that I care and don't want her to see her harmed? Am I worthy of her trust—not just in the maze, but in all things?

*Callie* ... My mind whispers her name, wavering on the edge of the knife that is both Light and Darkness, tipping toward one choice irrevocably.

Instantly, my consciousness is rocketed backward, as though I'm sinking through time into the depths of the most ancient Light imaginable. When I come to a halt, a ghostly image of a woman appears in front of me. I sense she's an Earth Manipulating Seer, and Ensoloradan too. She has Mom's wavy black hair, tawny brown skin, and amber eyes.

But she's also something else. Something sinister.

She's a Shadowmancer.

"My name is Saeli Nerida, the creator of the Rognaga." An enormous hole in her chest exposes the Seer's blackened heart covered by tentacle-like vines in place of skin. It's a horrifying wound. She looks forward stoically, but I can see how much pain she's in, and not just physically. She wishes every wrong thing she did could be erased forever.

Just like me.

"As atonement for the evils I committed as a Shadowmancer, I devised a plan to prevent my former Luminaut, Elara, from regaining the fullness of her Darkness until Living Light rebirths anew."

The memory shifts to Saeli in Shadowmancer form using Darkness alongside another Shadowmancer, killing Luminauts and Seers. World Divers are crushed by wave after wave of Darkness until all the Light in the stars and beyond shatters and fades from the multiverse. But I can't comprehend the loss. I'm too horrified by the face of the second Shadowmancer, the Luminaut Saeli called Elara.

It's Queen.

*Diver, was Queen your Luminaut?* I ask.

*Yes, Not-Our-Luminaut.* Diver's grief presses down on me, as deep as the ocean, engulfing my heart until it feels like I'm drowning in the overflowing tide. Saeli's remorse strikes as painfully as Diver's ceaseless anguish.

"I poisoned the earth I love on every world we set out to destroy," ghostly Saeli goes on…

Another flash of memory. Saeli surveying the desolate landscape of Tremurheim—ashes of trees and endless Mist. Her satisfaction turns to sadness, and she realizes too late the harm she's done. She places her palm on the deadened earth, desperate tears falling down her cheeks, until a tiny sprout rises at her fingertips. So much hope fills her eyes it makes my chest ache.

A new kind of resolve blooms inside the sprout: a desire to make things right.

"Allying myself with remnant Luminauts, five Light Cores were hidden on each multiverse-anchoring world. I bound my Darkness to their locations, tethering Elara and her Darkness in the Shadow Plain. We couldn't repair what I'd broken, but we could save what remained."

Ah, so that's how Queen was imprisoned. The Light Cores aren't keys, they're tethers. Very clever, Saeli.

"If Elara's ultimate destruction never comes to pass," a dark warning permeates Saeli's voice, "I've ensured great calamity will befall any who disturb my greatest creation."

Saeli stands in front of the Rognaga gate, using her Earth Manipulation to carve every pathway in the labyrinth before sending Darkness in after it, melding with stone and earth around a Light Core in the center Pit. Saeli herself inscribes the Tremurheim runes on the map Toran's translating.

"Anyone who enters my Rognaga will be met by Darkness," Saeli's voice floats over the vision, "and only a true sacrifice of

Living Light will free the Light Core from the Pit. Those deemed unworthy will perish."

Living Light? What is that? Some kind of super-powerful Luminaut?

Saeli reaches forward, touching Diver's Prism. "I'm sorry your Luminaut failed you, old friend, and even more sorry for the pain we caused. If any Light remains to revive me, I'll forever be faithful, as much as a Seer can be."

The memory abruptly ends, and Callie and I zoom through time and reality, back to the present in our hiding-spot crevice. I find her gaze, her shock matching my own.

"That's kind of a big deal," she says.

"Which part?" I ask. "The part where Queen was Diver's Luminaut? Or the part where the maze will kill anyone except Living Light?"

"All of those parts." Callie looks like she's struggling to collect her tumbling thoughts. "Oh, and a woman I watched die in Diver's memories was actually the second Prime Shadowmancer."

"Who was Queen's Earth Manipulating Seer." Queen never spoke of her Seer, not even once. "She always blamed her imprisonment on the Light Collective, but it was her former Seer who trapped her in the Shadow Plain. A fellow Shadowmancer."

Which puts everything she ever told me into question once again—and explains why none of Queen's subsequent Shadowmancer servants lasted long before she accused them of betrayal and ashed them.

"Um, Nate." Callie's face goes white with horror. "Don't look, but I'm pretty sure the wall behind your head is growing teeth."

I don't have to look because the hairs on my neck stand straight on end when a pair of fangs press against the base of my skull. The same curved, monstrous teeth inch through Callie's hair to ensnare her shoulders, dripping with what looks like a mixture of blood and mud.

"Run!" I grab her hand and dash out of the crevice and into the Rognaga just as the rock-turned-mouth snaps closed like some kind of stony Venus flytrap. "Boy Scout!" I tap my spear against Callie's comm to unmute it. "Toran, Ayla, Heike, come in!"

"Hello, Luminauts!" Bad time to be cheerful, Princess Airhead. "Did you have a good rest?"

"Just what do you think you're doing?" Toran's grouchy voice hits my ears. "You're running entirely the wrong direction!"

What? How?

"Which direction are we supposed to be going?" All I see in front and behind is a labyrinthine path stretching into infinity. No turns, no twists, no sign of the rock curving or turning. It's like we got spit out of a literal mouth into a whole new section of the maze.

"Turn around and go the other way," Toran snaps. "Didn't I say taking a rest was a terrible idea? Next time, you'll listen to me."

Keep telling yourself that, Boy Scout.

Switching gears, I sprint the opposite direction with Callie, the way Toran said. But dizziness spins me around, like the Rognaga is twisting itself into a funhouse mirror gone wrong.

"Stop running." Callie tugs on her hand in mine. "We need to get our bearings. And let go of my hand."

I stop running, but I don't let go of her hand. A pack of sleek, mountain lion-sized cats with dark purple fur the color of the night sky, glinting fangs, and iridescent black eyes melt away from the walls. Phantasmic gazes center on Callie and me, and when we back away, the pack follows.

"Don't you dare let go of my hand." Callie squeezes my fingers tight as the cats circle in like a school of feline-shaped sharks on the hunt.

"What's going on?" Boy Scout demands, obviously annoyed. "Why did you stop *again*?"

"Because monsters have surrounded us and are about to attack."

Ayla gasps audibly. "Oh, dunes! How dreadful!"

Yes, Princess Airhead. Very dreadful indeed.

The first wave of cats leap, and in a matter of seconds, fangs and fur bury us alive.

# CHAPTER 15
# CALLIE

THIS VICIOUS GHOST CAT situation is going to make me hate cats, and I don't want that to happen. Cats are so cute and fluffy. I begged Mom for a kitten when I was ten, but she's allergic. Kitty dreams denied.

The cat monsters attacking me are not cute, not fluffy, and *definitely* not here to snuggle. Unless by snuggle you mean claws and fangs trying to tear me to shreds.

"How did you get taken out, Nate? Oh, I was mauled to death by a pack of saber-tooth cats that melted out of a Darkness-infested rock. How about you?" Nate talks to himself while slicing yowling cats with his spear. But no matter how many he turns to Darkness ash, the cats keep coming. I blast cats to my left and more to my right, then Light bomb another group sneaking up in front.

"You're running out of time to reach the first safe house," Toran barks over the comms. We realize we're in deep crap, but thanks for pointing it out.

"Give us five minutes." Nate sweeps more cats aside when they make a leap for his shoulder.

"Five minutes?" I give him a look. "Are you joking?"

"Come on, Callie, I thought you were better at picking up my sarcasm." Nate swings his spear wide, lobbing the heads off of some Shadow cats before they crumble to ashes. "That's four for me. How about you?"

I aim a Light orb and let it fly, flashing bright when my blast hits its mark. "Ten. Maybe eleven."

"I bow to your superior skills." Nate hacks away at more slinking cats before they claw him to pieces. "Never send a half-Luminaut to do a real Luminaut's job, right?"

Half–Luminaut. Because his other half is—

"You know a lot about Shadowy things. Since all these traps involve Darkness, how do we outsmart them?"

Nate stiffens at my back, and it has nothing to do with the tidal wave of cats pouring from the Rognaga walls.

"I'm not going to become the Shadowmancer." Nate is definitely not being sarcastic now. "Besides, Queen would be on us in a millisecond."

"You think she doesn't know where you are?" Heike's voice over the comms is so quiet I strain to hear her over the squalling cats. "You're bound to her in Darkness."

"That's a morose observation, Captain Obvious," Nate points out. He must have heard Heike too. "You aren't turning into Boy Scout, are you?" Hack, slash. "One scowling pinecone per multiverse is more than enough."

"I am not a scowling pinecone!" Toran pipes up.

"Okay, fine, a frowning prickly pear." Nate never resists an opportunity to roast Toran, even when we're trying not to die.

It *is* really weird for Heike to say something like that, but I don't have time to ponder it. I need Nate to think like his other half if we're going to escape alive.

"You're a Shadowmancer that decided to betray Queen for

the sake of the multiverse, just like Saeli," I remind him. "What would a Shadowmancer do to get past these cats?"

"Darkness is all about trickery and manipulation." Nate takes out a few more screeching cats. "Which makes sense, because everything in this maze has been trying to trick us since the crumbling staircase debacle."

"If the cats are a clever trick, how do we manipulate them?" Use your very smart brain, Nate, and do it fast.

"Okay, I got it." Nate eyes the rocks above our heads while he takes down a couple more cats. "Those jagged overhangs don't have cats pouring out of them. They're solid."

I glance up, noting he's right. "What's your point?"

"Either there's no Darkness in those rocks, or it's not worried about us, which means we can use the maze against itself." Nate turns and looks over my shoulder. "I'll get the cats to chase me, and you'll Light blast the loose rocks around the overhang on top of them. Then bomb the whole pile of trapped cats. Theoretically, that should work."

"I would like to point out that this is extremely dangerous," Ayla announces. I'd bet she's wringing her lightning fingers around each other and pressing her lips.

"If I die, at least I got taken out by Callie and not Darkness." Such an angsty reply, it's peak Nate. "On my count, give them all the Light you've got." Nate maneuvers himself into position. "Three, two, one."

As soon as Nate turns tail, my Light builds, controlled and competent. My feet leave the ground, Light carrying me above the cats before turning the nearest ones to ash. The remaining pack cowers, then do exactly as Nate predicted—launch themselves after him when he bolts.

Nate is fast, but not fast enough to outrun more than a dozen angry Darkness cats. The head of the pack leaps, flying toward Nate's shoulders.

Immediately, the cats take him down.

"Nate!" I scream, but my voice is far from me, lost in Light. He slashes his attackers with his spear and attempts to get back on his feet, but there are too many cats. If he goes down for good, I'm on my own to complete the Rognaga.

*Would that be a bad thing?*

If only Living Light can win the Rognaga's Light Core, it makes Nate a potential problem. He's a half-Luminaut with Shadows still attached to his undead heart. What will the Rognaga do when it's Darkness figures out what he really is?

A fearsome shriek as more cats pile on Nate. The Light in his spear fades. He can't hold them back on his own.

*The last thing we both want is for Callie to get hurt …* Truth was all I felt in his flickering Light. No deception, no games. The Shadowmancer I knew in Verona Beach wanted to win at all costs. The boy who followed me into the Rognaga needs me to survive.

And I need him, too.

Light fills the maze path until it dims the moon, competing with the brilliance of the stars. The walls crumble, falling away. Cats scream and try to flee, but it's no use. Light is too powerful, and the ones who aren't crushed by toppling rocks fade to ashes.

When the last cat is gone, I float to the ground, recalling most of my power until only a little remains in my hands, just in case.

"Nate!" I peer through the dust and rubble. "Nate, where are you?"

"What happened, Callie? Is everything all right?" Ayla's voice sounds gravelly on the comm, like my Light disrupted the transmission quality. "We heard static and saw an explosion."

"I Light bombed a bunch of Shadow cats, but now I can't find Nate." And I'm starting to panic that he was caught up in the fallout.

"Perhaps he died." Wow, Heike, want to care a little more about the person who risked his existence getting you out of the Shadows?

"Nate!" His name sticks on my tongue, coming out as a half-cry instead. Did my Light ash him too? *No, no, no. I can't have killed him. I just can't …*

"Callie?" Nate pulls himself and his spear from under a pile of loose dirt and small rocks. He's wobbly on his feet and has a few claw marks here and there, but nothing severe. He grins ear to ear when he sees me. "That was totally rad! Not exactly what I had in mind in terms of strategy, but—"

I throw my arms around his neck. He's filthy, mixed ash and sand coating his clothes and skin, but he's okay. It's all I care about.

"We're hugging now? That's cool." Nate drops his spear and curls his arms around my waist. They slide into place as perfectly as they always did, only this time he's softer. Gentler. The sharp edges are gone, and in their place, steady warmth.

A tingle zips up my spine when his fingertips land on the curve of my hips, pressing just enough to light a spark in my belly.

This hits different than the infatuation I felt before. An entirely new sensation ignites when he touches me, deep and yearning, like an undertow pulling me into uncharted waters I've never surfed. There's freedom out here. Wildness. I can't explain what it is, but it feels … *electric.*

"You don't like hugs, do you?" I pull away, oddly breathless. "I forgot you didn't want Ayla to hug you. Sorry."

"Princess Airhead is a different story." The smile on his lips sets the butterflies in my stomach dancing. "You can hug me anytime you want."

"You hugged? That's so wonderful!" Ayla's voice on my comm startles me, followed by Toran clicking his tongue in disapproval.

"If you two are finished," he grouches, "I'd like to navigate you through this quadrant. We're running too short on time for you to engage in romantic embraces, in case I didn't make that *perfectly* clear."

"Romantic embrace?" I leap away from Nate, and Nate does the same, throwing his hands high. "Hugging a person you were worried about isn't romantic."

"Yeah, this was more like, I'm-relieved-the-screeching-Darkness-cats-didn't-claw-your-throat-out," Nate agrees. "No romance involved."

"Sometimes people deny their feelings when they're in love." Ayla clearly considers herself an expert on this topic. "I believe you fall into the pretending-to-be-enemies category of denial. It's my favorite, personally."

Why does Ayla insist an enemies-to-lovers romance between me and Nate is a thing? Besides, we're more reluctant allies than enemies at this point.

Nate rolls his eyes, exasperated. "You watch way too many soap operas, Princess Airhead." He snatches his spear and looks around. "I don't know what you're seeing on your end, Boy Scout, but Callie blew up the place."

"Excuse me?" Toran's voice speaks through my comm's static. "What do you mean she blew it up?"

"Kaboom. Alas, poor paths and walls. We knew thee well."

Snark aside, Nate isn't wrong about the state of the first

quadrant. Light blasting rocks onto cats was more violent than I meant for it to be. There's no longer a path for us to follow — no bends, turns, nothing. Just a wide field of bombed-out boulders and dust, and on the farthest side, a glowing panel beside a door in the only wall left standing.

"Look, the safe house!" I point to our destination.

"Hey, that was easy." Nate nudges me with his elbow. "Maybe you should Light bomb every quadrant."

"Except now the Darkness in the maze will see that coming." We pick our way through the rock field. The moon and stars glimmer brightly overhead without sawtooth maze walls blocking their light.

"Did you ever pretend you were an astronaut when you were a kid?" Nate asks, moving some pebbles around with the tip of his spear. "This is how I pictured a moon crater."

"No, I used to pretend I was a sea turtle. My vibe is like, if I lay on my back in the sun, I'll never get up until I die."

Nate laughs, but instantly stops. The rocks at our feet pile atop one another to form a gigantic, humanoid creature held together by swirling Darkness. The monster staggers upright and spots us as soon as a pair of glowing red eyes sprout from its craggy face.

"Uh-oh. That's not good."

"Stop being vague," Toran gripes on the comm. "Explain yourselves."

"Or, we could run away instead," Nate says, because the rock monster has learned it has legs and can use them.

"Yeah," I agree, "running is good."

We take off for the safe house door, and the rock monster gives chase. I'm not sure how to open the safe house door, but there's a glowing panel, so maybe it's touch activated? All the other doors in Ensolorada seem to be.

I press my hand to the panel and sure enough, the door pings open. Nate and I dart inside, and it swishes closed just before the rock monster slams into it. There's a *boom* at our backs, and the door crunches inward when the monster crashes into the wall. But we're safe at last.

"Welcome, competitor, to the first safe house." The female voice that welcomed us into the Rognaga entry gate speaks again. "Congratulations on surviving Quadrant One. The door to Quadrant Two will open in twelve hours."

"Finally!" Toran heaves what could only be described as a sigh mixed with a frustrated raspberry. The hologram map of the Rognaga disappears, and his face takes its place. "You arrived earlier than I expected."

"We saved time, just for you." Nate grins. "You're welcome, Boy Scout."

"I didn't thank you." No, really, Toran?

"Is the safe house cozy?" Ayla appears next to Toran with Nemo on her shoulder.

It's pretty sparse, honestly. There's a counter with a wash basin on the left wall, and a tiny cot with blankets and pillows on the right. Not much in terms of fancy Ensoloradan tech, and definitely not enough room or space for two competitors.

"It's, uh, tiny." Nate sounds as uncomfortable as I feel.

"There's only one bed," I add.

"I couldn't care less about the sleeping arrangements, only that you sleep enough to survive tomorrow," Toran announces. "I'm muting the transmission so I can review the map of Quadrant Two."

"One last thing," Ayla adds before I cut communication. "Don't forget to watch the archival footage I sent. And if you kiss, tell me first!"

"Thanks for the reminder about the footage, Ayla. Have a good rest of the night." I mute my comm and tap the interface, putting it in rest mode.

"So. Um. Yeah." Nate glances at the bed, and then back at me. Clears his throat. Wow, so awkward. "You can have the cot."

"Are you sure?" I shift on my feet and cross my arms.

"Yeah, sure. I, um, don't need sleep."

"You look tired," I observe.

"Nah, it's the ash dust from the cats." But his sloping shoulders give him away. "Let's just watch the footage Ayla sent."

"Good idea." I sit down on the cot and lean back against the wall, pulling off my boots. Ah, so much better! "Sorry if my feet stink."

"On a scale of rotten eggs to Shadowmancer ash, they're closer to rotten eggs." Nate smiles when I aim a teasing kick his way, and sits down on the floor.

"Why are you — don't sit on the floor, there's room up here for you." I scoot over and gesture to the half-cot at my side. Nate joins me, and I slip my comm off my armband. The avatar face that acts as an operation system manager pops up.

"Good evening, Callie James," the avatar greets me with robotic pleasantry. "How may I assist you?"

"Please retrieve the archival footage received from Crabby McButthead's comm," I say.

"Affirmative." The avatar disappears momentarily to perform the command.

"What's your avatar's name?" Nate asks. "Is it Terry?"

I make a face. "Why Terry?"

Nate makes a face right back. "Why not Terry? What did Terry ever do to you?"

"You are so weird."

"Thanks, so are you. Do I have a nickname in your comm?" Nate's smirking grin turns the corners of his mouth. "Sleazebag Grodypants, or one of your other favorite middle-school insults?"

"Sleazebag Grodypants is a good one. I'll keep it in mind."

The avatar pops up, their featureless face accompanied by a small video icon. "Here is the requested footage from Crabby McButthead's comm," they announce. "Would you like me to play it for you?"

"Yes, please. Thanks."

A hologram like a miniature TV screen floats above my comm, and in the footage, a young Mariasol appears with Serai. They're in a training facility wearing some type of sleek body armor, and Mariasol holds the crystal spear Ayla gave Nate. It glows in her hand just like it glows in Nate's, and when she smiles, she could be Nate's twin.

"Mom!" Nate's eyes light up at the sight of Mariasol. She's no older than us in the footage—seventeen, or barely eighteen. She slings her spear around, Light extending like a long whip from the tip to lasso some rocks Serai sends flying. The Light ensnares them easily, and she swings the heavy stones into a far wall.

"I've got to learn how to do that." Nate's eyes remain glued to his mom's face. Another section of footage plays, one where Serai lectures Mariasol like the bossy big sister nobody asked for. Mariasol ignores her, finger-crocheting a string she made from Light. She holds up an intricate, leaf-like Light pattern and grins. Serai shakes her head around a smile.

"Mom was always spunky and funny like that." Nate tries to touch Mariasol's face, but his finger passes through the holo. "She had so much love, you know? People made a lot of assumptions about her because she had brown skin and an accent, and never saw her as anything except ordinary. But she was special."

For a moment, he's silent, watching with a sad smile. "I used to wonder why Mom left Ensolorada if coming back would save her life, but I get it now. She never wanted to do this maze, never wanted to cause harm if she somehow unleashed Darkness. She made a choice to save her home at all cost, even if it meant she died." Nate's gaze finds me across the cot. "You didn't want to be a Luminaut either, did you? I forced your hand, and you had to make an impossible choice."

"I …"

Despite Mariasol's beauty and grace with Light, it's easy to see her smile is a plaster for misery while she fulfills everyone's expectations but her own. She gave up everything to Dive to Earth, and in doing so spared Ensolorada Queen's horror. Mariasol lived the life *she* chose.

And I chose the same.

I Dove because I knew what would happen if I stayed in Verona Beach. I'd spend every waking moment living up to Mom and Dad's expectations, forever playing a role to make them happy, never using my Light so I could be "normal," unhappily stuck in the status quo. All the while, Queen's Shadows would fester just below the waves, but I'd be unprepared to meet them. Even if Nate's deception forced me to Dive sooner than expected, I'd never let my family suffer because of the Darkness I unleashed.

"I don't blame you for the Dive I made that night," I say. "Maybe I did once. But in the end, the choice was mine."

"Mom made her own choice too." Nate watches Mariasol on the holo, her charisma and charm demanding attention. "I wanted her to make different choices, ones that guaranteed her survival. But I couldn't control her, so I tried to control everything else, and — well, we all know how that turned out."

Nate's eyes fill with raw, aching sorrow, ripped in two over that terrible choice he made in grief, a choice that altered his entire existence. I used to think I'd choose differently if I were in Nate's shoes, certain I was morally superior compared to his apparent deficiency. But now that I see him confronting his greatest loss, more vulnerable than I knew him capable of being, that certainty feels more like doubt.

"Speaking of choices," Nate says, soft and quiet, "I want to start making choices like Saeli, ones that will atone for my Darkness. I'm tired of fighting so hard against the Shadows. I'm especially tired of fighting you."

"I'm tired of fighting you too, Nate." And I mean every word. "I think this maze has shown us we make better friends than enemies. If I'm going to beat this thing, I need a friend like you."

"Friends?" The sweet sincerity in his voice is an ember glowing inside my heart. "Are you serious?"

"I'm serious." Nate is witty, resourceful, smart, and trying so hard to change for good. Every second we're together, I trust and believe in him more. I can't find the Light Core in the Rognaga without him.

But this feeling latches onto a part of my heart decidedly deeper than friendship — the part that's growing, changing, seeing anew. And it's getting harder to deny the longer I look into his beautiful, dark brown eyes.

*Keep it in check, Callie.* Crushes make winning death mazes a lot more complicated, especially where Nate is concerned.

"If you really want to choose Light, you have to learn to be a Luminaut." I open my backpack and pull out Mariasol's journals. "These are your mom's. Think of them as Luminaut Powers 101. Since you don't sleep and I do, you can read while I doze off."

Nate cradles the journals in his hands with a tender smile. All the love in the multiverse fills his eyes, as if the little books are Mariasol herself. "I knew she wrote these, but I didn't think Dad kept them."

"I borrowed them for a while, but they're yours now." I stretch my arms over my head and yawn, tossing my rotten-egg feet over Nate's legs. "I expect your skills to surpass mine by the time we tackle Quadrant Two tomorrow."

And I'm sure, knowing Nate and his competitive streak, they will.

"Loud and clear." Nate moves my feet out of his way, his hands almost warm on my exposed skin. Funny, he used to be so cold. "Thank you for the journals."

"You're welcome." Another yawn and I pull the blanket over myself, settling into the pillows. "Goodnight, Nate."

"Goodnight, Callie."

The rustle of pages and Nate's glowing Light are the last sensations I register before bone-tired sleep overtakes me. I just hope there aren't any more cats in Quadrant Two.

# CHAPTER 16
# TORAN

LANDS BEYOND, the anxiety of guiding two Luminauts through a maze actively trying to kill them is going to be the death of *me*. Adding to my stress, the menace Nemo has been pinching my ears all night, riding on Ayla's shoulder where he knows I won't try to harm him. The second she sets him down, I'm kicking him across no less than three dunes.

Guiding shouldn't be so difficult, should it? Even with all of Tremurheim's monstrous predators, I managed the task. It must be because Callie and Nate are Luminauts, and therefore, chaos embodied.

For now, they're safe, and we're one night closer to finding the Light Core. My plan with Manu is working flawlessly.

"I'm glad that's over." Ayla stands and stretches her arms. "I think I'll take some air."

"Of course." I fix my attention on the Rognaga map, focusing on Quadrant Two.

Just when I think she's gone, Ayla's soft touch on my shoulder startles me. "Would you like to come too?"

Ayla wants *my* company? Why? "I, uh—"

"You've been very tense," she elaborates. "Your shoulders are in knots."

My shoulders are always in knots, but the fact Ayla noticed is not something I'm used to. It makes me feel strange, like my insides have flopped over to face a new direction, and I can't force them back to normal.

"There's a whole quadrant I have to review," I say, desperate for an excuse to remove Ayla and feel centered again. "I'm good at reading maps, and—"

Heike takes my comm with the map. "I'll review Quadrant Two," my sister suggests. "Remember, I was a better Guide than you."

I glance between my sister and Ayla, at a loss for words. I had a plan for how I would spend the rest of my night, and now it's disrupted. My mind reels, trying to form a response as it simultaneously refigures my agenda, my schedule, my list of things to accomplish.

"Perhaps you could explain the map to me out on Diver's shoulder," Ayla suggests. Heike nods in agreement.

"That's a great idea," my sister says.

"All right, I'll accompany you." I rise and follow Ayla out the hatch door.

The stars have shifted over the course of the night, and the array of shimmering lights overhead looks entirely different than it did when Callie and Nate entered the Rognaga. Before us, the maze grows silent for the first time. A cursory glance reveals a large part of the first quadrant is indeed bombed away. Before, there were tunnels and paths carved into stone. Now it's nothing but a rocky plain.

That Callie's power could accomplish such destruction affirms my resolve to ensure Manu takes that power away from her—permanently.

"It's so nice to have a breeze." Ayla turns her face to the wind and smiles. "Refreshing, don't you think?"

Pale blue gems stud her earlobes, reflecting starlight onto her cheeks. She seems completely oblivious to me staring at her — but she's oblivious to most things. I turn my face away before my cheeks flush and burn.

"What do you want to know about the Rognaga map?" Perhaps it's blunt, but I don't know any other way to be. Ayla doesn't seem to mind my forwardness.

"In truth, I don't care much about maps. I've been longing to talk with you. You're the first Seer my age I've ever met, and I'd like to be friends." She sits on the Diver's shoulder and pats a spot next to her. Luckily, Nemo is on the opposite shoulder and can't reach my ears. "I think we might have more in common than our violent first encounter suggests."

I doubt I have anything in common with Ayla, but I sit next to her anyway. "I didn't know any other Seers before I met you," I say. "And your mother and Richard."

"One of each element, isn't that good luck?" Ayla's voice radiates hope. "I was reading some Lore on your comm while you were busy with the map, and it takes one Seer of each element using their powers simultaneously to open a new gateway."

"Fascinating." Why we would need to create more gateways, I don't know. There are millions of them overhead, dotting the expanse of stars. Tiny windows to other worlds, and only Ayla and I can see them. My Seer's Eye glows, as does hers, but for the first time, I don't feel the need to hide it.

"Can you use your Manipulation for things other than ice?" Ayla seems content to ask questions and let me answer. Which is good because I'm not much of a conversationalist.

"Yes, I just prefer ice."

"Why?" Ayla catches my eye. "A hidden metaphor, perhaps?"

"Ice is the most practical form of water." Where Ayla wants to mine for depth, the truth is disappointingly shallow. "I can do much more with it than vapor or liquid."

"How old were you when your Manipulation manifested?"

I turn away, my shoulders rounding toward my chest, and what little moisture exists in the air forms frozen prickles along my arms. This topic of conversation brings up some of the worst memories of my life.

"I was sixteen. Almost seventeen." Right after my selection as Guide, an unforeseen disaster that turned my life asunder. I had planned my whole future as Gravenskov's next Archivist, but in the blink of an eye, that future was snatched away. No reading side by side with Papa, who had always ignored me in favor of his books and could now continue doing so indefinitely. Yet learning I was a Seer made me more bitterly angry than the Village Council's cruel slight.

How is it still so raw and near a whole year later?

"Are you all right, Toran?" Ayla places a warm hand on my arm, and the chill of disappointment fades.

"I'm fine." I suppose the polite thing to do would be to ask her the same question. "How old were you?"

"Eight," she says.

"Eight years old?" I can't hide my shock. "You were just a child! Is that typical for female Seers?"

"Most Seers are sixteen or seventeen when their Manipulation manifests. You're quite normal in that regard. I was a special case." Her gaze remains on the many gateways dotting the night sky above our heads. She lingers on one in particular, but before I pinpoint which it is, she looks away.

"It was unpleasant enough discovering I was a Seer at

sixteen," I remark. "I can't imagine being half that age."

"It was terrifying." Ayla's eyes glaze with sadness. "My mother and father—my parents at birth—were more scared of my powers than I was myself. I was sent away, and lived alone for a year before …" She trembles, horrified by something she can't name. "Anyway, I was able to find my way to Mama. She taught me to harness my Manipulation and use it properly."

I think Ayla and I define proper use of Manipulation quite differently. "You still managed to electrocute me."

My comment makes her laugh. I didn't intend to be funny, and normally I would bristle, assuming contempt. But coming from Ayla, I don't mind.

"Yes, I suppose I did. But I've said I was sorry, and we're friends now."

*Friends?* Is Ayla my friend? Speaking to her is a strange comfort. Her story makes mine feel less of an anomaly or a cruel joke. Both of us were terrified of our Manipulation at first. We both faced rejection and fear from our families and communities for being Seers. Perhaps she was right when she said we had more in common than meets the eye.

"Have you seen them since your adoption? Your birth parents, I mean." I lead with a question for once.

"No, how could I?" Ayla looks rather disconcerted by my question.

"Well, you're from Oasis III, which Serai said is not far from Cordonanza. I thought perhaps you visited them occasionally." Did I ask a bad question? This is why I don't converse.

"Oh, I see what you mean," Ayla says. "No, I haven't seen them since I was found wandering Oasis III after my accident. My family lives in Aure—" She catches herself, going completely still. Electricity sparks around her entire body, and the air crackles and pops against my skin.

As quickly as Ayla lapsed, the sparks disappear and the air calms. Behind her smile, newly forged steel forms, as if her carefully guarded secret almost came to light but she threw up her protective wall just in time.

Perhaps we *do* have more in common than I assumed.

"Let's talk about something else. Your sister is alive, that must make you happy." Ayla switches the topic.

"It does." What makes me even happier is that Heike has realized Callie is dangerous, too, but Ayla is still firmly on the side of her "bestie." Best not to speak against her.

"And you have your beloved books back," Ayla adds.

"I do." I've managed to hide them away from Nemo before he shreds them.

"And now, you've guided our Luminauts to the Rognaga. When they win, we'll be one step closer to defeating Darkness." Ayla seems to think this satisfactory conclusion to the story is inevitable. I snort through my nose before I can stop myself. She tilts her delicate chin, a scowl on her brow. "You don't agree?"

"Callie is not my Luminaut, and she will not defeat Darkness." The words slip from my tongue before I can stop them. "She's foolhardy at best, and doesn't care if she hurts others to get what she wants."

"I don't think that's true at all," Ayla disagrees. "She seems to care about others very much." From her opposite shoulder, Nemo claps his consensus.

"Only while they benefit her. When they don't, she leaves them behind." Just like she left Heike. By sheer luck, my sister is with me, unharmed by the Shadows. "When Heike was attacked by Darkness in Tremurheim, Callie didn't save her."

"Didn't? Or couldn't?" Ayla's gaze searches uncomfortably

deep. "There's a rather large difference between those two words."

"Even if she *couldn't* save Heike, that only proves she's not strong enough to defeat Queen or save the multiverse from Darkness." I shake my head. "I know you think our Luminauts ought to be like second siblings, but I already have a sister, and I don't need a Luminaut, especially not Callie."

"If you think Callie doesn't stand a chance at defeating Darkness, why are you helping her solve the Rognaga?" Ayla shifts away from me, and the air grows cold in spite of the heat radiating off the dunes. Nemo peers around Ayla's bouncy curls and growls.

Dramora spawn, this was an absolutely terrible idea! Talking to Ayla puts me too much at ease, and I admitted things I never wanted her to know. How to salvage this?

"I'm helping because—well, even if I think our chances of success are slim, trying anyway is still the right thing to do." Another lie leaves my lips easily—except now, I can lie and sound like I mean it. My palms grow sweaty, and I rub them on my pants, swallowing back the disquieting realization.

What's even worse is Ayla believes me completely. The air surrounding us warms and her bright smile returns. "Doing the right thing, even if it's hard, is the most important lesson Mama taught me."

"Your mother taught you that?" Surprise sends my eyebrows inching up my forehead.

"I don't blame you for doubting." Ayla sighs, understanding etched across her face. "Mama can come across as severe, but above all, she believes in doing right. We just happen to disagree on what the right thing is at present, and how to accomplish it." She slouches, setting her chin in her hand. "All the nonsense with Manu and his failed power extractor makes her brusque and anxious."

"Failed power extractor?" Those three words halt any further flow of thought. "I thought the solar coils were failing."

"The solar coils are old. We need newer, more efficient models," Ayla says. "The power curfews are meant to preserve their efficiency until new ones can be developed for our technology. Mama leads the committee funding the project."

"New solar coils are already in development? And Serai is leading the charge?" Manu didn't mention that at all. He made it sound as if Callie's Light Cores were Cordonanza's last hope and Serai was callous to the people's welfare. What Ayla said is either completely untrue or Manu purposely omitted things.

My chest tightens and I force a breath. I've never questioned whether my actions or loyalties might be wrong, but Ayla's version of Manu's story leaves more questions than answers. "Why does Manu Carosti want to use Light Cores, then?"

"The only power Manu actually cares about is political." Ayla rolls her eyes, a rare display of sarcasm. "What he fails to mention in forums is that Light Cores don't create power that can be converted to electricity. Mama is having a difficult time convincing others of the truth. They see Manu's power extractor as new and innovative, but it will never work. Cordonanza will suffer at the expense of his ego." She looks at me, more serious than I thought possible. "People forget what shouldn't be forgotten and mistakes get made. Ones nobody can take back."

I should have said no to chatting with Ayla. She's given me even more questions to resolve, whereas before I was already assured of the answers. "The sun will be up soon. We should sleep."

Ayla yawns, and Nemo mimics the movement of her hands before nuzzling her with affection. "That's true. You're very practical. I always stay up too late."

"I suppose that's what friends are for." The grin turning my lips feels … not insincere.

"I'm so glad we're friends." Ayla stands, extending her hand to help me to my feet. I don't need her help, but I suppose this is yet another way to be friendly, and she can't suspect anything about my secret plot. So I take her hand and rise.

My stomach twists again, just as it did when she touched my shoulder in the Crow's Nest. Her fingers are longer than I expected, but then again, she's very tall. With her curls hanging loose around her cheeks and shoulders, the top of her head reaches my chin. I never noticed before. She's a good height.

"Goodnight, desert! Goodnight, moon and stars!" Ayla waves to the wide sea of dunes before disappearing into the hatch with Nemo, but I hang back, rapidly considering every new revelation. Is Ayla simply repeating well-rehearsed lies Serai told her? Or could I have been wrong about Manu's intentions?

The only recourse is contacting Manu covertly to learn the real truth. I'll do so tomorrow night, after Callie and Nate have finished Quadrant Two.

*If* they finish Quadrant Two.

It's lucky Heike is here to translate and decode the map alongside me because I'm afraid I'll be too mentally distracted to focus—not until I've learned what's true and what's a lie once and for all.

# CHAPTER 17
# NATE

"GO LEFT AT THE next pass."

"No, Heike, it's right."

"It's left."

"No, that's not right. They need to go right."

Ayla and Heike picked a seriously bad time to argue left vs. right. The goopy, mud-encrusted, reptilian sand ogre chasing us will swallow me and Callie before they arrive at an answer we needed five minutes ago.

Where in the ever-living crap is Toran when we need his bossy self-assurance? We'd like to not die down here, and between Princess Airhead and Captain Obvious getting into tiffs every three seconds, our odds of survival are dwindling.

*GRRRAAAAAAWWWW!*

Gag me with the ruffage. The sand ogre's bad breath spews from its cavernous mouth. Actually, it's mostly mouth. Big mouth, tiny eyes, t-rex arms and legs. It would be comical if it weren't trying to eat us alive.

"Is it left or right?" I shout. "Make up your minds!"

Whoopsie! Guess what? While everyone in the Crow's Nest wastes our time, the walls of the Rognaga shift, and Callie and I are lost. Again. If this death maze has taught us anything, it's that even Luminauts can get lost if the walls move. Everything around us is brand-new … except for the sand ogre. It's still there. Still roaring, still reeking up the place with stink-breath.

Quadrant Two has been a barrel of laughs.

"The walls just turned." Callie halts, panting. "We need a reroute."

"In that case, it's left," Ayla says.

"No," Heike argues, "it's right!"

More arguing, simply delightful.

How do I know the monster trying to eat me and my distractingly lovely fellow Luminaut is a sand ogre, you ask? First, it emits an echolocation signal to make sand traps. Second, the only two words it knows how to say are "ssssaaaaaaand" and "oooooooooogre." Articulate monsters are articulate.

"It's left now, I'm certain." You better be certain, Ayla, because in case you forgot, I'm being chased by a very carnivorous thing.

"Left it is." Callie Light blasts her way out of a sand trap while I slash my spear at the ogre's head. Callie's not gonna get snarfed if I can help it.

"Are you okay?" I help her stand when she trips.

"I'm good." Her eyes meet mine, golden brown and gorgeous. I haven't been able to think straight since last night when she faced me in truth and gave me the last physical piece of Mom that exists. Every vulnerability I tried to hide was bare in that moment, but she never once looked away. Her soft smile and even softer brush of her fingertips struck a match in the deepest part of my being, igniting an inextinguishable spark.

In case you somehow missed the clues, I have a *huge* crush on Callie James. It's bad, okay?

"How about you?" Callie asks. "Holding up?"

"I—" Get it together, Nate, you're being chased. Quit staring at Callie's pretty face. "I think we better haul it out of here."

"Agreed." Callie and I take off, but the sand ogre opens up a pit of quicksand with its echolocation inches from our toes.

"Watch out!" I skid to a stop, holding Callie back with my arm before she barrels into another trap.

"Thanks for the assist." She smiles. I melt.

"Anytime." Ooey-gooey squishy Nate picked a bad time to show up, didn't he? Quicksand before us, sand ogre behind, and I'm standing here all googly-eyed because she's touching my arm.

"Light blast some rocks into the quicksand, and we'll hop across. Ready?" Callie makes a giant Light orb. I make one too, ignoring the nausea and blurry vision. "And—go!"

We each bomb one side of the maze wall, sending boulders crashing into the quicksand. A few hops, and we're across the pit. The sand ogre roars, angry its meal is getting away, but its small legs can't leap the distance.

"I'll man the comm now, Heike." Finally! Toran is back!

"Impeccable timing, Boy Scout. We've got a major monster issue." I shove down the urge to hurl that still accompanies any use of Light powers and sprint—okay, hobble at a run— down the path with Callie.

"Give me a few moments to reroute," Toran says. A few moments is time we don't have, but beggars can't be choosers.

Callie realizes I'm slowing down and stops when I stumble to my knees. She reaches for me, takes my hand, and squeezes her support. "Clear your head, Nate. Let it pass."

Hard to let it pass, and frustrating it still happens in the first place. Mom's journals didn't have any helpful hints about my passing out problem, but she never anticipated training her half-Shadowmancer, half-Luminaut kid from beyond the grave. I give my head a hard shake, and my vision clears.

"Better now?" Callie's grasp tightens around my fingers. I'd make a witty comeback about holding my hand, but all I want to do is ground myself in her Light. At last, I stand.

"I've just finished rerouting you." Good, thanks, Toran. While you were busy being safe, the sand ogre figured out how to cross the quicksand pit, and it's racing after us. "Head straight. Go right at the next turn."

"It's left," Heike interjects.

"Don't start this again!" Ayla is beyond frustrated.

"Which is it, right or left? We're coming up on a T." Callie Light blasts the ogre over her shoulder, but it doesn't do anything except make the thing even more pissed.

"It's right," Toran says.

"Are you sure?" Why is Heike arguing?

"Of course I'm sure," Toran growls. "I'm the one who was officially a Guide, sister, you were merely—"

"TORAN!"

"BOY SCOUT!"

Callie and I scream at the same time.

"It's right. Unless the walls have shifted again." Of all the times I don't need Toran to second-guess himself, it's now.

"Right, cool." Way to be decisive, Callie. Except now there's a problem.

"The path to our right is closing." And Darkness pours from every nook and cranny of the maze to stop us moving forward. We must be closer to the safe house than I thought if the maze is desperate to keep us from winning another quadrant.

What would Darkness do in this situation, and how to

outsmart it? The foggy mess surrounding us equally surrounds the charging sand ogre, which means if we can't see, it can't see either.

I turn to Callie. "You know what an anglerfish is, right?"

"Is this you flirting? Random questions about sea creatures?" She tries to Light blast the ogre, but the orb disappears inside Shadows without hitting its mark. "Super sweet, but terrible timing."

She thinks my flirting is sweet?

"No, I'm not flirting with you, this is a legit strategy thing. Make a Light ball like an anglerfish. We'll lure the sand ogre into the shrinking path and let the walls crush it."

"Who says the walls won't crush us?" Hmm, good question.

"We have to trust we can run faster," I say.

"Okay, let's do it." I really like that Callie's not a time waster. She spins a large, shimmering orb, piercing the surrounding Darkness. Immediately, the sand ogre's jaws appear out of the Shadows. Snapping teeth inches from our faces send us racing into the rapidly closing path to our right.

"That worked."

"Yeah, too well." Despite its tiny legs, the sand ogre can hustle, and it's gaining on us quicker than I anticipated.

Callie's Light orb bounces above our heads, doing its job of luring our pursuer, but the walls are closing in and swirling Darkness is ever-present. If we stop, we're toast. Faster and faster we run until Callie and I emerge onto the other side of the path.

Behind our shoulders, there's a sickening crunch, a roar, and the sand ogre explodes when the maze walls snap closed. Ash and goop spray everywhere, completely coating me and Callie.

On the plus side, my plan worked.

"Yuck. That's disgusting." Callie shakes gunk off of her arms before using the bottom of her shirt to wipe her face. Don't look at her stomach, Nate, do not—too late, I did. A sensation strangely akin to a pulse hammers through my frame, and I quickly avert my gaze because the dip of her hips near her belt is *definitely* not something I should look at either.

"I don't think that shirt is any cleaner than your face." My hands ache to wipe the smudges of ash flecking cheeks, but that would mean cradling her face in my palms, and I might be tempted to do more than just help clean her up.

"It's a lost cause," Callie agrees.

"Well, did you make it?" Toran's voice on the comm sounds muffled from ogre ashes. "The safe house should be at the end of the path."

"We made it, and we're in desperate need of a shower." Callie points to a glowing spot on the wall a short jog away. "Look, Toran's right."

Oh good, the tiny room with only one bed. We drag our exhausted selves to the door. Callie activates the touch screen lock, and *ping*, the door opens.

"We're in," Callie announces to our three guides. The door shuts behind us, locking us in for the duration of daytime, and the voice congratulates us on surviving another quadrant.

"Two down, two to go. And the last one is in a massive pit." That should be kicks and giggles, shouldn't it?

"Worry about the Pit later." Toran sounds relieved this quadrant is past us too. "We're signing off."

"Rest up, everybody," Callie speaks to the hovering faces on her comm.

"See you for Quadrant Three tomorrow, Boy Scout. Glad you showed up when you did back there."

Toran's hologram face raises both eyebrows. "Really?"

"You gave us the correct route, and we made it to the safe house because of you. So, thanks."

"I, erm. You're welcome. Goodbye." Toran abruptly cuts the transmission, and Callie powers down her comm for the duration of daylight.

"Aw, how sweet!" She plasters on a syrupy smile. "You'll be in a bromance before you know it."

"The sweetest bromance ever!" I fake a cheesy grin. "Actually, I thought it might be good if I stopped being antagonistic to the guy in charge of the death maze map."

"Smart call." Callie sets her pack down and assembles the docking port to charge her comm. "Did using your Light back there make you want to pass out?"

"Unfortunately, yes."

"But you finished reading your mom's journals, right?" She sets her comm on the dock to charge. "I saw you doing blasts and orbs out there. You picked up on everything *way* faster than I did."

"Are you complimenting me?" I laugh when she gives me a distinctly Callie shut-your-face look. "After coming up with the anglerfish idea, I'm due for a nice compliment or two."

"Your humility never ceases to amaze me," Callie deadpans.

"That's a good one. Now, tell me the facial scars give me street cred and make me look roguishly handsome."

"In your dreams, lima beans." She stands and approaches, suddenly serious. "Is the reason you pass out because you haven't given up the Darkness?"

"More like can't. 'Haven't' implies I don't desperately want to." I heave a sigh. Maybe she's semi-right about the broody thing.

Callie purses her lips, staring ferociously at the wall beyond my shoulder as though she can force answers out of stone. "There has to be a way for you to live without Darkness."

To *live* without Darkness. What would happen if I lived … if I tipped off the edge of the knife and went all in? What then? Is it even possible?

"No known Shadowmancer ever came back," I admit.

"I know." Callie's dismay sinks all the way to my useless heart. "But I want it, don't you?"

Of course I want it. I want to teach El how to play ball and which chemical reactions will blow stuff up. I want to know if Dad and I can forgive past hurts. But more than anything, I want to anchor myself in Callie's smile and be a part of her adventures, not just watching her float past through the Shadows. A second chance at a human lifetime makes room for Light and love, all the things I took for granted before — and her.

"I guess the reward for surviving two quadrants is a shower. And it has blacked-out glass." Callie moves past me, any sparks that might have floated between us evaporating. "You go first, then we'll switch."

"Sounds good." There's some awkwardness tossing filthy clothes over the shower door and passing back clean stuff from our respective backpacks. By the time Callie steps out in fresh desert gear, wringing her hair, bone-deep weariness has caught up to us. She drags her feet and stifles a yawn.

"Okay, time for sleep." Callie flops onto the cot. "Are you going to rest too?"

"I don't know. I haven't mastered Mom's Light whip with the spear." Or I could do what she suggests and let my body recoup from being attacked and on edge for two straight nights.

"You're exhausted. You have the darkest circles I've ever seen under your eyes." Callie puts one pillow on one end of the cot, the other on her end. "Don't make it weird, just keep to your side and don't kick my head."

Whoa whoa whoa. Hold the phone. Is this happening? Am I dreaming, or did she just say I could share the cot? When she doesn't laugh and tell me to stay on the floor where I belong, I know it's for real.

"I won't kick your head." I settle down, but not comfortably. Partly because there's only one bed, I'm sharing it with Callie, and my feelings for her make this a semi-inappropriate situation, but also because something is poking my thigh. "Your elbow is—"

"Oops." Callie turns over. "Better?"

Nothing sharp anymore. "Better. How about you? Any rogue limbs jabbing you in the wrong spot?" Do not make a dirty joke, Nate, *do not make a dirty joke.*

"You're good." She pauses. "Geez, dude, you have gigantic feet! Seriously, they're bigger than Toran's and he's taller than you."

"Finding flip-flops in my size was always a pain." I nudge the back of her head, grinning. Her hair is really soft on my toes. "How do you know how big Toran's feet are?"

"Because he kept trying to kick Nemo across the Crow's Nest in Tremurheim." She leans up to glare. "Don't go there with your lewd insinuations. And I told you not to kick my head. Unless you *want* to sleep on the floor ..."

"No thanks." I close my eyes, giving in to how tired I am, how much my muscles and bones have needed this rest. "Sleep well, Callie."

At first, I think she's already dozed off. Then she says, "If you *can* come back to the Light all the way, what would you do first?"

"I'd eat a boatload of pizza." Her giggle is so cute my chest hurts. "Then I'd ask you on a date."

I know I said I wouldn't make it weird, but the words blurt from my lips unchecked. Backpedal, Nate. "I mean, you'd probably say no. I wouldn't blame you. Just ... shooting my shot."

"Dates aren't something friends do," Callie says.

"No, they aren't." My voice feels hoarse, almost choked. "Isn't that the point?"

Oof, there it is. Why did I say that? I all but admitted I *like* her. More-than-friends like her. It's not like I've done a good job at hiding it, but it's too soon to admit aloud.

"So after pizza"—commence anxious verbal diarrhea—"which is obviously the top priority, I'd be begging for a date." No, that's worse. "Er, not begging. Hoping you believe that I'm not a total jerk when I ask you out. And on that note, I'll shut up now. Goodnight."

Silence. Never a good sign.

Wow, I really struck out with that one, didn't I? Dumb, Nate. Why didn't I say the pizza thing and drop it? I was ahead of the game—she even giggled. But emotions don't play by the rules, especially crushes on girls. It's why I never really let myself have them. Too much scary vulnerability and potential heartache. But Callie is—always has been—the exception to everything.

"Are you awake?" Callie sits up, and I do too, so fast I almost whack her forehead with mine. Cool your jets, man.

"Yeah." I'm very eloquent in these situations, aren't I?

Callie rests her arms on my bent knees. She's so close I could close the gap between us in a millisecond.

"Listen, Nate." My name on the tip of her tongue makes me almost lose it. "I hope you get to eat your pizza. I really, *really* do."

*Oooooooh,* she's good. What a trick play, I never saw it coming.

"Just my pizza?" I lean in farther and my gaze flits to her mouth—the softness and perfect bow shape, the way her lips part ever-so-slightly. Is this too much? I can be a trick player too, if she wants me to be.

Callie doesn't back away. Instead, a smile bright enough to eradicate every last Shadow in the Rognaga lights her face.

"If you decide you want to share your pizza, you could ask me." Her words flutter over my lips like a teasing half-kiss until all I can think about is the real thing. "I'm always down for pizza."

"Maybe I'll share." Should I wink? No, that's overkill.

"Maybe," Callie agrees in a way that sounds very much like the flirting she promised would never happen. So help me, if she comes any closer, I'm going to kiss her.

Either this girl is a master strategist or I'm in it way deeper than I thought. Does she know the effect she has on me? She'd stay cool, say she wasn't purposely playing hardball with my heart, but I know better. All she has to do is throw the first pitch and I'll swing away with everything I've got.

Callie settles back onto her pillow, and I lay down too, closing my eyes. The warm firmness of her body next to mine lulls me into secure rest.

"Incoming transmission from Crabby McButthead." The sound of Callie's comm wakes me up.

Wakes me up? I fell asleep? Callie snoozes, and I don't know how much time has passed.

"Incoming transmission from Crabby McButthead."

Didn't Callie power down her comm? Or did she just cut the

transmission so it could charge? I ease myself away, making sure I don't wake her, and take the comm from the charging dock. I'm not about to wake Callie so Toran can info dump about some extremely dangerous booby trap we'll encounter face-to-face in a few hours. But as soon as I tap the screen, Ayla's face appears instead.

Ugh, Princess Airhead.

"What are you doing?" I hiss. "Trying to wake up every monster in the maze?"

"Oh, Nate, I'm so glad it's you. I was worried no one would answer." Any thought of grouching at Ayla fades when I see how worried she looks — afraid, even. "The sun will rise soon, but I had to wait until Toran and Heike were asleep to contact you."

"Why, what's the—"

"Something's wrong with Heike. I think she's … possessed." Ayla shudders at the word, and so does Nemo. He clings to Ayla's curls like he's scared for his little robot life.

"Possessed?" I scowl. "Really?"

"It's difficult to explain, but there appears to be something living inside her that isn't human." A shiver runs down my spine. "Earlier, when I was guiding and told you to go right, she said left. Do you remember?"

"How could I forget?" It was mass confusion, arguing, and almost getting eaten for fifteen solid minutes.

"Heike wanted you to go left because the path dead ends, and the sand ogre would have killed you."

Wow, that's quite an accusation. As weird as Heike has been since we left the Shadow Plain, insinuating she's purposely trying to get Callie and I murdered is a big deal. "How do you know for sure?"

"I watched her carefully after Toran came back inside. When

you said you survived the ogre attack, she was *angry*." Ayla trembles, and Nemo pats her for comfort. "Her face became pure white with black around her eyes, and somehow they — changed color. They were darker. Insidious. I felt cold standing near her, as though something evil and twisted inside her was trying to freeze me to death."

"Come to think of it, Heike's face shifted when we were in California too." It happened when she made a joke about dying during our Dive, and passed so quickly I thought my eyes were playing tricks. But if the same thing happened again …

Something's telling me Heike's short time in the Shadows left more of a permanent mark than anyone knew.

"We've only got two more quadrants. So far, Callie and I are doing okay." Even though we're not Living Light, the thing Saeli said could beat her maze, we've been holding our own. "Does Toran know what's going on?"

"I don't think so." Ayla presses her lips, betraying her doubt. "He wouldn't believe me if I mentioned it. Heike would contradict me, and he's loyal to his sister above all else."

She's definitely pegged Toran in the short time she's known him. Maybe Princess Airhead is way less of an airhead than I assumed.

"Listen, Sparky." Yes, a much better nickname. Two syllables, easy to say, far more accurate. "Watch out for any sign of trouble in Quadrant Three. Don't say anything to Toran yet. I'll tell Callie what's going on, but try not to be alone with Heike. Sounds like she won't try anything sketchy if Boy Scout's around."

"No, I think she finds me rather obtuse."

I wince a little because I found Ayla obtuse too, and didn't mind telling her so. Reformed Monster Nate needs to work on being less broody and sarcastic, and kinder to everyone — Ayla and her chokehold hugs included.

"Thanks for the heads-up, Sparky." I flash a genuine grin. "That's good intel to keep in mind, especially tomorrow."

"I thought I was Princess Airhead," Ayla points out.

"To be honest, it wasn't very nice of me to call you that." I can admit when I'm a jerk. "Sparky is, you know, because of the electric hands."

"Sparky, yes. I see." Ayla smiles. "I'm glad you believe me about Heike, Sparkle Friend! That's a good nickname too, don't you think?"

"Sparkle Friend?" I just threw up in my mouth a little. "No. Absolutely not."

Ayla frowns. "Why? You're very sparkly when you use Light."

"Leave the nicknames to me, okay?" Sweet sentiment, but stay in your lane, Ayla.

"Very well. Just Nate, then." There, that's better. "Oh! Are you sharing the one bed with Callie? Did you kiss her yet?"

"Ending the transmission, Ayla. Go to sleep." I cut the hologram feed before Ayla decides to ask any more intrusive questions that are none of her business.

I wonder how Callie will take the news. She was close with Heike in Tremurheim, so bringing up Ayla's suspicions might not go over well—especially given the level of unflinching loyalty Callie has for her loved ones. Then again, if Heike's been infected by Darkness somehow, Callie deserves to know what's up.

Callie trusts Ayla's word, too. The question is, which friend does she trust more to tell the truth?

"Nate? Are you awake?" Callie peeks up from her pillow. "Is everything okay?"

"Ayla called your comm. She's worried about Heike." I set the comm on its dock to finish charging.

"Is she all right?" Callie sits up a little more.

"Sounds like being in the Shadow Plain might have left her with some lingering creepiness." I ease myself onto the edge of the cot. "We just need to be extra cautious." That seems like the best way to phrase it, and Callie nods in agreement.

"Yeah, 'kay." She yawns. "Is it sunset?"

"No, it's just now dawn. Go back to sleep."

"You too." She tugs my wrist until we're side by side on the cot. If she weren't disoriented by exhaustion, there's no way she wouldn't kick me to the curb. Floor. You know what I mean. But hey, I'm not complaining about the new arrangement. Especially not when she snuggles up next to me, her warmth spreading through my Light. "G'night."

"Goodnight."

I could get used to her drifting off in the crook of my arm if I weren't so worried about what we'll be facing in Quadrant Three. Sure, there will be monsters, Darkness, traps, and all other manner of things trying to kill us. That's expected. What I didn't expect is not being able to trust one of our Rognaga guides.

Something like a rush of wind flies past my ears, and I hear Queen's voice, icy and venomous. *I'm watching you, Nathaniel. Did you think you'd escaped?*

"Where are you?" But when I look around the safe house, nothing's there. We're alone, just me and Callie, who's fast asleep.

I stare at the ceiling, feeling Callie breathe and listening for Queen's threats until sleep — real, actual sleep — wins out.

# CHAPTER 18
# TORAN

I CLUTCH MY COMM to my chest, checking the position of the sun on the daylight tracker every few minutes. Ayla and Heike slumber, but I've been awake for hours, too anxious for sleep.

Sixty-one minutes until sunset.

The most important thing I've learned during my short time in Ensolorada is if I want to do something in secret, I have a small window between sunset and moonrise to accomplish it. There's an important transmission to make, and in order to maintain privacy, I must do so outside—narrowing my window further. If I step onto Diver's shoulder too soon, I risk getting sun sickness in a place where we have only basic first aid. If I wait too late, I risk being overheard, or worse still, not being able to contact the person I desperately need to speak to.

One hour until sunset. It's time.

I rise, taking a small sip of water from my ration canteen, and carefully open the hatch door so it doesn't creak. The sun's sinking rays feel as hot as a bonfire on any exposed flesh, and the sky beyond the horizon hasn't finished its transition from orange to purple. I have horrific memories of being lost beneath that orange sky, certain I would meet my ancestors on the dunes.

I press the memories into my subconscious where they belong and tap my comm. The avatar face hovers above the glass.

"Good evening, Toran Rykjiersen. How may I assist you?"

"Initiate a private transmission to Manu Carosti," I say.

"Affirmative." The avatar face disappears, and I tap my feet anxiously. Maybe I'm being overly cautious. Is this call truly about warning him his power extractor is doomed to fail? Or am I seeking to assuage my own uncertainty?

Thirty seconds pass, then a minute. What's taking so long?

At last, Manu's face appears in holo form, floating above my comm. He glares, paled by fury. "This had better involve good news about my Light Core."

'Good news' meaning I have it in hand, which I don't. But I can give him an update on our progress. "I successfully led Callie to the Rognaga, and she's deep inside, hunting it. You'll have the Light Core in two more nights."

"Is that all?" Manu quirks an eyebrow. "Any useful intel you learned from Serai's daughter? It's crucial to keep our enemies close."

Enemies? I once thought of Ayla that way, but that was before I spent time with her. She was sincere when she called me her friend. It would be nice to have a friend, especially one like Ayla.

But what Manu asks would betray that friendship to the core.

"I also wanted to let you know—erm, before you go to the trouble of building your extractor—that Light Cores can't be used to make electricity. Better to save yourself time now." To my surprise, Manu rolls his eyes as though he's expecting my word of caution.

"Ayla Alindia spoon-fed you that nonsense, didn't she? And you believed her." He *tsks* his tongue and shakes his head. "It benefits Ayla to keep her mother in power. She'll tell you anything to convince you I'm the villain." He smirks meanly at my dismayed expression. "Let me guess, she batted her pretty eyelashes and you fell for her line."

Dramora spawn, of course Ayla would protect Serai! Why was I such a fool not to see it? It's because I *do* find Ayla pretty. That's the only explanation.

"Stop wasting my time and get back to work." Manu's voice grows cold. "If Ayla is clouding your judgment, just remember, transmitting a signal to my comm means I can track your location. I *will* come for that Light Core in two more nights, and your fate is at my mercy. Who would you rather have as an enemy: me, or Ayla Alindia?"

"I …" My mouth goes dry, and swallowing doesn't help.

"Are you backing out of our deal?" A steely glint flashes in his eyes. "Revenge on the Luminaut doesn't sound as good as flirting with Ayla, does it?" He scoffs, shaking his head in disdain. "You're disloyal and a liar. I never should have trusted you."

"That's not true." My fingers grow needles of ice when I remember my sister swinging her lantern on the Hem, flailing against the Shadows until Darkness took her. Everything I have done has been for Heike — to protect her and keep her safe. How can he say I'm not loyal?

Unfortunately, my comm is now frozen in my hand. Lands Beyond, I don't like these comms. I have half a mind to throw it into the dunes forever.

"Glad to hear it." Manu cocks his head, searching me. "Anything else you'd like to add before I sign off?"

I would like to end this transmission as soon as possible. The sky is more purple than orange, and soon my companions will rise.

I shake my head. "Nothing else."

"Very well." Manu gives me an irritated look. "Next time you get the urge to contact me, don't. If I need you, you'll know."

My comm goes blank, and I tap the screen to power it down. That did not go well.

"What are you doing out here?"

I tense at the voice. Heike stands in the hatch door. Her hair hangs halfway out of her braids until the whole thing resembles a red-brown nargush nest. Purple circles around her eyes sink deep into pale, drawn skin.

"Are you all right?" I pry my comm from my icy hand and pocket it, Manu's threats instantly forgotten in my worry. "Didn't you sleep?"

"Of course." Heike's response sounds oddly monotone. "Were you speaking with that politician?"

"Yes, I was. I needed to find out if something Ayla said is true." And for all that trouble, I'm no closer to answers than I was an hour ago.

"You trust this man?" Heike raises an eyebrow. "We don't need outside influences to complicate things. We only need each other."

"I agree." I put my arm around her shoulders, but she stiffens and I pull back. Heike has never avoided my touch. Why now? "This is all for us—for you. We just need to deliver Ensolorada's Light Core to Manu, and all will be well. Light will never hurt you again."

"You don't have to give him anything. He's useless. A distraction." Heike growls, low and menacing. "Let Callie find the Light Core for Manu, if you insist. We certainly don't need two Luminauts to accomplish your goal. Eliminate the spare."

"You want to kill Nate?" I can't believe Heike would turn her back on Nate after he got her out of the Shadow Plain. "Why?"

"He can pretend to be a Luminaut all he likes, but he's a monster. He'll never be anything else."

*A monster. A Shadowmancer. Not even human.* The things Heike says sound just like … me. A mimic of words I would say to convince her to go along with my plans, but the Heike I know always has other ideas. She would rather dig her heels in and do what she believes is right, even if she's at odds with me. To hear her hold up this mirror with her words is even more terrifying than her emotionless smile.

"But Nate is—"

"An inevitable pile of ash with a weak spot for Callie, one we'll use to our advantage." Heike's cruel assessment feels like a slap in the face.

"And what about Ayla?" I wrap my arms around my middle, suddenly cold. Is it my icy Manipulation? Or Heike's words?

"What about her? She can float back to Cordonanza if she likes, or rot in the dunes in that fancy dress."

Who is this person standing before me? "Heike, I—is something bothering you?"

"The only thing bothering me is your lack of decisiveness," my sister snaps. "You've never wavered in your convictions."

"I just … feel like you haven't been yourself," I say.

"I'm more myself than I've ever been," Heike argues before the last syllable crosses my lips. "Isn't it enough that I realized you were right?" Her eyes flash behind her curtain of hair, lips curling into an uncharacteristic snarl. "I'm starting to wonder what happened to *you*. Where's your loyalty, brother? With me, or with Ayla and Nate?"

"Nothing happened to me." I blink, and when I open my eyes again, Heike's dark expression is gone, replaced by neutrality. "I've never wavered in my loyalty. It belongs with you, always.

Everything I do is for you."

"Then forget about Ayla and Callie. We'll take care of them later. Tonight, we'll sit back and let Quadrant Three eliminate Nate." Her buoyantly happiness plotting the imminent death of one of the people stuck in the Rognaga puts me on edge.

"How do you know something in Quadrant Three will destroy Nate?"

"Trust me, brother." Heike sounds almost like herself except for the undercurrent of malice rising to the surface. "You can always trust me. Only me."

A shudder ripples down my neck until the tiny hairs stand straight on end.

"Of course, Heike." And yet, I only halfway believe it.

Heike spins on her heel and makes her way through the hatch door, almost stepping on Nemo. She doesn't acknowledge him like she used to, doesn't stop to pat his head. It's like her little mech friend no longer exists.

Nemo hangs back until my sister is gone before wheeling onto Diver's shoulder. I tense, anticipating his imminent attack, but the mech makes no move. He waits, watching.

"Come to take a swipe at my ankles? Try it and see what happens."

Nemo makes a gesture with his claw-hand I assume is vulgar, then climbs down Diver's shoulder. Is he leaving?

"Where do you think you're going?" I try to snatch him before he loses his grip, but Nemo shakes his head fiercely and pinches my fingers in his claws. He resumes the descent, hanging on by loose bolts and bends in the larger mech's frame. "Fine. Have it your way. I'm glad you're leaving."

Nemo ignores me.

"Good riddance, you menace!" Where Nemo plans on going,

I have no idea. Nor do I care. If he has it in his mind get himself lost in the desert, it saves me the trouble of doing it myself.

*Callie will be worried he's gone.* But soon, Callie might be gone, too. There's still a very real possibility the maze will kill her. And if Heike's dark prediction is correct, Nate won't last the night.

It feels like a stomach punch to realize—as if for the first time—that Callie and Nate could *die.* Callie and I will never argue about anything again. Nate will never laugh in that slightly maniacal way or call me Boy Scout. It will be as though they never existed in my life at all.

This is what I planned, isn't it? What I always wanted. No more Luminauts, no more Light. No more dangerous folk with magic. Just me and Heike. My sister is all I need.

I turn away from the desert and head into the Crow's Nest, preparing myself for the inevitability that tonight someone will die, and I'll have played a part in the cause.

# CHAPTER 19
# CALLIE

I'M NOT GOING TO discuss waking up with my cheek pressed to Nate Ormandi's armpit, open-mouth breathing and drooling all over his shirt.

Maybe some other girl stuck in a one-bed scenario with a boy would make the most of the opportunity and wake up all cute and perky, but not me. The only thing more embarrassing than my morning breath is knowing my slobber left a mark.

If Nate thought the drool was gross, he didn't say anything. He just flipped his gorgeous, wavy hair—because of course *he* didn't wake up looking like a train wreck—and made some pithy remark like, "On a scale of no sleep to oh-so dreamy, did I make a good pillow?"

I rolled my eyes and told him to get moving … except he *does* make a good pillow. I slept better than I have in ages lying next to him, and the answer to his question was oh-*so* dreamy.

I ought to be way more confused about this situation. Not long ago, I thought he was dead (all the way dead, not just undead—which is confusing in itself). Before that, we were sworn enemies, pitted against each other in a race for Light Cores each was determined to win. I tried to Light blast his head off once, before he could get a single word out in self-defense.

Now, we're sharing a cot inside a death maze. When he smiles, it reaches the depths of his eyes and makes my insides dance with a kaleidoscope of butterflies. He wants to take me on a date. I want to say yes because it seems like the most right and inevitable thing in the multiverse.

Which makes the fact something could kill us over the course of the next two nights all the more terrifying. I really, *really* don't want to think about what that "something" could be.

"Quadrant Three is kind of a let-down, huh?" Nate's astute observation draws me back to the present.

"Yeah, we've been walking around for hours and nothing's attacked us." I look up and down the maze's jagged walls and myriad paths. It's dark, but not with Darkness. The rocks and boulders littering the ground remain rocks and boulders without transforming into monsters before our eyes. The path lies open and clear.

In other words, this is really off-putting. I'd gladly take any other horror-movie scenario over the unnerving silence.

"I don't like it." Nate says exactly what I'm thinking too. "It's like the maze forgot we were here except for—"

*Click-click-click.*

"What was that noise?" Toran demands over the comms.

"They've already said they don't know," Ayla's voice crackles. My comm has sustained some pretty heavy damage the last couple of nights.

"It's the same weird clicking noise we heard as soon as we entered Quadrant Three," Nate tells Toran. "No clue what's making it, no clue where it's coming from."

"I'm sure you'll find out soon." Why does Heike sound like she *knows* we'll find out soon?

Nate's warning that something might be wrong with Heike comes back to me. Yesterday, I'd have thought she was making a joke. Her sense of humor can be pretty dry, especially if Toran's around. But now I can't help wondering if I should worry.

*Click-click-click.* A creeped-out shiver runs up my arms.

"Okay navigators, which way?" I stop and assess a series of turns coming up along the wall.

"The area up ahead is tricky. Several of the turns loop into other turns and crisscross multiple pathways." Toran opens up the holo map of the Rognaga to demonstrate what he's talking about. Holy complicated maze, Batman.

"Yeesh, it's an ant farm," Nate says. "It reminds me of ore wyrm tunnels." I don't like how he says those words.

"What's an ore wyrm?" And can it please not be in this maze? Pretty please with a cherry on top?

"Really nasty predator from Ictari," Nate explains. "El ran into one once. Lots of pus was involved, and no, that's not some gross joke."

*Click-click-click.*

Nate and I spin around at the same time, scanning the maze for the source of the clicking. But nothing is there.

"Okay Boy Scout, which path do we take?" Nate shudders when he speaks, his voice on the edge of a freaked-out tremble. "I'd like to be done with this quadrant ASAP."

"Me too." I put my hand on his arm, ignoring how firm and swoony his bicep is. Okay, not ignoring, but yeah. Anyway. "Is the clicking freaking you out too?"

"Very much," Nate replies, keeping his voice low for semi-privacy with a live comm. "It feels … weird in here."

"Weird?" I frown. "How so?"

"There's a different kind of Darkness in this quadrant," Nate elaborates. "It's like two competing forces fighting for control—one trying to protect the Light Core and the other trying to destroy it."

"But I don't see any Darkness." I glance around for squirming tentacles or sentient shadows out of place, but nothing looks ominous or deadly. Just well-worn maze paths flooded with moonlight.

"It's not showing itself yet. But when it does …" He jerks his shoulders and grabs my hand. "Stay near me. Please."

*Kick-thud* goes my heart, a sweet ache blooming around its beat. "Of course I'll stay with you. We're finishing this maze together."

The trusting look in his eyes anchors me. "Thank you, Callie."

Only Nate could say my name in a way that makes me question my resolve and reaffirm it at the same time. Yet as I'm learning about Nate, everything that should or could be between us is flipped around on its head.

I have to remember we're here to survive and win. Staying focused on our task is critical. It would be catastrophic to let my gaze stray to his lips, trace the shape of his mouth in my mind while my body aches to kiss him … kind of like I'm doing now.

Gosh, his mouth is inviting, though. That pouty bottom lip makes it hard to concentrate. The way he looked at me last night, with so much tenderness I thought I would melt into a simmering puddle of Callie-bloops, I know he wants to kiss me, too.

"Heike and I worked out the correct route." Toran's voice startles me out of my thoughts. "There's a narrow path coming up on your immediate left. Take it, and then the third right."

"You mean the path that's barely wider than my shoulders and incredibly dark?" Nate glances to his left. "Yeah, that's not happening."

"Even from here it looks dangerous," Ayla adds. "There must be another way."

"It's the only way," Toran replies. "Heike double checked."

"Heike thinks this is the right path?" I exchange glances with Nate. He gives his head a slight shake.

I don't have a good feeling about this either. But just because Heike's been acting a little creepy, it doesn't mean she'd purposely steer us wrong, right?

"Don't you trust me, Callie?" Heike's voice comes in over my comm. She sounds just like my friend I traveled with across the Hem—eager and entirely earnest. Familiar brightness replaces any malevolence I thought I heard in her voice, and when her hologram face pops up between me and Nate, she smiles as broadly as ever. "You know I was a better Guide than Toran."

I look at Nate. "It's true, she's better at Guiding than Toran."

Nate wavers a moment. "What do you think, Sparky? Is there another way, or is this it?"

"I would have to look more closely at the map." Ayla's nervous reply hovers between panic and uncertainty. "It's possible that—"

"It isn't possible. This is the only way." Heike doesn't give Ayla time to form a complete thought, much less look at the map.

"Get going before the clicking sound decides to make the most of your hesitation." Toran unsurprisingly agrees with his sister.

"The quicker we get out of this tunnel," I say, "the quicker we can rest at the next safe house."

Nate's eyes betray his doubt we'll live to see said safe house, but he wordlessly follows me into the path. Over my shoulder, haunting clicks reverberate up and down the rock walls—closer this time. But it's too tight a squeeze to turn and look.

"Third turn on the right, you said?" I confirm the correct turn the deeper we go. I can't see anything in the tunnel. I form a Light orb, holding it just above my palm.

"Yes," Heike replies. "You're getting closer. Keep going."

I take the turn in question, and that's when I hear it again. *Click-click-click.*

"Callie, I feel it. It's here." Nate sounds completely, totally panicked.

*Click-click-hisssss.*

Okay, the hiss is new. Not good. "What's here?"

"The Darkness," Nate answers. "The — the *thing*."

*Click — HISSSSSSS.*

Above our heads, an enormous skeletal insect crunches through the Rognaga's walls, gnawing rocks with jaws the size of an excavator claw. Its school bus-sized body stretches to squeeze into the narrow path, a cross between a centipede and a cockroach. Under the moonlight, its back reflects the stars while the half of its body inside the path goes completely black with Darkness.

Camouflage — that's why we couldn't see it following us. Thanks, I hate it.

I scream and launch my Light orb into the insect's mouth. It doesn't even dent the monster's jaws. The monster snaps harder at my face, as though eating my Light is a tasty snack and it wants more.

"Nate, get out of here!"

"What's going on?" Ayla cries over the comms.

Heike says nothing. Neither does Toran.

Nate can't talk, his face is sheer terror. We stumble our way backward, the gigantic insect eating through the maze in pursuit. My pulse thunders in my ears and drowns out all noise except for the gnashing insect's jaws. Darkness swirls through the tunnel, trying to devour my Light. It's colder than the rest of the Darkness in the maze, more venomous and sinister. Almost ...

Almost like Queen's.

*Luminaut, the maze has been breached.* Diver reaches into the Darkness to connect to my Light.

*What do you mean, breached?*

*This Darkness is not of the maze. The monster has been corrupted by another.*

"It's too much, too much." Nate's Light fades in and out when we emerge into the Rognaga's main pathway. I grab his arm, holding him upright when his knees buckle.

"Fight it, Nate."

*Not-Our-Luminaut is in danger, Luminaut.* Thanks Diver, but trust me, I know.

The insect exits the narrow tunnel and fades onto the rock wall, fully camouflaged from sight. I have no idea where it'll attack again—it could come at us from anywhere.

Taking Nate's ashen face in my hands, I turn him toward me. "You've got to get it together. Focus on Light."

"Callie." He grabs my wrists so hard they hurt. "She's controlling it."

Queen. That's who he means. Because this Darkness doesn't just care about keeping us from reaching the Light Core—it's trying to kill us.

"Why is she attacking now?" I search Nate for any sign he knows Queen's motive.

"She only needs one Luminaut."

The bone-like insect appears behind Nate's shoulder, and I Light blast it before it can snap his head off with saw-toothed scissor jaws. The monster hisses angrily, gives its skeleton-like face a shake, and retreats into the wall, concealing itself to attack again.

"We need to be rerouted, and fast," I speak into my comm. "There's an insect infestation, and this Darkness is of the even-deadlier variety."

"I, uh …erm …" Toran stammers. "It will be difficult to—"

"Dunes, they're going to die. Give me that!" A scuffle erupts between Ayla and Toran, but the clarity in her voice means she's winning. "Go straight down the path for now."

"Give me my comm!" Toran lands with an *umph,* a failed attempt to retrieve the tablet.

"No! You're going to get them killed!"

*Seriously* bad timing for a spat, Seers. I take Nate's hand and drag him along, racing down the path the way Ayla said to go. I can't see the insect or track its movements. It could appear out of nowhere and cut me in two before—

*HISSS – snap!*

The insect's enormous jaws gnash inches from my nose. I barely duck in time and skid into a wall with Nate, who crashes face-first.

He pulls his squished cheek away and groans. "Ow."

"Sorry." There's no time to check that he's okay because the insect has a new toy—a long, boulder-like abdomen it swings with the force of a battering ram. I pull Nate out of the line of fire before it catches him from behind and crushes him.

"What's going on? Where's our new route?" I bellow into my comm.

"Keep distracting it, I'm trying," Ayla replies, followed by another jumble of noise. "Toran, I *will* electrocute you!"

"Anytime you want to hurry it up, that would be—*umph!*"

The insect swings its abdomen—at least, I think it swings its abdomen because something I can't see slams into me, sending me flying into a rock wall. Stars burst in front of my vision, and the back of my skull erupts in ferocious pain. I crumble to my knees like wet tissue paper, numb nausea choking me as my head swims. There's no way I can prepare a Light blast. Not when I can barely see.

"Callie!" Nate calls somewhere in the distance. I try to answer, but my tongue isn't working. The world moves slowly, as if I'm watching through a blurry lens at half-speed.

Before my eyes, the insect reappears, jaws open to strike.

And then there's only Light. Another Luminaut—one just as powerful as me—joins the fight. It takes me a moment to realize who it is.

Nate faces his opponent, Light filling the space around him. There's no confusion, no hesitation, no almost passing out. Just Nate standing in Light, ready to fight the creature attacking me until one of them wins.

"Hey, Jiminy Cricket!" Blazing Light swings from the tip of his spear around the insect, holding tight and firm. With a tug, Nate burrows the creature's jaws into the earth, digging a trench with its saw-like teeth. "I know you've got *her* Darkness in you. Did she give you orders to kill a Luminaut tonight?"

Another swing of Nate's Light whip catches the insect around its legs. I've never seen Nate use his Light this way—so controlled and precise, doing the same trick Mariasol did in her footage. He's a true force to be reckoned with.

"You can tell your Queen Bee we're not going down that easy." He forms a Light orb in his hand and launches it like he's throwing a baseball to catch a runner. The insect screeches in pain.

Strength slowly returns to my hands and legs as my vision

clears.

"My power isn't yours to manipulate." Nate keeps throwing Light orbs at his captive monster, releasing all his pent-up fury as he talks to Queen through the giant insect. "And if you think about hurting Callie again, you'll find out exactly what my Light can do."

Light surrounds Nate, fills him, flows through him. His feet rise from the ground, and with a snap of his spear, the lasso cracks. A piercing shriek fills the air as Light explodes around the insect. The monster falls, then disappears from sight. Only Nate and his Light remain.

"Nate!" I hobble to him when he comes back to the ground, his Light fading until only his spear glows. "That was amazing!"

"Is it dead?" He's unsteady on his feet, and his eyes aren't focused, like he's about to lose consciousness. I grasp his shoulders to keep him standing. "Did I get rid of her Darkness, at least?"

"I don't know." I look around for the monster insect, scanning the place it fell. But it's gone. "Maybe we—"

*Luminaut, Not-Our-Luminaut, the creature is still there!*

Out of nowhere, the injured insect appears. Swinging its long abdomen, it catches Nate and sends him flying into a far wall. His entire left side hits the jagged rocks with a sickening crunch, and he falls to the ground, lifeless.

"No!" I run to Nate, but the insect is faster, even with all its Light scars and wounds. It slithers over Nate's form, rearing back to strike.

"Over here!" I shout, throwing Light at the insect. "Leave him alone!" But the monster ignores me.

*Luminaut, you must retrieve Not-Our-Luminaut. He is injured.*

Tears spring to my eyes at Diver's words. *I'm trying, Diver, but*

*I need a miracle.* The bug looms over Nate, jaws opening and closing like pincers to bite him in two.

Please, miracle, show up. Any time would be nice.

From the maze walls, Darkness pours like a tidal wave. The Rognaga crashes down, yet boulders never crush me—the Darkness cares only about eliminating the insect and its power, the Darkness Queen controls. Its jaws leave Nate, snapping at the slithering maze tentacles wildly.

The Rognaga's Darkness wraps itself around the insect and crushes it to ashes. Tentacles of icy Shadow fly away, and above me, Darkness forms the outline of Saeli's face, watching Queen's power flee.

*"STAY AWAY, ELARA. THIS IS YOUR ONLY WARNING."* Saeli's booming voice echoes through the desert night.

And just like that, her face is gone. Darkness retreats into the earth, leaving me and Nate alone in a wide field of ashes. A short distance away, the touchpad mechanism signaling the safe house shines like a beacon of hope.

"What's going on? Is Nate all right? Are *you* all right, bestie?" Ayla's anxiety is nothing compared to my own. I crawl to Nate and push his hair away from his face.

"Come on, wake up." The lump in my throat makes the words come out squeaky. "The safe house is just over there. The big, bad bug is gone, we can make it." I shake his shoulders. "Nate, if you're messing with me, this isn't funny."

"Finally! My comm!" Toran announces his triumph over Ayla. Wanna worry about how your crappy navigation might have killed Nate? Jerk—and that's not even the worst I want to call him.

Nothing from Heike, not even a sound.

Light fills my hands, and I press them to Nate's face. "Please,

please."

*Wake up. Be okay.* After a half-second that feels like a thousand years, Nate's eyes flutter and he groans miserably.

"Freaking son of a—" I'm not going to repeat the long string of expletives that pour from his lips, but it's impressive he can fit that many swear words into a single sentence.

"Thank the stars!" Ayla sighs.

I help Nate ease into a sit before I throw my arms around his neck. "Don't scare me like that again." He winces sharply, clutching his arm.

"Back up! Back up!" Nate grits his teeth, and when I pull away, he's pale with pain. "I think that thing dislocated my shoulder. There's a couple broken bones in my arm, too."

Nate's left arm hangs loose at his side, useless, and his shoulder blade sticks out sharply, pulled tight to the skin. Just beneath his elbow, his arm turns strangely aside, confirming the fracture.

"I need a sling and a splint. And I probably have a concussion. Guess I should be glad I'm undead. No brain damage."

"Are you sure you're undead?" All I see right now is a human boy who's in agonizing pain and desperately needs medical care. "We have to get you to the safe house."

I help Nate stand all the way, and when I put my arm around him to help him walk, he's cold again—but not with vampiric Darkness. He's clammy, shaking, and soon his teeth chatter.

"Does it hurt a lot?" I ask.

"Y-yeah." Nate barely manages one syllable.

*He's going into shock from the pain,* I realize. Which seems like a really human thing to do for a supposedly undead guy.

*Luminaut, you must get Not-Our-Luminaut out of the Rognaga.* Even Diver is worried about Nate.

*I wish there were a way, Diver.* Our last hope is winning the Light Core tomorrow night.

I press the touchpad to open the safe house door, and Nate falls on the cot inside. The robotic voice congratulates us on surviving — barely.

"I'm cutting the transmission," I inform the Rykjiersens and Ayla. "I'll check in with you later."

Nobody cares, all of them arguing amongst themselves about who was responsible for Nate getting hurt — Ayla thinks Serai and Dr. Ormandi need to come help get him out, but Heike and Toran argue for her to leave the adult Seers out of it.

Have fun losing that Seer brawl, Toran. Not my problem anymore.

I drop to my knees and root through my backpack for the box of first aid supplies. I don't know what will function as a sling, but maybe there are pain meds. Anything is better than nothing.

"There it is!" A sterile, white box, long and slim for easy packing. I snap it open, tossing aside anything useless. There's a salve for concussions that I rub on my temples, pocketing it for Nate's head injury before going through the rest of the contents. "Let's see, bandages, ointment, an adrenaline shot in case your heart stops …"

"How about an orthopedic surgeon?" Nate stares at the ceiling, jaw clenched. "I could use a CAT scan too."

"You're out of luck," I reply. "But I found a vial of fast-relief pain meds and some kind of sci-fi syringe. I can make a sling from some of your ashy desert gear, and we'll use the first aid box for a splint."

"Fast-relief better be *fast*," Nate groans.

"Where should I stick this needle?" I press a sleek injection device into the bottle of meds. A button on the side turns blue when it's full.

"I don't know, I don't have a functioning circulatory system." Nate uses his right arm to push himself up, and I look away from the V of muscle at his hips. But I'm too weak not to sneak a peek at his abs when he readjusts his shirt. "Stick it as close to the scapula as you can. Then hit my arm fracture."

Scapula? Oh, his shoulder. Said shoulder pokes from his skin with unnatural sharpness before his whole arm twists strangely to the right beneath the elbow. I feel sick thinking about the amount of pain he must be in. He cries out—yet another swear word—when I stick the needle in, but calms when the pain meds take hold. I refill the injector and give him a second dose close to the bone break.

"Does that help?" He doesn't reply, but his face relaxes. I unload his pack and find his ash-encrusted shirt from the other night, tearing it into a long strip. "I'll work on making a sling, but I can't promise I'll do a great job."

I tell the avatar on my comm to look up splint slings and start with step one of the procedure. Nate watches me with an increasingly lopsided grin.

"You've had a front-row seat to all my deepest vulnerabilities in this maze." Yeah, those meds are definitely kicking in. "Hashing out my crap choices that led me to Darkness. Mom dying. Being injured, in pain, and needing help. My massive, unrequited crush."

I go completely still at the words "unrequited crush," and Nate laughs. Do I have a weird look on my face? It's not that I didn't know he had a crush, because it was obvious—more that he thinks it's unrequited.

"Whoopsie!" Nate giggles uncontrollably. "You weren't supposed to find out." He presses his working index finger on my lips until they part slightly. "Shhh, don't tell Callie."

"Your secrets are safe with me," I promise.

"Safe with you…" His gaze lands softly on my mouth, our faces inching forward. My breath catches when he caresses my lower lip, pausing at the corner. "You have the cutest freckle by your mouth. Did you know that?" He leans in, pausing a hairsbreadth from a kiss, and my gasp like a sigh floats into the air between us.

"Callie," Nate's whisper makes me tremble all the way to my toes. "My stars."

*Ensoloradans only use "my stars" for the people most precious to them.* I look deep into his dark eyes, fingertips trailing through his wavy hair, nodding my consent to whatever happens next. This has gone so far beyond a crush, beyond infatuation. It's seeing and being seen inside someone's heart. What started as a fragile spark manifested by Light has led to this moment, a kiss I've wanted—*ached* for—so long it steals my breath. Nate lingers, fingers shaking, his lips so close I can almost taste them—

"Oof!" Nate loses balance, his injured shoulder and arm crashing against my side. Quickly, I help him upright, taking weight off his bad side.

So much for that kiss.

"Come on," I say, "you're a loopy mess from the meds. We need to finish patching you up before they wear off." I turn my attention back to my comm, fixing a splint on his fracture and setting his shoulder in a sling. "It doesn't look great, but it'll do for now."

Nate leans back onto the pillow, and I pull the concussion salve from my pocket. "I'm sorry, but I don't think you'll be able to be the big spoon tonight," he says. "Which is sad because I was looking forward to being the little spoon."

"Yeah, sucks." I rub some of the salve onto his temples, and his sigh of relief reverberates through my whole frame. "It's my lifelong dream to be the big spoon."

He smiles weakly. "Sounds like we missed the boat. Again. But that was Queen's plan all along."

"What plan?" I put the pain meds and injector into his backpack for later.

"She told me she was going to take you and El into the Shadow Plain and torture you until I did what she demanded," Nate says. "She's too smart to show her hand like that—she knew I'd do anything to prevent it, even putting myself into situations where I'd wind up dead all the way." A wry grin lifts the corners of his mouth. "Guess I gave her one less Luminaut to worry about after all."

*One less Luminaut …*

"People don't die of broken arms or dislocated shoulders." I pull the cot blanket up around him. "You need sleep. We'll tackle the Pit and Queen's schemes tomorrow."

"*You'll* tackle the Pit." Glassiness pools in Nate's eyes. "I wanted you to trust me, to prove I was serious about making all the wrong things I did right." He reaches for me with his good hand, cupping my cheek tenderly in his palm. "Out of all the people I hurt with Darkness, hurting you feels the worst. I'm so sorry, Callie."

I press his palm to my skin, and close my eyes. There's no Darkness in this moment, only Light. His and mine, entwined. Our Light becomes one and the same, dancing together in and around us.

"By the way," he murmurs, "you're the Luminaut meant to defeat Queen. I know you are."

The question is, can I defeat her if Nate isn't by my side? What if Darkness destroys everything I've worked so hard to protect, starting with Nate?

"Just promise me tomorrow you'll—" Too late, he already drifted off. Or lost consciousness. I snatch the extra pillow from the cot and lay down on the floor, keeping an eye on him until a restless slumber overtakes me too.

# CHAPTER 20
# CALLIE

A BLINKING LIGHT close to my face wakes me earlier than expected.

"Incoming transmission from Crabby McButthead."

I sit up with a moan, sore from having slept on the floor, and check my comm's screen. Sure enough, Toran—or somebody using Toran's comm—is trying to call.

"Nate, are you asleep?" I glance at the boy on the cot. He twitches fitfully under the blanket, his eyebrows pinched tight in a grimace of pain, but he isn't awake. He needs sleep to recover as much as he can. We've got the Pit to tackle in a couple hours, and he's down a working arm, plus his dominant hand.

I take my comm to the far corner and tap the screen. Heike's face pops up in holo form above the glass. Is her skin turning ghost-gray, or is it the dim light in the safe house?

"Heike, what's going on?" I greet her in a half-whisper.

"Is Nate dead?" Yikes on several freaking bikes, Heike, you're going to lead with that?

"No, he's not. He's sleeping." I make sure our voices didn't wake him. Nope, we're good. "Why did you call?"

"Everyone is worried about Nate's ability to compete in the

Pit." Her expression tries to imitate care and concern but ends up almost twisted. "He needs a physician."

"Yeah, I totally agree." Except I'm less coldly clinical than Heike. She talks about Nate like somebody might describe a spider they're about to squish. It makes me want to shudder. "But transports might not find the way out here, and I don't think Diver can get him out either. The maze walls are too narrow."

*Luminaut, be careful with your words.* Diver's voice, filled with suspicion, strikes deep in my heart. *Everything is not as it appears.*

*Nate needs help before he's hurt even worse, buddy.* Doesn't Diver care about Nate? He was terrified last night when the giant bug attacked. Why the shift?

*We do not mean Not-Our-Luminaut.*

Oh. I see.

"If nobody can come down to you, *you* need to finish the maze and win the Light Core. Then you and Nate can get out." Heike's smile twitches rapidly at the corners. She narrows her gaze until it's sharp as a dagger, muttering to herself. "It must be won. It *has* to be won. And she must do it now."

Something isn't right with her. Not right at all.

*Luminaut, use wisdom. Do not be fooled.* Diver thinks something isn't right with Heike too.

I watch her carefully through the holo. Her eyes are darker than normal—a hint of inky black peeks through the blue-gray. "Heike, are you okay?"

"Of course!" Heike stares, unblinking through the comm. "Don't you think Nate would want you to go ahead and win the maze? If you were injured, you'd tell him to do the same." Heike makes a valid point, despite the fact I don't like it. "The sun just set, soon it will be moonrise. If you leave now, you can be in the Pit and out again before he wakes up."

"But the only way to win in the Pit is—" I stop myself from admitting the truth about Living Light and how to defeat the Rognaga. *Be careful with your words.* Diver's warning rings out like a siren. "I mean, yeah, you're right. I have to get Nate out of the maze, and I can't do that until it's beaten."

"I'll guide you through the Pit," Heike assures me. Her chilly tone sends a shiver down my spine.

I don't want Heike guiding me anywhere, much less somewhere as purportedly dangerous as the Pit. But one look at Nate is enough to make up my mind. Aside from the pain, he might lose the use of his left arm completely if he can't see a doctor.

He'd do this for me if our places were reversed. I know he would.

"I have to change clothes and eat, I forgot last night." I was so anxious about Nate, food hadn't even crossed my mind. "Give me fifteen minutes."

"Don't take too much time." Heike's simple reminder sounds like a thinly veiled threat. She ends our transmission, and her holo face disappears.

I stand and look at Nate, still slumbering. Every so often he startles and moans when the reflex reaches his left shoulder. His face, normally a golden shade of perma-tan, is paler than Toran's and clammy-cold. I don't like leaving him alone, but I don't see how I have another choice. He'd put himself at too much risk going into the Pit in his current state.

"I should leave you a note, shouldn't I?" I find a small piece of paper and a pen in my backpack and scribble a hasty explanation for my absence in case he wakes up.

Dear Nate,

> *I'm going into the Pit for the Light Core so we can get out of this stupid maze for good. I don't want you to risk your whole existence trying to win with me. We made it this far together, now it's time for me to finish it. I want you to know I trust you the way you trust me, and I promise nothing between us is unrequited. The multiverse needs two Luminauts. I need you, too. In other words, don't follow me.*
>
> Love, Callie

Did I say too much? Especially the unrequited part? Too late to change it now. I'd rather he give me endless amounts of crap about it than risk him becoming a doomed pile of Shadowmancer ash. Just thinking about it makes me want to cry.

I set the note on the cot beside Nate, then crouch down next to him, brushing a few waves of brown-black hair away from his forehead. He's honestly so beautiful. Not just how he looks, but everything—even the scars. I never thought we'd get here together, but I'm glad he's been with me. I still want him with me.

After all, he owes me a pizza date.

"Enjoy sleeping in, sleaze-bag. I'll be back soon." I stand, shouldering my pack, and grab my comm. Time to be a Luminaut. Living Light. Whatever I have to be, I'll be it.

"Okay Heike, guide me into the Pit so I can get out of it as fast as possible." I strap my comm into place on my armband and survey the landscape outside the safe house. It's … different.

The Pit isn't a labyrinthine quadrant, it's a barren crater, as if an asteroid crashed in the desert and left a mile-wide divot in the sand. There are no pathways and turns, no jagged, saw-tooth walls, and no visible Darkness. Just a wide expanse with a giant hole in the center.

From the depths of the cave-like hole, I feel the Light Core. The gentle hum inside the rock calls to me, drawing me deeper into the Rognaga to the heart of it all. The only thing standing between me and victory is this crater.

And, like, probably a thousand Darkness monsters that will emerge the moment I take a step.

"What are you waiting for?" Heike's voice over my comm startles me with its urgency.

"I'm surprised there's no traps, that's all." I look warily at the pebbles littered around the smooth surface of the Pit. Is the earth infected the way the rest of the walls and floor of the Rognaga have been? Is an even bigger monster waiting to pop out and devour me?

"Make the most of the stillness," Heike says.

"This stillness is what scares me." I take a few cautious steps. A few more. Still nothing.

Better do this fast because if I learned anything in the Rognaga, "nothing" won't remain nothing for long.

I break into a run, Light in my hands, shooting blasts in case something pops up in my peripheral, but everything remains still. Does this mean I've passed Saeli's test of Living Light? Or does it mean I ought to save my strength for something worse awaiting me at the bottom of that hole?

*Luminaut, you should not be where you are. Return to Not-Our-Luminaut in the safe house.* Diver's footsteps boom above the crater, and he comes to rest at the top of the wall, looking as though he's going to jump in here after me.

*Diver, can you come down here and get Nate out?*

*The Darkness must be defeated first, Luminaut. Our Light will be attacked.*

Makes sense, but it still leaves me and Nate stranded until the Light Core is found. What doesn't make sense is Diver's Crow's Nest being completely void of people. *Diver, what happened to the Seers and Heike?*

Before Diver answers, Nemo whizzes up to me, clutching my ankle. His claw hands scratch the bare skin of my lower calf as he tries to climb up my leg.

"Nemo?" I snatch my little buddy and hold him close. "How did you get down here? Are you okay? What happened?"

Nemo wildly gesticulates, pointing at Diver's Crow's Nest with maniacal rage. He's even more angry than he was when I found him destroying the Hall of Machines after he set it on fire. Something — somebody — made him furious.

"Did Toran try to hurt you again?" He probably attempted to kick Nemo to the curb at least five times a night, but it's Toran, and that's standard for his relationship with my tiny mech. Nemo shakes his head and taps my shoulder, my face, my hair.

"Toran tried to hurt *me*?"

Nemo shudders and shakes his head again. If Toran isn't the problem, that means —

"*Heike* tried to hurt me?"

My heart sinks when Nemo nods.

"Why?" I channel Diver's Light. "Buddy, I need some answers ASAP. Where did everyone go?"

*Not-Our-Luminaut's Seer channeled her powers to go back home. The girl stole a device to contact Luminaut, and Luminaut's Seer went into the desert as soon as the moon rose. We do not know where he is. We believe he is looking for his sister.*

Toran can't find Heike? She stole his comm to talk me into going into the Pit alone? And Ayla inexplicably went back to Cordonanza without telling anyone? What is going *on* up there?

I swear, I leave two Seers and a thirteen-year-old for three nights and they end up swiping each other's tech and flying off who-knows-where. And Toran says Luminauts are pure chaos? He needs to look in the mirror.

*I'll figure this out later, Diver. I've got to finish the Rognaga. Nate is depending on me,* I keep my eyes on the dark depths of the Pit. *Do you know any tricks to win?*

And please, let me know the answer quickly, Diver, because this big hole is coming up fast.

*Luminaut must win by making the choice,* is Diver's cryptic reply. Non-answers when I'm barreling head-first toward uncertain doom? Cool, thanks.

*My choice is already made.* I set Nemo on the ground and pat his head. "Where I'm going, you can't follow."

Nemo tries to rush after me, but I sweep my hand wide, encasing him in a Light pen to protect him. "I'm sorry, Nemo. This is the only way."

*Luminaut, please. Do not do this.*

I don't answer Diver's desperate plea. There's no going back.

I move across the Pit, reaching the bottomless hole at its center. There are no stairs leading in, no way to go down except to leap. At the bottom, there's a Light Core … or destruction.

And so, I jump in.

But before I fall a foot, Darkness flies from the darkest parts of the earth, pushing me back into the crater with a force like a tornado. I sprawl flat on my back, catching my breath.

Ouch, that was bad.

A new wave of Darkness spews from the Pit, and I barely have time to Light blast a sweeping tentacle trying to take me out. Another comes for me, and another. There's so much Darkness, I can't see anything else.

"Okay, so the Pit is basically a gladiator battle between a Luminaut and Darkness. Funsies."

Shadows pour from the Pit like a giant set of squid tentacles, and where I cut off one leg, three more regrow. Squid-Hydra-Shadow-Monster. This has got to be the worst obstacle yet. It's an unending onslaught of Darkness, and I'm already fading from lack of sleep and anxiety.

This maze sucks. In case I haven't said it enough lately, it really, *really* sucks.

*Diver, do you have any locked-up memories about how I can become the Living Light thing?* Because if that's what it takes to beat this heinousness, I need to figure out the secret, fast.

*The answer is already inside Luminaut.*

Seriously dude, not the time for cryptic replies. More blasts, more Darkness, more running for my life, only to find there's nowhere to hide. It's just one defensive maneuver after another, and sooner or later I'm going to get sloppy.

Sloppy equals dead.

*Assuming I don't have any answers, could you tell me in the most direct way possible?* When I needed answers about the source of Darkness in the Rognaga, Diver had them. Why can't Diver help me now? Is literally everyone going to abandon me? *Any memory I can unlock for you that holds the magic key? Please, I need a clue. Anything.*

*Luminaut already knows everything there is to know.*

Except I don't, but yeah, sure. Okay. All things considered, my Rognaga journey has been pretty scratch-free so far. I guess I'm past due for some peril, pain, and possible death.

Before me, Darkness shifts, coalescing into a solid shape in the center of the crater. I form a Light orb between my palms, but when I launch it, the Darkness absorbs and destroys it—a small part of my power entirely erased. I feel a little less than I was before, and more terrified than ever that this Darkness will end me.

The solid Darkness becomes humanoid, and menacing red eyes open in its formless face. It walks on top of the swirling tentacle storm, and a voice speaks in my mind.

*"My creation is not yours to destroy, and the Light Core is not yours to take."*

It's the ghost of Saeli's voice, but not just her — the whole maze cries out in anger. Every ounce of Darkness I've fought since the zombie hands attacked under the stairs screams at me to abandon my fight while I have the chance.

*"Turn back and survive. Journey on and perish."* The humanoid Darkness comes closer still. *"I know your heart and what you desire. You seek selfish things. Your Light is unworthy."*

"You're lying." I find strength in my voice again, snapping back against the accusation. Selfish? On what planet am I selfish? I prep another Light bomb. "I'm here to help my friend. The only way to get him out of here is to win."

*"You desire his safety because your selfishness caused him pain. But you will happily cause harm to anyone who stands in the way of what you desire."*

"That's not true."

But is it? Toran always said I couldn't see the threat my Light posed to others, but what if it wasn't Light that was dangerous, but *me*? My inability to see another point of view if I don't like what that person says, even if it's true?

No, this Darkness is wrong. Everything is different now. I didn't put Nate in harm's way on purpose, he insisted on coming in here with me because …

… Because I hung an ultimatum over his head and said this

was the only way he could earn my trust. I knew I could manipulate him at that moment, and I did. I manipulated Ayla into helping me find Nemo and Diver against her mom's wishes. If it caused her harm, I didn't stop to think about it. And how many times did I use Persuasion, even though I knew it was wrong?

Maybe in that way, I've been selfish. But I don't see how wanting to win this Light Core makes me unworthy. It will help me defeat Queen if I win.

But why do I want to defeat Queen in the first place? Is that the big question? The ultimate test?

*"Your doubt betrays you."* The humanoid Darkness stares at me, burning red eyes blazing across my skin. *"You left your home to prove you were not a failure. You believe yourself a failure still. Only by proving otherwise do you believe people will love you."*

A stab of guilt, anger, and shame pierces my heart, and I wonder, just for a moment, if this monster sees my truth more clearly than me. My whole life, I was the family loser. My parents and siblings never saw me as special or worthy of praise unless I did exactly what was expected. I left California ostensibly to protect them, but was that *really* why I Dove? Is my entire Luminaut journey about saving people because they deserve saving? Or is my need to finally win everyone's approval, with no compromise or concession, driving all this?

Who's right and who's wrong? Me or this all-seeing Darkness? The answer is life and death.

Of course this Darkness is wrong. Darkness is all about manipulation and trickery to achieve its ends, isn't that what Nate said? This is a ploy to get me to slip at the very end.

*"You believe I'm lying?"* Crap, I forgot the monster reads minds. Or sees thoughts. Whatever. It sucks. *"You are the one who*

*is lying to yourself. Your power and choices may be your own, but have you used your gifts well? Or will you repeat the mistakes of those who came before you?"*

Oooh yes. I see exactly what's happening here. This Darkness wants to use my Light for its own ends and prevent the rise of another Light Collective. Nice trick, I almost fell for it, but I'm smarter than this. Fury builds until it bursts like a flood of fire on my tongue and breaks free in my Light, my words.

"I see through your games." The shout on my lips is half-rage, half-sob. "Everything I've done has been to save my loved ones from Darkness like you. There's no way you can call me selfish and unworthy. Believe whatever you want, but I'm a Luminaut, and only I can beat this maze. Stand aside."

*"You may be a Luminaut, but that does not make you Living Light."* The Darkness monster rises into the sky above me, prepared to strike.

Sentient tentacles of Shadow wrap around my ankles, wrists, arms, and legs, dragging me across the ashy earth toward the deepest depths of the hole. Terror grips me the closer I get to the edge, and Darkness rises from the deep, blocking my vision until all I see is Shadow.

The last thing I hear before Darkness swallows me is a scream. Mine, or someone else's? I don't know. My world collapses into Shadow and ash until that's all there is.

# CHAPTER 21
# NATE

IF YOU'VE EVER WONDERED how it feels to get hit by a bus, I can promise you one thing: it hurts.

Granted, I didn't get hit by an actual bus, just a bug the size of a bus, but it all equals the kind of pain that makes me want to instantly puke, except there's nothing in my stomach. My insides feel cracked and splattered, a scrambled-egg mess of vital organs, but miraculously, I didn't die. Always look on the bright side of life. Undead life? I'll work on it.

But my relief to be awake inside the safe house is instantly replaced by fear. Somebody who should be in the safe house with me is gone.

"Callie? Are you there?" Her pillow is on the cot next to me, still warm, but her backpack and comm are nowhere to be seen. When I lean painfully on my good elbow, I spot a note at my side. Two seconds after scanning her loopy handwriting, I groan, crushing the note in my fist.

"Seriously? Why?" She went into the Pit alone to get the Light Core. Because she values my safety, doesn't want me getting hurt again, and she needs me. Of all the dumb, brave, but incredibly *dumb* things she's ever done, this takes the cake.

"I have to find her before she gets killed." I like talking to myself, it's a quirk.

How am I going to find her in the Pit with only one working arm and a sloppy brain, much less help her fight Darkness? What level of physiological functioning does a guy need to fight against Darkness, anyway? Three-quarters? Half? A smidge? Does it even matter if I'm undead and stuck in perpetual limbo? The answers to these questions and more when we come back at nine.

If I come back.

"Okay, time to save the girl who's supposed to save the multiverse from herself." I inject myself with another dose of the pain meds Callie left behind, slip my pack with Mom's journals onto my good shoulder, and grab my spear, which feels unnatural in my right hand. I'll do the best I can with my non-dominant side today. "Hey Diver, you got any leads on Callie?"

Diver doesn't respond. His Light is lost in grief, a sensation I'm all too familiar with. That Diver would feel it now, when Callie is out there by herself, makes my stomach sink to my toes with dread.

"Diver?" I try again to connect. "What's going on, Big Guy? Talk to me."

*Luminaut has been taken into the Pit.*

"What?" No, please, Callie can't be gone. If this panic isn't enough to kickstart my pulse, I don't know what is. "Where is she? How do I get to her?"

*Not-Our-Luminaut must find her before she is lost forever.*

Soft tapping on the safe house door startles me. "Callie?"

Hope springs from my heart. Maybe Diver was wrong about what he saw and Callie is okay. Maybe she already won the Light Core and came back for me. I *ping-swish* the touch screen lock mechanism.

"Callie, is that you?" But she's not standing beyond the threshold. All I see is a barren crater full of ash piles, the remains of which rise into the air and block the moon and stars. It's dark. Dismal. Unsurvivable. "Callie?"

A tiny, whirring squeal by my feet forces my gaze down, and Nemo touches my foot, blinking up at me.

"Nemo? How did you get down here?" I lower my right hand, and he crawls up my arm to my shoulder, cowering beside my neck. Something serious must have happened if he's seeking me out. "Where's Callie, buddy? Did you see where she went?"

Nemo nods, trembling. His tiny arm extends from his body, and he indicates a nope-looking hole at the center of the crater, one still surrounded by faint tentacles of slithering Darkness.

"Oh, no." Agony rips me in two, threatening to tear me away from consciousness into a swimming, nauseous free fall. I stumble, gritting my teeth against the pain, and race out the door of the safe house into the Pit.

I promised myself I'd keep Callie safe from Darkness. That she would be the Luminaut who defeated Queen. My failure is too overwhelming to comprehend, even as it stares me in the face. Ashes and more ashes. An entire world composed of blackish-gray, reeking mounds: a hellscape vision of Queen's future multiverse. It's the most awful, terrifying thing I've ever seen, worse than the remains of Aragusti that El and I stumbled upon. Worse because Callie might be part of these ashes.

"Callie!" I maneuver around the ash piles and pray to the origin of Light itself that one of them isn't her. "Callie, answer me!" One mound, two more. None of them are human-shaped, but would they be? "Callie are you—wait a minute. Is that Boy Scout?"

Far across the crater, Toran Rykjiersen sprints in all his

scowling, angular glory. He smiles (yes, smiles!) when he reaches Heike, who's walking toward a gaping center hole.

"Heike! Why did you run off? I was so worried!" I strain to hear Toran's distant voice. "Don't scare me like that again! Come, we aren't safe. This place is full of Darkness."

Heike shows zero response to his warnings about the lingering Shadows. Her hair, normally braided in a circle around the crown of her head, hangs in a matted mess. It grazes her shoulders and covers her face like a mask.

I pause my search, moving in to watch them more closely, Heike in particular. Callie went into the Pit. Heike now stands beside it … is she the reason Callie left the safe house in the first place?

"Heike, what's wrong?" Toran doesn't notice me approaching. He steps back and puts a hand on his sister's wooden shoulder. "Heike?" He gives her shoulder a shake. "Sister, speak to me!" The desperation on his face to know what exactly went wrong matches my own.

Finally, I'm close enough to see it—tentacles of Shadow part Heike's hair, revealing a sliver of exposed skin on her neck. Skin that's turning necrotic with pulsing, oozing Darkness.

Whoever Heike was before, that's no longer her—and Boy Scout is in serious danger.

"Toran! Get away from her!"

Toran's scowl returns when he spots me. Predictable. "Nate?"

"The Great," I add. "Stand back. She's not who you think she is."

"Help me get Heike out of here." Toran completely ignores my warning. "She won't move. She won't speak. Something is wrong."

"She's got some kind of lingering Darkness from her imprisonment," I say. "Until we figure out how to get it out of her, back off. Unless you want Darkness invading your body too."

Toran, turning to the Dark side? No sir, I don't like it. Being impaled with Shadow-sicles doesn't sound like my idea of a good time.

"I won't leave her," Toran insists, reaching for his sister's hand.

A low, menacing laugh pierces the air, growing louder, more diabolical. Heike looks up, her hair falling aside to reveal her whole face. I leap away, shielding Toran with my body and spear. Her eyes are completely black with Darkness, and the veins in her face are black too, moving around under her skin like writhing worms. Darkness tentacles emerge from her mouth in place of a tongue when she speaks.

"One Luminaut has been eliminated. One remains." The Darkness speaks through Heike. "My old Seer has proven useful after all."

My old Seer? Heike never had a Seer, she's not—wait a minute. Old Seer. Saeli. I see what's happening, although I wish I didn't.

"Queen? Are you in there, you nasty piece of work?" I point the tip of my spear at Heike, who smiles malevolently.

"Don't hurt her!" Toran tries to push me away, but even with my left side useless, I'm stronger. "If you hurt my sister, I will—"

"That's not your sister, Boy Scout." I hold him back, but crap man, this guy's bony limbs suck next to my dislocated shoulder. "She's possessed by Queen's Darkness."

"She needs me. Stand down." Toran's eyes blaze fiery blue, and he holds his hands wide, drawing water from the depths of the desert to form ice pikes. Huh, new trick, very cool. Not so cool when he shoves them in my face. "So help me, Nate, if you keep me from my sister, I will run you through."

"Just try it, Toran." I slice the end of his pike with my spear, a clear warning. "The more time you waste arguing with me, the Shadows gain an advantage."

"You've already lost, little one." Heike speaks again, her words cold and venomous.

So, I'm back to "little one," huh? She's punching down at this point.

"Heike, it's me." Toran throws his pikes to the ground and grasps both his sister's hands. "Come back to me. Fight whatever is controlling you."

"Silly little boy." Heike pulls her hands from Toran's grip. "Your plans and schemes to protect the girl have been for nothing. But don't worry, I won't hurt her much longer."

"Heike!" Toran screams his sister's name as a lightning strike tears the sky. An earthquake rumbles through the crater before a fireball lands in the ashes, spinning like a cyclone of flame.

Fire and earthquakes and lightning, gasp! I sense some additional Seers have arrived.

At the edge of the crater, Ayla and Serai stand next to Dad and El, Diver at their backs. All of them descend into the ashen crater on Serai's well-controlled rock slide. Ayla builds a lightning strike large enough to electrocute five Torans just above his head. That is, if Serai and her Vines of Doom don't strangle him first.

"Ayla, what have you done? I told you to leave them out of this." Toran draws so much water from the desert depths I have an ankle-deep puddle at my feet in seconds.

"What have *I* done? You and your sister purposely guided

our Luminauts into danger in the Rognaga!" Ayla's voice cracks more than her lightning, and sounds just as hotly dangerous. "They could have died because of you!"

So the bug thing was partly Boy Scout's doing—should have known. There's a very specific word I want to call him, but it wouldn't be acceptable to say in front of polite company.

"What good would two dead Luminauts be unless you're secretly conspiring with Darkness?" Serai's vines speed across the water to ensnare Toran's legs.

It appears Sparky and her Mommy Dearest are rather angry. Dad's not particularly happy to see Darkness Heike and her sketchy brother, but he is happy to see me. El is too. The kid throws his spindly arms around me in a fierce hug when he reaches me. Better than getting punched in the gut, right?

"Nate!"

I hug El back the best I can, ecstatic he's unharmed. "Dad! El! You're okay!"

"Of course we're okay." Dad almost looks like he wants to hug me but doesn't. "Serai was quite a generous hostess once we realized our mutual desire to find our children safe and sound." Dad eyes my injured arm, his worry apparent. "What happened to you?"

"Stupid dümfo got himself hurt," El states the obvious. Gosh, I missed this kid, though.

"As much as I'd like to sit down over a nice cup of coffee and regale you with tales of my heroism," I tell Dad and El, handing off Nemo to safer companions, "I have to find Callie."

"Where is she? And how do you expect to do anything with your left arm in a sling?" Dad whips his head around, looking for the other Luminaut who ought to have won the maze but somehow was taken by Darkness instead.

"I'm improvising at being right-handed today," I reply. "Oh, by the way, Heike is possessed by Queen's Darkness. Might wanna keep an eye on her."

"The girl is possessed by Shadow?" Serai's vines tear Toran away from his sister's side, depositing him a safe distance away. He struggles against the restraints, slicing them with ice, but Serai is faster. "Move quickly to save your friend. The Darkness will only spread."

*Not-Our-Luminaut, hurry. Luminaut needs you.*

*I hear you, Big Guy. I'm on it.*

"Be careful, Nate," Dad cautions, casting a look of sheer dread at the hole just beyond my hurt shoulder.

"Don't die for real," El adds.

"I'll try, I promise."

The edge of the Pit looms, and Callie's Light cries to me from the bottom, her fear striking deep until it becomes my own.

*Nate! Help me!*

*I'm coming. Just hold on.*

I step over the edge and everything fades away. The ashes. The crater. Dad and El. The Seer brawl that's about to go down. Heike, standing like a motionless vessel of Darkness, spewing Queen's hate. The lightning, ice, and fire mixed with destruction. I descend as deep as time itself, until Darkness catches me, and suspends me in the void. A humanoid figure appears, its glowing red eyes locked on to mine.

"*Why have you come?*" The creature's voice appears in my mind. I know who she is—it's Saeli, but also not Saeli. She was separated from her Darkness, and a small part of her consciousness is all that remains to protect her creation. The rest of her is gone, buried. At peace.

"I need to find Callie," I reply. "Tell me where she is."

*"What you seek cannot be found,"* the Darkness that belonged to Saeli says.

"I felt her Light down here. Queen is possessing her friend. I don't know why you took her or where she is, but please, let her go." Whatever this Darkness thinks it needs from Callie, I need her more. Heike needs her. The whole multiverse needs her.

The Darkness tilts its head, searching me with a burrowing gaze. Barbs of Shadow attach to my bones. I bite back a scream of horror and pain. What kind of answer does the creature want? Or is it only here for torture?

*"Did you come to claim the Light Core and destroy my creation?"*

"No. I don't care about finding the Light Core." Honestly, Light Cores can go screw themselves right now. "I care about finding Callie."

*"You care about atoning for your mistakes,"* the Darkness argues. *"She is one of those mistakes. You fear you are too far gone to be redeemed. That you are a shame to those you love, unworthy of Light."*

"Yes, and?" This Darkness wastes precious time telling me things I already know, but if I don't answer, the Shadows will swallow me. Swirling tentacles wait for the signal to attack or retreat. The creature wants more than I've revealed.

"I've owned up to the fact I'm a giant sleaze," I add. "I'm not trying to pretend I'm not what I am, or act like I didn't make a lot of awful choices. But Callie isn't responsible for those. Don't make her pay for them."

*"Are you the Living Light?"*

"No." As if this Darkness creature doesn't already know it. "I'm not even a whole Luminaut. There's still Darkness in me, which I'm sure you can sense, given what you are."

*"Then why come into this Pit to claim what can never be yours?"* The Darkness circles tighter, worming around my limbs and

threatening to snuff me out forever.

"Because it should be Callie's. Maybe she makes mistakes and runs into trouble before she thinks about the consequences, but it's because she wants to do the right thing and protect the people she loves." I close my eyes, begging my Light for the right words—words that will save Callie before Darkness finishes me.

"I don't think anyone will ever be worthy of winning your Rognaga, but I know why you made it and what you hope to protect. You want to make sure nobody else has to suffer for the choices you made. I want the same thing."

The Darkness creature remains silent. I don't know if I'm supposed to keep talking, but emotional word vomit takes over. I've had a lot of emotional word vomit lately.

"I may not know what Living Light is," I tell the Darkness, "but I know Callie has a good heart. Maybe that's not enough reason for you to let her go and give her the Light Core, but I know she's worthy."

*"This is not about her. I am asking about you."* Darkness tentacles press into my skin, threatening to ash me out of existence should I answer the next question wrong. *"Why should I do what you request? Why should I let her go and give up the Light Core?"*

And there it is. It all comes down to this one answer. The truth rises through the Shadows still stubbornly residing in my heart, and my whole chest aches, heaves, and flutters as I speak the most important thing.

"Ever since my mom died, I've been hiding. I hid behind anger, behind winning at all costs, distracting myself with school, sports, being a music snob. I hid behind Darkness and schemes that took me far from Light in some boneheaded search for the truth I knew all along."

Words flow freely, and everything I've held inside bubbles to the surface.

"I don't have to hide from Callie. She sees me—all the scars and flaws, all the vulnerability and failure—and she accepts every part. She makes me want to come back to Light. To love something—somebody—so much I'd give up everything. Because of her, I remembered how to love like that again. Maybe I felt it for the first time. But power without love is no power at all."

*Power without love is no power at all.*

To love enough to give up everything. To love something more than life itself—I get it now. I understand the words Mom embedded in me before I formed memories, the words Light didn't let me forget, and why, even in death, she was victorious in her fight. When she told me to seek Light, even in the Darkest places, she meant in me: in my heart, where I knew that love was my true power all along.

All the fight, all the struggle and shame, all the grief—I would give that up for Callie, to know she'll come out of this Pit alive, even if it means I don't. I would make that sacrifice for her. I would make it for Dad, and El too. For the whole multiverse of people I haven't met but who deserve to live and know love instead of Darkness.

The Shadows loosen their grip on my soul, and Light glows bright and warm. No pain, no swimming vision, no nausea. Just Light building around my heart.

"I humbly ask you to let Callie go." I plead one last time with the creature of Darkness at the heart of the Rognaga. "She's more important to me than any Light Core or victory. I might not be Living Light, but if you accept a promise made in love as truth, then you'll have the answer to anything that remains."

*"Love is the answer to anything that remains."*

Darkness floats away, and tentacles withdraw from me. The feeling that I'm about to be ashed by Shadow fades as Light burns through the entire Pit. Brightness cocoons me, sends me soaring through everything and nothing. It feels free and wild. Unknown, yet known.

And here, in the pure Light of love, I'm alive.

*My stars.* Mom's Light reaches out, holding mine tight. *I'm so thankful you're here.*

*I miss you, Mom.* I miss her with every atom that forms me. But I know this was Queen's last great lie. She told me that in dying, Mom was separated from Light forever. Mom didn't get separated from anything—just the opposite. At long last, she went home.

With a gasp, I open my eyes. My feet are on the ground in the crater. Callie stands before me. Around us, the Seers and El stare. But they aren't staring at me or Callie. They're looking at something else.

In my hand, glowing like a star and humming contentedly, is Ensolorada's Light Core.

"Nate." Callie's eyes widen like she can't believe I'm real. Finally, a smile draws her lips, brighter than the Light Core and stars combined. "You did it!"

*I did it.* I won the Rognaga. I claimed Ensolorada's Light Core. In being willing to sacrifice everything for Callie—my victory, the Light Core, even myself—I was judged worthy as Living Light. But more than that, I freed her from the Shadows. She's here, and I'm here, and all I want to do is hold her and kiss her until neither of us can breathe.

I wish I didn't have an audience for this, but oh well.

"You're okay." I drop the Light Core and cup her face in my hand, hardly able to hear myself speak around the muffled pounding in my ears. It's thunderously loud, and I'm hot and shaky. My legs wobble, and my arm trembles when I wrap it around her.

"Thanks to you." She looks up at me, all the joy in the multiverse shining in her eyes. I never thought Callie would look at me like this. Something deep inside leaps into my throat, and I can't swallow it down. "I thought I told you not to follow me. You didn't stick to the plan."

"I stuck to *my* plan, which was — not exactly a plan." For once, I didn't have one, except to save Callie from the monstrous Darkness in the Pit.

"Look at you, being spontaneous," Callie says with a grin. "I'm rubbing off on you."

We forget the whoops of victory from El and Dad, the lull of the Seers staring in awe, of Heike laughing maniacally for whatever reason Darkness has to laugh in the face of its own defeat. Callie and I exist on another plane, standing in each other's Light.

"It was so dark and cold down there." Callie turns serious and shudders. "I couldn't feel any Light, not even my own. I was so scared … but I knew, as soon as you came for me, I'd be safe."

"Really? How?"

She winds her arms about my neck, softly tracing my cheek to the corner of my mouth and down my chin. "Because once your Light found me, it felt like the whole multiverse inside one person."

I want to tell her that to the fragile Light in my scarred heart and crumbled soul, she *is* the multiverse in one person. But my tongue is thick, and the words fail to come. So I pull her closer still, until the last breath of space between us disappears.

"Callie, can I …"

"Take me on a pizza date? Yes." She takes my face in her hands, pulls me down, and kisses me.

Holy crap, this is real, this is happening. I've wanted it for so long, and now, I don't know how to react. So, logically, I don't. I just stand there like a puckered statue while she presses her soft, perfect lips to mine.

Wait, why am I letting her do all the work? I'm good at this! Ten out of ten! Come to your senses, dweeb! Kiss her back!

I part my lips against hers, gentle and hesitant at first, then stronger, deeper, telling her everything I feel without words. The hammering in my ears gets louder, her breath caressing my cheek in a sigh that makes my knees quake. Everything fits between us—arms, lips, my hand raking back her hair. Light dances until I can't tell where she ends and I begin.

"Hooray! Finally!" Ayla claps enthusiastically. Hooray all you want, Sparky. Just go for it. I know I am.

Suddenly, Callie pulls away, a startled look on her face. Yeesh, was I bad? It was good for me, but if it wasn't a good kiss for her, then—hold on. Something red and wet stains her cheek. She touches it, staring at her fingertips in disbelief.

"Is this blood?"

Why, yes. That would be blood. My blood. Because I'm bleeding.

Blood runs down my face, flowing from my scars before dripping onto my shirt. Which means I'm alive. Not metaphorically, either. A living, breathing, heartbeat kind of alive.

There's no more Darkness inside me. Only Light. The thunderous pounding in my ears is my pulse—I'd forgotten what it felt like. Everything looks bright, shiny, and new, no longer tainted by lingering Shadow. I let it all go in the Pit, finally choosing one power over the other. When only Light remained, so did life.

I'm … me. Just Nate. A Luminaut.

"Congratulations, Nathaniel. My last servant to betray me will be the last to die."

Queen's voice speaks one last time through Heike, and the girl turns her face to the sky. Darkness pours from her mouth like smoke from a wildfire, flying back to the Veil where Queen emerges on top of the zombie-wolf Vredis with her army of Shadowmancers. Through the blurry haze of gathering Darkness, Heike falls to the ground, lifeless. Toran runs to her, screaming her name as chaos erupts all around.

Man, she can't even wait two minutes after I kissed the girl of my dreams, alive and filled with Light, before she attacks. Typical Queen, harshing my vibe, threatening death and pain and ashes.

"I'm so pleased you survived my insect," Queen leers down at me, "because now I have the pleasure of killing you myself."

# CHAPTER 22
# CALLIE

HEIKE FALLS TO THE GROUND as Toran's incomprehensible sobs tear the Shadowy air.

Darkness swirls everywhere, filling the entire Pit.

Earthquakes, lightning, balls of fire, and ice shards rise from the sand, swallowing every inch of the desert along their destructive path.

My feet slip and slide through freezing, ashen mud, and I hold Nate tight as an onslaught of Shadows encircles us, blocking the stars and the last sliver of the moon. It feels like the start of the apocalypse down here.

Maybe it is.

This is happening too fast. One minute, I was trapped in the darkest part of the Pit, terrified of dying. Then there was a flash of brilliant Light, and the Pit was no more. The Darkness in the Rognaga faded until everything was peaceful. Suddenly, I was standing in the crater with Nate. He won. The death maze was defeated, and I knew he'd finally let go of Darkness for good. He was alive and human again. We kissed, because of *course* we kissed. It was a freaking amazing kiss too.

Now Queen is here, and her Darkness threatens to steal my

happiness and Nate's future before it ever gets off the ground.

"No time like the present to try on the big boy Luminaut shorts." Nate launches the largest Light orb I've ever seen him create at Queen. Her zombified Vredis screeches when the blast hits its leg, taking out the joint at the knee. He flashes a cocky grin. "That was most triumphant."

"Don't let it go to your head or anything." As we speak, Queen builds a tidal wave of Darkness at the edge of the Pit, one aimed at me and Nate.

I grasp his uninjured hand so tight my knuckles turn white. It's the first time it's felt truly warm in mine, and the last thing I'll let Queen do is turn it cold again. "She's targeting you because you're hurt and exhausted. I want you to stay with Diver. You'll be safe with him."

"No." I should have expected Toran-level bluntness. Nate preps another Light orb in his right hand, trying to aim it for launch. I blast some Shadowmancers sneaking up on us from behind. "I'm not leaving you to whatever torture Queen wants to put you through."

"She'll ash you if she gets the chance. I won't risk it." He's given so much already, and now he has so much to actually *live* for.

Nate faces me, his lips I just kissed (and very much want to kiss again, as soon as humanly possibly) slightly parted. "It'll take a lot more than a giant zombie dog and a Darkness wave to ash me out. I had to defy time, space, reality, the multiverse, and death itself just to get a date with you."

It's *seriously* a bad time for him to be so kissably romantic.

"Nate!" El and Nemo dodge Shadowmancer tentacles, rushing through the minefield of Darkness while Seers create a storm of fire, lightning, and flying boulders.

"El, Nemo! Over here!" The boy and my little buddy arrive at Nate's side, cowering under the wing of his left arm in the sling. Nate Light blasts any Shadowmancer stupid enough to come within five feet of El.

"Why aren't you in Diver, dingus?" Nate glares at El like a worried big brother.

"Why aren't *you*, dümfo?" El counters. "Richard and I aren't letting you ditch us again."

"This is no place for children." The Richard in question is still half on fire when he joins us. He places the hand that's not inflamed on El's shoulder and looks at Nate with concern. "Both of you should get out of here."

Nate shakes his head. "Not happening, Dad."

"You're injured," Dr. Ormandi counters.

"And you're eighty years old."

"Can we have this argument later?" While Nate stands there chatting with his Dad and El, Darkness fills every last nook and cranny of the crater. "I'm only one person, you know."

"Yep, sorry." Nate's Light blasts are a lot more powerful now that he's fully Luminaut, but only being able to use his right hand slows him down. Every time anything comes near his injured side, he grits his teeth, swears, and has to regroup. We're playing with time, and both Luminauts standing huddled near one another makes us a big target.

"As much as I hate to say this, we need to split up." Our gazes find each other. "She chose to attack because she expects we'll lose easily. We have to do what Queen doesn't expect if we want to escape long enough to regroup and strategize."

"I knew you'd eventually start thinking like me." Nate grins. "Dad, El, and I will draw her toward the center. You go help Serai and Ayla. Toran's not mentally or emotionally present for the assist."

I cast a glance at my Seer, shielding his sister's fallen body with his own while he tries to shake her awake. Serai and Ayla are deflecting as much Darkness as they can, but they need a Luminaut.

"Got it," I say. "I'll call Diver."

"We've got your six," Nate assures me. "El, hold on to this Light Core, and whatever you do, don't let go. Come on, Dad, let's show her what a couple of pissed-off Ormandis can do."

Dr. Ormandi smirks. "With pleasure."

The old man lights himself fully on fire, and he and Nate work to draw the Shadowmancers away. El follows, clutching the Light Core to his chest, and Shadowmancers instantly attack the Light he holds, leaving me in the ashes of their wake. I sprint for the other three Seers, Light blasting as I go.

Just as I predicted, Queen's attention is split between me and the Light Core, and the Darkness wave she's building scatters haphazardly. More chaos means less control on Queen's end, which is exactly what I hoped would happen.

"Callie! Is my Luminaut all right?" Ayla's lightning strikes are way less contained, and electricity sparks in every direction.

"He and Dr. Ormandi are going to distract Queen. I'm helping you guys."

"We're grateful for the assistance." Swear drips down Serai's forehead from the exertion. Handling all those big, heavy rocks and gaping chasms with your powers can't be easy.

"I'm sorry I left the Rognaga without telling you," Ayla says, blowing away creeping Shadowmancers with a strong gust. "I thought you would be angry I went to find Mama after what happened in Cordonanza ..."

Serai scowls very quickly at her daughter before she squishes some Shadowmancers with boulders. "I'm not *that* bad, Ayla."

"You tried to arrest us," I remind her.

Serai shrugs. "You vandalized my house."

"Okay, that's fair." I touch Ayla's shoulder briefly before I get accidentally zapped. "I'm glad you did what you did. We were really up a creek."

"I don't know what creek you're talking about," Ayla says and smiles. "I'm so pleased you and Nate finally kissed! I knew it would happen. I have a sense for these things."

"You definitely called it." Now let's finish deflecting Queen's assault so Nate and I can get back to doing more kissing.

Speaking of Queen …

I survey the scene, assessing the remaining Darkness and how much effort it will take us to make a sizable dent in the Shadows, but she and her monstrous Vredis are nowhere to be seen. Shadowmancers writhe through swirling Darkness and impenetrable Shadow, but Queen herself is gone.

To sneak away while we're distracted instead of facing us head-on? That's not like Queen. She's planning something truly nasty.

*Diver, can you come down and get us? The Rognaga dissolved, and the situation just took a nosedive. We need to bail ASAP.*

*Yes, Luminaut.* I can't hear the rumbling groan of Diver's familiar footsteps over the glass-shattering shrieks of thousands of Shadowmancers, but I know he's coming. His Light grows closer, promising safety is near.

"Okay, Diver's on his way down. We need to get ready to meet him," I announce. "Toran, that includes you."

If Toran hears me, he gives no indication, unaware of the Darkness battle raging around him.

"Heike …" He touches his sister's face, laser-focused on

reviving a girl I'm not sure is revivable. Heike looks all but dead, barely clinging to life as shallow breaths lift her chest.

"Toran, Diver is on his way." I grasp his shoulder. This time, he glances up. I've seen the same sadness in his eyes before—the day Heike vanished into the Shadows on the Hem, seemingly lost forever.

"Don't make me leave Heike." He clings to her frail body all the more tightly as desperation and grief cover his body in cracking shards of ice.

"I won't. But right now, we need your help." I can't lie, a Seer who can control the groundwater beneath the desert, combined with my Light, would take care of a lot of our problems.

"Heike needs help too." Okay, I guess Toran really *can't* see the Darkness turning the crater into Shadowmancer soup.

"Callie, there's too many of them!" Ayla's lightning erratically strikes the Shadows drawing closer, and soon she'll be overwhelmed. Where are Nate and Dr. Ormandi? Weren't they supposed to be distracting the Darkness so it would stay *away* from us, not circle in tighter?

"I'm on it." I blast some Darkness before turning back to Toran. "It's too dangerous to stay down here. Let's go."

"No. You forced me to leave my sister once before. I will go nowhere unless Heike comes too." Toran, my dude—I know it's your favorite thing ever, but it's not a great time to argue with me.

I glance at Heike, my friend through the Hem and beyond. Toran might be a jerk sometimes, but Heike didn't have a choice to be infested by Queen's Darkness. She's innocent, a pawn in Queen's game to weaken her opponents and sow seeds of division before a calculated strike. And if nobody removes the Shadows from her heart, she'll die before we make it back to

Cordonanza.

I press pause on Shadowmancer blasting and place my hand to the girl's chest, channeling Light into her body to fight the Darkness.

"What are you doing?!" Toran shrieks. He tries to tear my hand away, but Light is too bright for him to see. "You'll hurt her! Stop! She'll burn!"

"No, she won't." More Light, and still Heike doesn't stir. I make one last attempt to ignite the Light around her heart before and my power fades, settling into her fragile body. *Please wake up, Heike.*

"You've done well, Callie." Serai covers Heike's body in a soft dirt mound until only her face remains for breathing. Toran panics, ice piercing the earth around him.

"What are you doing? She can't breathe!"

"She can. I assure you, this is for her protection. The earth will allow Callie's Light to do its work, and make it difficult for Shadows to reach her." Serai gives Toran a sharp look filled with suspicion and fury. "I'm not doing this for you. We'll deal with your actions later."

*Diver, tell Nate to come to us. I need his help.*

Instead of Diver, Nate's reply answers through my mech's Light. *Yeah, so, uh, splitting up may not have been the best call.*

Fear sinks deep into my chest like a hooked barb pulling my heart into my throat. What the crap does he mean? *Where are you? What happened?*

There's no reply. Please let him be busy fighting and nothing more.

"Do you really think your powers over the child can defeat my Darkness?" Queen snarls at Serai. "I had many years of experience with Earth Manipulators, I know how weak you are."

The Prime Shadowmancer couldn't have reappeared at a worse time. Behind my shoulder, she emerges from the Veil on her Vredis, sneering with so much malevolent glee it's like she's already won. I Light blast her, but Queen easily dodges, disappearing beyond the Veil and reappearing in front of us a split second later.

*Nate, please! I need you!*

"Are you looking for Nathaniel and the old Fire Manipulator?" Queen's eyes burrow into me like she can uproot my deepest fear with a single stare. "Here they are."

From out of the Darkness, Queen draws three figures tied up by twisting Shadows: Nate, Dr. Ormandi, and El, valiantly clutching the Light Core. They're alive—for now—but with a snap of her fingers they'll be ash, and Ensolorada's Light Core will be Queen's to destroy.

"Callie, I'm sorry." Darkness licks Nate's skin when he speaks. "I tried to fight her, but—"

"You're a child, playing games meant for the powerful and wise." Queen whirls on her former servant with a snarl so fierce I half-expect her to snap him in two. "I never should have trusted you, or anyone, for that matter."

Queen's vitriol as she regards Nate might look like well-placed fury, but I'm starting to see through her mask. Reading between the lines, everything she said—everything she's ever done—betrays what I suspect might be her weakness: her old Seer.

As heartless as Queen makes herself out to be, I know for a fact Shadowmancers feel emotion. Nate is proof. And being betrayed by your best friend—her sister, as Elara called Saeli in Diver's memory—has to hurt. All she knows to do is hurt me the same way she's been hurt, but I have to be smarter. I have to turn this tide. Queen doesn't notice me, she's too busy glaring daggers at Nate. And she doesn't see Diver coming down the crater's side either.

*Can your Prism reflect Light blasts, buddy? Amplify it to be more powerful?*

You may try, Luminaut.

Okay, let's try.

I rise into the air with my Light, above Queen and her Darkness, and throw an absolutely enormous Light blast at Diver's Prism in the Crow's Nest. The crystal catches the Light as he approaches, amplifies it, and sends my power shining throughout the crater. Shadowmancers and Darkness tentacles disintegrate. The chains around Nate, his dad, and El disappear. Queen cries out in shock and slips beyond the Veil just in time. Light fades under my heart as the last Shadows flee, and peace settles over the scene.

"Nate!" I rush toward him. "Are you all right?"

"Whatever you do, don't get distracted." He takes my outstretched hand and grips it tight. "She'll be back."

"Diver's almost here." I spy my mech lumbering through the crater. "El, you're amazing. Keep holding on to that Core, okay?"

"You got it." El grins, and Nemo emerges from his collar, shaking as he peers around for signs of Shadows. "You better stay hidden," El advises, and Nemo nods, more than happy to disappear again.

"T-toran?" Heike's whisper is faint, little more than a sigh. "What happened to me? Where are we?"

"Heike!" Toran digs the earth mound away from his sister with tears in his eyes. "I was so scared I lost you!" He looks at me, gratitude and amazement meeting in his gaze. "You … you saved her."

"Of course I did. She's my friend." Looks like Heike's going to be okay, but we won't, if we don't move. "Come on, everyone, let's get into Diver, before—"

Darkness rips the air, surrounding us before we can counterattack. Shadowy chains slip around me and every one of my companions, holding us tight. Shadowmancers emerge next, screeching and hissing to announce the arrival of their leader, the Queen Beyond the Stars, who stares at us all with a mixture of triumph and loathing.

"This is getting tiresome, isn't it?" Queen surveys her prisoners, shaking her head. "Why do you insist on making things difficult?"

The world goes dark, Shadow closes in, and the Light under my heart cries out as Darkness threatens to take my power—and life—for good.

# CHAPTER 23
# CALLIE

"YOU SEEM TO BE rather tied up, Calliope. Whatever could have happened?" Queen rides atop her zombified Vredis, shambling through the Darkness. "In a bit of a bind, aren't we?"

She wants something, otherwise she'd have ashed us already. Instead, she's making jokes about being tied up, suspended by the Darkness she controls—Darkness that makes no move to cause harm.

What game is Queen playing? I catch Nate's eye, and an imperceptible nod tips his chin. *Keep her talking. Buy us time to figure this out.*

"I'll give you one chance to leave us alone and go back to the Shadow Plain." I try to sound as confident and in control as Queen. "If not, I promise you'll regret hurting my friends."

"Regret? You don't yet know the meaning of that word." Queen laughs, low and menacing. "Perhaps you're inviting me to show you, is that it?"

If she wanted me to regret something, she'd kill us—Nate first, then El for the Light Core, and then everyone else. Queen's got an agenda here. But what?

It's a risk, pushing this next button. I'm going to try it anyway.

"Just like Saeli showed you what regret is, right?" At the mention of her old Seer's name, Queen's face shifts ever so slightly—little more than a twitch near her eye, but enough to see I guessed her trigger correctly. "Don't tell me I touched a nerve, Elara." Another twitch, and I smirk. "I know your Luminaut name—not what the egotistical Shadowmancer calls herself in the Shadows. You're Ictaran, aren't you? Do you miss your home world? How about Diver, do you miss him too? He was your mech once, wasn't he?"

"Your tongue is easily ashed." Queen's enraged, but not furious enough to slip and reveal her endgame. Rats. Taunting didn't work, so maybe negotiating will.

"But you haven't ashed me. Why?" Our Shadowy bindings are close enough to intimidate, but not to kill. "Tell me what you want because I know you want something. Maybe we can make a mutually beneficial exchange."

"I'm tired of your games." But she's not tired. She can do this all day. "I've come for the Light Core."

"Why put on such a show for one measly Light Core? Because you think I need all five to beat you?" I raise an eyebrow when Queen curls her lip. Bingo. "You don't really want to destroy me, not until you've got all five Cores—and you're assuming I'll agree to find the last one for you if you can pinpoint the thing I'd never risk losing. That's a dangerous bet."

Dr. Ormandi glares and barks a warning *"ahem."* Serai narrows her flinty eyes. Did I cross a bridge too far? Oops. Sorry, adults.

Nate looks forward, unblinking, and doesn't dare speak. Queen would never negotiate with her former servant, and he knows it. I'm the only one with a shot to strike a deal, and I have to make it count.

"Do you like danger? I do too." Queen's Darkness shrieks its impatience, and her Vredis paws at the ground viciously. "You seem to be in a wagering mood. What would you be willing to bet for a Light Core? Your Seer friends?"

Darkness curls even tighter around Ayla, Serai, Dr. Ormandi, and Toran, close enough to ash the edges of their clothes and flake off bits of exposed skin. Their faces contort in agony, but nobody can move an inch.

"Mama! Help!" Ayla is completely terrorized. Wind rushes, pelting us with ash and dust.

"Whatever you do, Ayla, don't move," Serai calls to her daughter, equally afraid.

"Let them go!" I shout. "Your fight isn't with a bunch of Seers, it's with me."

"The Seers aren't enough, hmmm?" A vicious smile lifts Queen's thin lips. "What about the children? Are you willing to wager their lives?" Queen tightens her stranglehold on Heike and El next. El bravely grips the Light Core, his face drawn but determined. Heike is helpless.

"Sister, no!" Toran can't do anything to prevent Darkness from worming into the earth around Heike. Any time he moves, the Shadows slice into him, leaving ash marks all along his arms. "Don't harm her, I'll do anything! Please!"

"Oh, you've done more than enough, Toran Rykjiersen." Queen speaks directly to Toran, who pales like a ghost when face to face with Queen's horror. "It was so easy to manipulate you into believing every word I put in her mouth. All I had to do was say exactly what you wanted to hear, and you fell right into my trap. Perhaps I should make my arrangement with her permanent."

"I—I can't—please—" For the first time since I met him, Toran has no words. Queen laughs cruelly.

"You think you're incredibly clever. All you are is a scared little boy, grasping for control." Queen leers over Toran. Tentacles of Shadow reflect in his horrified eyes. "I ought to thank you for being so predictable. Anger makes for the best kind of fool—and you're especially foolish."

Toran looks as shocked as if he'd been slapped across the face. His mouth opens and closes like a stunned goldfish flung from its bowl, gasping against the air. The ice spikes piercing the desert melt into puddles at his feet.

"Toran is angry because of what you did to his sister." I draw Queen's attention away.

"Correct. He is angry because his greatest fault is his most obvious one. But your weakness lies elsewhere." A wicked glow sparks Queen's blood-red irises. "Perhaps it's Nathaniel? Your last fellow Luminaut in the multiverse. Will you wager on him?"

Queen's Shadows wrap tight around Nate. He grits his teeth when tentacles of Darkness graze his broken arm and caress his scars with malice. The blood on his face becomes ash, falling onto the nape of his neck.

"*No!*"

I scream, my heart leaping into my throat as power explodes out of me, uncontrolled in my fear. Light flies through the Darkness, breaking my restraints, blasting Shadows in a dance of desperation, but nothing I do matters. With the fourth Light Core activated, Queen is almost returned to her multiverse-shattering power. She could kill everyone with a snap of her fingers, and I'd be helpless to stop it.

"I must admit, I'm somewhat impressed." Queen leans on the Vredis's head, resting her elbow between its ears as she watches me panic and scream. "You know your Light isn't strong enough to save all your friends. Some would die, and you would be forced to choose who. Still, I believe you'd try. Your spirit is not yet broken."

She pauses, holding up her hand, and Darkness stills. I pant around gasps, trying to anticipate her next move. It's a still-life of a stand-off, both of us frozen in time.

"Perhaps a larger wager is needed." Queen is the first to break the silence. "Come, Calliope. Let's have a private discussion."

Shadows latch on to the base of my spine, and I descend deep into the Shadow Plain.

Surrounding me are hordes of Queen's Shadowmancer minions. Millions of red-eyed, snarling monsters, all of them waiting to destroy people, cities, and whole worlds at her command. It's enough to make me physically ill. There's no way I can fight these Shadowmancers alone, and even if I tried, Queen would only make more.

"Welcome to the Shadow Plain, Calliope." Queen appears before me, suspended in the Darkness. "Although, you've been here before." Her hair floats around her face when she surveys her queendom. "Funny you'd mention my old Seer, because she helped me build this. She cut so deep into the earth we left the multiverse entirely. But my plans were always grander than hers. You see how vast it is? How eternal the Darkness? That is *my* handiwork." She locks her hypnotic, black-and-red eyes onto me and tilts her chin. "For all your power, what can you say you've created? Nothing but a mess, and friends who may become ash, should I choose to end them."

A chill like ice mixed with poison flows through my veins instead of warm, life-giving blood. I'm cold. So cold. My teeth chatter and my bones quake. "Why did you force me to come here? What do you want from me?"

"I want to offer you a choice. The ultimate wager." In the distance, just beyond the sea of Darkness populated by her horrors, a gauzy, curtain-like barrier appears. I know it immediately—the Veil. It's how Nate came and went between here and the human world, how he spied on her orders, planning with her how to steal Earth's Light Core. And now, I'm on the other side.

An invisible force pushes me to the edge, and I look through the Shadows at—home.

Verona Beach lies before me, the vibrant colors slightly grayed but no less familiar. Tourists mingle with locals on the beach, the haze of sunset casting a golden sheen. Hungry gulls and brightly patterned kites fly overhead, and the pier reaches for the endless blue horizon. I smell churro carts, taco trucks, oak-pit barbecues, and my mouth waters for a taste. My heart skips when I see Will straddling his shortboard in all his messy-haired, puppy-eyed Will-ness, chatting with … Emily Sawyer? Yes, it's Em! She surfs now? Did Will teach her? They smile and laugh together, and I swell higher than the waves with happiness when he leans over to give her a quick kiss.

Will and Em! Oh my gosh, Will and Em! I seriously ship this so hard. Unbelievable joy for my friend burns through the Shadowy cold as I watch him paddle to the head of the surfer lineup and catch a wave. He rides it a few wobbly yards and wipes out, but Em cheers for him anyway. She's so proud she glows.

"Oh, Will. I'm so happy for you." I wish I could hug him, and hug Em too. The Veil moves away from the beach to a place entirely different but no less familiar.

"Mom. Dad."

My parents are so close I feel like I'm sitting at the kitchen table with Dad while he sips his cold coffee. Mom bends over the counter, giving directions to a perpetually bored Ryan in server garb while scribbling in her notebook where she keeps the catering menus for each summer wedding. The scent of chili in the slow cooker mixes with Tyler's bag of spicy nacho chips. He looks at least two inches taller despite sitting down, but that's nothing compared to Olivia. She's grown into a little girl, explaining the difference between a Tyrannosaurus Rex and a velociraptor to Dad. Jase, my older brother and sometime-nemesis, saunters in from the basement and asks Mom about ironing his slacks and red dress shirt before they head out to set up service.

My family, going about a typical Saturday. Love for them builds a lump in my throat, and a weight lifts from my body until I'm lighter than I've been since I Dove away from home. My brothers and sister, my parents, all of them acting … normal. They're safe. The reality of Darkness and the horror of its chaos never touched them.

But maybe it could all go sideways. Queen's letting me see them once more before she takes them away. Everyone I love gone in an instant, depending on what I say or do next.

"Why are you showing me this?" I swallow my raw emotions and face Queen, who smiles like a snake. "Are you going to hurt them?"

"Hurt them?" Queen shakes her head, her hair moving with her. "I don't desire to hurt anyone, only to bring them peace. To free them from suffering and pain caused by Light."

"In other words, you're going to ash them." I gag, horrified. My parents, my siblings, my friends and the beachgoers—all of them ashes and dust in a world so deadened with Darkness it would never regrow.

"I know you're skeptical of my plan for the multiverse and would prefer I *didn't* bestow my peace upon your family and friends," Queen replies. "So, I'll leave them alone. I'll also free your Seer friends, the children, and even my former little one, Nathaniel. They'll exist and suffer freely until their natural human deaths. If ..."

"If I give you the Light Cores." The tethers to her prison — she wants them destroyed. In giving them to her, I'll lose the multiverse to the stronghold of Darkness.

"That's an excellent place to start." Queen grins with all the cool confidence of a cobra about to devour a cornered, defenseless mouse. "But I require more."

What else is there besides the Light Cores?

Oh ... wait.

"You also want me." More than drawing me into the Shadow Plain to negotiate terms, she brought me here to see if I can survive in the Darkness, so I can watch while she tears the multiverse apart.

*This* was her plan all along.

"Five Light Cores and a Luminaut in exchange for the pitiful human lives of those you care for most." Queen spreads her hands wide. "A fair trade, don't you agree?"

"And what about Nate?" I make sure to reveal none of the feelings I have for him. She can't know or she'd kill him. "He's a Luminaut too."

"Nathaniel has already betrayed his greatest weakness, and it's you." Queen's expression turns callous and cruel. "He will do anything to save you from the Shadow Plain, but he's not strong enough to defeat me."

There it is, the key to clinching victory. All Queen sees when she looks at Nate is someone lesser who betrayed her, same as

Saeli—a Shadowmancer she once trusted who returned to Light. She assumes he's a nonissue, too weak to pose a threat, but Nate and I know how to destroy the Shadow Plain. Queen doesn't.

It's a misjudgment we can use to plan a counterattack.

"I still haven't found the fifth Light Core." I stall for an excuse to escape. "Nate can't do it. He has no World Diver. Let me go back to Diver and Toran, and we'll hunt it down. There are three Cores at Cordonanza's Hall of Guardians too. I can't get them from inside the Shadow Plain."

"I'm sorry to say this, but I don't trust you." Queen doesn't look the least bit sorry. In fact, she saw this coming. "My Seer betrayed me. My little one, Nathaniel, betrayed me. All my servants were unworthy. You think a Luminaut is more worthy of my trust than those I called into Darkness?"

"I'm not your servant." I keep my face earnest, open, but more importantly, revealing nothing that's true. "And I never asked to be a Luminaut. I thought finding the Light Cores would keep everyone I love safe, but their safety is exactly what you're offering me. I've never wavered in my quest to protect them. I never will."

Queen stares deep into my eyes, searching for lies, anything she can exploit. But I'm not lying—not exactly. I'm just omitting certain facts.

"You have three days to find the last Light Core with your World Diver and Seer," Queen says, laying out her final offer.

Mental fist-bump, self! I can totally Dive across the multiverse and plan a heist in three days, especially if I've got Nate, all four Seers, and El, Nemo, and Diver on my side.

"Three days is more than fair," I agree.

"If you don't believe I know how long three human days are in the Shadow Plain," Queen adds darkly, "I assure you, I know more than you think. I have many watchers at the Veil, ready to keep you on track."

Thousands of Shadowmancers rise behind her to emphasize her point. Yep, nice Darkness flex, I got it. Shadowmancers will attack if I veer off course.

"Toran, Diver, and I will find the last Light Core," I promise. "And I'll return to the old Rognaga Pit to give you the Cores and myself in three days."

"I knew you could be reasoned with if I reminded you what was at stake." The Veil shifts, and we're back to Ensolorada. All my friends restrained by Darkness appear beyond the gauzy curtain as though no time passed at all. "And just to make sure you know the seriousness of the situation …"

With a snap of her fingers, Queen draws Heike into the Shadow Plain. She's disoriented and weak, but when she realizes where she is, her eyes go wide with fear. Shadows encircle her like chains, and she couldn't move even if she tried.

"What happened? Where is Toran?" She catches sight of Queen, blood draining from her face. "No. Not you again. No, please! Let me go!" Heike sees me and cries like an animal being taken to slaughter. "Callie, help me! Make her let me go!"

"This was *not* part of our deal." I whirl on Queen. "Release her. This is about me and you. Haven't you tortured Heike enough?"

"She's been so useful to me already, I couldn't possibly let her be free just yet." Queen pats Heike's hair and the girl sobs, choking on tears. "Nobody leaves my Shadow Plain without collateral. Saving your Seer's beloved sister ought to keep both of you focused on completing my task, don't you think?"

"Hurt her and the deal is off." If I can't get Queen to let Heike go, the least I can do is make sure she's unharmed.

"Never fear, she won't become a Shadowmancer yet." Queen's smile could freeze even the deepest Arctic glacier. "Not for three more days."

That absolute monster.

"Hurry, Calliope." An invisible force pushes me to the edge of the Veil, and Queen's last warning rings like a death knell behind me. "Time is slipping away."

The Veil spits me out onto a field of ashy mud, and the Darkness in the Rognaga disappears. The Seers are free, El is free, and the Light Core of Ensolorada remains whole. Nate's free, too.

Without a word, I run to him and brush the ashes off his neck and face before I throw my arms around him. Nate's grip on my waist is a little too tight, but I don't care. I want him to hold me until the chill of the Shadows fades away, but there's not enough time. The clock is ticking.

"What happened?" Dr. Ormandi immediately descends with questions. "What did she make you promise? I hope you weren't foolish enough to agree."

Yeah, about that …

"My life for yours. Everyone's, actually. And all the Light Cores. Otherwise she's going to ash everybody standing here and everyone in Verona Beach. Oh, and she'll turn Heike into a Shadowmancer."

"What?" Toran looks ready to pass out when he hears his sister's name and "turned into a Shadowmancer" uttered in the same sentence. "I will not let that happen."

"Neither will I," I say. "Which is why you and I have to go get the last Light Core in the multiverse, and Nate needs to find the ones Manu stole in Cordonanza. And hopefully get his injuries treated first."

"I won't let her take you." Nate's eyes flash. "Everything I've done has been to protect you. Don't let her defeat you like this."

"You think I'd have let her take you instead?" I say. "This is the best chance we have."

*Calliope, I'm watching you …*

Screw you, Queen. *Believe me, I know you're watching.*

Before Nate argues with me about the deal I negotiated with Queen, a sinister laugh rings in my ears, one that has nothing to do with Queen or her army of Shadowmancers.

Manu Carosti steps out of a passenger transport that just landed with four other men and women, plus a whole mess of guards with blasters and yellow energy shields.

# CHAPTER 24
# TORAN

HEIKE WAS JUST HERE. She was lying on the earth at my side, surrounded by ropes of Darkness, but she was alive and well enough to recover if The Queen Beyond the Stars hadn't pulled her into the Shadows. I never dreamed she would steal Heike again or point out my every flaw as clearly as Morning Drums breaking the Mist.

My sister is lost once more to Shadows. And I'm laid bare.

Manu Carosti stomps carelessly over the earthen mound where my sister once lay, his yellow-amber eyes locked on Serai and the Light Core in Elion's hands. There are people with him—guards and other City Guardians, if their manner of dress is any indication. One of the women holds the hem of her fine overcoat up around her ankles, glaring at the mud and ashes as though they were placed purposely to offend her.

Those ashes could easily have been Heike. Could have been me. But I'm here and she's not. My sister is gone to a place I can't follow.

"What is he doing here?" Callie's face falls in dismay when Manu approaches, triumph flashing in his eyes.

Callie is the only reason Heike is alive. She's the only reason any of us are alive, having negotiated our survival with her own life. Without Callie, I'll never find out how to save my sister — even if it means going into the Darkness myself.

But because of me, my one last hope is about to be robbed of her Light powers forever.

"Manu." I reach for him when he passes, catching his jacket hem. "My sister is alive. She was just here and was taken. I need to renegotiate our terms or else — "

"Let go of me, boy." Manu snarls, jumping out of my grasp. "You've got ashes all over you. Disgusting." He walks past as though I don't exist except to annoy him and make him dirty.

What happened? Why is Manu behaving as if we're strangers? I led Callie and Nate to the Rognaga, just like he asked. They found Ensolorada's Light Core for his power extractor. The disgusting state of my clothes and skin are all due to protecting the Light Core from Darkness. How can he behave as though he doesn't know me?

He was supposed to help me once I helped him. We had a deal.

"Didn't I tell you Serai Eradah sent those teenagers to find the Light Core in the old Rognaga? All to prevent me from accessing it for my extractor." Manu points at Serai, his finger sharper than a Volorad pike. "She'll do anything to keep Cordonanza in crisis, even seek the help of a dangerous Luminaut, all for her own political gain. This is treason of the highest order!"

"Serai didn't send us to find the Light Core," Callie's protests.

"Yeah, she actually tried just about everything to prevent us from going after it," Nate adds. "Lots of vines were involved. Not fun."

"The two young people went into the labyrinth of their own free will. They were led there by Toran Rykjiersen, using a map he *somehow* managed to obtain from you. I had no part in it." Serai faces her opponent, shielding Ayla with her outstretched arms and daring Manu to contradict her. "Be careful what you accuse me of doing because I have alibis and witnesses."

"Alibis? You mean the Luminaut, Callie James? We all know Luminauts are *so* trustworthy." Manu smirks with triumphant cruelty. "This girl arrived in the World Diver standing before you, the one Mariasol Zaira stole sixty years ago. Does it not stand to reason the girl was sent here by her predecessor to finish the traitorous mission she abandoned?"

"My wife is dead, you blithering idiot!" Richard's dark eyes flare with anger, and Light flashes in Nate's hand. Manu's eyes go wide with fear at the sight of such power.

"Watch what you say about my mom."

"*Two* Luminauts?" Manu smiles like he couldn't have planned Nate's reveal any better himself. "And one of them Mariasol Zaira's son?" He spins on his heel, facing the politicians. "Nothing they say can be believed. We all remember what Mariasol did, the active warrant still out for her arrest. Like mother, like son. Traitors to the last."

Serai's brown cheeks draw tight as the politicians buzz with hissed whispers and suspicious looks.

"Next time you feel like opening your impulsive mouths," she says to the Ormandis, "please don't."

I've never agreed with Serai until now.

"Tell me, Manu, what brings you this far out into the desert?" Serai crosses her arms. "How did you know we would be here? You didn't order a tracking beacon placed on my comm without my knowledge, did you?"

More fitful whispers from the group of politicians, but Manu seems prepared.

"Why track your comm when I have friends in the right places, ones who tell me everything I need to know? Friends like your very informative houseguest, Toran Rykjiersen." Manu nods at me, suddenly remembering I exist.

He remembers me now? Why not before? Am I just another political maneuver to be disposed of when I'm no longer useful?

Of course I am. Why couldn't I see the truth before? I'm as destructively foolish as the Queen Beyond the Stars said I am. Richard, Nate, Elion, and Serai all stare in silent disappointment and rage. Callie gasps, and Ayla's eyes widen. Guilt overwhelms me, adding to the heavy weight of Heike's loss.

"Callie, I'm sorry, I—"

"I knew you were lying about the map! And after all we went through to find it, you were planning to steal the Light Core for Manu Carosti the whole time?" Callie's hands blaze with Light until it matches her fury. "You two-faced, son of a—ugh, I hate you, Toran!"

She *hates* me. I didn't know Callie knew how to hate. Even at his worst, she didn't hate Nate, but I'm beyond reproach and forgiveness. My stomach twists so hard it burns all the way up my throat, and shame sinks down to my darkest depths.

Callie and her Light were never the enemies to fear. It's so clear now. She may hate me, but she will never loathe me as much as I do myself at this moment.

"Toran, is it true?" I can't look at Ayla. More than Callie's hatred, hearing Ayla's heart break with every word is more painful than I imagined. I betrayed her in every way. When I gather enough strength to look up, the beautiful sparkle leaves her eyes.

Wasn't I the one who so proudly announced I don't need friends? Ayla was little more than a means to an end—until she wasn't. Only now, I've realized my many errors too late.

"Manu," I say, "let them go. They didn't do anything—"

Manu ignores me as though I'm little more than an insect flying about his ears, an irritation he can swat away. Instead of acknowledging me, he turns to the four politicians, clicking his tongue and shaking his head sadly.

"As you can see, Serai conspired with dangerous Luminauts and Seers and plotted with them to steal this Light Core—the last one I need for my extractor. Serai cares nothing for Cordonanza, she only cares about advancing her agenda to rebuild the failing solar coils. For putting our city at risk, and for endangering the people with the presence of Luminauts, she should be arrested. These traitors must stand trial."

The guards circle in to arrest us—all of us, myself included. Me? I'm not a traitor, I helped Manu. The scope of his betrayal clarifies instantly.

"If anybody conspired with anyone," I announce, heat flushing my face as an angry hum fills my ears, "you conspired with me. You gave me the Rognaga map. You told me to bring you the Light Core no matter the cost. But your power extractor won't even work!"

"Is that true?" The female politician holding her overcoat looks between me and Manu, unsure who to believe. "Did you turn against your fellow Guardian to conspire with the boy?"

I stare at Manu, daring him to contradict me. But he fixes me with a look of pure disdain and draws his comm from his pocket. What is he doing?

"The boy is delusional. *He* was the one who suggested conspiracy to *me*, willing to do anything to kill the Luminaut who murdered his sister."

Manu turns to the politicians, playing a heavily edited

transmission he recorded of our first conversation—the one that makes me look guilty of everything he accuses but leaves out his part of the plot. Forest spare me, he recorded everything. That filthy dramora spawn!

"Who will you believe, Guardian Bereda?" Manu asks. "Me or him?"

Nothing I say will be believed by anyone. I have doomed myself, my sister, and everyone else to Darkness.

I never should have trusted Manu, but I was too blinded by fear and anger to see. Now the friends who might have stood at my side hate me to the core. And it's all my fault.

"You treacherous rock serpents." Vines fly from Serai's wrists toward Manu and me before she catches herself. The vines retreat quickly. "So help me, I will—"

"No need for violence. I think we've seen enough." The oldest man in the group waves his hand through the air. "Guardian Eradah, you and your companions are under arrest for conspiracy. Manu, begin construction on the power extractor. We'll hold a formal trial at tomorrow evening's forum."

"Yes, Guardian Xereia." Manu's smile is all triumph. He faces the guards he brought to accompany his party. "Make sure the Luminauts and Seers are placed in bronze cuffs, and seize the fourth Light Core."

Armed guards rush forward. Elion shrieks and kicks when they grab him tight, calling them all stupid dümfos. Callie and Nate attempt to use Light in self-defense, but both are so tired from their previous battles that the guards tackle them to the ground before either can form a blast, applying bronze cuffs that cover their whole hands. Richard and Serai are just as easily overpowered, evidence of exhaustion and defeat etched all over their worn, wrinkled faces.

One of the guards hands Manu Ensolorada's Light Core, and he grins, self-satisfied and smug. I betrayed every friend and ally I possessed to find it for him. And now I'm the one betrayed — the biggest fool of all.

I can't let this happen. I have to fight back, for Heike's sake. There will be no hope of saving her before she becomes a Shadowmancer, and no hope of anything exists for me if she's lost.

"Diver, now!" Callie cries, and at the exact same moment, I draw up water from beneath the desert, freezing the feet of half the guards and several politicians, including Manu, on the sand.

The World Diver steps into the fray, scattering the remaining guards as they flee from his sweeping hands. A few guards blast themselves out of their ice casings, aiming their weapons at Callie. One shot hits its mark at her hip, and she crumbles to the ground before passing out. The World Diver ceases his attack with Callie injured, and Nate shouts and curses as the remaining guards drag him into the transport.

I don't have cuffs on my hands. Neither does Ayla, but the guards are moving in rapidly.

"Ayla, run!"

Together we sprint as far as we can up the side of the crater, but without Serai to move the steep rock walls into easily climbed footholds, we slip and slide. The remaining guards free themselves from ice and give chase, blasters drawn.

"Diver, go! Go now!" Nate's voice from inside the transport is barely audible over my heartbeat in my ears. Soon the guards will be close enough to fire on us.

The World Diver lumbers toward me and Ayla. With his long strides, he outpaces the guards and scoops us up in his hands as blaster fire opens upon him. Such weapons are useless against a giant bronze mech, and Ayla and I take refuge on the Diver's shoulder as he climbs easily out of the crater, leaving the guards and politicians behind.

Transports rise into the air, taking everyone back to Cordonanza. I suppose Manu doesn't care that I escaped, or Ayla, for that matter. He has his Light Core, and Serai and the Luminauts are arrested. What harm could I possibly cause? I've proven completely incapable of retaliation and too stupid to counteract his schemes.

And yet, if I don't prove him wrong, Heike will succumb to a fate worse than I could ever imagine.

"Ayla, we must follow them," I say. "We have to free Callie and Nate, or else—"

A fierce gust blows me off Diver's shoulder, and I plummet, halting a hairsbreadth from the sand. Ayla holds me suspended, unable to move breathe, as she descends on a breeze. Her Seer's Eye flashes like the terrible lightning she uses to electrocute me.

"Ayla!" I cry over the agony of white fire coursing through my limbs. She ignores me as lightning bolts extend from every finger into my body. "P-p-please!"

"Everyone I care about—my best friend, my Luminaut, my mother—were taken from me because of you." Ayla zaps me harder, lightning intensifying until my brain swims and black-and-white spots explode in my eyes. "You pretended to be my friend, but it was all a lie so you could plot and scheme with Manu Carosti. Are you happy, Toran? Did you get everything you wanted?"

Consciousness fades until all that exists is pain, electrifying my insides and turning them to soup—until suddenly the pain is gone. My cheek rests in the desert sand, and so does my shuddering chest. My heartbeat slows, and I crawl to my knees, gasping air and shaking my head to clear my vision. Over my shoulder, a soft sound reaches my ears.

Ayla cries, hugging her middle tight. Tears flow freely down her cheeks before falling onto the sand, the picture of pure misery. Seeing her this way is even more painful than being electrocuted.

"Hurting you won't help." She can hardly speak over her sobs. "It never helps. But sometimes I wish it did."

"Ayla, I'm sorry." On trembling legs I stand and face her. "I made a huge mistake, but I want to make it right."

"You're sorry far too late," Ayla replies bitterly. "Do you know what will happen to them if they're convicted of conspiracy against Cordonanza? The punishment is a traitor's death." She sobs again, a wail tearing from her lips. It stabs my heart like a hot knife. "Why did you do it, Toran? Why?"

"Manu promised to eradicate Callie's Light powers so they could never harm Heike or anyone else ever again." It never occurred to me he meant to do so by killing her, but looking back, I realize that's exactly what he meant all along.

"And how, exactly, do you think he planned to do that?" Ayla's terse question reiterates my foolishness.

"I was wrong." My chin dips onto my chest. "I blamed Callie for Heike falling into Shadow, but it wasn't her fault. Her Light saved my sister from certain death. But now, because of me, the Queen Beyond the Stars will win."

The entire multiverse—Tremurheim and beyond—will be ashes because of my choices. If I could trade places with Heike and subject myself to torture and punishment in her stead, I would gladly do it. I deserve to be the one turned to ash in the Shadow Plain.

"She hasn't won yet. Neither has Manu." Ayla's voice shakes, but remains resolute. Uncertainty and determination meet in her eyes, and she wipes the tears away, sniffing back sorrow. "There's still the fifth Light Core."

"It's a whole multiverse away," I remind her, "and we're two Seers. We can't Dive to find it. It's hopeless."

"Nobody is ever without hope," Ayla says firmly. "Manu's argument against Mama is that she wanted Ensolorada's Light Core for herself, to harm Cordonanza by preventing him from building his power extractor. But Mama doesn't need Ensolorada's Light Core because she already has one — Aureloria's."

"Aureloria?" I recall the name of that world from the Hall of Machines. An ancient Fire Manipulator from Aureloria stood on a pedestal there. "The fifth world in the multiverse?"

"The fifth world with a Light Core tether," Ayla corrects me.

"How in Lands Beyond does Serai have Aureloria's Light Core? And where?" Nothing Ayla says makes sense.

"Mama has Aureloria's Light Core because it came here with me." She takes a deep breath and squares her shoulders, facing me in full truth. "I'm not Ensoloradan. I'm from Aureloria, and the fifth Light Core is still attached to its original earth tether at Mama's estate in Oasis III."

Lands Beyond, the fifth Light Core has been in Ensolorada this entire time! Ayla's strange slips about her past, her near-admissions regarding her origins and home that made her catch herself in fear … it all makes sense. She's Aurelorian, and she and Serai have been hiding a Light Core in plain sight. Serai isn't just protecting Ayla. She's protecting the whole multiverse, should the Light Core fall into the wrong hands. Manu's hands, specifically.

"If we can get the fifth Core, we'll bring it to the trial and show the other Guardians that Mama never conspired to steal a Light

Core from the Rognaga because she didn't need to in the first place." Ayla's skirt billows behind her, flapping excitedly when she paces. "It will prove Manu lied about Mama's intentions and cast doubt on his testimony. The Guardians will be forced to acquit everyone."

I have many, *many* questions for Ayla, Aureloria, the fifth Light Core, and everything in between, but the most immediate one blurts from my lips. "How are we going to get across the desert to Oasis III before sunset? On foot? Will you blow us on the wind like you blew yourself home to Cordonanza?"

There's a loud groan when the World Diver bends at the hip, extending his palm for me and Ayla. Her eyes sparkle at the sight, and she grins.

"I believe Diver will take us!"

"How? World Divers only obey the command of a Luminaut." Perhaps Ayla keeps forgetting we're Seers, although it seems a strange time not to remember how helpless we are without our Luminauts, who were just arrested.

"And the command Callie gave the World Diver when she entered the Rognaga was to listen and obey us." Ayla pats the mech's rusty finger. "Nate told him to come after us and save us from the guards. He'll do as we say, as long as our Luminauts are alive." Ayla sits on the World Diver's palm, her skirt fluffing out around her. "Diver, please set me on your shoulder."

Shockingly, the World Diver lifts Ayla onto his shoulder. She claps her hands and steps off the mech's hand, giving his head a fond pat.

Now is as good a time as any to test whether Diver will listen to me too. I clear my throat, feeling awkward. "Diver, pick me up. Please."

The mech hesitates. His anger at me is palpable, and even

though I cannot hear his voice the way Callie can, I'm sure he's giving me a piece of his mind. At last, he lowers his hand, and I'm lifted to his shoulder to join Ayla.

"Do you know the way to Oasis III?" I ask.

"As long as you have your comm, I can find it," Ayla answers. A surge of something like hope fills my downtrodden soul. I actually smile when I pull my comm from my pocket and hand it to her.

"Lead the way."

"I shall." She takes my comm, then turns on her heel, scowling at me over her slim shoulder. "Don't smile at me. We are no longer friends. I'm simply working with you so everyone I care about isn't killed as a result of your scheme."

Her willingness to help me free Callie and rescue Heike is more mercy than I expected to receive. "I understand."

I follow Ayla into the Crow's Nest, hoping we can accomplish our task before Manu's sham trial starts or the Queen Beyond the Stars and her Shadowmancer army come searching for the last Light Core in the multiverse.

If Ayla and I don't succeed, everything will be lost, and it will be my fault.

# CHAPTER 25
# NATE

THE GOOD NEWS IS, the bad guys were nice enough to set my dislocated shoulder and treat my broken arm. They sent me to a med bay where a mech popped my shoulder joint into socket and put this thing on my arm called a "bone sleeve." It absorbed into my skin and attached to the break, setting and healing my fracture from the inside out. Coolest thing I've ever seen, for real. No more pain, and I'm a leftie again. I didn't enjoy my brief time as a righty at all.

The bad news is, they only fixed me so my bronze, whole-hand handcuffs would fit properly before they threw me in jail. I can't use either of my hands, and I can't use my Light. The bronze in question is the same kind of metal used to make World Divers, and Light can't penetrate them.

Now I'm in solitary. Should I sing a song? Quote movies to entertain myself? Consider the elusive source of my nagging, existential dread while I quietly ponder life's big questions?

Just kidding, I'm freaking out hardcore. Climbing on the sparse furniture to inspect the ceiling for outlets or vents, overturning said furniture to look for weaknesses in the walls and floor, kicking the door and screaming obscenities ... you know, that kind of freaking out.

If I wanted to punch Boy Scout in the teeth, the feeling has amplified by a thousand. Thanks for getting the only two known Luminauts in the multiverse arrested, Toran. Forethought is *not* his specialty today.

"Hey, can anybody hear me?" Endless stream-of-consciousness swearing isn't getting anyone's attention, maybe coherent sentences will. "Just wanted to let you know this is a really bad time for you to put a couple Luminauts on trial. There's a Darkness monster on the loose. Do you guys care about that, or are you cool with your whole world becoming a pile of ash?"

Speaking of a couple Luminauts …

"Can somebody tell me where Callie James is?" No answer. "You know, the girl one of you jerks stunned with a blaster gun?" Silence. Probably shouldn't have called them jerks. Considering the circumstances, "jerk" is a grade-school insult compared to what I'd like to say. "Answer me! Is she okay? Tell me where she is!"

Nobody's going to tell me where Callie is. Nobody cares if she's okay. Being human again has some unfortunate pitfalls, and the physiological response to emotions like anger, panic, and fear are my least favorite. My heart races, chest tightens, palms sweat (inside brass cuffs—even worse), and a low buzz in my ears makes it hard to focus.

I've got to get out of here and make a plan so she doesn't go through with the horrifying bargain she made with Queen. There's no way Queen will honor it. Once she has Callie trapped in her net, she'll go back on her word. Queen always lies.

I wonder if Callie knew that when she was negotiating her crappy deal.

Before I reinspect every inch of the cell door for signs of

weakness, it ping-swishes open, and a guard shoves Dad and El inside. Dad's cuffs are similar to mine, covering the entirety of his hands, but El's are regular wrist-only cuffs. I bolt for the door, but it shuts behind them just as fast. At least I'm not alone, and they both look okay — singed and covered in ashes, but physically fine.

"What did they do to you guys?" I approach Dad. "Did you see where they put Callie?"

"I didn't see where they took either Callie or Serai," Dad answers, "but I'm sure they're detained elsewhere."

"Then how did you get put in here with me?" I appreciate the company and all, but I'd rather be released than have a lockup reunion.

Dad shrugs. "I was very loud about wanting our family in a cell together, and eventually they listened."

"He called the guards a lot of bad names I'm not supposed to repeat," El adds, sinking onto the floor. "I think they just wanted him to shut up."

Pays to be a cranky old man with a laundry list of complaints. "Come on," I say, "help me find a way out."

"A way out? Unlikely." Dad snorts.

"So we should sit here and do nothing?" Yeah right, like that's gonna happen. "I have to find Callie. She's the key to everything, and they tossed her in a cell like she was nothing."

"We were all tossed into cells, if you recall. I heard some of the guards say they're rushing the trial for the sake of political expediency." He takes a seat in the single chair at the far end of the cell. "You're overly emotional because of your obvious affection for Callie, but the best thing you can do is remain calm."

"I'm not overly emotional."

"You're totally emotional," El pipes up. "Everyone saw you kissing Callie in the crater. It was like two ore wyrms trying to eat each other, mouth-first." He makes a fake-barf sound for emphasis. Lovely child, isn't he?

"Can it, dingus."

"*You* can it, dümfo."

"El, the disgusting sound effects are unnecessary." Dad's eye twitch is back, would you look at that! "Listen, Nate, we must proceed cautiously, and not let strong feelings cloud our better judgement."

If I expected Dad to be anything besides condescending in this scenario, I was dead wrong—which isn't even a good pun anymore, now that I'm alive again.

"'Oh, hi son, nice to see you alive.' Thanks, Dad, I appreciate the show of concern. Now that you're here, I'll gladly sit on my butt and do nothing, basking in the glow of our big, happy family jail cell."

Sarcasm bleeds out of me before I can check myself, but seriously, Dad's poorly timed professor lectures are not helping. I survived more than I thought I ever could, came back to freaking *life,* Queen tried to kill me, and Callie just bargained herself and all the Light Cores for me—and got shot by a blaster before we were thrown in jail. So yeah, I'm edgy. Just a tad. And I'm *not* going to sit around if I can figure a way to bust out and reunite with Callie.

And kiss her again. El can make puke noises all he likes.

"I haven't sat on my backside and 'done nothing,' as you imply," Dad counters. "Serai and I went through all sorts of trouble trying to track down your location, and I was more than happy to assist in our doomed battle against your former mistress of Darkness." Ouch, passive-aggressive much? "I was merely pointing out that making poor choices based on emotions is not—"

"Please, spare me the diatribe about crap choices. Trust me,

I've made a million. But just for you, I promise I won't have any more emotional outbursts or show any reaction whatsoever to Callie bargaining her entire life away to Queen." I swear, Dad has the worst timing in the entire multiverse, and I guess I do too. What comes out of my mouth next isn't kind, but it comes out anyway. "I'll be just like you. Emotionless and rational."

"There's no need for derision. We're on the same side." Dad continues on in his cool, reasonable tone. It was how he talked down to me after Mom died, too. *We have to be grateful she's no longer in pain.* I'd have been more grateful if she were alive, but I couldn't say that to Dad. He'd have brushed me off, just like he's doing now.

"Oh, we're on the same side? Thanks for that clarification," I sneer. "Were we on the same side after Mom died and you ignored me for three years? Except when baseball was involved, then you'd show up. It was the only way I could get your undivided attention, and I was out behind home plate, not in front of your face. What about when Darkness called me while I was drowning? Were we on the same side then? Or were you back in a lecture hall a week later, pretending it never happened?"

Dad startles like I just punched him in the gut, but I can't hold back, especially knowing that Callie is lost somewhere in this jail, and I can't use my powers to help her. I'm useless and stuck.

Does that have anything to do with Dad? Not really. Is this the greatest time to hash out our past relationship? No way. But when is it?

"Emotions weren't scientific enough for you, so I shoved them down and pretended I didn't have any," I go on. "Hiding the complicated parts of myself for your convenience was the reason Queen Turned me into a Shadowmancer in the first place.

But I'm not hiding how I feel anymore. You wanna show you're on my side? Help me get out of here so I can find Callie and make sure Queen never hurts her or anyone else again."

Dad and El's faces are so still I think they might be frozen. As soon as the words are out of my mouth, I wish I could take them back. Why did I say all that? Stupid, Nate. In my powerlessness, I unloaded on my only living parent in the most unfair way possible.

"I'm sorry. Just because you show you care in a different way than me doesn't make it wrong. If anyone is wrong here, it's me." My voice is raw, speaking truth to Dad for the first time ever. "I'm sorry I turned to Darkness and took away the last person you had. I'm sorry I used my power to hurt you. No matter what went down between us, you never deserved that, and I—"

"Nate, stop." Dad chokes up. I've never seen him close to tears. He didn't even cry when the hospice nurse told him Mom was truly gone. But his eyes glisten, and he swallows hard before he can speak.

"There isn't anything to apologize for," Dad says. "You're right about everything. I wasn't there for you the way I should have been. You were fourteen years old and had just lost your mother, but I expected *you* to stop grieving because *I* couldn't handle my own grief. It's no wonder you turned to Darkness. A father is supposed to love his son through the pain, no matter what, but instead, I emotionally abandoned you."

Wow. I didn't … I can't believe Dad felt that way this whole time.

"We both did things to each other that hurt, whether we meant to or not," I say. "If we make it out of here, we can start over. It won't change all the time we lost, but it's better than nothing." And if somehow these political schmoozers manage to end us, at least Dad and I made peace.

Dad actually smiles at my suggestion. "I would like that."

"The best thing we can do right now is agree this situation is bogus, and that Callie *can't* exchange the Light Cores and her life for all of us. We all know the trial is a sham, so the best course of action is to play their game and win before the Guardian forum convenes."

"We agree on all counts." Dad nods and wipes his eyes on his shoulder, once again the composed, logical Rick Ormandi. "However, I don't believe it will be easy getting out of this cell." Dad holds up his cuffed hands. "I can't use my powers, and neither can you. Unless you've had a moral change of heart about Persuasion..."

"Absolutely not." I shake my head. "And you never should have encouraged Callie to use it in the first place."

"I did no such thing, she unintentionally used it on a local co-ed, and I simply explained—"

"Can we get back to the escape plan?" El interrupts impatiently. "If I had a key, I could get your cuffs off. Mine are normal, see?" El holds up his simple wrist restraints and twiddles his fingers.

"But you don't have a key," I point out. "Where's Nemo? Maybe he can swipe a key."

Nemo peeks out of El's shirt collar, waves, then hides again. Good call, little dude.

"Even if the mech finds a key," Dad says, "we have to steal four Light Cores from a heavily guarded facility."

"Plus, Boy Scout and Sparky are who-knows-where in the desert with Diver." Could things be worse? I don't think they can, but maybe there's a bright spot I'm not seeing. Maybe Ayla will completely zap Toran to shreds for getting us into this situation in the first place. I just wish I could be there to watch with a big, buttery tub of popcorn.

"You got the guards to move you in here," I come up with a plan even as I speak. "We can use you to get us out too."

"How?" Dad raises an eyebrow. "Please, enlighten me."

"You're an old guy." Yes, this can totally work. Genius, Ormandi! "You're basically one bad fall or bout of indigestion away from death's door."

"Death's door?" Dad's nostrils flare. "I will have you know, at my last stress test with my cardiologist, I was informed I have the heart of a forty-five-year-old."

"Whatever." I didn't ask what your cardiologist said, Dad, I'm plotting. "The point is, you can fake some illness or injury, they'll open the door to help, and we'll bust out of here."

Dad balks. "You expect me to humiliate myself?"

"Pride cometh before the fall, as they say."

"Who says that?" El asks, looking between me and Dad.

"The most obvious flaw in your plan are these." Dad holds up his whole-hand cuffs. "We can't unlock any touch-activated doors."

"I can do that stuff," El says with a grin. "And me and Nemo will steal the key."

"I believe you could steal a great many things, if the way you raided Serai's kitchen cupboards was any indication," Dad deadpans.

"Awesome, we're doing the plan," I say.

"No," Dad argues, "we're not."

"Yes, we are." I kick the door loud enough for any guard in the corridor to hear. "Help me! Somebody, help! My dad is hurt!" I turn to Dad and hiss, "Quick, lay down on the floor and pretend you're dying."

"Absolutely not."

"I could hit you for real, if we need some blood." El's always happy to suggest actual violence.

"If you hit me, I'll set your pants on fire the moment these cuffs are off." Dad rises from the chair and makes his way to the door. "I'll lean on you and look ill. That is my compromise."

"Fine." I can work with that. I kick the door a few more times, shouting at the top of my lungs. "Please, you have to help us! This is a medical emergency! He could die!"

El whacks the door with his cuff-chain and yells too. "Help us! Seriously! I promise we're not lying!" Ugh, this kid. El, I swear, if you give us away …

The door ping-swishes open, and a couple frowning guards stand just beyond the threshold. I guess dying old dudes in potential distress is enough to get people interested, or they want Dad alive enough to attend his trial. Dad's not a terrible actor when he chooses to be, and he looks believable, faking like he's about to faint.

"What's all this about?" One of the guards steps forward to assess Dad and holds his comm to his mouth. "High alert, need a MedTech team in the containment center."

The guard's blaster sits in a hip holster. Since we're cuffed, we're not a threat. Well, buddy, have I got news for you.

Once the door is open, the three of us barrel out, slamming into the small group of guards left behind as sentries. El presses the touchpad to lock the guard in the cell inside, which is a really excellent move and I'll compliment him later. One thing brass handcuffs *are* good for is whacking guards, and Dad and I incapacitate the small contingent left in the corridor near our cell. El roots through the contents of their holsters once they're all grounded.

"No cuff keys," he says with a look of dismay.

"Crap." At least we can scout around for Callie and Serai. The corridor stretches long and white, mostly sterile. It looks more like a hospital than a jail. "What's this place called, again?"

"The Hall of Guardians. We are in the containment center, where convicts are kept prior to trial." Dad and El walk fast to keep pace with me. "According to Serai, the Hall itself is much more elaborately decorated."

"You're friends with Serai now? How easily you forget she captured you with a bunch of sentient vines."

"In her defense, I attempted to light her on fire." I guess Dad's got a point about the fire thing. "Besides, she was also your mother's Seer before me. So we share a Luminaut as well."

"She's actually pretty nice," El agrees. "Her house has a lot of food, and she let me swim in her garden pool." Give an eleven-year-old snacks and a pool, and you're automatically best friends.

"Our previous cell was this way." Dad nods his chin to indicate the long line of white, windowless doors in front of us. "Perhaps the others are down here as well."

"El, you've got the only free hands." I turn to the boy at my side. "Start trying doors."

El presses his palm to the first touchpad on the left, but the room is empty. Same with the cell on the right. But two doors up we get lucky. Serai rises and strides toward us, looking like a majorly ticked-off queen whose rightful throne is much grander than her little plastic chair. She's restrained by the same kind of cuffs as me and Dad. Somebody must have made them specifically to prevent people with powers from using them.

"You aren't who I expected to see, but I'm pleased nonetheless." Serai glances up and down the corridor. "Were you followed?"

"Not that we're aware of." Dad shoots a smirk my way. "My

son had a plan for escaping our cell, but not much strategy beyond."

Watch it, Dad, or I'll make you feign old-man frailty again.

"The keys to our cuffs will be outside the containment center in a relic catalog room. These are old, from the Light Collective era." Serai seems more than happy to take over as master strategist. "The difficult part will be getting from the containment center to the catalog room without being spotted."

We'll worry about being spotted later. El continues trying cell doors, but none of them are Callie's. Where the heck is she?

"Callie!" I call her name. Maybe she'll hear me and bang on her door so we can find her. "Callie, where are you?"

Soft cries reach my ears along with muffled taps inside a cell in the opposite direction. Callie! I run for her with El, and he opens her touchpad door.

"Nate!" She limps forward, a blaster mark still visible on her hip. "I'm seriously so happy to see you guys."

El gags and makes gross-out noises when I bend to kiss her. El can suck eggs.

"Any sign of Toran or Ayla?" Callie looks around for the Seers in question. "Did they get captured too? Where's Nemo?"

The tiny mech waves joyously from El's collar before disappearing again. Callie smiles, relieved.

"It appears Ayla and Toran escaped with the World Diver, although where they went, we don't know," Serai replies. "I only hope my daughter is safe and keeps her distance until Manu is exposed."

"If Toran hurts my mech, I swear I will—"

"I think we all want to cause Boy Scout significant bodily harm, but that's got to wait. Serai knows how to get out of here."

"Theoretically." Okay, Serai. Semantics.

"I've got to get the Light Cores. I need them." Callie has trouble keeping up with the rest of us on her injured hip, every step a sharp wince. My arms ache to carry her. Stupid cuffs.

"Are you okay?" I ask. Callie's grin is half-grimace.

"It hurts, but I'll be okay."

"We have to talk about the bargain you made with Queen." I keep my voice low. "She's not going to keep her promise to you."

"I know," Callie replies.

"Then why did you make a deal with her in the first place?"

"Because I learned subterfuge and wordplay from the best." She sends a sly wink my way. Clever girl. If anybody proved they can outplay Darkness, it's Callie. She outplayed me several times, and I've never been more proud to lose. "Agreeing to her demands buys us three days to make a plan to defeat her. Although I didn't expect this detour to take up so much time. Thanks for nothing, Toran."

"All we need to do is escape jail, heist the four stolen Light Cores, find the fifth one, and Light blast Queen and the whole Shadow Plain to ashes before three days are up." I smile, but all the dried blood caked on the left side of my face makes it more like a half-ish smile. "Totally doable."

"We've got this." If Callie and I weren't cuffed, we'd walk out of here hand-in-hand like a rad power couple to meet our Lightbound destiny head-on. The cuffs are *seriously* wrecking our moment.

Dad scoffs and mutters something about the misplaced optimism of youth. Serai's chuckle tells me she agrees. Laugh it up, elderly curmudgeons.

"Prioritizing our immediate escape, I suggest we stick to the Hall of Guardians back corridors, closest to the filing rooms," Serai informs us as we walk. "Those areas are sparsely populated."

"An excellent suggestion." Dad sounds like he's relieved we aren't planning five steps ahead anymore.

"The exit is this way." Serai marches on. "If I've guessed the time correctly, we have about an hour before the forum gathers, and by then we'll be—"

"Going somewhere, Serai?"

Manu the Dangling Dipwad stands in the exit, blocking our path with a whole slew of guards, all of them armed with active blasters and force shields. It's not like we can defend ourselves, but he just had to send his ever-present goon squad to point live blasters in our faces. This freaking guy, man. He twirls a bronze key on his finger and smiles devilishly.

"Were you looking for this?" Manu waves the key in Serai's face, and she snarls like she wants to vine-choke him. I'm pretty sure we all want to light this guy up, so there'll be a line. "I guessed you'd escape and head straight to the relic catalogs to find this. I'm not as stupid as you think I am."

Don't give yourself *that* much credit.

"What are you doing here, Manu?" Serai grinds her teeth when she talks, and I wouldn't want to be in Manu's shoes when she gets those cuffs off. But Manu's smile widens until his teeth gleam like a razor in firelight.

"The timing of your attempted jailbreak could not have been better," Manu announces. "Your conspiracy trial is about to begin. I've come as your personal escort to the forum."

They moved the trial up an hour. This escape heist just took an unexpected plot twist, didn't it? Knowing Queen, she's sitting in front of the Veil watching with glee as this idiot does all the messy work of screwing us over. Queen was always strategically lazy.

I hope you're happy you set all this up for us, Boy Scout. Ayla better electrocute him before she rides to our rescue with Diver. That the last great hope for the safety of the multiverse rests in Sparky's hands only worries me a little.

Okay, it worries me a lot. Because the second she gets distracted by a sappy holodrama, or sees a picture of a cute puppy, or becomes too scared of her own Seer power to function, we're all doomed.

# CHAPTER 26
# TORAN

**ONE TIME,** when I was a little boy, Heike and I got into an argument so fierce she refused to speak to me for several days. I no longer recall what started the fight—something inconsequential that to children seems like a tremendous offense. When I complained to my parents about my sister's behavior, Papa offered me his rarely-bestowed wisdom:

*"Silence is sometimes the loudest rebuke of all."*

That very day, I apologized to Heike and the silence was over. Now, it's deafening. Never has silence been more tangible as Ayla and I march through the desert toward Oasis III in the World Diver, preparing to extract the last Light Core.

She hasn't said a word.

I pause my organizing of the Crow's Nest. Evidence of Heike remains everywhere, staring at me like a ghost I desperately wish to breathe back to life. Hair ties for her braids, her handwriting and drawings on random paper scraps, the covers of her favorite vinyl albums scattered by the record player. She might as well be standing behind my shoulder.

But she's gone, lost in the depths a villain's plot against Light. A toy to borrow and break until the game is ultimately won or lost. My scheming has all but assured the victory for Darkness. Why did I think Manu was the answer to my problems? That he could alleviate my grief and fear? Instead, I've only added to my misery.

Ayla sits in the Seer's chair, staring blankly out the window at the dunes and brilliant night sky. She was always so open before, so kind. The opposite of me in every way, but in an odd twist of fate, so much like me too. I would gladly listen to her chatter about her favorite holodramas for hours if it meant she would speak to me again.

Silence is sometimes the loudest rebuke of all.

"Is the, uh, World Diver still following the coordinates you gave him?" I suppose I must speak first because I can't take not speaking any longer.

Ayla bristles at the sound of my voice. "We're on course."

"That's good." I cautiously approach the chairs and lower myself into a soft leather seat. Ayla doesn't object or move. She remains focused on the desert as though purposely avoiding my gaze.

"You didn't alert Manu to our activities, did you?" Ayla darts a glare across our chairs. "The last thing we need are your political friends showing up uninvited."

"Manu is not my friend. He took what he wanted from our arrangement and left me a fool." Why did I think I could hold my own against him? What experience do I have with such games and betrayals?

"A fool who lost all his friends and his Luminaut in the process," Ayla says sharply, reminding me of my dire situation.

"Yes." I can't disagree with her assessment, as much as it stings.

"Was it worth it?" Ayla finally looks at me, but her eyes are guarded, almost cold. She's never looked that way before.

"No, it was not."

"I'm glad to know you're capable of remorse." Ayla crosses her arms over her chest as if she's protecting her heart from me. If I had another chance to go back and do things over again, I'd never give her a reason to feel she couldn't trust me.

"We have to pass through a port of entry when we arrive at Oasis III," Ayla says matter-of-factly. "After that, it's a quick transport ride to Mama's family estate. It's small, used to assess mining operations. That's where we've kept the Light Core." A smirk draws her mouth. "Our secrets are safe there. Unless you decide to spread them."

"I promise I won't." I'll do anything in my power to protect Ayla from further harm.

"Good." Ayla sighs, her eyes clouding with a far-off look I can't name. "I first fell from Aureloria into the desert not far from here. I still remember how hot it was on the dunes, how the sun burned my skin and made me see things that weren't there. Oasis III was the first shelter I found."

"May I ask—and I realize you probably won't answer—how did you get through a gateway with Aureloria's Light Core in the first place?" My curiosity gets the better of me, despite Ayla's righteous suspicion and anger.

Her shoulders hunch defensively around her ears. "I don't owe you my story."

"I understand." I remain quiet, looking out at the stars. In between them shine a vast multitude of gateways. I leap a little when Ayla's soft hand finds my shoulder, and she points to one gateway in particular.

"That's Aureloria." Beyond the opening, I see a wide meadow of flowers surrounded by lush forest. A babbling stream cuts the meadow, and beyond the trees, tall mountains covered in snow rise toward a pale blue sky. There's no sinister Mist, no violent predators. It looks idyllic. Peaceful. Serene. It isn't difficult to believe Ayla grew up in a place like that.

"It's beautiful," I say. "Do you miss it?"

"No." Ayla doesn't hesitate, not even a little. "The outside beauty hides plenty of inner rot. I wouldn't return to Aureloria in a thousand lifetimes. The worst memories of my life happened there."

"I feel that way about Tremurheim," I murmur. "Although the landscape there is admittedly bleak."

A hint of a smile cracks Ayla's aloofness, and my spirit soars. I miss her smile more than I realized.

"I told you I went to live on my own after my Manipulation manifested," Ayla says. I nod because she did tell me that. "However, I never told you *why* I was sent away. I had an altercation with a boy at school. He thought he could get away with teasing me because I was quiet, and wasn't perceived as very smart. One day he followed me home, throwing rocks and calling me names. Before I knew what was happening, I electrocuted him." She pauses, then adds, "He survived, but his family was very powerful. It was the final straw for my parents."

"I'm sorry, Ayla." It's clearly painful for her to recall the memory. I see now why she never wants to return. "For what it's worth, I think you are exceedingly intelligent."

"Thank you, Toran." Ayla grins at the compliment, but it quickly fades. "However, the boy and his family discovered the location of my safe house. They tried to burn it down with me inside. I escaped out the back just in time and ran to the only other building nearby—Aureloria's Light Sanctum."

"Light Sanctum?"

"The site where our Light Core was tethered to the mountainside," Ayla explains. "A cathedral of glass built to reflect the Light, and above it, a partially open-air gateway that never fully closed after the Severing. It was quite lovely until I destroyed it." She shifts in her seat, her eyes never once leaving the gateway to Aureloria in the sky above our heads. "In my fear, my uncontrolled Manipulation opened the gateway fully, and the Light Core and I were pulled through. I lost consciousness, and when I awoke, I was here in this desert." She shrugs. "Anyway, that is how myself and Aureloria's Light Core came to be in Oasis III."

"Thank you for telling me. I'm glad you trusted me with the truth."

"The truth is that my story has another point. Just because things look a certain way on the outside, that doesn't mean the inside is good." She fixes me with her deep, wide-eyed gaze, one that pierces all the way to my heart. "The things we believe about others might be lies our fears have told us. And the fears we have about ourselves might be our greatest strengths."

"I'm afraid there is nothing about me worthy of being called strong." What kind of person betrays his friends or allows Darkness to manipulate his sister without noticing? A selfish one, only concerned about himself. "I was so single-minded about protecting Heike, I never stopped to consider the harm I caused to everyone else. To Callie, to Nate… to you."

"Perhaps you aren't strong," Ayla says, "but perhaps you're wrong, too. I suppose we'll find out for sure because Oasis III is right there."

I look out Diver's windows and startle instantly. "Are you sure that's a water mine?"

The sight before us isn't what I expected. Mines in

Tremurheim are pragmatically carved into the earth, where miners extract ore and precious metals with no fanfare. Oasis III is a … beach. Under the thin dome of artificial sunlight, a strip of white sand edges an expanse of crystal-blue water. Lush gardens and parks surround the beach, and beyond is a small town full of houses, shops, and cafés. An outcropping of large buildings surrounded by pipes and tanks sits at the farthest end, and in the midst of it all, a massive estate.

"Where are the miners?" I can't see anybody dressed for work coming and going around the entry port. "And I thought you said all of Ensolorada's oceans were underground?"

"Mechs handle the actual mining," Ayla says. She rises from her seat, stretching. "This is an oasis pool, a place where the underwater ocean spills to the surface, forming an above-ground sea. People come here for vacations." When I show no response, Ayla tilts her chin. "Have you never had a vacation?"

"No." I don't know what that word means, but I get the impression I've missed out on something good.

"Perhaps you should take one. It would help you unwind." She motions for me to follow her. "Come, we don't have much time. Diver, please set us down and wait for us until we get back."

I cannot hear Diver's agreement, but he does what Ayla asks. Soon we're on the ground, staring at the port of entry, although I wish we were not.

Surrounding the entrance to the Oasis are hologram posters of me and Ayla. They announce to anyone coming or going our names, ages, and that we're wanted for conspiracy against Cordonanza and its Hall of Guardians. Dramora spawn! Manu must have put out some kind of alert to ensure our capture.

"What are we going to do now?" I lament. Ayla looks entirely undeterred.

"This way." She takes my arm and leads me into a small crevice between two buildings near the main entrance, one filled with old junk and rubbish.

"Is there an alley or a hidden passage of some kind?" I ask, looking around. I can't make out much except piles of garbage left behind by those coming and going.

"No. We're going to make disguises so nobody recognizes us." Ayla finds an abandoned tarp and ties it around her shoulders, making a hooded cape. Deeper in the pile are a pair of darkened glasses and a tattered cap. She places the cap on my head and finds brown-black grease on an abandoned piece of mining equipment, which she smears on my eyebrows and the tips of my hair.

"Your features are quite recognizable from your hologram," Ayla explains, applying my disguise. I don't like the feeling or smell of the grease, but I also don't want to be arrested. "There, now you have dark hair and eyebrows. No one will recognize you."

"Should I put these over my eyes?" I place the glasses on my face, and Ayla claps her hands.

"Exactly!" She adjusts her makeshift hood over her curls, which are her most eye-catching feature. "Now for our act. I'll pretend to be your old grandmother, and you're my grandson. We're here for our yearly family reunion trip, and you must escort me because I'm elderly and confused."

"I'm not very good at acting." Discomfort makes my insides twist.

"Don't worry, I'll do most of the talking." Ayla grins and takes my arm.

My insides twist again in an entirely different way—a good

way. I like her holding my arm when we walk out into the crowd, even if she's only pretending. We slip easily from our hiding spot and join the vacationers gathered around the entry port. Nobody notices us or spots my resemblance to the hologram. I can breathe easier. The disguises worked.

Ayla stoops over, her hair and face completely hidden by her hood in that posture, and we approach a sentry stationed beside the entrance.

"Clearances?" The sentry holds out his hand.

"Oh, uh—" We don't have clearances. Lands Beyond, do people have to have permission to even breathe here? I fumble for an excuse, but true to her word, Ayla does most of the talking.

"We do *not* need clearances, my good sir." Ayla makes her youthful voice gravelly and shaky as a nargush feather. I don't believe this sentry will fall for it. Sure enough, he raises an eyebrow incredulously.

"The Oasis is technically the private property of Serai Eradah of Cordonanza," he replies. "All guests must have proper clearances to enter."

"Of course it belongs to Serai Eradah! Do you think I'm daft? Grandson, can you believe the audacity of this young person? I never, in all my days!"

"Erm, let's not cause a scene." I flash a nervous look at the sentry. Too many people looking at us means it's more likely somebody will see through our disguises.

"I will cause a scene if I please!" Ayla raises a fist. "My grandson—this tall, handsome fellow here—is escorting me to our annual reunion. Serai and our family go back many generations. We've always had our celebrations at Oasis III and have never been asked for paltry clearances!"

"Madam, please, I'll have to look into this—" But Ayla

doesn't let the sentry finish.

"Look into it? Dunes!" Her voice becomes cracked and squeaky, and she fakes a sway so violent I have to hold her upright. "There will be no looking into it! My mother and Serai's mother were once the best of friends. They had a brief falling-out when Ferdan—my father, you see—asked for my mother's hand instead of Serai's mother's. My mother was a great beauty, and Lysa—that is Serai's mother—was greatly vexed. But then she met her own dear Orolin, and all bygones were—"

"Just let them in," an annoyed female sentry calls across the path to the sentry bothering us. "The old woman clearly knows the family. We'll sort the details later."

"Fine, go on." The sentry steps aside and allows us to pass.

"That's more like it! And I shall be having a word with your supervisor!"

"Be kind, grandmama," I add over Ayla's ranting, which she continues until we're out of earshot of the sentries and lost in the dispersing crowd. A long line of transports waits to take guests to their destinations, and Ayla and I find an empty one.

"That was great fun!" She removes her hood once the transport door closes behind us. "My plan worked, you see?"

"That was very good," I agree, wiping away the grease. "Nate Ormandi will be hard-pressed to defend his title of top strategist." I look around the Oasis outside my window, admiring the rough-hewn houses and unkempt but lovely sprays of pink flowers growing along the paths, each one leading to the white sand and crystal-blue water. "Heike would love this place." My gaze finds Ayla. "It's lovely."

"I think so too." Ayla smiles, softness reaching her eyes, and it strikes me that the beach is not the loveliest thing in the Oasis. Then she jerks her head away, as if remembering she's still furious with me and we aren't friends.

My stomach sinks. Working well together isn't grounds for forgiveness.

"Destination?" The monotone transport navigation system speaks.

"Eradah Estate," Ayla responds. "Access code 24785-612."

"Affirmative."

The transport rises into the air, and after a short ride, comes to a stop on the bright green grass of the enormous estate. All the homes in Cordonanza are made of white stone and crystal, but this one is pink stone with accents of wood and colorful tiles. Many arches surround the lower level, and expansive windows soar to the golden rooftop, gleaming in the simulated sunlight. Manicured flower gardens tended by mechs, filled with small pools and crystal fountains, surround the grounds.

"When you said your mother maintained this home to assess mine operations, I imagined it would be smaller," I tell Ayla, sauntering across the wide park.

Ayla shrugs. "It's smaller than our home in Cordonanza."

I suppose that's true.

Ayla presses a touchpad lock on the front door, and inside the entryway, a Light Core sits ensconced in half of a broken stone pedestal with a cracked glass sphere. The last Light Core in the multiverse, a piece of Aureloria brought here by the Seer standing beside me. It's remarkable. My Seer's eye blazes in its presence, and so does Ayla's.

"They're pretty objects, aren't they?" Ayla takes a moment to admire the Core. "Who'd have thought they would cause so much devastation?"

"Don't touch it!" I put a hand on her shoulder, halting her when moves in for the Core. "It will summon the Queen Beyond the Stars."

"Not if a Seer touches it." Ayla brushes past my grasp. "One of Mama's ancestors, a Seer named Saeli Nerida, created the original earth tethers, but the Cores themselves can only be activated by Luminauts." Ayla carefully sets the glass dome on the floor and picks up the Light Core, giving it a quick toss as if it were a ball or some other plaything. "No Darkness. No trouble." She hands the Core to me. "See for yourself."

"So light." A Light Core hardly weighs anything. It's remarkably cool to the touch and smooth like hollow crystal or glass. Nothing like I thought it would be, but hasn't that been true of all the magic and powers I've encountered across the multiverse? Even my own Manipulation, which at first felt like a burden, proved far more useful than I realized.

Perhaps Ayla is correct when she says the way things look on the outside is not the whole truth.

"Warning: intruder. Security breached. Stand down."

There might not be any Darkness swirling through the entryway, but there is certainly trouble. No less than two dozen guard mechs swarm us, their glowing eyes zeroed in on the Light Core when they draw their blasters.

"Dramora spawn!"

"Dunes!"

Serai must have programmed them to attack if the Light Core is touched or moved by anyone except her. I'd be impressed with her level of security and planning if I didn't have so many blasters pointed at my face.

"Warning: intruder. Security breached."

Before the mechs open fire, I spy a sliver of hope—a small fountain bubbling in the corner. I call the water in the basin into my hands before they finish aiming and freeze half the mechs solid. Ayla swirls her fingers, electricity forming a lightning strike in her palms, and she launches it at the remaining mechs. They fall to the floor, electrified, and we dash out the door with the Light Core.

"Warning: intruder. Security breached."

More mechs? Forest spare me, how many of these things does Serai have, and where do they keep coming from? It's like they spring up, fully formed, from the garden beds to chase us across the grass.

"Mama certainly doesn't make things easy, does she?" Ayla blasts some mechs with effective lightning strikes. Her targets topple over, crackling and sputtering.

"No, she doesn't." I use water from the garden pools to freeze even more approaching mechs. "This seems to be a common recurrence with her."

"With you as well." *Zzzzplat.* Ayla's lightning eradicates a group of mechs on our left. "Perhaps you have more in common with Mama than you want to admit."

"Or perhaps all Seers are inherently troublesome." More water, more frozen mechs. The transport is within sight, waiting to take us back to Diver with our prize.

"You must mean all Seers besides Air Manipulators." Ayla scatters mechs into the swaying trees with a strong gust. "I'm never troublesome."

"Yes, you are—oh, you're joking." I leap into the transport and hold out my hand to Ayla.

"Of course I was joking. And you were taking me too seriously." She takes my outstretched hand, holding up her skirt, and hops into the transport after me. The few remaining mechs fire on the closed door as the transport rises into the air and we fly away to safety with the Light Core. Any lightheartedness between us fades as Diver appears beyond the transport window and our final destination becomes real.

"They'll have started the forum by now." Ayla places the Light Core in my satchel at my hip, fumbling with the clasp. "Diver must get us back to Cordonanza quickly. If we're too late …" She trembles, and I curl my fingers around her shoulder. It's smooth and soft. And she doesn't pull away.

"It will be all right, Ayla." Some lies don't feel awful to tell — and in truth, I don't know if I'm lying.

The transport docks at Diver's shoulder, and Ayla and I race to the seats at the front.

"Diver, take us back to Cordonanza," I command. The mech turns with a groan, moving away from the outskirts of Oasis III and traveling back into the dunes under the open nighttime sky. I turn to my companion, her face increasingly ashen as she watches the horizon. "We'll make it, Ayla. Your mother will be spared. I know we—"

I don't finish my sentence because above our heads, the sky breaks. A rift forms between the stars, opening a hole in space as deep and dark as time itself. From this gaping chasm, Darkness pours across the desert, a syrupy-black fog that oozes and writhes, suffocating the beauty of night.

And it's heading straight for Cordonanza.

"What's happening? Callie said Queen promised her three days." Panic for my sister floods my lungs and throat with ice as I watch Darkness fill the sky.

"Three days to find the Light Cores, and three days until she turns Heike into a Shadowmancer," Ayla corrects my assumption. Horror fills her eyes as she follows the slithering Darkness leaving tentacle trails of ash across the sand. "She never said she wouldn't attack Cordonanza."

"Diver, go as fast as you can!"

The World Diver breaks into a headlong run, racing for Cordonanza as Darkness blocks the light of the moon and stars. I pray to the Old Spirits of the Clans, Tremurheim's most ancient deities, that we won't be too late.

# CHAPTER 27
# CALLIE

MANU CAROSTI IS A big fan of the sound of his own voice.

I mean, I guessed that about him when I met him in jail my first waking hour in Ensolorada, but he's going out of his way to confirm my suspicion. He spent the first forty minutes of this "trial" droning on about all the perceived slights Serai committed against him and his dad—not actual crimes, just political maneuvers he's still carrying grudges about. Now he's been on his Luminauts-are-evil speech for twenty minutes.

In front of me, all four of the Light Cores Nate and I hunted glow and hum inside a glass case, stolen trophies from our capture rubbed in our faces. All the while, a cold chill travels slowly up my spine. Something Dark and dreadful is coming, but nobody in the forum makes a move to stop it.

"He's basically asking Darkness to swoop in and destroy those things." Nate nods at the Light Cores. It's like he can read my thoughts—or he feels the drawing threat of Shadow too.

"Talk about handing Queen the multiverse on a silver platter," I agree. "Aren't they going to let us defend ourselves against Manu?"

"Highly doubtful," Serai whispers. "The Guardians have

already made up their minds. This trial is to make sure things look copacetic to the public."

"What public?" Dr. Ormandi scoffs. "Darkness is coming, and they're trying to kill off the only people who can save them."

This room full of Guardians will be ash. My family and friends in Verona Beach will be ash. The entire multiverse and all its Light, gone. An unending Shadow Plain will be all that's left of existence.

*Do you still think you'll win, Calliope?* Queen's voice slithers through my mind. She enjoys watching us suffer. *It will all be over soon.*

The Light Cores' hum becomes agitated, and venomous cold inches up my arms.

*Luminaut, Darkness is coming.* A flashing vision of Diver's fear appears in my mind. Inky Shadows swallowing the desert, racing through the dunes, spilling from the Shadow Plain just outside Cordonanza.

It's coming to take the Light Cores for Queen.

"Darkness is almost here." Nate stiffens next to me, his jaw clenched in dread.

*Diver, hurry. As fast as you can.*

*Yes, Luminaut.*

I've got to get the Light Cores before the Shadows reach them. They're dangling like a proverbial carrot in front of my nose, but yeah, handcuffs. Son of a buzzkill, Manu! He still has the key in his pocket, but we've got a trick up our sleeve Manu doesn't know — an expert key-swiper hidden in El's collar.

"Nemo, I have a job for you." I speak so quietly my lips barely move. My tiny friend peeks around El's curls, waiting for my instruction. "You see that blowhard talking over there?" Nemo spies Manu and nods. "He's got the handcuff key in his pocket.

Go get it, and give it to El. Everything depends on you."

Nemo puffs himself up, his confidence inflated sky-high now that I'm relying on him to save us. He slips out of El's collar and climbs down the boy's leg, disappearing stealthily among the Guardians crowded inside the forum. Nobody notices a teeny robot whizzing around their feet. Their eyes are glued to Manu and the Light Cores.

"Good luck, buddy," Nate adds. "We're gonna—oh, no. Callie, look."

Flakes of ash fall like black snow from the ceiling, awakening memories of the Verona Beach High School gym the night I Dove from California. Lights flicker overhead, and Manu stops talking, glancing at the falling ashes. A frown creases his brow, and soon the rest of the Guardians stop paying attention to the trial, staring at the ashes raining on their heads.

"How is this possible?" somebody near me mumbles.

"What's going on?" A panicked cry from the back of the room.

"The Luminauts are causing this!" Manu points an accusatory finger. "They're working with Serai and the old Fire Manipulator!"

"Oh please," Dr. Ormandi mutters, rolling his eyes.

"Didn't I tell you they were—DUNES, NO!"

The forum erupts into chaos as Shadowmancers tear through the roof, descending on the Guardians like twitchy, tentacle-mouthed sharks on a school of defenseless fish. Screams pierce the air as the monsters tear into everything, leaving ashes in their wake. Horrified Guardians rush the doors, and Serai directs a few to hide in the defendant's box with us, but most are caught up in tentacles of deadly Shadow.

"No! Get away from them! No!" Manu rushes for the Light Cores inside the glass case, but a group of Shadowmancers encircle him with shrieks like shattering glass. Manu's fearful face turns a sickening green at the sight of their tentacle mouths. The monsters wrap themselves around his frame and—*puff*—turn him to ash.

"Welp, the guy with the handcuff key just got ashed," Nate deadpans. "This is going great, isn't it?"

"Where's Nemo?" If Nemo didn't get the cuff key before the Shadowmancers ashed Manu, we have no hope of fighting back—which is exactly what Queen wants. No wonder she sent Shadowmancers in her stead. Why bother wasting energy?

"Come on, Nemo!" El calls into the fray, but my little buddy is nowhere to be seen.

*Please, Nemo, please please please …*

Shadowmancers spot the Light Cores in the case, the prize they came to claim for Queen. The Cores' hum becomes a scream, rippling through me with fearful fire. Shadowmancers tear apart the walls, the doors, exposing a wide square filled with fleeing Cordonanzans. Darkness pours through the city, turning everything it touches to ashes. Trees, fountains, transports, mechs, people—nothing is safe.

*Whir-whirrrr!*

"Nemo!" My tiny mech whizzes through the chaos, the handcuff key in his tiny claw hands. "Awesome job, buddy!"

"Way to go, Nemo!" El takes the key from my little mech, uncuffs himself, and then the rest of us. Nemo glows with well-earned pride.

"Get somewhere safe," Dr. Ormandi instructs the boy. "Take the little mech with you."

"I'll see you guys soon. Don't die!" El puts Nemo on his shoulder and joins the remaining Guardians who survived the attack in running away to find shelter.

"Awesome, free hands!" Nate flexes his Light-filled fingers and sends a blast rocketing into a group of Shadowmancers chasing down terrified civilians. Another blast mixed with fire and flying boulders saves even more people across the street, allow-ing them to hide in a charred building.

And, of course, people are filming the entire battle on their comms.

I bomb through the Shadowmancers climbing the Light Core case, sending Darkness flying, then kick open the glass and retrieve the Light Cores, safe and sound. Queen's minions shriek angrily at the loss of their target.

*Boom. Boom. Boom.*

*Luminaut, we are coming.*

Finally, backup!

Diver stomps through what remains of Cordonanza, Ayla and Toran front and center on my mech's shoulder. As soon as Diver comes to a stop, he puts them down, and they run headlong through the ashes, fighting furiously with their powers.

"Hey, Sparky!" Nate smiles at his Seer. "I thought for sure you'd have electrified Boy Scout."

"I did a little." Ayla swirls some Shadowmancers up in a mini-cyclone, steering them away from a group of kids taking shelter in a locked-down school.

"A little was enough to shock some sense into me," Toran adds.

"Did Boy Scout make a pun?" Nate laughs. "Oh my stars, he made a pun! Ha! Good one, man!"

Toran approaches me cautiously, water from some nearby fountains forming ice pikes in his hands. "Do you still hate me, or will you let me fight with you?"

"Under the circumstances, I'll gladly take the assist."

Toran and I work to finish off the Shadows attacking Cordonanzans to our right while Nate and Ayla eviscerate the monsters to our left. Once they realize the Light Cores are out of reach in my grasp, the Shadows flee, leaving Cordonanza a burnt-out ruin in their wake. Ashes float through the air until the white marble buildings turn gray, and the deepfake sunlight fades out, revealing a night sky torn in two by Darkness.

*You've won this time, Calliope, but don't think I'm letting you off easy. I will see you in the Pit. Don't be late, Luminaut.*

"Mama!" Ayla falls into her mother's arms, tears in her eyes. "I was so frightened!"

"I'm so happy you're here, my stars." Serai's whole face relaxes until she's as close to peace as I've ever seen. She caresses Ayla's curls and sighs. "You're all that matters to me."

"Before anyone Light blasts me, or vine-chokes me, or sets me on fire, I have something to say." Toran holds his hands high, shoulders hunched beside his ears like he's anticipating trouble. "I'm deeply sorry for all the trouble I caused, and I promise I will do whatever it takes to earn your forgiveness."

"Your buddy Manu got ashed." Nate still speaks about people being ashed with remarkable nonchalance. A holdover from the Shadow Plain, probably.

"Thank you for bringing Diver back." I'll play nice with Toran, since he didn't abandon my mech in the desert and just helped me fight off Darkness. "But unfortunately, getting arrested seriously cut into my time to hunt the fifth Light Core. We've got to make a game plan to find it before—"

"I can help with that." Toran actually smiles. When he opens his satchel, I understand why. Nestled inside is the elusive fifth Light Core.

"What the crap, man!" Nate stares at the Core in awe. "How

did you find it?"

"Surprise!" Ayla throws her arms wide. "It was in Ensolorada the whole time, at Mama's estate in Oasis III! I'm not actually Ensoloradan, I'm from Aureloria, and the Light Core came here with me. Isn't that lucky?"

Lucky? I'd call it a miracle.

"I have about a bajillion questions right now," I tell the Seers, "but unfortunately, they're going to have to wait." I deposit the other four Light Cores in Toran's satchel, careful not to touch the fifth and accidentally activate it. "We've got to get to the Rognaga and finish this fight while we have the element of surprise on our side."

"I agree," Toran says.

"You agree with me?" I quickly check my pulse. Yep, still alive. "Sorry, I thought I might be dead for a sec because you agreeing with me is not something I imagined happening in this lifetime."

"Maybe he's got a fever." Nate presses his hand to Toran's forehead.

"Forest spare me." Toran swats Nate's hand away. "I agreed regarding one single thing."

Ah. Toran is still Toran. Whew, I was worried about him.

"Hey, lazy dümfos, look what I found!"

El pulls up, driving a transport. An actual transport. As in the egg-shaped flying cars. And he's grinning like a cat in the front driver seat through the open door, a lifeless mech driver draped over his shoulder. "I thought it might come in handy when we go kill the monster lady. You can deactivate the driver and program these things from comms, did you know? It's super-easy. I'm surprised more people don't steal them. Come on!"

"Did you sneak off and steal that while we were fighting the

Shadows?" Dr. Ormandi dad-glares and a grin crinkles his worn, ashy face. "You sneaky little genius! We'll make an Ormandi out of you yet." He catches Nate's eye and hops in the transport with El. "Remind me to keep a very close eye on that boy in the future."

"I'll accompany Richard, you four take the World Diver. We will follow." Serai joins her crew, and Toran and Ayla head for Diver, looking remarkably chummy. There's a weird, not-like-Toran gentleness in his eyes when he looks at her, and wow, do I want to be obnoxiously nosy about it.

Maybe he gave her an elaborate apology when they were Light Core hunting. Maybe she forgave him. I hope so, and I hope they remain friends. I hope nothing but happiness finds all of them because in a couple hours, we'll be facing Queen for the last time. And what I know what I have to do to win—going into the Shadow Plain to destroy it—means I might not come back out alive.

In fact, I'm certain I won't.

*I have to fight Elara, buddy.* Diver's sharp pain at Queen's human name gives way to unfathomable sorrow. *I know she was your Luminaut once, but I have to make sure she can't hurt anybody I love. You know what that means, don't you?*

Diver knows better than anyone, having seen death and destruction befall so many humans over his long years. But still, he's uncertain. Why?

*Our old Luminaut hurt many people. She hurts them still.* Diver's anguish at what Queen became is the deepest kind of grief, one that squeezes you to the bone and never, ever leaves or fades. It's been centuries of this kind of sorrow for Diver, heavy enough to drag me to my knees, but my mech remains standing.

*I'm so sorry,* my heart whispers. *I know she hurt you worst of all.*

*But our old Luminaut loved us once. She loved her Seer as her own sister. She loved her friends before they were killed. The Light Collective stole too much, and our old Luminaut began to hate.* Diver's Light sparks a glimmer of faint hope, as frail as a leaf clinging to a branch in the bitter wind. Even after all she's done, my mech doesn't hate Queen. He loves. *Luminaut must never let love give way to hate.*

*Power without love is no power at all,* I assure Diver.

*Do not forget, Luminaut. No matter what.*

I won't forget. But not forgetting doesn't mean I'm not going to destroy all the Darkness it's possible to destroy, including the Darkness in Queen.

"Hey, we better get going." Nate grazes my fingertips with his touch. "No time like the present to go slay some Shadowmancers, right?"

*No time …* I thought we'd have a lifetime, but now, even a few precious seconds would be a gift. I bask in the glow of his Light, feeling loved, wanted, enough—everything Nate makes me feel in my soul. I wish I could pause this moment forever because what happens next has too much at stake to lose. The outcome is final.

Which makes this goodbye more painful than any I've made yet.

"Nate." I trace the veins in his arms until my hand finds its way into his. Hopping onto my tiptoes, I kiss him.

An ache of love blooms under my heart, settling into my Light until I know, at last, what it means when people say love and Light are the same. I press my lips way too hard compared to the tender way he holds my face, but I have to feel this, every inch of him. I want this kiss imprinted on my memory so that when I'm inside the Shadow Plain, facing down my destiny, I'll remember this moment and know this kiss told him everything my faltering words couldn't say.

*I love you. I'm sorry. I hope you understand what I have to do.* Speaking the truth aloud would break me, fracture my resolve. Instead, I linger as long as I can in his arms, kissing him softly until inevitably, we part.

"What was that for?" Nate's lips shine, slightly swollen from our kiss, and it takes everything in me not to kiss him again.

"No reason, I just wanted to." I gulp down the lump that forms in my throat and smile at his bemused grin. "When this is over, we'll go on our pizza date. Sounds good?"

If Nate knows I'm lying, he doesn't say. He tucks a loose lock of hair behind my ear, his fingers slipping down the strands like he's memorizing every last one of my features.

"Sounds perfect."

Perfect. Yes. It would have been. We walk hand in hand to Diver, who waits to take us to the Rognaga one last time.

# CHAPTER 28
## CALLIE

THE ROGNAGA PIT LOOKS LIKE an abandoned war zone. The barren ground is wet with mud, ash, and blood, scattered with craggy stones that once formed the old Rognaga walls, all of them toppled in the aftermath of our false victory. It's a reminder of everything that was almost sacrificed here and all that might be sacrificed still. The crater's heights loom like an open grave waiting to receive us, and not a single star shines in the tangibly black sky.

Will I be judged worthy of facing the Darkness this time? Failure isn't something I'm willing to contemplate. The multiverse depends on us winning this final fight. All we need now is an opponent.

Guess what? Queen hasn't shown up. Am I surprised? No.

"She's playing with us," I murmur. Toran nods silently at my side.

It's part of our hastily concocted plan. Toran holds the Light Cores in his satchel and will pretend to hand Queen her prize. Diver remains hidden behind a large bend in the crater, waiting to snatch Toran and me. The rest of the Seers and Nate will hop out of El's transport, Nate will blast Queen to distract her, and the

Seers will use their collective powers to create a new gateway to the Shadow Plain. Then Toran and I can rescue Heike. No amount of arguing would convince him not to come into the Darkness with me. Getting them out together — and alive — should be fun.

The last piece of the puzzle is Queen herself.

"Perhaps she doesn't know we're here," Toran suggests.

"She's watching from the Veil." I shake my head. "Either she's taking her sweet time strategizing or she's waiting it out until we get distracted."

"So it would seem." Toran's gaze remains on the empty horizon. "What's it like inside the Shadow Plain?"

He's nervous. He ought to be. "Imagine the worst kind of horror you know. It's a thousand times worse than that."

"Then I see why Nate would choose to go there after his mother's death."

"Really?" I glance at Toran's many angles, softened by regret. "Why?"

"Because escaping to a place that's worse than a thousand horrors sounds easier than living with grief." When Toran looks at me, I see nothing but sadness lining his face, making him appear far older than seventeen.

"If Queen had come to me after I thought Heike died, I'd have joined her cause without a second thought. But after everything you've been through, all the losses you suffered — leaving your family and friends, knowing you'll never see them again — you didn't run away from what was hard. You chose to sacrifice your happiness over and over again so the multiverse will survive. I don't know why the Rognaga judged you unworthy as Living Light, but I think you're more worthy than anyone I know."

I hope I'm as worthy of my destiny the way Toran says. Maybe I went into the Rognaga for selfish reasons, but I came out of it knowing the truth: Darkness has taken too many innocent lives, and I could never live with myself if I let it destroy more. Queen exists in the first place because Luminauts looked away when ignoring evil was easier than facing it head-on. Light wasn't broken by Shadows, it was broken by apathy: hidden, politicized, and made villainous by the last place in the multiverse that remembered.

Luminauts are supposed to choose love and Light, but the five raw pieces of Light in Toran's satchel prove even Luminauts can forget the truth. But maybe the brokenness can still be made whole. Love and Light are always choices we have the power to make.

*Power — and Light — without love is no power at all.*

"I'm sorry we didn't learned to get along and be friends earlier." I offer Toran a smile of apology. "At least we can prove we're the most awesome sister-saving dyad ever, right?"

Toran smiles, a rare sight. "Right."

Across the expanse of the crater, the Veil appears. From its depths, Queen emerges on the Vredis. No Shadowmancers follow, and no Heike either. A terrible smile parts her lips when she sees me standing with Toran.

"Hello, Calliope," she purrs. "Your Seer has come with my prize. How kind of him."

"Where is Heike?" Toran speaks, his deep voice booming. "I've brought your negotiated price in exchange for my sister's life, and earlier than stipulated. I demand proof she's unharmed."

This is all part of the plan. So far, it's going swimmingly. I stand silent and wait. It's not time yet.

"Once I've taken what I'm owed into my Shadow Plain, I'll return the girl." Typical ambiguous Queen response. We expected this. "However, I have some concerns."

Queen's smile becomes poisonously cold, and the sky overhead fills with Shadow. Obstacles were always built into what happens next, but depending on what she throws down, we might have to improvise.

I've basically improvised this entire journey by the seat of my pants, so why stop now?

"You found the fifth Light Core *much* faster than I expected. I'm starting to believe you're working together, plotting against me."

Any last trace of the moon and stars fade as Shadowmancers spill across the Veil, snaking through the crater, sniffing out Light. The Cores in Toran's satchel whir ferociously, and the monsters gather close, tentacle mouths reaching for us.

"Why betray me now, Calliope? Doing so will only bring your loved ones the worst kind of pain."

Betrayal: the one thing Queen can't tolerate. It's what she's always wary of, and it's why she expects my next move to be a trap. For as powerful as she is, I hold the keys to destroying her, putting us on equal footing.

"You're getting what you want," I say carefully. "Me and all five Light Cores in the Shadow Plain. Isn't it time to let Heike go?"

"I'll set the girl free in due time."

"The time is now." Water rises from the desert sand to form ice daggers in Toran's hands. Queen grins triumphantly when she sees his mounting rage. Angry Toran is distracted Toran.

*Luminaut,* Diver says, *Not-Our-Luminaut says your Seer needs to slow his roll. We do not know what that means.*

*I know what it means.* And I very much agree with Nate's assessment.

"Toran, it's okay." I place a hand on my Seer's shoulder,

watching for any moves Queen might unexpectedly make.

"I see you finally learned some restraint, Calliope." Queen gives me a mocking round of applause. "Unfortunately, you learned too late. The deal is canceled. You and all your friends you've been plotting with, hiding with your World Diver, will be the first to die."

"Like hell we will."

Nate and Ayla leap out of the transport zooming across the crater, powers flashing. Ayla uses her Manipulation to float them to the ground while Nate blasts Queen with so much Light it crumbles the Vredis to ashes. Dr. Ormandi and Serai follow next. Fire blazes across the earth while flying boulders ricochet around a fog of Shadowmancers spilling from the Veil.

"Hi, Callie! Bye, Callie!" El and Nemo wave at me before he guides the transport back into the air. The getaway vehicle is a go.

*Diver, it's time, buddy.*

*Yes, Luminaut.*

My mech steps away from his hiding spot, rumbling across the crater, crashing through Darkness and fire and lightning. Queen is busy with Nate, each of them slinging their powers so fast I get whiplash.

"Okay Toran, game time." I take the satchel with the Light Cores, and he raises his palms.

"I hope this works."

Water floats into the sky where it forms a ring at the edge of the crater. Dr. Ormandi and Serai add their elements to the ring too. Ayla is last, adding lightning and wind, and in the center of the ring, a crack forms. It starts small, a piercing bright spark that grows wider and brighter. Blue water bonds with green-brown earth, orange fire, and white-hot air, all of it swirling together in a plasma-like expansion of elements until it snaps and distorts.

It's as if space itself is split, a fissure growing larger until it encompasses the whole elemental ring.

On the other side, the horror of the Shadow Plain shows itself. Glowing red eyes of a million Shadowmancers peer at us, waiting for what comes next.

"Toran, now!"

Diver picks us up the very second our gateway appears. In the Crow's Nest, I put one of the already activated Light Cores in the Prism, allowing us to pass through with a brilliant flash of Light.

Even from this height, Queen's scream of rage as Toran and I barrel into the Darkness reaches my ears. And there, lying prone and suspended in the Shadows, is the person Toran came here to save.

"Heike!"

## Toran

My sister lies in Darkness like a corpse on a pyre, waiting to begin the final journey back to our ancestors in the Lands Beyond. Darkness lurks around her, a slithering, writhing pile of grubs on a rotted log. It hasn't been given a command to consume her, but eagerly listens for the call.

"We must get Heike. She needs us."

"Toran, wait," Callie says. Shadowmancers surround the World Diver, trying to eat through his bronze and glass. "We have to stick together or they'll ash you."

If I'm destroyed, turned to ash before I reach my sister, Callie will have to choose between destroying the Shadows or saving Heike. I can't ask her to do both.

"Do what you must to defend us."

Callie calls Light into her hands, forming a ball that she

enlarges into a protective cocoon around us. It isn't perfect, and if we don't move together in sync, Darkness will seep in.

"This would be a good time to start acting like a bonded dyad without trying to go off and do our own thing or fight about who's right," Callie advises.

I'm in perfect agreement.

"Once we get Heike, take her back to Diver at all costs." Callie catches my eye to see that I understand. "Is that clear?"

"What about you?"

Callie doesn't answer — her grim, determined expression says enough.

"No. You can't." For the first time, fear fills me at the thought of losing the person I have always known — even reluctantly — is my Luminaut. Callie has too much to live for to sacrifice everything now. "What about Nate, your mechs, your friends who love you?"

Callie's eyes are immensely sad but resolved to see things through. Light builds around us, and gnawing tentacles of horrid Darkness grow louder by the second.

"No matter what happens, get out of here with your sister. She's suffered more than enough as Queen's pawn."

I shake my head. "But—"

"Being a Luminaut, fighting Darkness, and hunting Light Cores — that was my choice. I own the consequences." Callie audibly gulps, facing the last barrier between us and the Shadow Plain. "Okay Diver, let us out."

The hatch door creaks open. Immediately, Shadowmancers assault the Crow's Nest. Callie's fierce Light blocks them from overwhelming us, and together we move forward, past the threshold. The door slams shut behind us.

I hang on tight as we float, unable to walk. I can't control my movements. Darkness attacks any part of me that ventures too far from Light. Callie's power protects her and deflects Shadows, but I have no such shield.

"Dramora spawn!" Pain as a sharp as a pike slices my skin, turning my flesh to ash where a Darkness tentacle touches me. The throb cuts as deep as the bone.

"Stay with me." Callie grabs my arm to keep me near. No Shadowmancers can touch her in such a powerful state. She glides toward Heike, stopping at last before my sister's form.

"She looks like a sleeping maiden from a fairytale," I whisper. Heike loves fairytales. I was too proud to see anything good in them, but now I desperately cling to the fragile hope of a happy ending. An act of love always triumphs—I love my sister more than my life. Will that be enough?

Screeching, hissing Shadowmancers descend on us, their malicious red eyes glowing like ember coals. Heike can't move to save herself, and she doesn't wake up. Once their tentacle mouths latch on to her frame, they'll turn her to ash.

I refuse to let Heike die like this. She's too good, too worthy of life. More importantly, none of this was her choice.

"Toran, your water bottle!" Callie points to the object on my hip, a small bottle of my element I looped through my belt on our way to the Rognaga. "Use it!"

"I don't think I can." My hands are gray and cold and stiff. Being trapped in the Shadow Plain is killing me. It's becoming harder to breathe, and my movements slow down, my vision deteriorates. I can hardly tell Shadows from the black spots in my eyes. It won't be long until I perish.

Callie sees what's happening and touches my shoulder. Her Light temporarily warms me, but the creeping chill of death remains.

"On the count of three," Callie says, "we're going to hit them as hard as we can, and you're going to take Heike. Then I'm going to wrap both of you in Light and toss you out of here through that open gateway."

"What about Diver?"

"You'll be dead before you make it to the Crow's Nest with Heike in your arms." As much as I don't like to admit it, what Callie says is true. "Trust me, Toran. I've got you both. Okay?"

Trust her: the hardest thing I've had to learn since I found her in the forest outside Gravenskov. This requires I relinquish control to her completely and place all my faith in her Light. I never trusted anyone but myself, but if I don't fully trust Callie I'll die, and so will Heike.

"All right, we'll do it." I snap open the bottle and form the sharpest, most deadly ice daggers.

"Three …" Callie's Light fills the ice. "Two …" Light fills the space around Heike. Darkness can't approach. "One."

Ice daggers whiz through the Shadow Plain so fast they create a whistling noise as they pierce monster after monster. Glowing red eyes shutter and disappear with haunting screeches, and Light overtakes the Dark. It looks, for a moment, like we cleared a way forward.

But hope is dashed. Shadow upon ceaseless Shadow swarms in around us. How could our attack accomplish so little?

"Just grab her, Toran," Callie advises, "and hang on tight."

Reaching through from the safety of Callie's Light, my exposed arm is met by an onslaught of Darkness. Tentacles latch themselves to my limb, turning it to ash. Excruciating gnawing turns flesh and bone to ash from the inside out.

I cry out, unable to grit my teeth against the agony any longer.

"Hang on, Toran!" Callie Light blasts the Darkness away, and with what little is left of my hand and forearm, I grasp Heike and pull her close, clutching her to my chest.

Her body is cold—so very cold.

"It's time." Light encases my sister and me, and through the brilliant glow, I catch sight of Callie's golden-brown eyes. It may be the last time I ever see my Luminaut—a thought that rises through the pain and fear and turns into panic.

She must come too. She must stay with me and Heike and soar through the gateway to safety. I've been foolish not to realize she's my friend, but now that I do, I can't let her sacrifice herself this way. Too many people need her. *I* need her. A Seer without a Luminaut is never quite whole.

"Callie, wait—"

"Goodbye, Toran."

With a forceful push, Callie sends Heike and I flying through the gateway. There's a brilliant flash, and we emerge onto the ashen ground surrounded by Darkness, fire, rubble, and furious Light—but not Callie's. It's Nate, battling Queen alongside Ayla.

"Callie?" I look over my shoulder. There's nothing. No gateway to the Shadow Plain. No Diver, no circle of elements creating a fissure in reality. Just the wall of the crater staring at me like a stony punch in the face.

Heike and I made it through, but Callie didn't. She stayed behind to finish what she set out to do.

Agony fills every void inside of me—for my ashen limb, my lifeless sister, and my lost Luminaut. So much pain I can hardly breathe, and the tears in my eyes freeze as they fall down my cheeks.

One Luminaut is gone. Only one remains, holding the fate of the multiverse in his hands.

## Nate

"Sparky! Watch your freaking six before those Shadowmancers rip you a new one!"

Between making sure Ayla doesn't get eaten alive and keeping Queen away from the gateway to the Shadow Plain, I'm pretty busy. That doesn't include watching out for Dad and Serai, doing whatever geriatric Seers do in a melee, and El, who might fly his hot-wired transport into a cloud of Shadowmancers or a rock wall.

These dingbats know how to keep a Luminaut busy, that's for sure. Blasting Darkness on the offensive and the defensive has me beat. Especially because, oh, that's right, *I'm the only person here with Light powers.* Callie and Toran sure are taking their sweet time bombing the Shadow Plain, but I'll admit, it's a pretty big job. All I can do is fight my tormentor/former boss while these old people, children without pilot's licenses, and oblivious Seers try their best to get themselves ashed.

Needless to say, it isn't going well.

"What's a six? I wasn't aware I had one." Ayla shoots some lightning at a group of Shadowmancers. They disappear, then reappear to my right. *Sparkly sparkly boom boom pow* goes my Light and they're gone, but more come through the Veil just as fast. "And what new one will they rip me? I don't like the sound of that."

Please, somebody—and I mean Callie James, specifically— show up to end this. Pretty please.

"Stick close, don't turn your back on them." I'm trying to answer Ayla with less snark. She responds better that way. Case in point—

"Oh yes, I see what you mean." She turns so we're semi-back-to-back and throws down a cyclone to trap Darkness in its spiral. She sends the whole thing my way, and a plume of Light catches the wind, depositing Shadowmancer ashes in its path.

"That was a good trick!" Ayla claps her hands, pleased with herself. I swear she doesn't notice the imminent danger she's in. Maybe all that electricity shorted a few circuits.

But yeah, it was a cool move we did.

"Don't lose focus. Watch for Shadowmancers sneaking up on us." One awesome Light tornado doesn't mean we're making headway.

"Are you struggling by yourself, Nathaniel?" Queen floats above me, controlling her Darkness with ease and dominance. "You are untested and getting angry. We all know what an angry Luminaut can do."

Mass destruction, yeah, I know. Queen still likes to bring up the negative things Light has done throughout the ages, as if I'm going to change my mind about what I am and go back to her side, or toss my hands and give up, or something equally stupid in the middle of the fight for the multiverse.

"Goading isn't going to work." She's dealing with *me*. I learned to see through her insults and needling taunts a long time ago.

"Yes, that wasn't one of your many weaknesses." Queen agrees with me? That can't be good. "But you never try to hide when you care for something. It will be your downfall."

"Loving people is a weakness?" To Queen, of course it is. Love exposes a person to loss—which is defeat, according to her. "Only because you pretend you don't know how to love and never did, but I know that's a lie. You loved people so much you turned to Darkness to save them. Just like me."

Queen's lips curl over her sharp, glinting teeth. "You and I are nothing alike. I am strong, all-powerful. You're a weak creature of Light, and human again. Which means you can bleed."

Queen's Darkness fills the whole crater until I'm choked by Shadows. I can't see anyone, not Dad, or Serai, or El flying around in the transport. I can barely see Ayla and she's six inches away.

It's easy to predict Queen's next move. She's going to break me by killing everyone and leave me alive to spend the next seventy-odd years alone, blaming her murderous actions on me for not falling in line. For daring to challenge her.

*"You brought this upon yourself, Nathaniel."* I can hear the line now, but I'm not going to give her a chance to say it.

Not today, Queen. Not today.

Light burns away the Darkness and explodes through the crater, saving everyone just as fast as Queen's power sought to destroy them. I don't feel pain or nausea—just power surging through me, sniffing out every last Shadowmancer. I suddenly become aware my feet aren't touching the ground, and Queen and I are eye-level. She looks momentarily surprised before she grins meanly.

"Impressive. To think you learned so much in such a short amount of time," she says. "Let's see what else you learned."

Light and Darkness pinball back and forth, each exploding around the other like a waltz of death and life. *Give in. Be angry. She's taken so much from you, and now she's trying to take everything else.*

The voice in my head says words I'm not ready to hear, *can't* hear if I want to maintain control. Rage makes me sloppy, and Queen's trying her best to rile me. As powerful as she is, she can play games all day. The second I tire, she'll be ready.

Come on, Callie and Toran. Let's get the Shadow Plain blown up already, huh?

A brilliant flash of Light explodes the gateway to the Shadows, and my heart beats hard, anticipating the end of the monsters and the slow death of Queen's Darkness for good. Yes, Callie, you did it! If anyone has enough power to destroy the Shadows, it's Callie. Queen whips around, staring at the gateway with momentary fear.

But what comes out isn't a multiverse-saving Luminaut—just a small ball of Light cocooning two people. Two. Not three. And no mech. The Light around them fades, and all my hope flickers and dies. Toran and Heike lay on the ground, barely alive.

Callie isn't there.

"Toran!" Ayla shrieks, remembering she actually cares about him despite the fact he's been a major dirtbag.

"Boy Scout! Heike!" I come back to the ground and run. A low, chilling laugh spills from Queen's lips. Toran looks like death itself, clutching his arm—what remains of it—to his middle. Heike hasn't moved.

"We need El's transport." Somehow, Toran's comm is still strapped to his remaining arm. How? No idea. I'm shocked Darkness didn't melt it off. But it's there, glowing. A miracle that means I can call El and the transport. I rip it off Toran and tap the command. "El, get your butt over here!"

"Did you win?" He comes in statically. "It looks like you're losing, dümfo."

"Shut up, dingus." I don't have time for this. I need to get injured people away from the mess and find out what happened to Callie. "Heike and Toran are hurt, we need to get them out."

"On it." El switches tone in a flash, and above me, the transport circles. I shoot a Light orb into the air as a flare, alerting him to our location.

"Ayla! Nate!" Toran tries to stand when he sees me, but he

can't hold Heike in his good arm and get his feet under him at the same time. "Help!"

"What happened in there?" I Light blast Darkness away from Toran and drop to his side, examining his injury. Holy freaking crap, that's bad. His entire right hand is gone, turned to ashes, and most of his forearm. The flesh that remains is necrotic. It has to be amputated before Darkness infects Toran's blood and bone, a slower, more agonizing death than if he'd gotten ashed all at once.

"Heike hasn't woken." Even grievously injured, Toran only cares for his sister.

Heike looks grayer than gray in Toran's arm. I touch her neck, checking for vitals. The faintest pulse, little more than a flutter, erratically beats.

"She's alive," I assure Toran. "But she needs to get out of here."

El lands the transport and opens the door. Nemo pops up on his shoulder, the mech's worry palpable. El glances around, noticing Heike and Toran — but no one else.

"Where's Callie?" El blurts the question of the hour.

"Let me carry Heike," I tell Toran. "You follow. Can you walk, or does Ayla need to help?"

"I'm not leaving." Toran can barely string the three words together, but those three words are as stubbornly resolute as ever. No use arguing with him if he wants to try and fight. Even injured, his Manipulation is sorely needed.

So is Callie. But that's another question entirely.

"Whatever you say." I lift Heike and place her in the transport. She releases a soft breath when I lay her down but doesn't wake. "El, get her to the MedFac in Cordonanza, if it's still functioning."

"What happened to—"

"I don't know. Just … take Heike to safety."

A sick feeling tells me I already know what happened, but I'm not going to give in. I can't sink inside the drowning weight. This moment—and the moments that follow—are too critical. El catches my eye, and I give the transport's side a loud tap with my palm, blasting the Darkness trying to sneak up from behind.

"Go, El! Now!"

El closes the transport door, then pilots it into the sky before whooshing off for Cordonanza's ruin.

Time for the truth.

Dad rushes up, demanding to know what happened to Callie, and Serai tries to reform the gateway in the rock with her powers alone, but it's useless.

Everything around me slows. My pulse all at once pounds and inches at a crawl, like my blood is stuck in my veins, unable to continue forward motion. Somehow I walk, one foot in front of the other. Ayla tries to help Toran, but all he can do is clutch his half-arm to his stomach. Something tells me the pain in his eyes is only partly from the injury.

"I know you're in level twelve of the pain cave, Boy Scout." I crouch beside him, and he turns toward me, his eyes swallowed by icy tears. "But I have to know what happened. Where is Callie?"

"She—" He gulps, and ice sticks up like needles from his frost-white skin. "She stayed. With Diver. To finish it."

The feeling of my soul being ripped in two cleaves my heart from my chest. It's like an ax cut me open to take me apart, harvesting my organs and leaving me broken and bleeding, less than a whole person. My brain screams quietly, a half-sob stuck in my throat as Light bleeds from me, falling to the ground like tears, and I stand dumbstruck with grief.

Callie stayed to finish what she started and made sure Toran and Heike got out first. It was always her intention to stay in the Shadows. She's going to save the multiverse the only way she knows how: by sacrificing herself for everyone she loves.

*Callie ... my stars.*

I can't wonder why because I know why. I'd have made the same choice. Even if we were only together for a moment as brief and bright as a shooting star, it will be enough. She'll live on in Light, same as Mom. One day, at the end of my lifetime, I'll join them both.

*I'll keep going for you – it won't be like it was with Mom. I won't become angry and stuck. I'll live my life for you because I love you. I always will.*

I hope, somehow, my truth reaches her Light.

"Well, Nathaniel?" Queen appears over my shoulder, suspended in Darkness. "You lost the Luminaut you loved and sacrificed everything for—your Darkness, your true power, your ability to avenge her. And for what? A humiliating defeat, surrounded by mud and ash."

"Stop talking like you won." Standing between Queen and victory are my Light, Ayla and her lighting, Dad's inferno, and Serai and her earthquakes. "If you want to plunge the multiverse into Shadow, you've got to go through me first."

"And me."

Toran stands, unsteadily raising his remaining hand. Water flows through the desert, fast and ferocious, until a massive wave builds around the edge of the crater. Ice encases Toran's injured arm, forming a hand to channel his power. Standing in front of his fifty-foot swell with a whole limb made of ice, he's a fearsome sight to behold.

Queen stares at us gathered in defiance—at my Light that burns brighter than ever. "Excuse me?"

"I said, you haven't won." I plant my feet, powerful in my truth. "Darkness was never my real power. Light is, and love. Love for my mom. Love for Callie. Love for everyone you'd kill in your unchecked rage."

Queen shakes her head. "You leave me no choice but to destroy all of you." Then she smirks. "Don't worry, Nathaniel. That was the plan all along."

Darkness races forward, and our collective powers rise to meet it. If Callie's destiny is to save the multiverse, my destiny has always been to help her do it. Queen won't win. Love will— always.

*See you on the other side, Callie James.*

Light flares in my hands, and I come face to face with the beginning of the end.

## Callie

Okay, so it's up to me, five Light Cores, and a mech to destroy an entirely separate reality that took millennia to carve into existence. And I've got to finish up said destruction derby in about twenty minutes. Give or take.

If I don't, Queen's going to use all this power to ash everyone I love on the other side.

The problem is, I have no idea what I'm doing. Giant Light blasts using my self-contained power didn't even crack the foundation of the Shadow Plain.

Obviously, this is a problem.

"Okay Diver, how do I do this?" The Cores in Toran's satchel practically scream in the presence of so much unrelenting Darkness, their vibration hurting my hip where they rest.

*Luminaut must channel the Light.*

"Yeah, I'm doing that and it's not working." Can't he see me blasting these monsters to no avail?

*Luminaut has to channel the Light in the Light Cores.*

"Cool. How?" It's part of his charm that he forgets I'm not as old and knowledgeable as him. "I'm a human with a seventeen-year-old memory. I need some ageless robot wisdom. If you've got any to pass on, I'd appreciate it."

*Touch a Light Core, and Luminaut's Light will channel it.*

Except I've held Light Cores plenty of times before, and all I can do with them is accidentally open gateways or summon terrifying Shadowmancers. Light Cores and I tend to have an erratic relationship at best. But hey, why not try everything, right?

I take a Light Core from the satchel, grasping it tightly despite my fear — an emotion that fades the moment I realize it's the one from Ensolorada. I feel Nate's Light where he held it, a feeling like his hand holding mine.

I close my eyes, fresh tears pricking the corners. This is as close to holding any part of him as I'll ever be again, and everything inside me aches with love and tremendous loss, all the way to the cells and atoms forming my bones. I wish we could've gone on our date because it would mean we had one more day — one more hour — together.

*I hope you know how much I love you, Nate. Enjoy your pizza for me, okay?*

Love fills my Light, flowing through the Light in the Core, joining with Light cosmic, until all the Light in everything at once unites in me. My Light, Nate's Light, they're briefly entwined, and I feel him shine. But it's not just Nate. The Light of every human being alive throughout the multiverse connects with me, with each other, all of us shining like a galaxy of stars. Light grieves with me, celebrates with me, loves with me. That's what happens when you give your heart to something and let it go.

And then, something strange starts to happen.

The Light Core in my hand melts into my skin, sending Light racing through my veins like a river of warm gold. Through the Darkness, I soar in freedom, as though I'm suddenly part of a greater kind of Light, the kind that once connected everything there is. Every world I've visited, and the ones I haven't. Every person, every animal, every plant. Rocks, rivers, oceans, and sky. The Light of the multiverse. A broken beauty, given rebirth.

*Diver, what's happening?*

*This is how it should be, Luminaut. How Light can be made whole.*

Everything Diver longed for is happening in me.

With newfound confidence, I take another Core from the satchel. Tremurheim's Core carries the great sorrow of rupture, but also hope that the world can return to the peaceful days of the past, before war and violence tore apart forests and Mist. Toran's hope can be restored too. He'll grow and thrive like the trees rooted deep in Tremurheim's scarred earth. All will heal.

The next Core is Ictari, El's lost world where people and Light were forced to hide underground, protecting themselves from the unseen and unknown. The Light of Ictari longed to be found, just like El. Eventually, both Light and El got what they wanted most, despite all the pain they've been through. They were seen at last, and known.

Aureloria is next. I feel Ayla in this Light, a power to look on and admire but not to get too close for fear of danger and destruction. This Light fled the bars of its gilded cage, and now there's no need to be afraid. Light and Ayla are strong and secure. They've learned to embrace truth and not dwell on past wrongs.

This Light is stronger than anyone knows.

The last Core is Earth. My home. Nate's home. Mariasol's chosen home, where she made her family and was buried in the same ocean holding this Light Core. But that home is no longer home for any of us. It's just a place because home is Light itself. The currents of the ocean will always flow, just like Light—never ceasing, carrying passengers—willing or not—to a destination they can't foresee.

I never expected my journey would end here after starting in the wild surf off the shores of Verona Beach. But Light has a way of drawing people along in its ebb and flow to exactly where they should land.

*Diver, what do I do next? I need your guidance. I can't do this alone.*

All the Light in all five Cores scorches away my blood and nerves. Soon I'll become more than just one with Light—I'll become Light itself. A part of Callie must remain to finish this task.

*The Shadows tremble, Luminaut. The foundations and the ends of everything have been shaken. Luminaut must channel the Light.*

Channel the Light. Concentrate and fire away.

I stretch my arms wide and let Darkness have it.

Light fractures Shadows, cracks Darkness, destroys Shadowmancers. The alternate reality of the Shadow Plain—the suspension of life, death, and time—fissures, and a glimmer of Light appears on the horizon. It's faint, barely noticeable. Then it's swallowed by the red, glowing eyes of monsters brave enough to venture close. They want to swallow me, take the Light inside and snuff it forever.

Another blast, this one less controlled. Horrific screeching, like sharp nails scratching a glass windowpane, erupt all around me until I think my ears might explode. I cry out, desperately clinging to my power. The edge of the precipice is within my grasp, but I'm slipping into a void.

Light flies into the Shadows like pure chaos. Light spins, swirls, explodes, consumes. A fireworks show of dazzling danger. Darkness shudders, damaged, but is it gone? Did I break this dark kingdom born in the fury of betrayal?

Queen's need to protect herself — her creation — is strong. But Light could be stronger …

*I have to be stronger than Darkness …*

One last blast and I hang limp, watching as Light and Darkness wage a battle above my head. Each power fights the other, sparks and ashes falling onto my cheeks. One side makes headway, another falls back. Which will triumph? Everything depends on the outcome.

Then it's quiet and still. The Shadows are nowhere to be seen. Beyond the edge of Darkness, a crack of Light forms, exposing a beautiful multiverse of cosmos in active creativity. Stars and dust, future and past, all meeting at once.

"Diver?" I whisper my mech's name. "Did we win?"

*Diver?*

*No, Luminaut. We did not win.*

A crack in the Shadows won't kill the disease. This is a small victory, but not enough to end the war.

Beyond my Light, at the edge of the Shadows, millions of glowing red eyes open. Queen's full army has awakened, hellbent on defending their home and destroying anyone who stands in the way of its sustaining ruler. Namely, me.

Even though I have the Light of all five Light Cores within me, the power goes inert. Useless, motionless, unable to move. Just like me. I can't lift my hand to blast a single Shadowmancer. My body has given all it has to give.

I watch, horrified at the realization that I lost the fight for the entire multiverse — all the lives it contains, all the Light and love. Defeat becomes a grim reality before my eyes, and a numb chill like death overtakes all sensation.

Tentacles reach for me, and Darkness closes in.

# CHAPTER 29
# CALLIE



*LUMINAUT. YOU ARE WITH US.*

Diver's hands materialize through the drawing Darkness. Shadowmancers disappear as he pulls me away from my assailants. His Light gives the illusion of warmth, but it's a temporary reprieve from the inevitable end.

*I lost, buddy. It's over. I wasn't strong enough to win.*

Everything will become ash because of me. I set out to prove I could be good, that I wasn't a failure, a loser, a slacker who didn't live up to her potential. I tried my hardest to be what the multiverse needed — to make every sacrifice to ensure the people I love will be safe and healthy and live long, happy lives, even if it means I never see them again.

I gave *everything* I had to give, but it wasn't enough.

Wet hair sticks to my cheeks while I cry—no, sob—uncontrollably. I wanted so much to be enough, and I wasn't. I never will be.

*I'm sorry, Diver. I wanted to make Light whole again, but I wasn't what the multiverse needed. I wasn't the Luminaut you needed either.*

*Luminaut, you are wrong.* Diver gently pushes me into the Crow's Nest, safe from harm. His agony as Shadowmancers devour him pierces my Light, but he holds strong. For now. I know he won't be able to last much longer.

*How can you say I'm wrong? I failed. We're going to die.*

*Luminaut is a part of us, always. We are with Luminaut in Light, and Light cannot die, no matter what Darkness steals.*

*Maybe you can't die, but I can.* And I will. Just like all my friends, my family, every single person in the multiverse.

Darkness grinds against the glass dome of Diver's windows until a crack forms — small, but growing larger. Swarms of Shadowmancers pile onto the weakness, attacking it with all their strength. Persistent, hateful relentlessness I couldn't overcome.

*My Light isn't strong enough, Diver. I'm not strong enough.*

The crack grows wider. We only have a few minutes left, if time passes here. It could be a millisecond or three hundred years, but it wouldn't matter. I'd still have lost. Darkness tearing Diver to shreds is the worst kind of anguish. Out of all the things I said I'd never do, hurting Diver worse than Queen did is one of them. But even in that, I failed.

*Luminaut is exactly what is needed to make Light whole,* Diver says. *But great victories are not won alone. Luminaut is not weak for needing us, just as we are not weak for needing Luminaut.*

Light sparks in the Prism, illuminating the Crow's Nest. The cracked crystal I repaired in the Hall of Machines pulses with more Light than the rest, a reminder that I *can* fix some things. Small things. Mistakes I made because I was angry and impulsive. I can fill the cracks of unspoken need.

*Luminaut will not hurt us. Luminaut loves us.* Diver's love shines bright in the Prism's Light, combining with the Light of the Light Cores, with my own Light. So much Light, all of it resting inside me.

*Luminaut can never say she is not enough because to us, Luminaut is *everything. We were alone before we met Luminaut, and trapped in the dark. Luminaut never abandoned us. Now Luminaut must let us help.*

The Light in the Prism pulses, calling me. Shadowmancers retreat, screaming in terror as Diver's Light burns them away. Light that is pure love—no longer in pain, unburdened by memories of failure and regret—shines all around.

Diver's Light, the Light of his past Luminauts. It's the same Light that exists in me, that's existed since Light first became. Even though my eyes are open, I'm suddenly wide awake.

*Luminaut never had to do this alone. She will never be alone, even after we are gone, because we love Luminaut and Luminaut loves us. Power without love is no power at all. Let us give the power we have to Luminaut.*

I turn on my side and shift my legs under me, strength building as I stand and make my way to the Prism. Diver's love and Light drown the Darkness and overwhelm my doubt.

This task—destroying the Shadow Plain, saving the multiverse from Queen, restoring what was broken—isn't a task I'm meant to do alone. I need my friends, fighting on the other side. I need Nate and the resolve he gained by turning from Darkness. I need Diver and his vast capacity to forgive.

Light isn't a power meant to be wielded alone. It's what Diver's been trying to tell me all along—*we* can do this, not *I*. It isn't weak to accept support, and I'm not a failure if I save the multiverse with the help of everyone who loves me. It's knowing that we're all connected by invisible threads of Light that makes us stronger than Queen.

*Luminaut, use our Light. Use the Prism. Focus the Light and try again. Darkness will fall because we are stronger together.*

*We're stronger together, Diver.*

I look out the curved window at the festering Darkness.

Despite the unceasing assault, Diver and I remain. The crack I made in the Shadow Plain remains too, barely visible, but it's there. With Diver's Light and mine, we can widen it until this whole place implodes.

Hope blossoms in the Light, and I know — this time — we'll triumph.

Touching the Prism, all the Light in me, in the Light Cores I absorbed, and in Diver mingles and becomes one. It dances briefly before melting together, shooting from my hands through the crystal in a brilliant burst. The Prism refracts it, channels it, and sends pure Light soaring into the Shadows.

Darkness shatters, unable to withstand. Shadowmancers fall, millions at once. Light spreads, covers everything, burns away the evil around us like a star shining through the darkest part of night. No more shrieking monsters, no more gnawing jaws, no sound at all. Just Light healing what was hurt.

My consciousness floats above Diver, watching Light do its work. Darkness can't fight back in the face of something so powerful — it simply ceases. The crack at the back of the Shadow Plain widens, revealing the beauty of infinite stars and futures and pasts hidden from the place made to destroy beauty in the first place.

Light will endure, even if it seems to fade.

Love will cover the cost of grief.

It's the truth the Shadows can't face.

Light will restore what's been broken — even itself. Because of me, because of Diver. Because of love.

Power without love is no power at all.

Glowing like the birth of a brilliant star, Light fills everything. All the Darkness in the Shadow Plain crumbles until it's gone, and the Light from the Light Cores floats away, joining the multiverse that lies just beyond. Light stitches together a gold band to connect it all, and I know, in my heart and soul, everything that was broken so long ago has been renewed.

It isn't the same. The gold band absorbs into the rest of the cosmos, a tenuous and invisible connection. It isn't a Lightbridge, because Light can't be what it was before. But it *can* be different. It can learn from the past and be better than ever before.

Shattering crystal brings me back to my body and to the reality of what Diver and I just did. I'm weakened, wobbly and dizzy. The Light Cores are gone. My own Light remains … but Diver fades. His Prism lies in pieces on the Crow's Nest floor, broken by the effort it took to focus Light.

*No, no, no.* The throb in my knees when I drop and gather crystal shards reminds me I'm very much alive despite everything, and Diver and I are sitting at the edge of a reality that's disintegrating. Soon, we'll disintegrate too.

"Don't worry, Diver, I'll fix you."

There's still a little time. Expanding Light hasn't absorbed us the way it's absorbing Darkness. We can make it. I'll repair the Prism and use my power to open a gateway out. I rush to gather crystals and put them back together. One here, another there. They don't quite fit, but I'll make it work.

*No, Luminaut. You must go.*

"I can't leave you."

*Luminaut is with us. We are with Luminaut, always—even if Luminaut cannot see us.* The crystal shards in my hands glow faintly with Diver's Light. Each piece is a part of him—his memories, his consciousness. I feel him in each glittering speck scattered across the floor, and I know his Light is part of me.

But I also know the rest of him is not going to make it.

*Hold the crystal from our Prism, Luminaut, and tell our Light where you wish to go. They will take you there. All the Light in the Light Cores has touched us, and we can open any gateway. Our last gift to our last Luminaut.*

"This isn't how it's supposed to happen." Tears fill my eyes when I look at the crystals, evidence of Diver's physical brokenness. All that's left of him is contained in my hands.

I gaze through what's left of Diver's window, watching Light stretch toward the remaining corners of the Shadow Plain. We could stay here and let Light take us. Become one with all Light in the multiverse, forever.

It would be so quiet, so still and calm. Peaceful.

Or I could go back to my friends and fight Queen and her lingering Darkness. Spend the rest of my life helping others mend the broken things in their worlds.

I never thought I'd leave once I came to the Shadow Plain, but Diver is offering me a chance to truly finish what I started and take the ultimate journey with Light—living my life for it. But I have to make a choice quickly, before it's too late.

"Diver, I ..." I wipe my face.

*Do not worry, Luminaut. We are not sad. We love Luminaut.*

"I love you too, buddy. You've been with me from the beginning. You made me realize I'm a Luminaut in the first place."

This is the final goodbye I'll share with my mech. The truth settles into every nook and cranny of my heart, and I wish he could come with me. But Diver is going to be with Light outside of time, with the Luminauts he loved, with everyone who gave their lives to save what Light always should have been. At last, he will be whole.

It isn't sad for him. But it's so, so sad for me to know I won't see him again.

*I'll miss you, Diver. Thank you. For everything.*

*Thank you, Luminaut, for giving us adventure and Light once more.*

I clutch the crystals close, whispering my destination. "Take me to Ensolorada, to my friends. Take me where I can use my Light to do good and rebuild what's broken."

Light from the crystals wraps around me, pulling me away from the physical remains of my mech toward the destination I gave him. I didn't think it was possible for a mech to open a gateway, but a small circle of brilliance expands before my eyes, revealing not only Ensolorada, but the ultimate truth: in love, the power of Light can accomplish the impossible.

*Goodbye, Diver.*

*Goodbye, Calliope, my Luminaut.*

Diver becomes one with Light, and the last corner of the Shadow Plain is erased forever. As easy and soft as a sigh, he fades into eternal Light and rest.

Meanwhile, I'm rocketed through a gateway into a battlefield.

And by rocketed, I mean I'm falling through the air.

In all fairness to Diver, he couldn't pinpoint an exact location to create this gateway while he joined himself with Light. But still, a better aim would have been helpful.

*Whooosh — splash.*

My free fall stops. I'm suspended in water, a tangle of arms and legs that feels just like the moment after I wipe out on my surfboard and the ocean breaks my momentum. I'm floating, safe and secure, in a gigantic wave.

A wave? Ensolorada is a desert.

My lips break the surface and I look around, taking in the scene.

Nate and Ayla sling Light and lightning at legions of Queen's

Shadowmancers. It's an all-out brawl, but they pause when they see me emerge from the wave. Queen's venomous expression shifts, betraying horror as her Darkness disappears, becoming ash before her eyes.

Ayla smiles.

Nate's eyes fill with awe and love.

Fire engulfs Darkness at the other edge of the crater, burning it away, and rockslides and flying boulders keep a hold on even more Shadows. But both Dr. Ormandi and Serai stop when they see me, disbelief penetrating the glow of their Seer's Eyes. I don't notice El in the transport, but I hope—*truly* hope—he flew Heike away from this mess.

Below me, at the edge of the wave, Toran, controls the water. Which means he just saved my life. Oh Toran, you secret softie.

"Hey, Crabbypants!" I call down to my Seer. I'm so weirdly glad to see his scowl. "Cool new ice arm. Wanna go surfing?"

"*You* can surf. I will stand here."

Gosh, Toran, I would have missed you being the bluntest blunt person that ever was blunt. Light travels from my heart to my feet, and I rise above everything, forming a platform like a Light surfboard. *So. Cool.*

"Elara!" Queen stands still as stone, staring at me on top of the paused tidal wave. "Your Shadow Plain is gone."

Queen doesn't move, but an expression I've never seen overtakes her features—surprise. It's the first time she's shown any level of vulnerability. Her silvery-blonde hair hangs around her face like regular hair, and her eyes—still red, black, and glowing with menace—become fearful.

"You're lying!" Queen calls for her Darkness, but it's weakening, moving erratically. Shadowmancers fly off-course before faltering and sputtering out into vapor.

"It's fading. You feel it." My Light surfboard glides under me when I come closer, watching Queen with more sympathy than I thought I might feel for her at this moment.

She's been so lost after deep betrayal, she doesn't know how to love. She's a monster through and through, and she chose her path. There's no excuse for the things she did in the name of Darkness. But monsters are made by other monsters, and Queen—Elara from Ictari—is no exception.

"I don't want to continue the cycle of Luminaut violence that started you on this path," I say. "But if you decide to fight on, I'll battle until your Darkness gives out. The choice is up to you."

"If you win, then you win." Queen's voice sounds more grounded, less poisonous—but she remains deathly serious. "I cannot, *will* not, surrender to a Luminaut."

Queen lashes out with Darkness, sending it flying like a hurricane of writhing tentacles across the crater. I angle my Light surfboard under me, and at the crest of Toran's wave, barrel down.

Elation at the wind in my hair, the spray of a wave on my face, fills me with ecstatic joy. I let out a whoop as my fingertips graze the water, Light and water becoming one. Nate's Light finds Ayla's lightning, making both of them even more effective in destroying Darkness. Fire and earth rise up, scorching or burying Darkness as Dr. Ormandi and Serai make sure their kids survive this assault. Parents will never stop being parents, even when their kids have superpowers.

"Hey dude, nice work!" I recall my Light surfboard into my feet, and Toran uses his Manipulation to angle the wave, alive with Light, around Queen.

"I'm not finished." Toran moves both hands—the flesh one and the ice one—in a wide circle. The wave responds to his command, and any Darkness it touches fizzles out. "I assume you can swim."

"Correct-a-mundo, duderooni."

"Never say anything that idiotic ever again." Don't ever change, Toran.

I Light blast Queen the same moment Toran's wave descends on her. Water swallows her and her Darkness, crashing with finality against the edges of the crater. Small bubbles of air—Ayla's power at work—encase everyone who isn't Queen or her Darkness, protecting us and keeping us from getting swept away in the current.

"Ayla comes through! Nice! Did you two plan that?" I turn to Toran in our safety bubble and grin.

"No." He seems startled that Ayla would save him. "She must have guessed what I was going to do and knew exactly how to help."

Awww, they're such adorable soulmates! It'll be even cuter when they realize it.

I raise my hand, Light forming an orb in front of me. "Withdraw your wave. I don't want Queen to die, I just need all the Darkness inside her gone. Ready?"

"What will you do, if not destroy her?" Toran looks surprised, but there's been more than enough death at Queen's hands. I won't add to the body count.

"I'll ask her to reconsider my offer to make things right," I say.

"You're granting her mercy. You prefer that, don't you? I don't understand it." He regards me with something I never thought he'd show me: admiration. "One day, perhaps, I'll learn it too."

"Never too late to start."

Toran's wave sinks into the earth, rejoining Ensolorada's underground ocean and turning the crater to mud, sludge, and swampy puddles. Ayla pops the protective bubbles with a flick of her wrist, and we find ourselves standing in a circle around a very defeated, very wet, and very quiet Queen Beyond the Stars.

She sits on her knees, surprisingly small for somebody who was once the cunning and cruel Prime Shadowmancer, and stares at her pale, soaked hands, then down at the muddy ground, placing her palms flat on the earth mixed with ash.

"Elara?"

She looks up at Nate when he says her Luminaut name, but only briefly.

"Saeli is here." Queen closes her eyes. When she opens them again, she stares at the sky, alive with shimmering stars as the sun peeks over the horizon. "I always wondered what happened to her after she abandoned me in my prison."

"She lived." Serai steps forward, standing before Queen. "Saeli Nerida is my ancestor. From her came a long line of Earth Manipulators sworn to protect Ensolorada's Light. I've done everything in my power to uphold this tradition."

"Then she got what she wanted. A legacy other than death and violence." Queen stares at the mud between her fingers. "You realize, Calliope, you can't destroy Darkness forever. You can destroy me and my Shadow Plain, but you'll never rid the multiverse of Shadow. Humans will always betray, always hurt each other. Not even Light can fix their condition."

"I know." I kneel before Queen, and she lifts her chin, expressionless. "But you could help us. We'll help you too. Come back to Light, and right your wrongs." I look around at the Seers, at Nate. He nods his agreement.

"You don't have to be lost in Darkness anymore," he adds.

"There's hope on the other side. You can atone."

"No. I don't want hope or atonement." Queen's words are bitter, something of their old poison seeping through, but she's weakening, both in body and spirit. Small flakes of ash float into the air from her rapidly dissolving form. "I'll never rejoin you in Light. Some hurts are too deep to heal."

More ashes fly away, joining with the stars. Queen keeps her hands on the ground, on the earth of Saeli's home, and points her face at the moon as everything becomes ash. The final remains of her physical form disappear into the night.

She's gone. Everything is silent.

It's over at last.

"Callie." Nate is the first to move. He takes me in his arms and holds me like he can't believe I'm real, and he's afraid if he lets go, I'll float away like Queen.

There's so much to say. Words of reassurance that this moment is true despite both of us thinking it would never happen, and promises of a long future together. But we have our whole lives to commit to those assurances, to make those promises.

All those words can wait.

I grasp his face, kissing his chin and jaw, his scars, his nose and mouth. Every inch I can kiss, I do. He kisses me back, our lips finding each other, and everything he is becomes part of my Light, my soul, my entire heart. I never again have to swim against his tide.

"I love you."

"I know," Nate whispers before kissing me again.

"Wait." I pull away and frown. "Did you just Han Solo me?"

He grins devilishly. That punk!

"So …" Nate's words are soft and sensual against my mouth.

"When do you want to go on our date?"

"I'll tell you as soon as I'm done kissing your face."

"I love happy endings!" Ayla's arms are around both of us before I can kiss Nate again, and then Serai hugs her daughter, wordlessly conveying immense pride. Dr. Ormandi even hugs us, and he's not a hugger.

"I'm so proud of you both. And I'm sorry I put so much pressure on you—especially you, Callie. I was not truthful from the start, and it was wrong. I'm sorry."

"You *were* a lying jerk, but hey, that's what it took to get my butt off your couch," I reply through the hugs and tears. "You literally only get one pass. Be honest from now on. I'm dating your kid, I have influence."

"Understood." Dr. Ormandi seems pretty happy with that.

"Come in for a hug, Ayla. I know you've been angling for one." Nate holds his arms open for his Seer.

"Really?" Ayla's face lights up like the Fourth of July, and she squeezes so tight I think Nate's eyes might pop.

"Ow! Ayla, *chill out!*" Nate grasps his throat when she backs off. "You almost crushed my larynx."

"I'm next!" I hug Ayla fiercely. "You're amazing, bestie."

"You're amazing, too, bestie." Wow, no joke, she really does need to work on not squishing tracheas.

"I'm glad I agreed to sign off on your release from jail, Callie." Serai half-grins, half-smirks. "Despite the mass destruction your presence has caused, Darkness eliminated my greatest political rival. I'll have no one running against me for reelection."

"Healthy perspective, Serai," I say.

Then my gaze finds Toran. He's shivering like he's about to go into shock as the real pain of his injured arm sets in post-adrenaline rush, but he's too stubborn to lay down and give in.

It's so like Toran to stand there, clutching his half-arm, and literally say nothing. But I don't think I want him to change. We couldn't be a good dyad if we didn't fight like siblings, and I need him exactly the way he is, just like he needs me the way I am. Opposite sides of the same coin.

I touch his shoulder, smiling. "I'd offer you a congratulatory fist-bump, but you needed a MedFac twenty minutes ago."

"A congratulatory what?" Toran scowls.

"A fist-bump. You know, that thing where I hit my fist against your fist, and then we do, like, twoodle-oo with our fingers."

Toran shakily rolls his eyes. "That is the stupidest thing I've ever heard."

I'd come up with a witty retort, but El's transport whizzes to a skidding stop through the mud. He grins as the door pops open.

"Hey, dümfos! You aren't dead! More good news, the MedFac didn't get ashed, and Heike's there now. They said she'll pull through." He waits while we stare, struck by his oddly cheerful announcement. "What are you doing? Get in! You wanna be stuck out here when the sun comes up? No way."

While everyone else shuffles into the open transport door, Nemo whizzes out and immediately gets trapped in the mud. He angry-robot rants that he can't wheel forward, so I rescue him, just like I always have and always will.

"Come on, buddy. Let's go." I deposit my muddy little mech on my shoulder. Diver may be gone, but I have Nemo to keep me on my toes.

*Diver …*

"Hey, what's this?" Nate bends and retrieves a glowing piece of crystal from the mud. It pulses through the grime, just like a miniature Prism. "It's …"

"It's Diver's Light." Tears fill my eyes, and I take the crystal. All the pieces I could grab before Diver pushed me through the gateway litter the crater. His gift to me wasn't just my chance to live, it was also the last physical pieces of himself, his love and Light.

"We'll need to build new World Divers. These can be the start." I put the crystals in Toran's satchel, still slung across my shoulder, and give them a fond pat before I grasp Nate's hand and squeeze tight.

"New Divers sounds great. But first, I'm going to get about a hundred stitches in my face, three MRI's, and then nap for a week." Nate's smile is pure happiness embodied. He pulls me close until I melt into his arms, and kisses me softly. "And by the way... in case it wasn't perfectly obvious, I love you too."

Beyond the crater, the sun rises over the golden dunes, and the last twinkling stars glitter like diamonds scattered across the endless horizon.

It's a beautiful morning.

# CHAPTER 30
# TORAN

"I THINK I LIKE fake sunlight better than Mist. Although, I wish we could see the stars."

Heike rests on a plush lounger surrounded by cushions in Serai's garden. My sister is too weak from her ordeal in the Shadow Plain to do much except rest, but she likes company.

"You don't miss the damp chill seeping through cracks in our windows every morning? I found it delightful." I practice Manipulating water from a fountain using my new cybernetic hand and arm. It's aligned with my nervous system and brain, and it moves and functions the same as a flesh hand. It's sleek and metallic, but not the same.

I'm not the same either. I'm trying to be better.

"Are you growing a sense of humor?" Heike smiles. "I'm so proud." She breathes deeply, as though taking in air and releasing it still requires effort.

"Perhaps you spent too much time outside." I release the water into the basin. "You should go in." But Heike rolls her eyes.

"I like being outside. Stop fussing over me."

Heike is right, she doesn't need to be fussed over. She only needs a brother who loves her. "If you'd like to go in, let me know, and I'll help you."

"I will." Heike turns her face into the false sunlight, and I resume my practice. "Are you excited for the party?"

"I have never been to a party." Events where the outcome is unexpected used to make me nervous, but this occasion is reason to celebrate. Adoption paperwork was officially signed by Richard, making Elion a permanent part of the Ormandi family.

"I think it will be fun." Heike takes a rattled breath. "I'm happy for El to have a real family, aren't you?"

"I think El and Nate being brothers now will give me an eye twitch," I say. Heike laughs. I missed her laughter so much. Never will I take my sister for granted—and never again will I try to control her. She's free to live life as she chooses, same as me.

"Why will you have an eye twitch, Toran?"

My heart leaps to a gallop at the sound of Ayla's voice over my shoulder. I spin on my heel, staring at her beauty in the dappled light. Pink gems stud her curls, the same color as her silky dress, and in her arms are party lanterns lit up by Callie's shimmery golden Light. I gape, slack-jawed, at the sight of her, a detail Heike doesn't miss.

"On second thought, I'll go inside after all. It's a little hot out here." Heike stands, catching her balance briefly on the back of the lounge, and meets my gaze. "I don't need help. I'll see you at the party."

Heike shuffles inside Serai's vast Cordonanzan home, leaving Ayla and I alone in the garden. She silently threads lanterns onto a string. Who will speak first?

"How's your new arm feeling?" Ayla asks. I glance at the arm, shining like silver ice.

"It's fine. I'm still getting used to using my Manipulation with it. But there isn't any pain."

"That's good." She continues working on her lantern string and uses her Manipulation to float them into the air, hanging them along the drooping branches. She's so graceful, but I feel I'm looking at her too much. Perhaps she doesn't want me here.

"I should go get the cake you made for Elion."

"Mama said she would bring it out later." Ayla's cool response is so unlike the warmth I used to know. She's warm to Callie, Nate, El and Heike, and her mother—everyone but me.

An ache burns through my chest, one of longing, regret, and something I have no name for, but it's gentle, like falling into soft down. Regardless of how her response might hurt, the words must be spoken.

"I'm sorry, Ayla." I sink to my knees, humbling myself before her. "I know promises mean nothing, and I must show you how much I regret what I did. It may take my whole life, and you might choose not to forgive me. That would be your right. But I've never been more sorry for anything than I am for hurting you. I care for you, and always will."

I've never admitted my true feelings willingly to anyone. I'm somewhat drained after my confession, but also lighter, freer. As though a weight pressing on my shoulders has been lifted.

"Toran." Ayla stands over me, a gentle smile on her lips. When she kneels at my side and takes my hands, the look in her eyes feels like coming home at long last. "Will you help me with the lights?"

She doesn't need help, but I'm all too eager anyway. "Of course."

"I used to think I had to help others to get people to like me." Ayla hands me the long strand and resumes placing lanterns in tree branches. "I wanted so badly to be wanted, I would go out of my way to do whatever anyone asked. But that's a good way to get taken advantage of."

"I understand." She's saying I used her. And in truth, I did. I feel worse about it than anything, but saying it won't change my actions.

"I also realized something else." She turns to me, lantern light sparkling in her eyes. "If I *want* to help a friend because it makes me happy, that's something I can keep. But *needing* to help others so they'll accept me is something I can discard." She tilts her chin. "Do you still understand?"

"Truthfully? No."

To my surprise, Ayla laughs. It's like music—a sound I knew as a child, but haven't felt in a long, long time.

"You should discard what doesn't suit you too." Ayla touches my shoulder. I don't see electricity wrapped around her fingertips, but I feel it all the same. "You made terrible mistakes, but I saw what you were willing to sacrifice to make things right. It's time to discard your anger, especially your anger at yourself."

"What about you?" I ask. "Are you still angry at me?"

"Perhaps a little, but it will pass." The glittering decorations turn the garden into a fairy land, like one from Heike's favorite tales. Only Ayla could make an already stunning garden more beautiful. "There, that's finished. We have much to celebrate, don't you agree?"

"I do." It's the truth. "I would especially celebrate getting to know you better, Ayla."

Ayla takes my hand, and I feel as though I could float away with her. "I would celebrate that too, Toran."

Bustling noise spills into the garden as all the others—Callie, Nate, Elion, Richard, Serai, and Heike—emerge from the house. Richard scolds Elion to stop eating all the food before anyone else gets a bite, Callie helps Nate carry another lounger for seating,

Serai holds Ayla's lopsided cake, and Heike, dearest sister, laughs and pets Nemo on her shoulder.

"Hey, Boy Scout!" Nate sets down his end of the lounge and Callie the other. "Your cheeks are pink. Did we walk outside mid make out?"

"No way, he'd be tomato red if *that* happened," Callie says. "I'm gonna guess sneaky hand-holding."

I will not confirm or deny her very correct assumption—not aloud, at least. Nate flops onto the lounger and Callie sits with him, leaning back against his chest. It looks comfortable. Would Ayla sit with me like that?

"Hey, El! Bro!" Nate waves at Elion. "Toss me some of those spicy puffs."

"No way, it's my party, I'm eating everything." Elion dumps a whole bag of the desired puffs into his mouth.

"We aren't stingy with snacks in our family," Richard chides, frowning.

"*You're* not, I am." Elion sits at the foot of the lounger, smacking his puffs in front of Nate. "Mmm, so good. You snooze, you lose, dümfo."

"Give me some puffs, or I'll chase you up a tree, dingus. I'm faster than you."

"Bet you're not." Puffs spill across the ground when Elion drops the bag of snacks, and Nate races after him.

"Those boys will put me in an early grave." Richard sinks onto the other lounger, pinching the bridge of his nose. Serai joins him.

"Lucky for you, Ensoloradan medical technology should keep you around to parent them for at least another forty years." Richard groans, and Serai offers him a steaming cup. "Tea?"

"Toran!" Nate hops from a nearby tree, carrying El—kicking,

flailing, and giggling—under his arm. "Come on, we're tossing the kid in the pool."

I balk. "Why?"

"Because he's a snack hoarder, that's why." Nate claps my shoulder with his free hand. "Let's go, before he escapes. He's still a little feral."

"Don't throw me in the pool, I'll pull you in after me!" But El is laughing, Nate is laughing, all the girls and Richard and Serai are laughing, and suddenly I feel a lump in my throat. I can't move, my eyes sting, and I can't speak. I'm completely overcome.

"Hey, are you okay?" Nate sets El down, looking me over with concern. "Is your arm bothering you?"

"No." I shake my head and wipe my eyes. "My arm is fine. I'm just … happy."

For the first time in my entire life, I'm surrounded by laughter. Abundance. People who accept me unconditionally, even when I am behaving horribly, and forgive me. They tease me, joke with me, and call me friend. Finally, *finally* I have a real home. A true family.

I've never been so happy.

"We're happy you're happy, Toran." Callie gives me a hug. My Luminaut, my friend, my sister in Light. I don't hold back when I hug her too. "I call spontaneous pool party!"

Elion whoops and bolts, and Callie, Nate, and Ayla run after him while Richard yells for them to please not swim until twenty minutes after eating. Ayla beckons for me to join.

"You come too," she says. I glance back at Heike where she rests.

"I'll be here, I promise," my sister assures me. "Go on, have fun."

She'll be here. So will I. But I can choose what suits me, and right now, I want to join the others in their games. A spontaneous pool party could be entertaining. I'll never know if I don't make the leap.

I quietly grasp Ayla's outstretched hand and run after my friends.

# CHAPTER 31
# NATE



*SOME TIME LATER...*

"WHAT IF THEY GOT HER eyes wrong? Or her smile? They might forget her dimples."

I nervously tap my feet in the back of the transport soaring through clear Cordonanzan skies toward the Hall of Machines with Callie, El, and Dad. Tonight, the project I've been spearheading for months will be unveiled: Mom's Luminaut statue. She'll join the other Luminauts in the renamed and refurbished Luminaut Gallery in the Hall of Machines, an honor she should have been given from the start.

To say I have a lot of personal feelings invested is an understatement. Confusing, heavy feelings I've avoided for a long time—feelings about Mom's death and legacy, and my part in her story afterwards, both in Darkness and Light.

"Don't worry." Callie laces our fingers before she runs her thumb down the length of mine. "I'm sure it'll be great."

Her touch eases my anxiety a little, but not enough. "What if it's not? What if—"

"Nate." Callie squeezes tight, applying firm pressure to my palm. "It'll be alright in the end."

In the end… because there's no changing it now, even if I wanted to.

"Besides," she adds, grinning, "you managed to convince the Hall of Guardians they should reopen the Gallery to the public instead of using it as a glorified garbage dump for old tech. I doubt they want to risk even more meetings with you by messing up your mom's statue."

A smile parts my lips. "I can be very persuasive in negotiations."

Callie and El make faces, and even Dad gives a start. "Persuasive?" Callie tilts her head. "You don't mean—"

"No, not *that* kind of Persuasion." Who need Persuasion when I have other talents? "I was incredibly persistent, stubborn, dare I say obnoxious. I credit being an only child for seventeen years, right Dad?"

"It was closer to eighteen years, but otherwise, you're correct," Dad agrees. His eye twitches for old time's sake.

"But you're not the only child anymore," El says with more than a little devilishness—as if I need reminding I had to bathe that kid in disinfectant before I bent him into a pretzel shape to trim his toenails for this occasion. Being El's big brother is a disgusting joy.

"Stubborn persistence aside," I continue, "preventing an impending apocalypse might have softened the City Guardians on the topic of Luminauts. Just a little."

"That tends to change people's minds," Dad laughs.

"Have you seen the statues, Callie? You work at the Hall of Machines now." El leans forward in his seat, tugging at the stiff collar Dad made him wear.

"Nope, I'm just there as an apprentice to learn mech design and programing. World Diver programming, specifically." A scowl crosses her forehead. Toran's teaching her proper scowling. On her face, it's adorable more than severe. "Did you say statues? Plural? I thought tonight was all about Mariasol."

"Actually," I figure it's as good a time as any to come clean about my surprise, "there are two statues being unveiled. The other one is for you."

"For me?" Callie's brow crease deepens. "Please tell me you did *not* commission a statue of me."

"Not of you," I promise.

"Who, then?"

"You'll see."

Somebody is about to win boyfriend of the century. In case it wasn't obvious, that somebody is me.

"Serai saw the prototypes, and said the sculptors did an outstanding job." Dad peers through the window at the Hall of Machines coming into view, and the fancy private transport parked at the front entrance. "It would appear she's arrived early, as usual."

No surprise. Serai is to promptness what Dad is to crankiness.

Our transport lands next to Serai's, and flashes of comms and joyous cheers overwhelm my senses when Callie and I step out. People insist on stopping us to take comm holos or chit-chat everywhere we go, thanking us for saving their granny, their aunt, their parents or kids, even themselves on the Night of Shadows — what Cordonanzans call the night Queen almost evaporated their city into desert dust. It's made going on dates interesting.

"Look, Nate, your adoring fans," El snarks.

"Take a hike, dork," I mutter through a smile, waving like Miss America for the gathering of well-wishers.

Callie politely exchanges hugs and kind words with a few

people, but Hall of Machines workers fend off onlookers before a legit crowd forms. We're here with an agenda.

"Luminaut!" Ayla rushes me, arms outspread. She goes for a side hug instead of a choke hold, because I've indicated I enjoy breathing now. "We are so proud of you!"

"We? You mean, Toran's proud of me too?" I put my hands over my heart and flutter my lashes. "I'm touched, Boy Scout. Truly touched. I'd hug you if I didn't think you'd stab me with your icepick fingers."

"I'm somewhat impressed you pulled this off." Oh, Toran, your churlishness always keeps me humble. "I'm also convinced the City Guardians acquiesced to your requests simply to get rid of you."

"Mama told them you'd never quit blocking two hour meetings until they agreed to redesign and open the Gallery," Ayla adds.

"She's right." The squeaky wheel gets the grease, even this far across the multiverse.

"I was on your side from the start." Serai places a hand on my shoulder. "Honoring Mariasol's memory is important."

"I firmly agree." Dad motions for us to make our way inside. "Shall we?"

Serai leads the way with Ayla and Toran, El badgering the latter about why Heike didn't come to the unveiling tonight. Callie and Dad hang behind with me.

"Are you sure you're alright?" Dad gives me a pointed look. "You were pale as a ghost in the transport."

I haven't been pale since I was a Shadowmancer. The nerves must be getting to me more than I thought. "I'm okay."

"I understand if you're not," Callie says. "It's the memorial your mom deserves, but with Gallery opening next week to the public, everyone will see her, not just us."

*Everyone will see her.* Tightness constricts my throat, swallowing my unvoiced reply.

Mom has always belonged to me and Dad, but soon, she'll belong to everyone else in a way she never did before. They'll see her face and judge her actions: if they were right, or wrong. That worries me more than how accurately the sculptor captured her nose.

"This is a moment to be proud, regardless of how the statue may or may not look." Dad grasps my shoulder. "No matter what happens, I'm proud of you. And I'm glad you're here."

He says that a lot now. "Here" meaning alive, his kid in the flesh—a second chance to be better to each other, more honest and real. "I'm glad I'm here, too."

"Hey, Dad." El rushes up, excitement in his eyes. "Serai said there's some new model droids in the small mech lab. Can we get one?"

"No." Dad doesn't miss a beat.

El frowns. "Why not?"

"We have one utility mech, that's plenty," Dad replies. "And Nemo comes around half the time."

"But I want my own Nemo," El argues. "Callie or Nate can animate him with their Light."

"One Nemo per multiverse is more than enough," Callie says. Thankfully, she left Nemo behind tonight, although I'm sure she and Ayla will come home to find their new apartment trashed with paper scraps.

"Isn't this exciting?" Ayla claps her hands in front of her fancy dress and smiles. "Both statues are going to be so amazing!"

"Wait, Ayla knows about the second statue?" Callie looks between me and my Seer.

"I know, too," Toran adds with an almost-devious grin. Almost, because it's Toran.

"How do Ayla and Toran know and not me?" Callie's eyes narrow with accusation. "Were they in on it?"

"Well, I *am* Nate's Seer," Ayla reasons.

"But you're *my* roommate," Callie counters.

"Ayla forces me to tell her everything. She's practically got Luminaut Persuasion in her ability to wear people down. And Toran and I hang out without you." I raise a brow. "You know, guy time, bro's chilling, boys being disgusting, gross boys."

"I have three brothers, I'm aware." Callie makes a face while Toran mutters something about me being gross, not him. "You *swear* you didn't commission some cringe statue of me?"

"It's not of you, I promise." I glance at the Seers. "Back me up, Boy Scout."

"If it was your official Luminaut statue, that would mean I'm on the statue, too," Toran says. "And you know I would never agree to such nonsense."

Callie laughs. "That's true."

"You'll love it," Ayla chimes in with a wobbly sniffle. "I could cry just thinking about it."

"Cry?" Callie looks more than a little concerned. "Why would you cry?"

Before anyone answers, Serai stops before a ceiling-heigh bronze door marking the end of the corridor. "Here's the Gallery now."

The entry looms wide, newly refurbished for the public opening and etched with stars and World Divers. Callie touches one of the Divers, sadness and grief overtaking her expression before Serai presses the touchpad beside the door. Two statues covered in drapes stand tall and silent at the end of an expansive room.

Floor to ceiling glass windows reveal silvery dunes silhouetted against the violet moon and twinkling stars, creating a backdrop for the proceedings. Luminauts and Seers of the ancient past flank either side of the Gallery, somber grayness reflected in the lighting overhead. After all, some of these Luminauts did horrible things in the name of Light—and the Light Collective isn't something to remember fondly. But even more of these Luminauts gave their lives protecting the multiverse, honoring Light with their love and sacrifice.

It's like Ayla always says, we can't erase the past, only learn how to never repeat it, and be better than the mistakes.

"The fruits of your labors, Nate," Serai says, coming to a stop in front of the statue to the left. "Mariasol."

My palms get sweaty and hot, pulse pounding through my veins. Seconds more, and I'll see her.

"Would you like to do the honors?" Serai picks up the silk tassel at the edge of the drape and offers it to me.

"Uh, yeah. Sure." I step forward and hold the tassel, motioning for Dad to join me. "Are you ready for this?"

"To see myself as a large, bronze thing? No." But his eyes are glassy all the same. "To see something like me standing next to something like her again? Yes."

With a tug, and the red, gauzy drape falls to the marble floor, revealing—

Mom.

Even in bronze, it's Mom. Her wavy hair spills around her shoulders, her athletic, tall frame stands proud, and in her left hand is the spear I used in the Rognaga. But more than that, it's her face embodying her spirit: lips quirked in a half-smile, her large, deep-set eyes looking toward a beautiful future. Her cheeks, her nose, her forehead, everything is perfect, right down to the way her right dimple was deeper than her left.

Even though it's not really Mom in the flesh, it feels like looking at her all over again.

"It's…" Dad leaves the word hanging in midair. All the tears he held back at her funeral pour down his face. He doesn't even see the bronze version of himself standing at her side. The picture of Dad the artist used was one he kept in his wallet from college, wearing his favorite Cal Track and Field sweater. It's a great likeness, and Serai's is just like her younger self, too. I read the words inscribed on the placard on the statue's podium aloud.

"Luminaut: Mariasol Zaira. Home world: Ensolorada. Seers: Serai Eradah—Earth Manipulator—Ensolorada, and Richard Ormandi—Fire Manipulator—Earth, who was also Mariasol's husband. Without Mariasol's intervention, Darkness would have invaded Cordonanza sixty years earlier, and corrupt politicians would have abused the power of Light for their ends."

"I instructed the sculptors to add the last part, even though it breaks with tradition," Serai says. "The truth deserves to be told at last." She puts her hand on Dad's shoulder, mourning and peace mingling in her eyes. "Didn't she come out well, Richard?"

"Perfectly." Dad wipes his cheeks and smiles the biggest smile I've seen in a long time, one that reaches all the way through his eyes. "Don't you think she's perfect, too, Nate?"

Looking up at Mom, I don't feel the need to cry. I thought I would, honestly. Episodes of horrifying Shadow memories and ceaseless nausea plagued me for the last month while the statue was being made. I showed up prepared for an emotional gut-punch.

But I'm not anything close to that breathless, stomach-churning devastation. I'm… satisfied. It's a more lifelike statue than I dreamed possible, and fitting that Mom has this place of honor in her home world. Seeing her again, all I feel is how much I love her, and how I wish she was here to see this, too.

"I think she'd say it's too much trouble and fuss, but yeah," I agree with Dad. "It's perfect."

"She looks like a girl version of Nate," El observes. He touches Mom's foot. "I wish I could have met her."

"Me, too." Callie smiles sadly. "She was a really special person. Beautiful, inside and out."

That she was.

"Now for the second statue." Ayla picks up the end tassel of the second drape a short distance away. "Go ahead, Callie."

"Okay, let's see what this big surprise is—Ayla, are you crying already?"

"Yes!" Ayla wipes her tear-streaked face. She's a blubbering mess and the drape hasn't even come down. "I can't help it! It's going to be beautiful!"

Toran puts his arm around her shoulder. When she leans into him, I give him a discreet thumbs up, drawing his less-rare-now smile. Way to go, Boy Scout, smooth move.

Callie takes the tassel from Ayla, and pulls. Before the drape hits the floor, her hands fly over her mouth, a sob breaking free. "Diver! It's Diver! Oh, my buddy!"

The statue is a perfect miniature of the giant old mech, down to the worn gears, the dents, the general age cracking through every part of him. But it also embodies his homey warmth, his kindness, and ability to forgive unconditionally, right down to the way the statue shines.

I hope the sculptor who did these things got paid *really* well, because wow.

"In honor of the last World Diver, known simply as 'Diver,'

who sacrificed himself in the Shadows so the multiverse would know Light," Callie reads the statue's inscription, her voice thick with tears. Underneath are the words that were so important to Mom, to Diver, to Callie and me. "Power without love is no power at all." A brilliant smile spreads across her face, and she hugs me tight. "Thank you for this."

"I miss the old scrap heap," Toran admits, reaching out to pat Diver's foot. "But he is at peace in the Lands Beyond."

"I miss him, too." Ayla blows her nose into a silk hankie that matches her pale blue dress. "He was the sweetest old Diver."

*Was* the sweetest old Diver. Callie winces, her shoulders stiffening in my arms at the past tense reference to her mech. She pulls away, pain shining clear in her eyes when she touches the sculpture of her friend. Despite being an exquisitely detailed replica, it's no substitute for the real Diver.

I can read a room, and I'm not the person Callie needs right now. The person she needs is gone, and only his statue remains.

"I think I'm going to get some air on the dunes," I tell Callie.

"Okay." She doesn't offer to join me. She wants to spend time with Diver's statue. I get it. There's probably a lot of emotions to process.

But I'm ready for a change of scenery, and I've got some emotions to sort out too. Ones that have been swirling through my heart and mind since Callie destroyed the Shadow Plain, after the reality of my life as a reborn human truly set in.

"Can I come outside with you?" El's eyes gleam at the promise of the great outdoors.

"Yeah, sure."

"Don't go hiking too far," Dad cautions. "Serai has a reception planned with the City Guardians."

"We'll stay close."

There's a touchpad door beside the expanse of windows leading out to the desert. A bracing wind sweeps across the dunes, cooling the sand and stirring the air to life. El pulls at his collar and unbuttons the top of his shirt-vest.

"That's better." He grins when the breeze blows through his silvery curls. "It was boring in there."

"We were unveiling two statues, and it took ten minutes."

"Yeah, and it was boring." El scoops up dune sand, letting it slip through his fingers. "Besides, Callie and Ayla were crying, Dad was crying, Serai was almost crying. Too much crying. Why didn't Heike come? She's not boring."

"Heike is still weak from the Shadow Plain, and school wears her out," I remind him. "She'll be at the reception."

"Does the reception have food?"

"Yes, you bottomless pit." El and food—some things never change. "And about the crying… it's not always because people are sad. Sometimes crying is good."

"I know." El brushes his sandy palms on his pants. "They all miss Diver. I miss him, too, but I didn't want to cry about it. The monster lady can't hurt him anymore"

"Yeah. You're right."

Queen can no longer hurt anyone—but Darkness isn't gone entirely. Memories of Shadows will always remain, especially for me. I have nightmares thinking about it sometimes. How much Darkness escaped the Shadow Plain before it was destroyed? And how do I stop it before another Queen Beyond the Stars—or King, for that matter—emerges?

Even after everything I did to come back to Light, I can never forget part of my existence was in Darkness. And I still have a lot to do to make up for that mistake.

"Hey, throw your Light for me," El says, changing the subject entirely.

"As much as I know you love chasing Light orbs near and far, Dad said not to go running off into the dunes." It's been an emotional day, even without the Richard Ormandi laser glare if El gets sidetracked.

"Just throw it from the top of the dune to the bottom," El suggests. "Dad can still see us if I run down."

"That's fair."

We crest the tip-top of the dune, and I draw Light from under my heart through my arms into my hands, spinning a few quick orbs. Amazing how easy it is to use my powers now, how instinctual. It's almost as if Darkness never blunted it at all.

Almost…

"Only five?" El wrinkles his nose at the meager number.

"You wanna get all sweaty before Serai's reception?" I give him a raised-eyebrow look. "Dad will make you take another shower, but if you're all about personal hygiene now, be my guest."

"No way." El fake-gags. "Five is fine."

I toss each Light ball down the dune, and El takes off like a shot after them. The glowing, silver-white Light bounces and bobs up and down, skittering across the sand. El will be occupied for a while. I sit down on the top of the dune, staring at the stars.

*Mom, are you there?* My Light calls to hers. I listen, holding my breath, waiting.

*My stars,* her Light answers.

It's a faint echo, but a reassuring sign she's there, just beyond my reach: safe and surrounded by love, Light, and peace. Darkness no longer shrouds my remaining memories of her, and the way I miss her aches with every breath. But the hurt doesn't break me like it used to. Some feelings no longer burn.

"Mind some company?"

I smile broadly at the sound of Callie's voice. "Yours? Never."

She sinks onto the sand at my side, and I turn to face her. Her golden brown eyes glow like warm honey under the blanket of starlight.

Eat your heart out, Mrs. Kim. What was that about a B+ in AP English?

"I can't thank you enough for making sure Diver was honored in the Gallery," Callie says. Her cheeks are still a little pink and damp from tears. "Everybody should know what he did. How much he sacrificed."

"It's the least he deserves. Diver made sure a lot of people survived that night—including you." I hold her gaze steady, drinking in the sight of her here, with me. A different kind of ache blooms in my chest when I think of how much I love her—and how close I came to losing her. "If not for him, we'd be unveiling your bronze memorial tonight, too."

Callie's eyes shine, freshly wet. "I didn't want to die in the Shadows, even if I was prepared for it. But I—" She swallows hard. "I miss him so much. And I wish he was still here." Suddenly, she straightens up and wipes her eyes. "What am I doing? We came to honor your mom tonight, and all I can do is cry about my mech. It's been months… I should be over it."

"No, you shouldn't." I take her hand and hold it tight. "You don't just 'get over' losing somebody you love. If the love was real, it doesn't go away."

She grasps my fingers like I'm her anchor and she's worried she'll drown if she lets go. "Does it ever get better?"

"Not exactly," I say with a sardonic grin. "I spent a long time being angry Mom died, and when I wasn't angry, I was obsessed with figuring out why she had to leave me the way she did." Nate

Ormandi, grief counselor? It's what Callie needs, so I'll do my best. "Even now, it feels like there's a hole in my chest where part of my heart should be. But you learn to make room for it."

"How?" Tears slip down Callie's cheeks. I brush them away with my thumb, but the flow is ceaseless.

"Find a way to walk the tightrope of moving forward while never forgetting." I nod towards the Hall of Machines. "I thought I'd be a wreck tonight, seeing Mom's memorial. Especially after I screwed up by becoming a Shadowmancer. But I wasn't. Doesn't mean I don't wish she hadn't died, but I'm learning how to remember her better. I closed the book on the angry part of my grief."

It hits me when I say it—I'm no longer angry about Mom's death. A lot of other emotions, sure. I feel those. But I'm not angry.

A weight lifts from my shoulders, and the last piece of old Nate that hung on so tight floats away. The statue is complete. Mom has been honored, the real truth about her actions told. I'll live in her absence knowing a part of her carries on within me— her Light and love. It exists in my love for Callie, El, and Dad. One day, if I have kids, her Light will shine in them, too.

At long last, the final chapter of that book has ended, and a new adventure awaits. I can choose a new path —the path of a Luminaut.

"We both have a second chance at a new life," I tell Callie, and point to the multitude of stars overhead. "The best way to honor Mom, Diver, and everyone else up there with them is to live."

Callie closes her eyes, tipping her face toward the nighttime sky. She's still, quiet. A breeze blows her hair away from her cheek. "Yes, you're right."

We sit side by side, gazing at the stars from the top of the dune in the pale glow of the moon. El's caught almost all of my Light orbs. Soon, our time will be up.

"We should grab him and head back," I gesture at El, "before Dad storms out and melts the sand into glass because El got disheveled."

"That would definitely kill the vibe. But it's such a nice night." She tips her head onto my shoulder, nestling perfectly into the crook of my neck. "The statues are done. What's next?"

"I've got a few ideas," I say, and Callie laughs. Nobody is ever surprised I have ideas, and it's never just a few. "Mostly, I want to figure out how to contain the spread of Darkness that escaped the Shadow Plain before it was destroyed. I could create some kind of a device, maybe like Light radar, that scans the whole multiverse and tells us where the Shadows are hiding. What do you think?"

"It's another ambitious project," Callie replies. "But if anybody can figure out how to track Darkness across the farthest reaches of the multiverse, it's you."

Through the Hall of Machines windows, I watch my friends, my family. Ayla and Toran stand off to the side, their smiles more flirtatious than I'd give either of them credit for. Dad and Serai admire the statues with pride in their eyes. El races around the dunes, panting and laughing while he chases my Light. And at my side, sitting beneath the vastness of the cosmos, is Callie — my entire multiverse in one person.

All of them are the people I live my life for. I thought Mom's death irrevocably broke me, destroyed my sense of self. And for a while, it did. What little of me remained, Queen's Shadows tried to steal. And yet, my Light persisted, as real as the stars and as fathomless as the ocean.

Even the Shadows couldn't steal my ability to love. That truth is Mom's greatest legacy of all.

"I was wrong, you know."

Callie glances at me, tilting her chin. "Wrong about what?"

"I told you once that love stories like ours don't have happy endings," I say, tucking her silky hair behind her ear. "I was wrong."

"Sometimes being wrong is exactly right." She leans in, kissing me softly. "For what it's worth, I'm glad you were wrong."

Me, too. More than she knows.

We walk together down the gentle slope of the dune, our backs to the heavens as we face the unknown future before us. But I'm never so far I can't feel Mom's gentle glimmer just under my heart.

*Nate, my stars…*

*I'm here, Mom.*

*I will be with you, always.*

The desert breeze carries the promise into the night, until the words are forever stitched into the fabric of the sky.

# EPILOGUE
# CALLIE

## *1 YEAR LATER*

"I STILL CAN'T BELIEVE you and Ayla bombed out on a test run."

"Believe it." Nate's throaty laugh reverberates through his World Diver. I can't see his face, I'm nose-deep in a busted mech's innards, but I know he's smiling. "You're making an El-level mess, by the way."

Eye roll. "Only because you and your Seer fried this beyond recognition. Nemo, I need that calibration wrench."

My work buddy grumbles and deposits the tool unceremoniously in my waiting palm before whizzing off to cause mayhem, his favorite activity.

The cockpit area of Nate and Ayla's World Diver is in complete disarray, but that's what happens when I've got to rebuild the control panel she imploded with way too much electricity. It's a damaged mess of wires, microprocessors, and Light-channeling crystal, but luckily it's salvageable. Just a few more tweaks should do it.

"Wow, that was like a shark got hold of a chum bucket full of fish heads." I emerge from the mech's inner workings, wiping my forehead.

"First, gross analogy. Second, Sparky's never been a Seer in a World Diver. You and Toran have the benefit of prior practice." Nate reclines in his Luminaut chair, dark eyes shining. "I heard a rumor you were so terrible at Diving once upon a time that you crashed in the dunes and almost died of sun sickness."

"Did El tell you that?" Of course El tattled. I put the last repaired microprocessor back in its casing and close the panel.

"Only about a hundred times. It's his favorite story. Pretty sure his whole class at school knows too."

It wouldn't shock me. El having Luminaut Nate Ormandi for a brother gives him major social clout.

"There, she's fixed." I put away my mech repair gear. "At least you were only practicing out in the desert, and we could bring her in for a quick fix."

"Speaking of a quick fix." Nate snags my waist in his arms and pulls me into him, reclining the seat all the way back so we can nestle side by side. "Ayla and Toran aren't going to show up with my Darkness detection devices for another" — he looks at his comm — "twenty-six minutes."

"Twenty-six minutes?" I brush his hair wavy away from his forehead, tracing the scars down his cheek. "Are you sure that's enough time to kiss me the right way?"

"Hmm, I don't know. Only one way to find out." His lips part against mine, and he kisses me in *just* the right way until I'm tingling all over and lost in him, no less in love than I was a year ago.

*Crash!*

"What the — Nemo!" Nate breaks our kiss and points at my mech, who's busy causing chaos in the back of his World Diver. "Leave that alone! It's important human stuff."

Nemo waves dismissively at Nate and gets back to his exploration.

Getting up to chastise Nemo isn't worth it, but Nate's still annoyed. "Does he listen to you? Is it me?"

"No, he doesn't listen to anybody. Especially not me." Nemo has yet to change, much less become sweet and compliant, but it's okay. He's perfect the way he is.

"Nate? Callie? Where are you?" Crap, Ayla and Toran are here early.

Nate and I scramble over each other. We resume separate seats as our Seers emerge into the cockpit carrying two of the Darkness detection devices Nate built. The little orbs send out a Light signal through the multiverse, and if any Shadow is found, a set of holo coordinates on a specific world will appear, communicated directly to our Divers. It's like a comm and a Prism combined with some awesome Light power wizardry, and I'm the proudest girlfriend that Nate came up with something so cool. Today, we're doing a trial test to see if they work.

If they do, we'll have our first mission through the multiverse together, just as soon as …

As soon as I have the courage to bring the World Diver I share with Toran to sentience.

"Hello!" Ayla grins. "You are both flushed. Were you making out?"

Toran rolls his eyes and crosses his arms. "They kiss every spare moment they can," my Seer grouches. "Not that they take responsibility for their public displays of affection."

"Gentlemen don't kiss and tell, Boy Scout," Nate replies with a wink.

"They just make not-so-subtle insinuations," I add.

"How's Roxanne? Has she forgiven me?" Ayla touches the

miniature Prism crystal, one of the shards from Diver's Prism given a new chance at life.

"She's all good, aren't you, lady?" Nate pats the control panel fondly, and a lights above his Luminaut chair flashes warmly. He brought his Diver to sentience last week so he and Ayla could do some test runs. I'm the only holdout. "Callie fixed her up."

"I was only trying to expand the air glider mechanism," Ayla defends herself. One of the new features I designed for each Diver is a component that works with each Seer's element. Nate and Ayla's Diver has air glider wings so she can fly. When expanded, they resemble something from a Gundam anime. He sent dozens of drawings to my comm that looked like a five-year-old made them, begging me to make his Diver "the raddest" and "cooler than Boy Scout's."

Nate can never, ever say I don't do anything nice for him.

"First step, air gliders. Next step, plasma sword." Nate glances at me with a hopeful smile. "You can manage a robotic plasma sword, can't you?"

Ha! How about no. "The Cordonanzan public might be cool with Luminauts and World Divers using the Hall of Machines as a base of operations, but I think a giant plasma sword is a bridge too far."

"You're no fun," Nate pouts. "You spend too much time around Boy Scout." He flashes my Seer a broad grin over his shoulder. "Just kidding, Toran. I'd never talk smack about you."

Toran snorts. Nate laughs. Typical Toran and Nate.

"At least Callie and I didn't name our Diver after a silly song." Toran gives Nate a look.

Nate clutches his hand to his heart, feigning shock. "How dare you imply Roxanne would be ashamed of Sting!" He points out the crimson bulb above his head, which flashes indignantly.

"She even loves her red light!"

More blinking lights, this time to the bass beat of the song in question. Roxanne has a sense of humor, just like her Luminaut.

"What is Sting?" Ayla looks between Toran and Nate. "And I was told the Roxanne song was the greatest masterpiece of the 1980s, whatever that means."

"They're just ribbing each other, like always." I hold out my hand. "Let's get that Darkness detector set up so Nate can calibrate it."

"And then you can bring our World Diver online," Toran adds with an impatient scowl. "Unless Nate and Ayla are the only dyad planning to take their first Dive."

*Bring my World Diver online* … When I stop installing the little orb mid-screw, Nate and Ayla immediately whirl on Toran.

"If she isn't ready, she's not ready," Nate defends me.

Ayla takes Toran's hand (they're *dating*, can you believe it?!) and shakes her head. "Don't force her, Toran. She already lost Diver. She might need more time."

"It's been a year," Toran argues. "We have work to do across the multiverse."

I look out Roxanne's windows at my new Diver sitting across from Nate's. It has the same two sleeping chambers under the cockpit, the same supply storage in the back, the same small piece of Diver's Prism on the control panel to channel Light. It's got cool water features too, like combo running-and-water-skis and a submarine mode. But none of that is functional until I complete the very last step.

"Yeah, okay." I stand. "Let's do it."

"Are you sure?" Nate asks.

"I'll be okay. I want to explore the multiverse again. Eventually see my family and friends in Verona Beach. Check on your

Dad's house as a second home base." And I do. I really, really do. I have my own apologies to make and wrongs to set right, just as Nate did. He nods, understanding. "More importantly, we've got a mission to find Darkness throughout the multiverse and eliminate it. Help people on other worlds fix what's broken. One Queen Beyond the Stars and evil Light Collective was more than enough."

I believe in our mission with all my heart. Diver would believe in it too. So why am I still holding back?

"Should I be there with you?" Nate searches me.

"Yes, let us know how you need us," Ayla chimes in. "You don't have to do this alone."

"I won't be alone." I face my rather scowly Seer. "Toran's going with me."

I grab Nemo and hop to the ground, crossing the World Diver hangar built into the Hall of Machines just for me to do this work (Serai's financial politicking for the win). These Divers aren't as big as my lost Diver. They're less humanoid and more sleek and practical, kind of spacey, sci-fi looking, but I love how they turned out. Building them has been a robotics nerd's dream come true.

Inside, I take a seat at the Luminaut's chair. Toran climbs up after me and slides into his Seer's chair across the cockpit. Before me is a Prism crystal in its new home atop my dash, the last remaining part of Diver — *my* Diver. The final step in bringing my new World Diver to life is giving it my Light.

I reach for it, but my hand hangs in midair. Tears sting my eyes, threatening to fall, and the familiar lump that builds in my throat every time I try to do this sticks around a swallow.

"I don't know if I can," I murmur. "I might not be ready ..."

"You can, and you are." Toran puts a hand on my shoulder, a comforting gesture he only displays when he means it. "Do you think Diver would want you to linger on his memory? Or would he want you to form a connection with a new World Diver so you could continue your life as a Luminaut? As *his* Luminaut?"

Okay, yeah, Toran has a point. But still, the worst question of all remains.

"What if I can't love this new one as much?"

To my surprise, Toran laughs in response to my fear.

"Um, sorry, is that an appropriate comment to laugh at, Crabby McButthead? No, it's not. Wipe the rudeness off your face."

"No, no." Toran waves his cybernetic hand. "I'm not laughing *at* you. It was just the idea you can't love something as much as you loved Diver. It's *you*, Callie. If anybody can love a mech, or a person, or any little thing in the entire multiverse, it's you."

Well, when he puts it like that …

Light flows from my fingers, coursing through the crystal into the mech I built. In my Light, I pass happy memories of Diver, of my friends across the multiverse. I pass sad ones too— losing so much in the fight against Queen, and how much it still hurts Diver isn't here with me to share in this moment. Mostly, what I give is my love, because that's what this new mech will need most. A Luminaut who loves him. If Diver proved anything, it's that love, in a way, is all we need.

It's so simple, yet so difficult at the same time.

When I've finished giving my new mech Light, I sit back, waiting. Listening for a voice, anticipating with excitement and dread how different it will be from Diver, but ready to meet it all the same.

*World Diver? Are you there?*

At first, nothing. Did it not work? Maybe I just can't have another Diver. My lot as a Luminaut is to be grounded while Nate and Ayla fly into the stars. I guess I can—

*We are here, Luminaut.*

That voice! It's … new. Different. Unlike Diver, yet entirely like him at the same time. All the mechanical lights glow in the cockpit, and Toran looks around, pleased, while Nemo flails his arms happily.

"It worked," Toran says. "I knew it would."

*What should I call you?* I ask the voice in the Light, pulsing in the new Prism.

*Whatever Luminaut would like to call us,* it replies.

I can't call this new Diver "Diver." It would feel strange giving him my old mech's name. But I don't think a casual human name feels right either. Nemo was named after a small, curious creature who wanted to see the unknown, and he embodies it, every inch. This new Diver deserves nothing less.

*How about Polaris? On my world, that's one name for the North Star. It's guided explorers for centuries, helping them find their way home. Now you'll be my guide across the multiverse.*

The new Diver is quiet, as if thinking. At last, he responds, his warmth spreading through my Light like an embrace from a new friend. *We like that name very much, Luminaut.*

Polaris it is. *Hi, Polaris. It's nice to meet you.*

*We are happy to meet you too, Luminaut.*

"Sorry to break up the proceedings, but we have a problem." Nate and Ayla rush into Polaris, looks of dread on their faces.

"Ayla, please don't tell me you electrified the control panel *again*," I groan.

"No, it's worse." She stands behind Toran while Nate quickly installs the Darkness detector and gives the orb a few taps to calibrate it. Instantaneously, it fills with swirling, shadowy tentacles. Darkness.

"Whoa, already?" I watch as a set of coordinates appears in holo form above the orb, reading our location. "It's in Tremurheim."

"What?" Toran leans forward with a jerk, his eyes wide and fearful. "What happened there?"

"Darkness happened, that's what," Nate says. "I don't know if Queen isn't as gone as we thought, or if this is some random cluster that made its way out of the Shadow Plain before it got destroyed. Either way, we have to stop it."

I look at my friends, a slow grin spreading across my face. "Guess we're taking our first Dive a lot quicker than we thought."

"Sync comms," Nate announces, tapping the command, and the rest of us sync ours too. "We'll see you there." He grins, clapping Toran's shoulder. "Looks like you get to go home first, Boy Scout. Lucky you! Watch out for skuddima on the ground!"

"Skuddima. Lucky me," Toran deadpans.

Nate and Ayla rush into Roxanne, Lighting her up, while I put my hand to Polaris's Prism. Toran presses a button on the control panel, and the enormous bay doors of the World Diver hangar open, revealing a desert sky full of billions of stars.

"Ready for your first Dive, Polaris?" I ask.

"Polaris?" Toran screws his face. "Absolutely not. That's an awful name."

"Nope, sorry, he already loves it." I channel Light into my mech while Toran grumbles. Polaris waits, ready.

*We are at Luminaut's command.*

*There's a set of coordinates in the holo above your Prism,* I say to my mech.

*We read them. Is that where Luminaut would like us to go?*

*You got it!*

Through the Prism, Light extends beyond the cockpit, connecting with Nate's Light from beyond his Diver. Air swirls around the Light, joined by water from deep under the desert sand that Toran draws to the surface. Together, the four of us form a gateway through the newly restored Light connecting the multiverse — the Light that Diver gave everything to renew.

On the other side, the vast, misty forests of Tremurheim appear, waiting for us to explore.

*Okay, Polaris.* I give my first command as this mech's new Luminaut. *Let's Dive.*

*Yes, Luminaut.* Polaris's running skis extend under him, and he takes off through the gateway, followed closely by Roxanne.

With a brilliant flash of Light, we fly through the multiverse to the other side of the stars, the first Dive of a brand-new adventure.

# BONUS SHORT
# NEXT TIME, WE'RE BRINGING A FIRE EXTINGUISHER

*LUMINAUT, THE SEER IS* very late. Roxanne's impatience mirrors mine. If my World Diver had a tongue to tsk and a head to shake, she would. With dripping derision, I might add.

I blow a frustrated raspberry, checking the time on my comm. Ayla was supposed to be at the Hall of Machines well over an hour ago, and instead of my curly-haired Seer, all I see (ha, Seer puns!) roaming the World Diver hangar are mechs of varying shapes and sizes.

*Tell me something I don't know, Rox.*

*We don't know what Luminaut doesn't know, but we can certainly try our best, if Luminaut really wishes. Although, we think Luminaut does not really wish.*

I smile, chuckling to myself. Roxanne should have been named SnarkBot, but I wanted to honor Mom when naming my World Diver, and "Roxanne" was one of her favorite songs. Mom listened to that single so much she scratched a hole in the vinyl.

*Thanks, Rox, but I was just joking around.*

*We know that, Luminaut.*

Another laugh. *That's my Roxy girl.*

*My* World Diver—I still can't really believe Roxanne is mine. The second Roxanne came to sentience, it felt like meeting a friend I've known my whole life in the space of a single second.

Ayla, on the other hand… sometimes I wonder if we're going to cut it as a Luminaut and Seer dyad.

"Come on, Ayla, where are you?" I check the time again, gritting my teeth so hard I get a headache. She either lost her comm and doesn't know what time it is (likely), or she saw some cute animal or baby and got distracted fawning over it in a suffocating squeeze-hug (even more likely).

Is the Luminaut-Seer dyad supposed to be so constantly irritating? Callie and Toran still bicker sometimes, but really made strides working as a team since we defeated Queen. Ayla is… I don't dislike her, she's cool most of the time, and she's my girlfriend's roommate. But hanging out with her and Callie socially is an entirely different context than Luminaut and Seer practice, and that's when she makes me want to pull my hair out.

In case it wasn't obvious, I'm about to yank a patch out of scalp any second.

*The Seer approaches at last, Luminaut.*

Finally! About freaking time, Ayla.

"Hello, Nate! I'm here!" Ayla calls, breezing into the hangar with no less than six enormous, fully-stuffed shopping bags.

What's that thing Toran always says? Forest spare me? It's a lot nicer than some other words I want to say that start with F.

"Decided to swing by the mall on the way to our previously schedule test run?" I spin in the Luminaut chair, crossing my arms. Ayla drags her overloaded bags up the steps leading into Roxanne's cockpit.

"I don't know what a mall is," she says, slightly out of breath. "Is that a California thing? I'd like to go to California one day. Callie told me all about the beaches, it sounds lovely. Maybe we can go there with Roxanne! Wouldn't that be—"

"Ayla. The bags." I gesture to her purchases.

"Oh!" There's the focus lightbulb, blinking to life. She holds up one of the bags proudly. "I bought some snacks! I know you like snacks." She dumps the contents of her bags on the floor — spicy puffs I usually compare to Cheetos, sweet custard cakes, reheatable flatbreads, dehydrated fruit strips you reconstitute with a moisture packet, juice pops, meat pockets like gyros but spicier, and veggie crisps. All in multiple flavors and quantities.

"Snacks?" My eyebrows rocket up my forehead. "You bought enough food to go camping for a month."

Ayla glances at the mounds of food around her sparkly, aquamarine skirt. "I suppose I was a bit too enthusiastic."

If a-bit-too-enthusiastic was a person, it would be Ayla. See what I mean about the hair-pulling thing? She doesn't know how to hold back. Restraint, thy name is *not* Ayla Alindia.

"I'll clean it up and organize later. We're late leaving for the test run, and I don't want to risk being out in the dunes at sunrise." I spin around in my Luminaut chair, facing Roxanne's control panel, and press my mouth into a line, holding back a groan.

*Luminaut is frustrated with the Seer again?*

The groan caught in my throat comes out as a hiss of air through clenched teeth. *Was it that obvious?*

*It was that obvious, Luminaut.* Thanks, Rox.

"Here is my seat," Ayla states the obvious, plopping herself down in the Seer chair with two sweet custard cakes. She holds one out to me. "Would you like a treat?"

"No, I want to get going."

Ayla shrugs, oblivious to my impatience. "More cake for me. Oh! I have a surprise for you!" She reaches for her dress pocket. "I know it's here somewhere. Perhaps I left it in one of the bags…"

"Well, isn't that special. But unfortunately, we're late, so surprises can wait." I press the touchpad linked to the hangar door. The gargantuan wall behind us slides apart, revealing Ensolorada's dunes beneath an ocean of twinkling stars. We aren't Diving anywhere in the multiverse yet. This test run is meant to see of Roxanne's air glider wings work properly with Ayla's Manipulation and how well I control her movement. I put my hand on Roxanne's Prism crystal, nervous adrenaline racing through my pulse.

*Okay, Roxy, ready to go?*

*Yes, Luminaut.* Roxanne's excitement mirrors my own.

*Let's start by making a right hand turn out of this hangar, then —*

A sound coming from the Seer chair distracts me. *Slurp-pop, slurp-pop, slurp-pop.*

What the actual crap, man. I spin in my chair, staring at Ayla sucking custard cake frosting off her fingers. "Can you keep it down? I'm giving Roxanne directions."

"Oh! I'm sorry!" Ayla grins. My eye twitches. I swear if she turns me into Richard Ormandi, we shall have words. Many, many words.

*Sorry, Rox. Let's try that again.* I channel my World Diver's Light. *Like I said, take a right turn out of the hangar, and —*

*Crinkle-crunch, crinkle-crinkle-crunch.*

More noise, more eye twitching. I turn so fast I almost get whiplash. Ayla's busy crumbling up her cake wrapper. She stuffs it under her seat with an apologetic smile. "Sorry again."

"Uh-huh." I fix her with a serious look. "This test run is for you, too, you know. We've got to see if the air glider wings work, or if Callie needs to make more adjustments."

"Yes, I know that," Ayla says.

"Cool, so maybe worry more about what we're doing presently, and less about cake."

Ayla tilts her chin, confusion creasing her brow. "I'm not worried about my cake, I enjoyed it immensely."

Facepalm.

*Is the Seer finished being noisy so Luminaut can give us directions?*

*I hope so.* I exhale, waiting for more irritating sounds. Nothing. Good. *Like I said, right turn out of the hangar, then wait for my signal at the top of the dune.*

*Yes, Luminaut.*

Roxanne maneuvers herself right, lowering the sand ski under her nose. It hits the fine grains a little too hard, lodging itself momentarily, before Roxanne dislodges it and tries again. Slowly she make her way out of the Hall of Machines and up the imposing dunes. At the top, she stops, just like I asked. That a girl, Roxy! I fondly pat her control panel.

*Very awesome, Rox!*

Roxanne's inner Light glows happily. *We are pleased that Luminaut is pleased.*

*Great to finally get out of this hangar, right? Let's stretch those wings.*

*We agree, Luminaut.*

"Yay! She's moving!" Ayla claps her hands, beaming. "Callie told me she ran Diver into a wall the first time she tried moving around with him. You're doing fabulously!"

"Yeah, I heard about that." Awkward throat clearing. Callie's first test run happened during the Darkness Time. I know Callie's forgiven me, but that doesn't mean I've quite forgiven myself, and definitely haven't forgotten. Lots to make up for still, ya know?

Ayla, as per usual, doesn't notice that I'd rather drop this particular topic. "She also said that was when you were still a

Shadowmancer pretending to be a ghost, and that you—"

"Circle back around there, Sparky. That's enough nostalgia rehashing for one evening. Once Rox expands the glider wings, you're up." Remember why we came out here to do this in the first place?

"Oh, yes." Ayla primly straightens herself in her seat. "I'm ready."

Sure you are.

*Is the Seer really ready?* Roxanne awaits my signal.

*As ready as she's ever going to be. Go ahead and get the wings out.*

Yes, Luminaut.

Roxanne's glider wings extend from beneath her sides, then rise halfway into the air, ready to soar the moment Ayla gets her act together and I give the command to soar. The idea is, Ayla will Manipulate the air around us, catching the wings and allowing Roxanne to fly. I'll direct the World Diver's movements, allowing us to turn directionally. That's the theory, anyway. It's supposed to test our skill as a dyad, but as we all know, Ayla's skills are limited to buying too much food, wearing nice clothes, holo-drama recaps, and gushing over puppies.

"Oooh, look at the stars reflecting on the wings! Isn't that beautiful?" Ayla does the exactly opposite of what she's suppose to do, which is Manipulate air. You know, since that's her job as my Seer, but sure, let's admire the stars some more. Like she didn't grow up in Ensolorada and never saw a star in her precious life.

"Ayla." I tap her shoulder. "Refocus, peanut."

"I thought I was Sparky," Ayla refers to my usual nickname for her. "Am I called Peanut now? I have to admit, I prefer Sparky. And you still haven't gotten your surprise. I swear I put it in one of my pockets..."

*"Ayla!"*

"I see. You were joking again about the peanut. You do that a lot, you know." No, *REALLY?!* Me, joke around? The audacity!

"You know what you're supposed to do next, right?" Even though we've discussed Ayla's part of the test run a thousand times, it ever hurts to double check.

"I'm supposed to channel the air so Roxanne will float, and you will tell her which way to fly." In theory, yes. She has the gist.

"Okay, then. Showtime."

She faces forward, staring at the ocean of sand dunes under the glittering purple sky, and raises her hands. Her eyebrows scrunch in concentration, and her Seer's eye blazes diamond white. A strong gust of wind slams Roxanne's side, rocking my whole World Diver at a ninety-degree angle.

*Roxy, stay upright!* The last thing I need is a Diver on her side.
*We are trying, Luminaut, but the wind is quite strong.*

"Ayla! You're going to capsize us!" I glare across the control panel. "Get the air *under* the glider wings, not above them."

"I'm sorry!" Tremors rattle Ayla's shoulders, and her fingers shake on the control panel. Electricity builds around her, culminating in lightning on her fingertips. "I didn't mean to—"

"Don't get sparky on me, Sparky." Too much electricity will fry the control panel, and we'll be up a creek in a hurry.

"Right. No sparks." Ayla hides her hands under the folds of her skirt. The wind calms, and Roxanne rights herself. Whew, close call. "I'll try again," my Seer says. She breathes deep, and closes her eyes. "Air flows, air moves. Air is me, I am Air."

This time, Ayla Manipulates the air beneath Roxanne's wings correctly. We rise into the sky, hovering above the dune steadily.

"Hover mode is go." Yes! We're doing this! Well, kinda. Maybe Ayla can focus up better than I give her credit for.

*Okay, Rox, ready to fly? Let's start small. Slow acceleration forward.*

*Yes, Luminaut.*

Roxanne glides over several dunes, not too high that I can't land her quickly. The glider wings work perfectly. Stars open up before us as Roxanne climbs higher and higher, and a thin band of golden Light appears on the horizon, connecting Ensolorada to the cosmos and the multiverse.

"We're doing it!" Ayla smiles broadly. "This is so—"

The second Ayla loses focus, Roxanne plummets, nosediving out of the sky, approaching the summit of a sand dune way too fast for my personal taste.

"Ayla, what are you doing?!" I frantically channel Roxanne's Light. *Roxanne, stay upright!*

"I'm sorry!" Ayla shakes in her seat, electricity building around her.

*Luminaut, the Seer ceased Manipulating the air. We are static without her.*

"Roxy can't right herself." Dread slams into me like wave a pure nausea when I see how close we are to hitting sand. Roxanne tries her best to stay afloat, but without Ayla, she's sinking fast.

*Pull yourself up as high as you can,* I command my World Diver, panicked. *We can't hit the ground nose first.*

*We understand, Luminaut.*

Roxanne valiantly tries to change course, weaving and bobbing up and down as Ayla loses every ounce of control of her Manipulation. Sparks fly everywhere, and her Seer's eye goes in and out, shifting between hazel and white so fast it's like a flickering strobe light on the verge of sputtering out.

"Ayla, get it together!"

"I'm trying!" Her voice breaks, and the sparks turn to lightning at her fingertips. She places her palms on the control panel, and with a cry, air rises underneath us. Roxanne flies upwards, away from the dune just in time.

"Okay, now put her down gently, and we'll—"

*Luminaut, the Seer has fried us!*

One glance at the control panel and my heart drops to my toes. Lightning wraps itself around every inch of the mounted tech. One more second, and the lightning might reach the Prism and burst it. I have no idea how to fix Roxanne if her Prism gets broken.

"Can it, Sparky!" I whirl on her, glaring. "Eighty-six the electricity. NOW!"

"I'm trying, but I don't know how!" Ayla shrieks, on the verge of tears, and I grab hold of Roxanne's Prism, shielding it with both hands. I'd rather I get shocked myself than blow her life force to bits.

"Yes, you do, you're an Air Manipulator." Need I remind Ayla she's a Seer? Why am *I* the one who has to constantly tell her how to do *her* job?

"I know, but I—"

*Luminaut, we are falling!*

Ayla completely shuts down mid-flight, or she's so worried about her electricity she loses her grip on the air beneath us. Either way, we make impact with a sand dune, skidding down the slope violently. I hang onto the Luminaut chair with all my strength. Lightning flashes before my eyes. Roxanne careens wildly through the sand, coarse grains and small rocks smacking her windows. Her glider wings catch the fine silt beneath us, and she turns onto her side before cruising to a stop. Ayla's snacks land on the far wall, and I have never been more appreciative of a safety harness in my life.

"Roxy, you okay?"

*Define okay, Luminaut.* Even if she's alright, Rox is beyond pissed. Honestly, I am, too.

*Can you maneuver upright?*

Roxanne doesn't answer, she just shifts herself so we fall into a vertical position. The snacks slide onto the floor, and I'm thankfully head-up again.

*I take that as a yes.*

Roxanne's Light burns with seething irritation. *We require repairs. Please make necessary arrangements.*

She's grumpy, that's for sure. And judging from the state of the control panel, I don't blame her. Nothing but singed, smoking wires that stink like an electrical fire. *I'll take care of it, Rox. Can you fly back to the Hall of Machines, or do we need carrier drones to come pick us up?*

*Drones.* Roxanne says the word like it's an insult to her character and every World Diver that ever existed.

*You got it. Sign off for a bit, I'll get ahold of Callie.*

*Yes, Luminaut.* Roxanne's Light fades in the Prism, a sure sign she's exited stage left, so to speak. World Divers can't leave their mechanical shells, but Roxanne retreats inside herself sometimes, especially when I'm gone or she needs a rest—or wants to pout, as in the present circumstance.

"If you're done wrecking my World Diver for one evening, I'm going to call Callie and debrief about—Ayla?"

My Seer isn't in her chair. But Roxanne's side door is open, and a sparkly, aquamarine figure miserably climbs the nearest dune. She's going to go have a cry, I guess. No time like the present, because Ayla is the last person in the multiverse I want to see. After what she just did to Roxanne, I don't think I could be nice to her if I tried.

In the meantime, Callie needs to know how much extra work

she's got ahead of her when we get back. I tap my comm's interface, sending her a chat request transmission. Moments later, her sunshine smile appears as a holo above my comm. I ground myself in the joy of it, releasing some of my tension.

"Hi, cute boyfriend!" Callie tucks her hair behind her ear, and her little mech, Nemo, waves at me from his place on her shoulder. "How did the test drive go?"

Yeah, about that… "Do you want the bad news first, or the worse news?"

Callie's smile fades, and worry fills her eyes. "Oh, no. What happened?"

"Well, the bad news is you're going to need to send about five or six carrier drones out to take us back to the Hall of Machines, because Roxy's grounded."

Callie's eyebrows rocket up her forehead. "That's the *bad* news? What's the worse news?"

"The worse news is Roxanne's entire control panel got fried, which is the reason we're grounded." A sarcastic smirk curves my mouth. "Hours of repairs, courtesy of Ayla."

Callie sighs deeply, resting her chin on her fist. Nemo mimics the same movement, his elbow disappearing into Callie's golden-brown hair. "Where is Ayla? Is she okay?"

"She left. Sobbing face down in the sand, probably." And she can stay there as long as she likes.

"You'd better go make sure she's alright," Callie advises. "Don't worry about Roxanne, I'll get her fixed up."

"I'm sure you will." Can she fix Ayla, too? Callie senses my irritation. Even in holo form, her eyes grow sharper, a sure sign she's reading me like a book.

"Nate. You've got to learn to work together with Ayla, and that includes making sure she's a capable co-pilot."

I try my hardest not to roll my eyes. Really, I do. But they slip towards the back of my skull anyway. "I'm pretty sure that's impossible. She lost her focus for one tiny second, we took a nose-dive, and instead of course correcting, her lightning almost blew up my whole World Diver." I groan through gritted teeth. "Bless Toran's little heart, he spends more time with her than me and hasn't lost his mind yet."

"I heard that!" Toran calls from somewhere behind Callie. Crap, they must be working on their World Diver together—aka, Toran is organizing, and Callie is wrangling Nemo.

"Sorry, Boy Scout!" I call. Toran mutters something incomprehensible, probably one of his many gripes with me despite the fact we're friends. I can deal with Toran's pickiness and reserve, but Ayla's big emotions get the best of her with catastrophic results.

"Listen, I know firsthand the Luminaut and Seer dyad is a tough bond to navigate," Callie says, and Toran chimes in with a "me, too." Saying those two didn't get along at first is an understatement. "But, if we're going to ever leave Ensolorada and assess the Darkness situation other places in the multiverse, you've got to learn to get along with Ayla."

"Why me?"

"Because she's trying." Callie remains gentle, but firm. "Between the two of you, you're the calculated strategist, nobody denies that. But there's something to be said for kindness, thoughtfulness, and gentleness."

Fine, she's got a point. It's well known, all the way down to ancient Lore, that Luminauts and Seers in a dyad are two sides of the same coin—meaning, complete and total opposites. That's been true of Callie and Toran. Go-with-the-flow-boho meets Type A Planner. Is there space for Mr. Strategy and Ms. Puppy Hugger to get along, too?

If not, I'm never going to be a Luminaut of the multiverse. I need a Seer, and like it or not, my Seer is Ayla Alindia.

"Okay. I'll go talk to her and help her calm down." The things I do sometimes, man.

Callie smiles. "Thank you, Nate. And I'll order those drones to come bail you out. Keep your location active on your comm so I can track you."

"Will do. See you soon." I cut the transmission, and breathe deeply in my Luminaut chair for a few minutes. It won't help matters to go talk to Ayla if I'm not calm, and giving her some space to get all the sniffles and sobs out isn't a bad idea, either. At last, I pocket my comm, making sure my location signal remains turned on, and grab some spicy puff balls before I make my way out of Roxanne.

"Ayla." I march up the dune. She doesn't look at me. I crest the summit and open up the puffs. "Want a snack?"

Ayla's face is buried in the folds of her skirt, her whole body a tightly-coiled ball. At the sound of the word "snack," she throws her head back and lets out an enormous sob.

"How can you think about food at a time like this?!" Gee, I could have said the same thing earlier. Tear-stains glisten on her cheeks, and her eyes are red and puffy. She's a wreck, that's for sure — almost as bad as Roxanne.

"Until the drones get here, there's nothing else to do. Might as well take advantage of your overspending and stuff my face." I munch on a puff, the salty, savory spices rolling across my tongue. Ah, yes, just like a Cheeto, but better.

"This is the worst night of my life," Ayla wails. "Even worse than when I was lost in the desert after I came to Ensolorada."

Really, she'd rather face Stage 5 sun-sickness than deal with a busted World Diver? Hyperbole much? "Why is that?" I ask.

"Because I broke Roxanne and you hate me!" Ayla wipes fresh tears away from her eyes.

"I don't hate you." That part is absolutely true.

"You wish I wasn't your Seer." Ayla catches my eye. The look in hers is absolutely anguished. "I know you think it, even if you don't say it."

Okay, she caught me. Wasn't I just lamenting to Callie the seemingly insurmountable task I have in working with Ayla? Saying I haven't secretly wished for a different Seer would be a lie. I wince, a move Ayla doesn't miss.

"See? I'm right. It's true." She rests her chin on her curled knees.

I breathe deeply, eating more puffs. What to say? Ayla really isn't into trite and disingenuous, despite her love of soap operas. Another breath, more snacks in mouth. I'm usually good with words, until I'm not. Then I turn into Richard Ormandi and can't talk about anything but science or sports stats. Should I wax eloquently about how good these snack balls are? Maybe a distraction would—

Wait—I'm eating. I'm breathing. And suddenly, I know what to say.

"You made a mistake, Ayla." I nudge her shoulder like I do with El when he's riled up about some jerk at school. "I know what it's like to make my fair share of mistakes."

"Yes, the Shadowmancer time." Ayla nods in agreement. "That was a mistake, indeed. But everyone forgave you."

"Doesn't mean *I* forgive me." I set the puffs down and face Ayla. "I lost so much time with Dad. I deeply hurt people I cared about—Callie included. I believed a lot of lies I should have been smart enough to see straight through. So yeah, calling it a mistake is majorly selling it short. But like you said, people who matter most forgave me. And I forgive you, if you forgive me."

*Do we truly forgive the Seer?* Roxanne's incredulous statement rings loud and clear.

*Yes, Rox, this is important.*

*Very well.* Roxanne's Light releases her frustration in one single flash, and she calms. *It is as you wish, Luminaut.*

*Thanks, Roxy girl.*

"What do I have to forgive you for?" Ayla tilts her head, clearly confused.

"For not doing my job as your Luminaut," I say. "You know how to get the air under Roxanne. I need to be better about helping you stay the course. I unfairly expected you to keep up with me without giving you grace that you're learning, too."

*That is true, Luminaut did not do a good job assisting the Seer.*

*Okay, Rox, we get it.*

"That's an easy mistake to forgive. Far easier than an electrified control panel." Ayla wraps her arms around herself, a guilty look on her face. "I will do better next time, I promise."

"Of course you will, because I'm going to do better, too." I grin around another bite of puffs. "We can't let Boy Scout show you up as the coolest Seer. What's soggy old Water Manipulation when you can make lightning with your hands, and help Roxanne fly? Clearly you win."

Ayla actually smiles, and a laugh breaks free. She reaches across to grab a puff ball from the bag, and perks up. "Oh! I forgot your surprise!" She stuffs the snack in her mouth and roots through her dress pockets. "I hope it didn't get electrocuted also—ah! Here it is!"

She hands me something that looks like a comm, but smaller and covered in tempered glass. I turn the object over in my hand, trying to figure out what this little tech could be. "Um, thanks. What is it?"

"It's a comm-ex data bar. It attaches to your comm and configures with the interface," Ayla explains. "It's how Ensoloradans access old documents and tech that have been archived."

"You're giving me an old document?" I pull my comm from my pocket and attach the little device.

"No, you'll see." Ayla shifts her legs under her, watching me sync the data bar with my comm. Her excitement is palpable. "It was Callie's idea for me to give it to you. She thought you might like it for Roxanne's first test run."

"So, Callie wants me to have an old document. I wonder what it—"

To my absolute shock, the album covers of all my old vinyls appear in the air above my comm, as well as the track listings for each one. I scroll through, completely awestruck. My records, Mom's records, memories of my childhood I'd forgotten in Darkness. Dancing in the living room to Bruce Springsteen when I was little, humming U2 while Mom took a chemo nap, Nirvana to annoy Dad, and Sublime, the Ramones, and Rage Against The Machine to drown out or drown in my grief over Mom's death. All of them are here. I tap Surfer Rosa by Pixies, and the acoustic strum and familiar wail of vocals feels like coming home.

"This is incredible!" I smile so big the scars on my cheek pull tight. "But, how? I thought all my albums got destroyed with Diver in the Shadow Plain."

"When we arrived at the Rognaga Pit, you and Toran were busy finalizing some planning, so Callie and I secretly snuck them onto El's stolen transport, along with Toran's books," Ayla explains. "She made me promise to give them to you if anything happened to her, and when the dust settled, we decided to have them transcribed onto Ensoloradan tech so you could keep them with you always."

"This is the best surprise I've ever gotten in my life. I mean that, sincerely." I'm so overwhelmed with emotion, I could cry. I swallow a lump in my throat and wipe the corners of my eyes. "Thank you, Ayla."

"You're welcome! I was a dual effort between Callie and myself." Ayla shrugs modestly. "She wanted me to gift it to you when Roxanne was ready to fly."

"Speaking of Roxanne—"

*Luminaut calls us?*

"You should both hear the song Roxanne is named for." I scroll through the holographic album covers until I find the right one. "This song is one of my mom's favorites. It's a masterpiece of the 1980's."

Ayla scrunches her nose. "What is the 1980's?"

*We are similarly confused, Luminaut.*

These girls—I'm stuck with them.

"Forget the 80's. Just enjoy the song." I press play, and Roxanne's namesake begins playing, chords floating into the desert night. Ayla bobs her head, curls bounding around her shoulders.

"I like this," she says. "It's quite—what do you say? Catchy?"

*We also like it, Luminaut.*

"Of course you both like it, The Police are an amazing band." I lay down on the sand dune, relaxing to the music while I eat my snack, and I feel like maybe, Ayla and I will be okay after all.

My Seer flashes a hopeful smile. "Will we listen to the Roxanne song again on our next test run?"

"Definitely," I reply. "But next time, we're bringing a fire extinguisher."

# ACKNOWLEDGEMENTS

Thank you so much, reader friends, for following Callie, Diver, Nate, Nemo, Toran, and Ayla on their journey to this final goodbye. I hope you laughed a little, cried a bit, and enjoyed the ride. I write books for you, my readers. Without you, none of my stories would exist anywhere but my own head. The biggest thank you of all is my gratitude for each and every one of you.

Shadow Ender was written in a period of extreme, chronic illness, both mental and physical, and the original release was something I wasn't sure would happen. I pushed my deadline back three times. There were unforeseen delays during the entire production process, including a whole shipment of stolen books. While I am proud of the original version released by my former publisher, Uncommon Universes Press, I also felt like this book could have been better. I don't remember writing half, much less the initial launch. All that to say, I'm grateful I have the opportunity to release what I consider the definitive edition of Shadow Ender. I hope you've enjoyed this last book as much as I've enjoyed reviving it into a book I had complete mental and physical health while writing.

Thanks to my Kickstarter backers, who supported this relaunch and all the cool bonus content I was able to include with their support:

Heidi Wilson, Michelle Kellog, Jennifer Dyer, Gretchen EK

Engel, Aunt Evelyn, Benjamin, C.J. Milacci, Brigitte, Tristan Ringhofer, Marie A Lynch, Cassandra Hamm, Liz Koetsier, Jason C. Joyner, Isabel K., Lauren Russell, Lauren Hildebrand, Cheryl Underwood, Kaitlyn Carter, Julie Fugate, Amy Hodges, Janeen Ippolito, Allie McDermott, Christine Wilcox, Amanda A Balter, Deborah O'Carroll, David Holzborn, Ari Azure, Michelle Bruhn, Rebekah Doose, Colleen Brown, April C., Karen Machado, Lizzy Hite, SM, EL, Andria Henry, Chad Abbs, Janine, Josiah DeGraaf, Sharon Hanson, and Stephanie Dooley, as well as several anonymous backers. Thank you!

Last, but not least, thank you to my family and friends for all of the love, support, and encouragement. Without you by my side, I'd never have made these books a reality.

# ABOUT THE AUTHOR

Haylie Hanson is an author, teacher, and disability educator who loves everything geeky. When she isn't dreaming of adventures in a galaxy far, far away, Haylie can be found drinking too much coffee and writing stories about kids with superpowers, a love of STEM, and snarky humor. Haylie lives with her family in Colorado.

www.ingramcontent.com/pod-product-compliance
Lightning Source LLC
Chambersburg PA
CBHW030329120726
47901CB00007B/1726